Crimson & Cream

The Oxbow Kingdom Trilogy
Book I

By C. M. Skiera

ISBN: 9781521759059

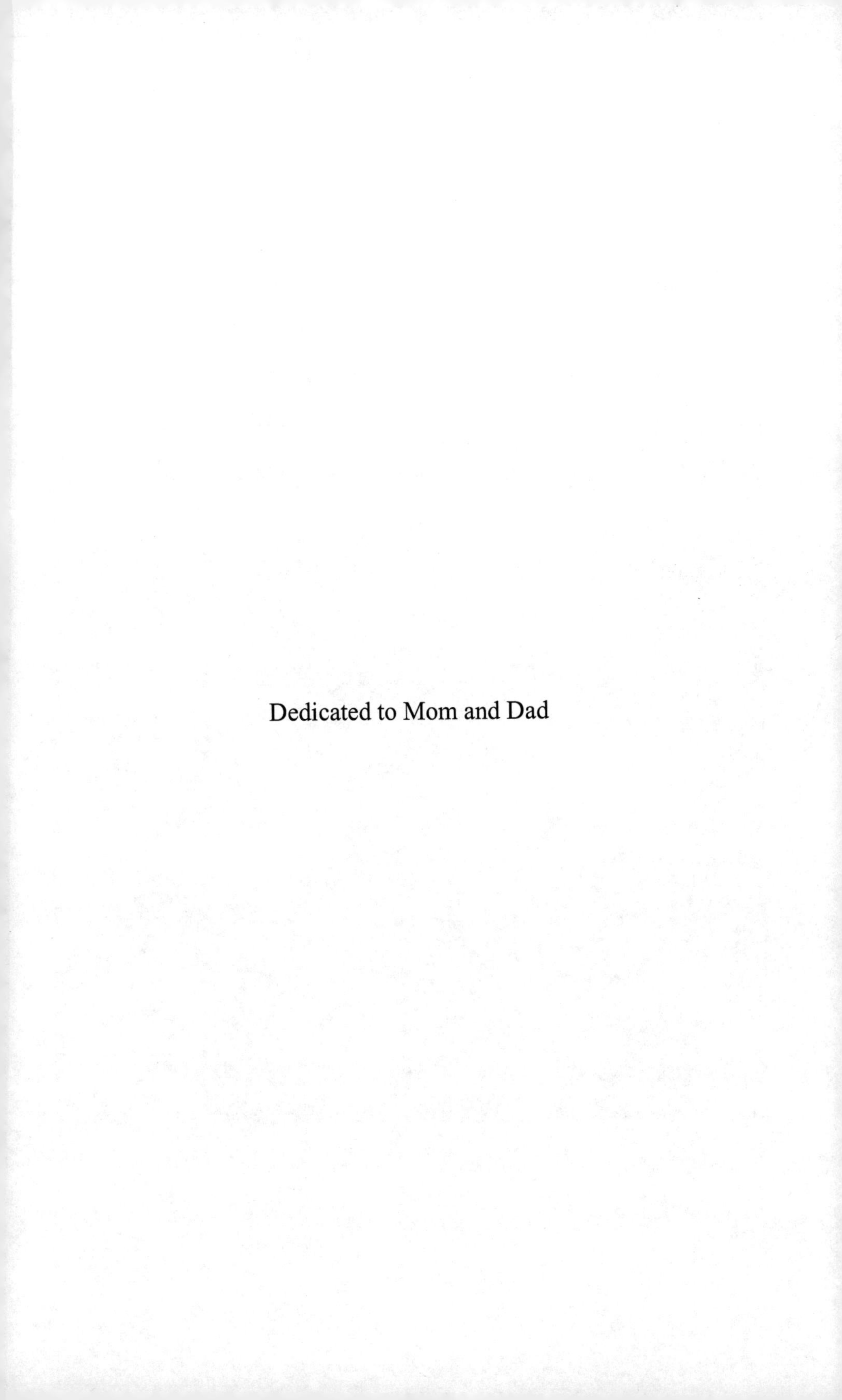

Dedicated to Mom and Dad

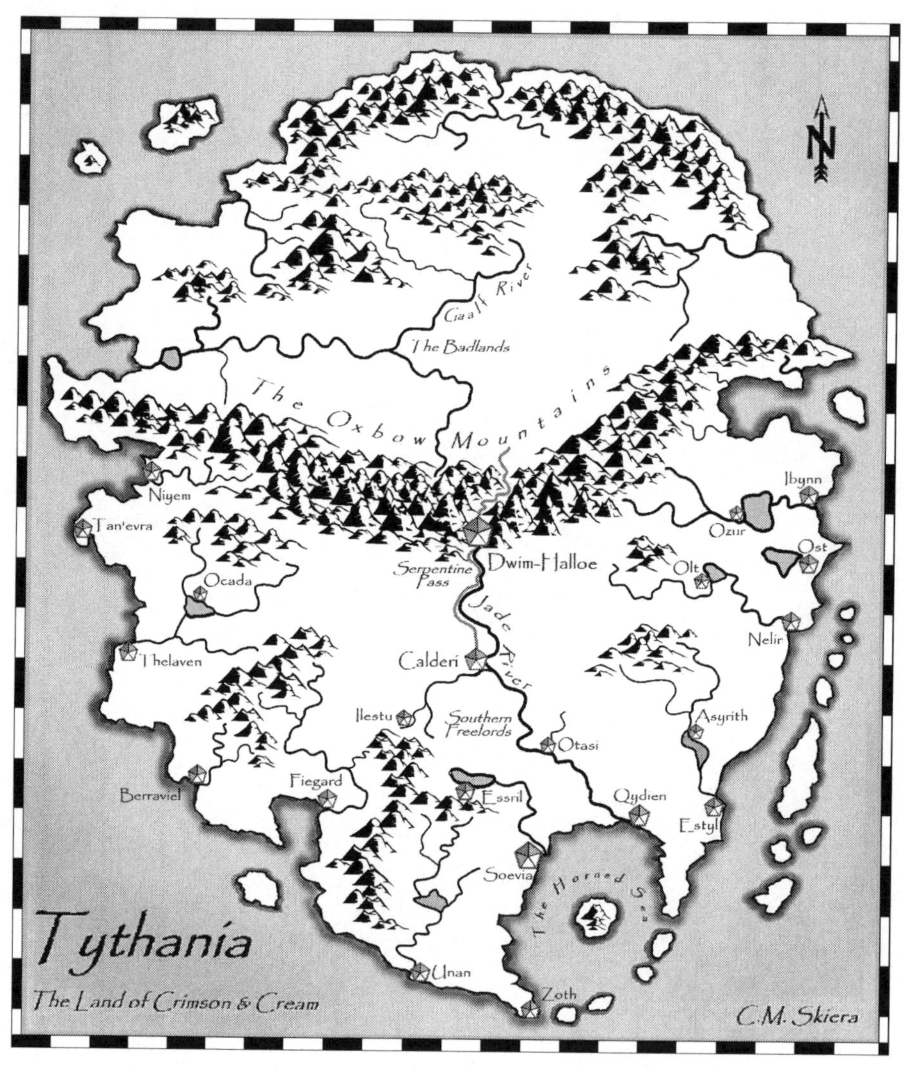
Gaalf River
The Badlands
The Oxbow Mountains
Niyem
Tan'evra
Ocada
Serpentine Pass
Dwim-Halloe
Jade River
Ozur
Ibynn
Ost
Olt
Nelir
Thelaven
Calderi
Ilestu
Southern Freelords
Otasi
Asyrith
Berraviel
Fiegard
Essril
Qydien
Estyl
Soevia
The Horned Sea
Unan
Zoth
Tythania
The Land of Crimson & Cream
C.M. Skiera

The Badlands
Gaalf River
Asigonn
Kierawaith
The Oxbow Mountains
Dwim-Halloe
Sylallian
Serpentine Pass
Jade River
Calderi
Copyright 2014 C.M. Skiera

Prologue

"Bloody unnaturals," Yduk Thiern murmured. He stroked the hairy mole on his chin, sliding his boot across a desiccated wolverine skull buried in the brushwood. "Always hated 'em. Always will." Now, past midnight on a summer's eve in the forested foothills south of Dwim-Halloe, he waited beneath an ancient tree-tower.

The breeze caressed Yduk's bald head, while his mustache hung too heavy to be bothered by a zephyr. An ash loomed before him, silvery bark magnificent in the moonlight. An Elven dwelling wound around the trunk, high in the branches. *Now the Elves are gone, and a fugitive mage lives there.*

With his hand on his sword hilt, Yduk examined the rangy tree. Without a ladder or low branches, he wondered how to reach the dwelling's elevated entrance. He suspected wards, illusions, or other perilous trigger spells might protect the tree tower.

After deliberating, he decided not to ascend. Though he stood tall and lean, even the lowest branch defied his reach. *Could wait him out,* he pondered, *he must come down, but that might take days.*

This particular unnatural wasn't necessarily evil, nor had he committed any atrocity Yduk knew of, other than practicing magic in the Oxbow Kingdom after the new ruler outlawed sorcery. *A decree long overdue,* Yduk thought.

He tapped his leather boot on the carnivore's cranium, debating his options. *Climbing the ash is not one of them.* Calling for the unnatural's surrender was also an unlikely solution.

His black-lacquered buckskin blending with the shadows, Yduk moved without a sound, collecting kindling. He ringed the tree with a wreath of dry wood, then retrieved a jar of torch pitch from his pack. *I'll buy more in Dwim-Halloe.* With a stick for a makeshift brush, Yduk slathered the viscous resin on the tree trunk and smeared the last gobs on the kindling. With his flint, steel, and tinder, he set the blaze. Then he pulled out a small pouch and emptied its contents into the fire.

Might as well use the whole bag, he decided. *Not gonna kill him,* Yduk lamented, considering the airborne dilution between the ground and the dwelling. *Just blister his lungs a bit.*

In the high branches, Yduk saw no sign of the unnatural. As the sumac burned and rose with the smoke, Yduk positioned himself upwind of the toxic fumes. Even with the breeze, he wanted no whiff of the poison. As the flames embraced the pitch and dead wood, smoke billowed. An eerie light emanated from the conflagration, casting dancing shadows in the forest.

Pondering the ghostly lighting, Yduk wondered if he stood far enough from the fire. He retreated further beyond the fiery illumination and admired his handiwork. The breeze died, allowing the acrid smoke to drift into the Elven tower. The animated fire crackled and popped.

Then Yduk's head felt a drop, and then another. *Of all the damnable luck!* He pulled a hood over his glistening head. The rain intensified, turning into a downpour. Moments ago, the night sky had been clear. *The unnatural,* he guessed, moving closer to a tree for shelter. The drenching shower continued for several minutes, and soon the flames were vanquished. Charred branches were all that remained of his blaze.

Whether it was the tainted smoke, or plain curiosity, the warlock peered out from his tower. Yduk discerned a silhouette against the night sky. *He's casting a spell!* Yduk slid behind a thick trunk, keeping one eye on the spellcaster. A moment later, the forest was awash in light. Yduk jerked his head behind the tree.

And waited.

Patience, he told himself, trying to quell his racing heart. His slick hands clutched his crossbow. In less than a minute, the incantation depleted, returning darkness to the forest. Yduk allowed his eyes time to adjust, and blindly spanned his crossbow and slid a bolt into the track. With the weapon against his chest, he craned around the trunk.

A rope ladder dropped from the tree. In the inky night, Yduk squinted at a robed form. He heard the unnatural coughing. *Must have got at least a whiff.* Yduk raised his weapon, taking aim. When the unsteady mage's feet touched the steaming ground, Yduk spoke. "Unnatural, ye've a bounty on yer head and I've come to claim it. On the ground. Now!" *I hope he complies.* When men refused, things became unpredictable, and unnecessarily bloody.

Wide-eyed and slack-jawed, the sorcerer spun toward Yduk, who noticed a wobble in the wizard's step. The spellcaster looked unprepared for a confrontation. *Probably the smoke.* Yduk glimpsed the terror etched on the mage's face.

Yduk repeated his command, but the man didn't obey. Instead, the spellcaster's hands jumped to life as an indecipherable phrase started on his lips.

Without hesitation, Yduk pulled the metal trigger, launching the bolt. The projectile ripped into the mage's chest, piercing the sinew between sternum and ribs. He collapsed backward against the trunk, his unfinished spell frozen on his tongue.

With faster hands than the incapacitated unnatural, Yduk spanned, reloaded, and fired. The second quarrel zipped clean through the sorcerer's neck, pinning him to the ash. Blood gurgled from the victim's throat as he breathed his last.

Yduk slept in the dead man's tree-bed, and in the morning, took proof of his bounty and set out north toward Dwim-Halloe.

From the clearing, Yduk could see distant torch light defying the darkness. The faraway brands lit Dwim-Halloe's outer rampart, where the sprawling fortification peeked above the Oxbow Mountain tree line. By midday tomorrow, Yduk would reach the bustling capital city and collect his reward. But tonight, he searched for a decent spot to camp.

As Yduk rode up the Serpentine Pass, shrill howling startled his horse. The ebony mount pulled up with a snort. "Bloody wolves," he muttered. With a soothing hand, Yduk steadied his anxious steed. "They're close," he said, grabbing his crossbow. He scanned the forest, ears guiding eyes.

Against the starry sky, he spotted a wisp of smoke. *Same direction as the caterwaul.* Yduk raised a bushy eyebrow and rode off the path and into the woods. Not far in, dim light from a dying campfire seeped through the pine branches. He heard growling more clearly—and panicked voices.

Yduk dismounted and tethered his horse far back from the fire. With crossbow ready, he crept toward the discord. Crouched in the brush, Yduk peered over a low ridge. Teeth bared and snarling, three wooly mountain wolves had two men up a tree. Neither man nor wolf detected Yduk's approach. He inched closer, and started up a tall pine himself.

He found a sturdy branch to support him and positioned for a clear shot. Yduk propped the crossbow against his shoulder. He closed one eye and aimed for the scruff of the largest wolf's neck. With a click, *swoosh*, yelp, and *thump*, the beast collapsed to the soil, mortally wounded.

The other two wolves sniffed their fallen alpha as Yduk reloaded and fired again. A second carnivore fell victim to his deadly aim, as the projectile tore through its ribs, crumpling the howler. The last startled wolf turned and snarled, catching a whiff of Yduk's buckskin. A third clean shot left this wolf pinned to the ground.

Yduk slid from his perch and landed without a sound. His thin dagger ended each wolf's misery. Yduk cleaned his bloody blade in the fur.

"Ye can come down," he hollered. "They're dead."

The trapped duo were mere teens, armed only with dirks that they didn't dare test against the mountain wolves. Nerves frayed, they all but fell from their perches.

"Thank ye, sir," they croaked in unison, eyeing the corpses. "Evil bloody buggers," the taller one mumbled, sliding a cautious step toward Yduk.

"Squirrel, they call me," said the lanky blond, extending his shaky hand to Yduk.

"I'm Weasel," said a black-maned youth, standing back, shoulders stooped.

"Flattering monikers," replied Yduk, shaking their sap-sticky hands in turn. Yduk scrutinized the pair. They were rail thin, with long hair and adolescent beards. The shaggy blond stood taller than the sable-haired boy. Their tunics and breeches were tattered and ragged, and too small for their lanky frames. They were dirty and unkempt. *Unprepared for traveling,* Yduk thought. *And there's no farms for miles.* "In over yer heads?"

"Afraid so," said the taller one. "Didn't expect wolves this near the city."

"Gathered as much," Yduk said, studying their torn packs, contents strewn on the ground. "Traveling long?"

"Only a stinkin' day," Weasel replied as he collected his scattered belongings. Yduk noticed Squirrel shoot his partner a dirty look.

"Yer from Dwim-Halloe, then?" Yduk questioned, picking up an empty flask and handing it to the young man. With a glance at each other, the pair nodded with trepidation. "Where ye headed?" Again they looked at each other before answering.

"South," Squirrel responded timidly, fingering the hole in his ravaged pack. "Mebbe far as Calderi. Lookin' fer work."

"Aye, work," confirmed the other.

Their eyes darted from his gaze. "What trade ye in?" Their faces wrinkled as if they were at an inquisition.

"Metal smiths we are," said Squirrel.

"Aye, smiths," said his echo. Yduk contemplated this response but a moment.

"Could ye not apprentice in Dwim-Halloe?" Yduk enjoyed watching them twist in the wind. Every simple query took longer to answer.

"Aye, could've. But we're seeking our fortunes south. Better weather," Squirrel stated. He assumed the role of spokesman. Weasel had been reduced to nodding.

"Ye've worked as smiths, but not under a master? How'd ye manage that?" Yduk tapped his foot waiting for the reply.

"Oh, we've an apprenticeship all right," Squirrel confirmed. "But our ol' master kicked the bucket, so we moved on."

"My sympathies," replied Yduk, restraining his grin. "What I've heard, King Valin keeps a tight hold on his tradesmen. Didn't think it was easy to leave."

"Aye, 'tis not, usually," Squirrel stammered. "But we've some connections."

"Connections, aye," Weasel repeated, finding his voice and bobbing his head.

"Off to a rough start. I'm heading north, but I'd gladly camp with ye tonight. I'll take first watch," he offered while adding a dry log to the waning fire.

"Much appreciated," Squirrel replied. "You've our gratitude." Yduk shrugged.

"Going to fetch my horse," he informed them, and then disappeared into the night. He found the black gelding where he tethered it.

"Smiths my arse!" he muttered to his patient steed. "Most surely runaway orphans." By the time he returned with his ebony mount, the ragged partners were asleep near the fire.

Daybreak rode in on a red sky, morning birds stirred with song, and Weasel and Squirrel awoke bound tightly. They struggled and squirmed, but could not wiggle free. When Yduk tied the knot, no one ever escaped.

"On yer feet, orphans." The tone in Yduk's voice told them he meant business. His sleek armor and deadly crossbow added to his imposing presence. *And they haven't even seen my bastard sword unsheathed.* A sneer stretched across his stern countenance. "Yer little adventure is over," he informed them. "Ye'll be going back to Dwim-Halloe where ye belong, and I'll be collecting my reward. Now march!"

Seems the Oxbows are rife with bounties, Yduk thought. *Between unnaturals and orphans, half of Dwim-Halloe's got a price on their head. But I've a bigger fish to fry.*

Bound together and tethered behind his horse, Squirrel and Weasel shuffled all the way back to Dwim-Halloe. There, they returned to their forced labor, and Yduk collected his small reward for their capture. In the Granite Capital, all orphans toiled for the king.

And they never left.

Chapter One

"Jetsam!" his twin brother Flotsam whispered. "Get down! We shouldn't be here." Jetsam's ragged pant leg tightened from his brother's pull. The second-hand breeches were ill-fitting for the growing youth. Jetsam's trousers, and his wrinkled tunic, were swiped from a peasant's clothesline. With a grunt, Jetsam jerked his leg free of his brother's grip.

Jetsam hung from the stone wall, transfixed on a maiden strolling in the garden below him. With the tip of his nose resting on the ashlar, his aching fingers clung to the bulwark's lip. Jetsam's nostrils flared at the fragrances rising in the warm night air. The toes of his shoddy boots wedged into the cracks between the blocks.

Upon first glimpse, Jetsam noticed the girl's eyes. Her crystalline orbs drew him in, mesmerizing Jetsam. Sallow moonlight danced in her locks, shimmering like waves. Willowy and angelic, the somber lass displayed a regal air. She meandered the flagstone path amidst flowers and shrubs, drifting like a leaf on the wind. Surrounded by low hedges, she moved out of earshot.

"Jet-*sssam,*" Flotsam hissed again. "Stick to the alleys. This is too dangerous!" he whispered. "Can't believe you sodding talked me into this."

Jetsam snorted. *Only had to pester you about it every day for weeks,* he thought. *If only you'd relax, then we could enjoy our birthday!* Jetsam was amazed he convinced his brother to go this far. For months he envisioned this special adventure for their special day, but convincing his cautious twin was another hurdle. Swimming the moat was hazard enough, but creeping inside the castle through a narrow drainage chute was risky indeed. *Must be the full moon,* he rationalized.

"Sheer lunacy, sneaking into the Citadel—birthday or not," the pragmatic Flotsam warned, whispering his brother's thoughts while maintaining his sense of reason. "Turn back while we can."

Despite the plea, Jetsam didn't budge. Logic fell on deaf ears. Captivated by the lass, Jetsam ignored his twin's urging.

"Seem rather *fond* of that wall," Flotsam teased. "Find a soft spot?"

"Always the jester," Jetsam replied with a smirk. "Come have a look," he whispered.

Visibly flustered, Flotsam scaled the rough surface alongside his brother. Inside the yard, trees rustled in the midnight breeze while their branches shaded flowers and bushes from the lunar radiance.

"Let's go inside!" goaded Jetsam, blue eyes flashing with enthusiasm. He glanced at Flotsam's stern face. *Bet he's hungry,* Jetsam connived. "Look at those apples!" Jetsam exclaimed in a high whisper. "Can you imagine eating one? Fresh and juicy—not some chewed-up core. Fill our sacks and not a one'll be missed." The trick to getting his brother over the wall was to convince him of the garden's bounty. A meeting with the mysterious girl would be Jetsam's secret birthday present.

"You're not looking at *apples,*" Flotsam retorted, "and she'll holler for the stinkin' guard. We've done just fine filchin' in town. Always enough for both of us, and then some."

"She won't rat us out. She looks lonely." Jetsam turned to his twin. "How long's it been since we talked to a *girl?* Can't even remember."

"Don't want to get dragged to the mines over a stinkin' lass!" Flotsam snapped with a scowl. "Just 'cause she *looks* lonely don't mean she won't go screamin' bloody murder when she spots our dirty hides."

"We've outrun the stinking guards before and will again," Jetsam countered, while remembering a few close calls. "Can't ignore that fruit." Jetsam even began to sell himself on the succulent produce. "Look, pears!" It was the girl, however, that drew him in. "*I'm* going over!"

With both hands grasping the wall's top, Flotsam could only object with a grunt. Jetsam scampered to the top, hunching cat-like before dropping on all fours into the grass on the other side. Jetsam crouched and watched the lass, who remained oblivious to him. Now he wavered, as uncertainty entered his head. With her radiant hair and immaculate gown, she looked so *clean.* With his greasy locks and tattered clothes, he felt ashamed. Although he acclimated to his own odor, he was certain she'd smell him. *Flotsam's right. I don't belong here.* He considered sneaking back over the wall.

"Hello?" the girl said in a melodious voice, slightly above a whisper.

Too late. Jetsam's heart raced. He didn't dare glance at Flotsam.

The lass kept her distance, her head tilted. Jetsam surmised she was a few years younger than he and his brother, but he had little experience with the fair sex.

"Who are you?" she snapped, standing hands on hips, a dozen paces from Jetsam, who was still frozen on hands and knees. He noticed her drawn lips and furrowed brow. *Oh, no—Flotsam was right.*

Jetsam tried to reply. His mouth even opened a bit, but no words came out. He sat back on his heels, raised his dirty palms, and met her eyes with a pleading expression. *Don't scare her off.*

The comely girl stood her ground, tilting her head now to the left. Her long blond hair shifted across her narrow shoulders. She glanced behind her, and then returned her attention to Jetsam.

"Are you lad or lass?" she queried, peering in the moonlight at the wide-eyed youth. Embarrassed, words finally jumped from Jetsam's mouth.

"*Boy!*" he proclaimed, in the deepest voice he could muster.

Thirteen years old this very day, the identical twins could pass for several years younger. Small and lean, with delicate features and long dark hair, they could also nearly pass as sisters.

"*So* sorry." She held back a grin. "Didn't mean to offend. 'Tis just, well, in the dark, I couldn't tell." Jetsam's face softened as he rose. Examining his damp, shoddy attire, the girl's eyebrows arched. "Why, are you an orphan?"

Jetsam sensed Flotsam's angry gaze burning the back of his neck. The familiar urge to flee tugged at his soul. But something about the girl rooted him in place.

"Worry not. I shan't call the watchman," she stated, as if reading his mind. "I've never met an *und'orphan.* 'Tis very exciting," she gushed. "My parents don't allow me to consort with lads my age." She paused and tucked a loose hair behind her ear. "You are awfully brave coming inside the castle."

"Not brave," he answered, "just hungry."

"Oh, I imagine." Her green eyes grew wider. Jetsam waited as she scanned him up and down. "Come, follow. There's an orchard where the sentinel shan't see us. The fruit's delicious. And I'll show you the gardener's basin for washing," she added.

Jetsam paused and thought of his brother. Before he could turn around, Flotsam landed beside him. The lass scrutinized the scruffy siblings. Her tiny nostrils twitched, but she withheld comment on their pungency.

"Oh, my! You are almost identical!"

"*Almost?*" Flotsam questioned. "No one can tell us apart!"

"I can," she declared with certainty. "There's a difference in your eyes." Flotsam's mouth curled with skepticism. Jetsam, however, believed her. Since he didn't want Flotsam arguing with their hostess, he spoke.

"This is my brother Flotsam. I'm Jetsam."

The twins had been dubbed Flotsam and Jetsam after being fished from the Jade River by the sewer orphans. Adopted into their clan eight summers ago, the siblings' real names faded away with other memories, like a dream of a past life.

"Pleased to meet you both. My name's Giselle."

Giselle, Jetsam repeated in his head. *The perfect name for the perfect girl.* "It's our birthday," he blurted.

"How grand! We shall do something special, then," she insisted. "Come now," she urged, turning and gesturing with her supple hand. "We need to move, before the watchman spots us."

The twins followed their guide as she escorted them through a maze of hazel and hornbeam, her lavender gown tickling the ground. Pointed slippers peeked from under her kirtle as she moved along at a swift pace. She led them past a pool and lingered long enough for at least Flotsam to get the hint. He jabbed his enamored brother in the ribs. They hurriedly washed their hands and faces in the cool water and moved on.

Near the garden's north corner, abutting the castle's outer curtain, sat the tiny orchard Giselle spoke of. Enclosed by high hedges, apples shined in the early summer moonlight as the western Mirrored Peak punctured the starry sky. As the threesome strolled, Jetsam relaxed, savoring the garden's serenity. He remembered the older orphans' tales of scavenging within its walls. The perilous foray proved bountiful, they assured. *Nobles throw away better food than the townsfolk eat!*

Upon entering the orchard, Flotsam scurried up the trunk of a tree and plucked a shiny apple. With a crunch, he bit into the ruby skin. Jetsam and the lass sauntered side by side. As Jetsam turned toward Giselle, he saw panic in her face. Like wildfire, the contagion spread to him. Before he uttered a word, she put an index finger to her pursed lips, halting him.

Then Jetsam heard the heavy footsteps on flagstone. They grew louder and quicker. Aware as well, Flotsam dropped from the tree, still holding his apple, and with a knowing look at Jetsam, tore off.

Jetsam, however, wavered, fearing for Giselle. She glared at him.

"The sentinel! You must flee!"

"What about *you?*" Jetsam begged.

"I shall be fine. I'm *allowed* in here. Now *go!*"

Still Jetsam delayed, his head swiveling toward the footsteps. He saw the guard round the hedge corner. The crimson and cream surcoat sent a chill down Jetsam's spine. The man was tall and meaty, but approached swiftly, chain mail rustling and his silver helm reflecting moonbeams. With his short sword drawn, the lumbering sentry spotted Jetsam. Below his furrowed brow, the watchman's eyes glistened. The sentinel closed, yelling "halt, knave" but once. Anger and greed filled his dull face, panting through his bushy mustache.

Jetsam still held his ground, paralyzed with indecision.

"Believe me, I'm in no danger. But you *are.*" With both hands, she shoved him. The push came as such a shock, Jetsam lunged sideways. After catching his balance, he broke into a sprint, trusting the strange girl.

Jetsam spied his brother's back, yards in front of him, racing from the encroaching guard. *Hope Flotsam knows where he's going.*

Like two mice in this giant maze of a city, Jetsam and Flotsam played a deadly game of cat-and-mouse with one of the King's hungry felines. Jetsam gained ground on his sprinting brother, zigzagging through the garden. The greenery presented a troublesome obstacle, blocking their path and their vision, slapping and tugging at them as they sped past. For a change, Jetsam enjoyed the luxury of following. With his brother fleeing at full speed, Jetsam had no choice but to trail. The burden of decision rested on Flotsam.

Jetsam understood that they ran in a direction opposite the drain chute where they breached the Citadel's outer curtain. He knew only one exit that didn't involve going through a guarded gatehouse, and he was running away from it. Jetsam peered over his shoulder, the sentry chugging closer with every blink. The crimson-clad sword-bearer maintained the advantage of familiarity, and a longer stride. With each misstep and backpedal, the sweating hunter drew nearer.

Through the foliage, Jetsam spotted the garden's exit. His brother was aiming for the open gate. What lay beyond, he couldn't guess. *Bet the guard knows where we're headed.*

By the time Flotsam hurdled a low hedge, Jetsam lagged by a few steps. They shot like arrows through the garden archway and into the north bailey. Jetsam glanced back and noticed the lagging guard. As the man's legs weakened and his armor sapped his endurance, the watchman's pace tailed to a jog. A sly grin spanned Jetsam's lips. *Now we double back to the drain.* Jetsam reached to tap his brother's shoulder.

The bearded man's feet stopped with two thuds and Jetsam craned back to witness the satisfying concession. But the weary sentry drew his horn and blew a piercing note. As the clarion broke the stillness, Jetsam's optimism faded. *Out of the pan and into the flames.*

Gasping for breath, Jetsam slowed behind Flotsam, who paused a few steps in front of him. With a panting guard blocking a retreat into the garden, Jetsam recognized they must push onward. A glance south showed a pair of soldiers emerging from the barracks, called to action by the horn blast. To the north lay an open courtyard and the foreboding outer wall. East sat a cluster of venerable houses, homes for the most elite of nobles. Their best hope sat in front of them. Jetsam tugged Flotsam's tunic and bolted east toward the cluttered alley separating the magnificent dwellings.

Aware of the two fresh watchmen on their tail, Jetsam cut south off the alley, up a narrow pathway between high hedges. He scrambled as fast as he could, leading Flotsam over bushes, under branches, and around corners. *And yet the guards follow.*

Exhaustion assailed Jetsam, and with a glance at his sweaty twin, he confirmed Flotsam was as tired, if not more so. Jetsam also understood there were plenty of soldiers to join the hunt. *Running in circles'll prove fruitless.* His legs burned and his soles ached from the pounding. His worn leather boots offered no comfort. Jetsam saw his brother gasping and grimacing.

Upon spotting a shed tucked among a stand of oaks, Jetsam grabbed his brother once more. A glance behind revealed the guards momentarily out of view. Still grasping Flotsam's arm, he pointed with his head and veered toward the shanty. Flotsam's face showed doubt and concern, but he followed Jetsam. With his twin on his heels, Jetsam slipped through the shed door, closed it after his brother, and slid the latch into place.

If the guard finds us, we're trapped like rats, Jetsam comprehended. *Then to the mines we'll go.* But running in circles was no longer an option. *Some birthday.*

Jetsam panted in the darkness, and between his and Flotsam's heavy breaths, he listened for the guards' footsteps and clinking chain mail.

So far, so good.

When Jetsam's keen eyes adjusted, he discerned they hid inside an old well house. He groped around the brick-encased shaft. The well appeared abandoned and without a windlass, as his hand waved in the void.

Jetsam sat on the bricks and listened to Flotsam bite his apple, carried through their hurried flight. The crunching fruit sounded louder than a rusty hinge.

"Quiet," Jetsam hissed.

Mouth full of apple, Flotsam murmured in concurrence. Jetsam shook his head, his spirits sinking. As Flotsam devoured the fruit, Jetsam wondered how long they should wait until venturing out. His heart stopped when the shed's door rattled.

For a few moments, the guards tugged, ultimately relenting to the door's deceptive strength. Jetsam gazed into the darkness, and through the cracks in the door spotted a thin blade poking in, trying to unseat the latch. In a matter of seconds, they would be caught.

As the short sword probed inward, a hand grabbed Jetsam's shoulder.

When the watchman pried the door, the well house was empty.

"Well, bugger me raw!" replied the latch specialist.

Jetsam held his breath as he listened to boots shuffle, then heard the door creak.

"Wait," said the bearded sentinel who trailed the boys from the start. He tromped back inside, leaned over the open shaft, and thrust his short sword down the hole.

The sharp weapon cut the musty air.

Jetsam smelled the odor of oiled steel as a sword tip stabbed past his nose. The flat of the blade nicked his flaring nostril. Jetsam pulled his head in like a turtle while the guard's sword waved but inches above his scalp. Sardines packed inside the narrow well shaft, the boys held firm. Far above the well's dry bottom, the duo braced themselves with hands and feet, pushing their backs into the rough-hewn rock. Barely wide enough to slither into in the first place, the hole squeezed even tighter now that discovery was imminent.

"Lantern," the guard commanded, nodding toward the void.

Wedged above Flotsam, Jetsam figured their sole hope was to squirm deeper into the mountain's bowels, past the oncoming lantern light. His fear of capture outweighed the certain death awaiting them after even the tiniest of slips. *I've no clue how far it is to bottom.*

Jetsam reached down to Flotsam's shoulder and tapped his brother.

"Deeper," Jetsam whispered.

Flotsam inched downward, hands, feet, and back pressing into the stone. Jetsam followed, not wanting to step on his sibling. The shaft scraped their backs as they slunk further down the black hole.

Jetsam listened to the guards above and saw the lantern's light cascading down the well. Simultaneously, he heard a disturbance below, with the sound of rocks falling and an ominous yelp from Flotsam.

Jetsam froze.

The lantern lowered, clanking against the shaft's sides, pouring eerie, flickering light down the abyss. Jetsam dreaded looking below and seeing an empty shaft. He tried to whisper his brother's name, but fear consumed him, stealing his voice.

He prayed Flotsam hadn't fallen with the loose rocks.

From above, the guards detected him as the lantern revealed his hiding place.

"Come on out, knaves, 'fore we seal the well shut atop ye!"

Jetsam craned his head to peer into the gap below him.

Flotsam was gone.

Chapter Two

Jetsam's eyes welled and a mournful sob passed his lips. *Flots?* As desperation immobilized him, he again glared up at the vile guards. They mumbled to themselves now, trying to puzzle out how to recover their trapped quarry. Tears ran down Jetsam's cheeks as the hatred for his pursuers brought back memories of the day his parents died.

Now Flotsam, too!

He nearly wet himself when a hand grabbed his ankle.

Jetsam jerked his head down and saw a thin arm protruding from the shaft wall.

"Over here," Flotsam hollered. "There's a cavern!"

An ear-to-ear grin erupted on Jetsam's face and he almost lost his footing as he descended toward his brother's voice. When his foot swung through an opening where the well shaft should have been, he crawled through the inadvertent breach and joined Flotsam inside a dark void.

"Where are you?" Jetsam whispered. The blackness was inescapable. When he felt Flotsam's grip on his arm, Jetsam pulled his brother close and hugged him. "Thought you were gone!" he blurted in a squeaky voice, teetering on the verge of tears.

Flotsam reassured Jetsam, "Always darkest beforc the dawn." It was one of Flotsam's favorite sayings, although it didn't fill Jetsam with confidence. *Things just always get darker.* Regardless, they were safe from the guards, whose voices trickled down the shaft.

"Knaves are gone! So much for the stipend."

"Serves the piss-pails, makin' us chase' 'em all 'round."

"Least we don't have to seal the well no more. Tired enough as it is."

"Gimme that rope." Jetsam recognized the gruff voice of the garden watchman who first spotted them. While Flotsam and Jetsam stared into the darkness, the lamp dropped lower. Light poured through the rift and the brothers spun toward the hovering lantern.

"See?" Flotsam said with a hint of *I told you so.*

Before it dropped another inch, Jetsam grasped the lamp. With a swift tug, he snapped it toward him into the cavern. The yank surprised the guard above and the lantern rope slid from his groping hands, snaking down the dank hole.

Curses echoed as Jetsam pulled the rope through the aperture.

"Ye dropped the bloody lamp, ye oaf?"

"Didn't drop it—something pulled it from me!"

"What, a sodding ghost, ye clumsy arse?"

"'Twas the soddin' knaves, I'm sure."

"Well, they're gone now. Knaves and me lantern."

Jetsam cloaked the lantern in front of him, keeping any light from reaching the breach. *Maybe they'll think we found the bottom,* he thought. The voices faded to murmurs and then disappeared when the shed door slammed.

After waiting to be certain the guards were gone, Jetsam lifted the lantern, letting its light spill into the room. The immense cavern opened like a flower at daybreak.

"Never seen nuthin' like this," Flotsam said, his head craning to take in the exquisitely-carved hall. "What do you think it is?"

"This place is a disaster," Jetsam replied, holding the lantern above his head while scrutinizing the crumbled walls and collapsed ceiling. Twin columns sprouted from the room's center, both sheared in half by whatever force ravaged this chamber. Yet even with the cracks and rubble and debris, the room stood an ageless testimony to craftsmanship. The undamaged portions were smooth as glass and decorated with ornate geometrical carvings.

As Jetsam watched the light flicker off the slick walls, the severity of their situation sunk in. *The lantern won't burn forever, and we've no idea how to escape this cavern.*

"There's no doors!" Flotsam blurted.

"We can't go back up," Jetsam declared. "Look around—there has to be a way in, or out." Within the lantern light, Jetsam sifted through the rubble strewn on the floor, and Flotsam followed his lead.

"Look at this," Jetsam said, pointing to a wall cleft.

"A staircase," Flotsam said, kneeling to inspect the cut stonework. "It went up—once. Now it's full of stinkin' debris." Flotsam stood and peered upward, hands on hips. "We'll never get out that way." Inspecting the collapsed staircase, Jetsam silently agreed. The spiral exit was more than just filled with debris; it was unusable, even if they cleared the rubble.

"What caused all this damage?" Flotsam asked. "A landslide?"

"Don't think you can have landslides underground. Trembler I bet."

Flotsam nodded while biting his lip. Jetsam and his lamp inched forward. He pushed over a chunk of rock with his foot.

"See that?" Jetsam pointed at the stone's surface. Flotsam crept in for a closer inspection.

"Looks like writing," he said. "Not that I know what it says."

"Me neither," Jetsam agreed. "But I *do* remember the alphabet, and those aren't letters we ever learned." He recalled beginning reading lessons inside his parents' comfortable house, the hearth's warmth, and the long-forgotten feeling of security.

"This is *old,*" Flotsam murmured, snapping his brother back to the present.

"Remember Ratboy's tales?" Jetsam asked. "Said smallfolk once lived under the city."

"Ratboy tells lots of ghost stories. Says monsters roam deep underground, yet we've never seen more than rats and bats and spiders."

"Yeah, Ratboy's full of it," Jetsam said unconvincingly. "There's gotta be another way out," he replied, raising the lantern higher. Jetsam stepped over chucks of rubble and worked his way to the wall, eyeing it up and down. He led Flotsam around the entire room, and the twins examined every crack and crevasse in each of the four walls.

Spiders wove webs between the gaps, catching blind insects in their sticky nets. Water trickled down cracks, eroding the stonework. Dust and mildew gathered on the floor, accumulating unfettered by the near-forgotten pacing of heavy boots. All signs of Dwarven inhabitancy disappeared from this subterranean setting ages ago.

"If there ever was another doorway, it's gone now," Flotsam moaned upon completing the circuit. "Bloody, sodding trembler."

"Think the guards are still up there?" Jetsam asked.

"Dunno, probably."

"Guess we'll have to wait 'em out."

"Even if they leave, I don't want to scale that well shaft."

"Don't see much choice. Might as well save lantern oil." Jetsam plopped onto the floor, and his impacting rump emitted an unexpected sound for a cavern.

"Hey! There's a panel here." Jetsam scrambled to his knees. "Help me dig it out." With the lantern on a nearby pillar chunk, the boys dug through the rocky debris to unveil Jetsam's discovery.

"Think it's a door?" Flotsam asked. He rapped his knuckles on the dusty wood. "Sounds hollow." Four hands brushed over the oak, clearing the gravel and dust, while searching for a handle. Once cleaned, the square panel revealed a surface flat as a table top.

Knees on the floor with hands on hips, the brothers mirrored each other.

"How do we open it?" Jetsam asked.

"Sodding dung," Flotsam hissed. "Mebbe it don't open."

Undaunted, Jetsam brought the lantern closer. He leaned to the ground, blowing the fine dust away as if he were extinguishing a candelabra. He ran his fingertips across seams, digging his dirty fingernails into the cracks.

"Devil's luck!" Jetsam exclaimed as his clawing hands slid a small panel to expose a hidden handle.

They lifted the heavy trap door, as rusty hinges squealed in opposition. Lantern light illuminated a winding stairwell, carved from the native stone. The siblings entered and circled deeper into the ground, following the stairway to a rough-hewn landing. Jetsam turned to his brother.

"Well?"

"S'pose we follow it," Flotsam resigned. "Mebbe it leads back to the underbelly."

Jetsam set the lantern as low as possible, giving off just enough light to see, trying to conserve the precious oil. Even in the dim glow, the devastation was apparent. As the passage slithered down, rubble hindered their every step.

Despite the treacherous footing and growing exhaustion, the boys moved at a steady pace. Jetsam's unspoken fear of the lantern burning out weighed on him. He and his brother were accustomed to traveling underground, their eyesight honed to the blackness. However, familiarity usually aided them, but they roamed in foreign territory now. The lantern proved a valuable ally. *For now.*

"This tunnel winds like a drunken snake," Flotsam complained.

"About as narrow as one," Jetsam replied.

They trod on, with the sound of their breath and their footsteps breaking the silence. *Flotsam's never going to let me live this down,* Jetsam lamented. He brushed an errant strand of hair from his greasy brow.

"How long you 'spose we been in here?" Flotsam asked.

"Seems like forever." Webs clung to Jetsam's face as his nimble fingers wiped away the sticky veneer. He had no idea how long they'd been plodding. Regardless, the lantern oil kept burning lower.

"I know," Flotsam concurred. "Sometimes it feels like we're going downhill, but just as often up."

A rat scurried beneath Jetsam's feet as he shuffled. Gambling on the rat's instincts, Jetsam followed the rodent. "The varmint'll lead us to the surface," Jetsam murmured, hoping he was correct.

"Don't get too close," Flotsam warned. "Don't want him running off." The furry rodent stood as big as a barn cat, and displayed no fear.

"He's lucky we're not hungry," Jetsam joked.

"If he gets us out of here, I'll spare him," Flotsam promised. "Can always find another rat if we're starving."

After following the rat a quarter furlong, the span widened and Jetsam detected the distant sound of water dripping. "May be nearing the surface." He hoped the passageway lead to a familiar part of the underbelly. He and Flotsam had memorized endless runs of storm sewer.

"Don't recognize any of this," Flotsam moaned. "And I thought we'd been everywhere in the underbelly."

With the rodent leading the way, Jetsam heard a low, guttural sound, and paused, turning back at Flotsam. The lagging sibling shrugged and arched his eyebrows. When Jetsam turned back around, the rat was gone.

"Blast!"

"What's wrong?" Flotsam asked.

"Stinkin' beady-eyes ditched us."

Jetsam plodded on, taking the lead from their truant guide. When they reached a fork, a decision was required.

"Where's a bloody rat when you need one," Jetsam bemoaned. With the lantern in front of him, he poked his head into each branch. After a glance at Flotsam, he chose the passage with a slight incline.

The sound behind them reverberated again. *Louder.*

Jetsam looked back. Within the lantern's radius, there was nothing beside his brother.

"Ditch-dung!" Flotsam blurted. "What the piss-and-pus was that?"

Jetsam swallowed hard and shook his head. *Whatever it is, I don't want to face it.*

Gasping for breath, Jetsam led onward, wanting a break, but fearing to stop. The lantern burned the last of its oil and blackness enveloped them.

From behind, feet thumped and claws scraped the stone floor.

"Grab the rope!" Jetsam instructed, and for a second, his hands slapped at Flotsam's, trying to exchange the lantern cord.

"Got it!" Flotsam yelped. With an assuring tug on the rope, Jetsam scrambled blindly up the shaft, knowing they were linked. Flotsam secured the twine around his waist and forearm, and followed close behind his twin.

With every step, Jetsam's ears told him the creature drew nearer. Jetsam stumbled and fell and scampered back up, Flotsam at his heels, still clutching the rope. Several times Jetsam crashed into the hard stone walls, scraping and bruising his forearms and shoulders.

Sobs burst from Jetsam, alternating with gasps to fill his burning lungs. He could only imagine what kind of vile monster nipped at their heels. In his years in the sewers, he never encountered anything like this. No giant spider or oversized rat chased them now. *A mountain wolf or wild dog maybe,* he thought. Still, the rhythm of the trailing footfalls made him suspect the creature ran on two legs—not four.

Jetsam recalled Ratboy's tales of beasts inhabiting the deep tunnels beneath the Citadel. Now he worried they were more than legend. He'd never seen a goblin, ogre, or troll, but he was afraid he soon would.

Then Flotsam screamed.

Jetsam pulled on the rope and felt tension. *He's still there.* Unable to speak, Jetsam feared his twin had been struck or bitten, for he'd *never* heard Flotsam scream.

"Flots?" he yelped.

Oh, Elvar, he lamented, *what have I gotten us into?* It had been years since Jetsam thought of his brother by his real name. He used his brother's birth name when they were first orphaned, and Elvar called him by his true name: Eidryn. But to the others, they were Flotsam and Jetsam, and soon, Elvar and Eidryn Lothyrn were no more.

"Flotsam?" Jetsam's voice cracked with terror, yet he received no reply. The tightening rope weighed him like an anchor. He peered back in vain, seeing blackness.

"Elvar!"

In the passage ahead, Jetsam discerned the faintest of lights. The flicker provided enough encouragement to shoot one last burst of adrenaline through his veins. He dragged his unresponsive brother up the steepening slope, all the while hearing the scraping, snorting, growling fiend snapping at their heels. *Feels like dead weight,* Jetsam lamented.

Time tortured Jetsam as he struggled toward the glow. *Moonlight,* he told himself, as if getting aboveground would be of any help at all. Salty sweat burned his eyes and his empty stomach churned. His sibling grew heavier, but as long as he felt the drag, he knew Flotsam was there. Though the coarse rope blistered his hands, the pain was his life-link. But the pull was heavy. *So heavy.*

Finally, the starry night sky shone through a small hole. With all his might, Jetsam yanked his brother to the opening, the clawing, faceless beast forcing itself up the narrowing egress behind them.

With a desperate lunge, Jetsam broke free from the ground, dragging Flotsam behind him, his slender body tangled in the lantern rope. Like seeds spit from the earth, the twins shot from the breach, landing on the bank of the Jade River. As they tumbled and slid toward the water, Jetsam spied a brief glimpse of his pursuer.

In the split-second before plunging into the cool river, Jetsam saw an ugly, rubbery-gray head with sunken, beady eyes.

Chapter Three

Dog-paddling in the wide river, Jetsam couldn't stop the memories from pouring back. This same Jade River had carried the twins from danger the day their parents died. Only five years old, Jetsam remembered the unrest in his household in the days leading to their murder.

Flotsam and Jetsam's parents taught at the Citadel's venerable School for Sorcery, and became unsuspecting targets of the king. With their innocent blood, a statement was made that insurrection would not be tolerated, no matter status or standing. The terrified brothers barely escaped the slaughter, jumping from a bridge into the frigid Jade River, to be rescued downstream by the orphans.

Jetsam shook off the painful memories and stole a glimpse at their pursuer. Foul breath spewed from the frustrated beast's salivating maw, Flotsam's shredded boot impaled on its bloody incisor. The panting creature struggled against the small hole, failing to squeeze its broad shoulders through the opening in the ground. Scratching the stone orifice with massive black claws, the beast's effort was to no avail. The growling troglodyte relented its assault on the moonlit earth. With a chilling howl, the hairless brute retreated into the darkness.

Jetsam fought the rushing water while still clinging to the lantern and rope. With Flotsam wound in the cord, the lamp proved an anchor. Jetsam held on anyway, not wanting to lose his brother.

He strained above the water, struggling in the current, legs kicking, searching for Flotsam.

As he reeled in the rope, Jetsam spotted Flotsam's frail body bobbing face-down in the swift current. Jetsam's feet stretched for the bottom while he reached for his brother. His boots swung without hitting sediment and he sank under water.

Jetsam swam against the undertow, sucking in frigid water while clutching the lantern rope. When he popped into the night air, Flotsam was nowhere to be seen. The fierce current tumbled Jetsam into a river bend and his heels struck a shallow, sandy bottom.

He dug in and worked his way to the bank. Half out of the water, he grabbed a low-hanging branch to secure himself. With his remaining strength, he reeled his sibling in, the wet cord coiling at his feet.

After an interminable struggle with the river's tenacious grip, Jetsam dragged Flotsam to the shallow bend and pulled his motionless body to the bank. Only then did Jetsam see the extent of his brother's injuries.

Jetsam propped Flotsam upright. Bloody river water poured from his lifeless mouth. Claw marks raked Flotsam's jaw and neck. The strike had torn away flesh, crushed his windpipe, and sliced his jugular.

Jetsam sat on the shore trying to revive his brother. *Come on, Elvar! Come back to me!* Drenched and shivering, his long locks clung matted and stringy to his bony shoulders. Tears and sobs poured forth in vain as the reality of Flotsam's death stared Jetsam in the face. He pounded the wet sand with his fists.

You can't leave me here alone.

Jetsam's mournful wailing echoed along the river bank and disappeared into the mountain pass. He gazed at his dead twin as if into a mirror. The face was his, and his own mortality mocked him. In Flotsam's colorless visage, Jetsam recognized the corpse of his lost hope. Every dream he had of growing up and escaping this miserable life included his brother by his side. *I can't imagine a future without you.*

In deep shock, Jetsam clung to Flotsam.

What do I do now? Glassy eyes staring to the heavens, the agonizing moonlight offered no answers. His mind a swirling void, Jetsam unwound the tangled, knotted lantern rope from Flotsam's body and discarded it on the bank.

Got to get him back to the lair, Jetsam decided, without any compelling reason. Achy and shivering, he stood on the uneven riverbank and tried to lift Flotsam. His hungry, tired, exhausted body failed him. Slumped on one knee, he surveyed the surging river.

Can't go back in the water. Too cold. Too fast.

His head pounding, Jetsam took a deep breath and leaned down to grasp Flotsam's wrists.

Must be a sewer drain nearby, he convinced himself. With every last bit of strength he possessed, Jetsam dragged his twin along the bank. He averted his eyes from Flotsam, unable to bear the sight of his sibling's lifeless head lolling.

When Jetsam finally encountered a drain, he bordered on delirium. Shock and exhaustion ravaged him. He pulled Flotsam into the dirty outlet, collapsed beside him and passed out.

Jetsam never remembered being carried back to the clan encampment. The solemn march never recorded as a memory in his tormented brain.

Jetsam awoke with a start, a blurry face staring at him.

"What— " he began, and it all came rushing back. *Elvar!* He broke down, sobbing.

"Easy, Jets, easy," Ratboy said, patting his friend on the shoulder. "Mole and Biter found ye and Flots at the drain. They thought ye both dead."

"Wish I was," Jetsam blurted, tear streaks striping his dirty face. "But only Flotsam,"

"What happened?"

Between sobs and gasps, Jetsam spit out what he recalled of his brother's demise. Whether the monster had killed his brother outright, or Flotsam had bled out or drowned in the river, Jetsam would never know. *Little does it matter.*

"A sodding knuckle-dragger," Ratboy shook his head. "Can't hardly, believe it, yet I saw Flotsam's wounds." Jetsam couldn't meet his friend's sympathetic gaze. He hurt too much. "Jets, we gotta bury yer brother. Ye up for it?"

Jetsam sniffled and nodded, and Ratboy helped him to his feet. Guided by Ratboy's hand on his shoulder, he proceeded to Flotsam's wrapped body. Six orphan pallbearers lifted Flotsam from the ground, and started on their way. Ratboy followed with Jetsam, supporting his wobbling friend.

Not a word was uttered as Jetsam's allies carried Flotsam's shrouded corpse into the catacombs. The uppermost sections of former mine shafts were converted into the final resting place for Dwim-Halloe's departed. To bury their deceased, folk ventured into the abandoned underground, carving crypts to house their beloved.

The orphans snuck Flotsam's fresh corpse into an empty tomb and sealed it with a scavenged slab. Visibly moved, Ratboy used the dull tip of his rusty dagger to scratch an 'F' into the stone. After his impromptu epitaph, the wet-eyed urchins left Flotsam with the other nameless dead, to be discriminated against no more.

His trembling hand pressed against the slab, Jetsam lingered.

"Come on, Jets," Ratboy whispered. Jetsam shook his head. "Grave diggers'll be here 'fore ye know it. We gotta go." Ratboy's urging fell on deaf ears. Jetsam obsessed on death, and waited for the Reaper to take him wherever the rest of his family already was.

"Mole," Ratboy called. "Gimme a hand." His friends hoisted Jetsam by the arms and lifted him from Flotsam's resting place. Jetsam never spoke a word as they carried him back to the lair.

Jetsam's subterranean dwelling seemed more depressing than ever. *I'm sick of the underground. Sick of scavenging and hiding. Sick of everything.*

Sick of living.

Inside his unmoving body, unbridled emotions tortured him. Sorrow pounded him for the loss of his brother. Guilt persecuted him for goading Flotsam inside the castle. And regret besieged him for allowing his passion to overrule logic, sealing the fate of poor Flotsam. Time stopped as he struggled with these demons.

Elvar's death flooded Jetsam with memories of the day his parents died. *The day Elvar and I fled from home.* The day they first ran from the king's guard. *The day the running started.* Trapped on a stone bridge, with soldiers rushing from each side, the twins climbed the rail and met the river's chilly embrace, leaving their life behind.

Jetsam recalled the envoy of king's men arriving unthreatening on his doorstep. He remembered answering the knock and seeing the towering captain in shiny armor. The impeccable soldier in flawless crimson and cream, politely asking for his father, saying he had a message from the king.

A message from the king!

Jetsam relived every bitter step as he ran to tell his parents. *Message from the king!* He saw his father's pained expression, and remembered being sent to his room, Elvar by his side.

Why isn't father excited by the message from the king?

Jetsam shuddered at how quickly things went wrong. *They struck without word or warning.* Their crimson and cream surcoats blurred into his parents' red blood and pale flesh. They were slaughtered unsuspecting. *For no reason at all!*

He remembered the faces on the murderous guards, the heartless words. "'Twill surely give those damned rebels something to think about." The fateful sentence echoed in his head, even though he tried to shut it out. The years had not made the recollections any less painful.

Now Elvar joined his parents as an excruciating memory branded in Jetsam's tortured mind.

"He's not doin' well," Ratboy said, nodding toward Jetsam, who sat huddled in a dark alcove off the cavern the orphans called home. No more than a series of low twisting tunnels, the dank underbelly was all the boys had. Curled in a ball, pale hands clasped across his shins, Jetsam was just another piece of rubble.

"Ain't even comin' out ta eat, he's not," Mole replied. "Some o' the others saying he ain't' gonna make it, he's not."

"Bullshit," Ratboy spat. Though loathe to admit it, Ratboy, too, struggled to envision how Jetsam would survive without his brother. *They never left each other's side.* Their scavenging skills were renown among the orphans, for they worked as a tandem almost telepathically, always sharing their surplus bounty with the clan.

“Gonna get sick, if he ain’t already, he is.”

“Not gonna just let him die,” Ratboy retorted. “We’ve had too much death ‘round here.” One of the few underbelly teens, Ratboy stood taller and more muscular than most others. Despite his physical maturity, Ratboy still had a boyish face, round and full, unblemished by facial hair. His sandy brown locks hung long and tangled, curling at the ends.

“W-w-what’re we s’posed ta do?” Mole asked. A summer younger than Ratboy, Mole appeared not nearly that old. Skeleton-skinny with beady eyes, the redheaded Mole contrasted Ratboy’s maturity.

“Not give up, that’s what.” Ratboy recalled the day he spotted the twins bobbing in the Jade River. Ever since their fateful exile, Ratboy had been their best friend. He served as the closest semblance to a leader the clan had, and orchestrated the rescue of the waterlogged youths that portentous day. He invited them into the group, bestowing the fitting names Flotsam and Jetsam.

Ratboy and the brothers had been close ever since. The three shared many adventures, both real and imaginary. *Endless days we spent playing hide-and-seek, bloody murder, and other games in the sewers, waiting for nightfall.* Sling stone contests and tree-limb sword fights, foot races and wrestling matches, these diversions occupied the waifs’ daytime hours. Once darkness covered the land above, the trio would apply their fertile imaginations to their imperative scavenging. By day, they rescued make-believe fair maidens and vanquished pretend giants, while by night they stole from real townsfolk and hid from armed guards.

Mole interrupted Ratboy’s bittersweet reminiscing. “Think Jetsam’s the one that’s given up,” he squeaked. “He gets sick, we’re all at risk, we are.” The orphans grew accustomed to death. With malnutrition and disease rampant, the Reaper made regular stops in the underbelly.

“I’m not about to lose ‘em both,” Ratboy vowed. Born a bastard, only-child to a rag-picker, Ratboy was sent to the mines after his mother died of typhoid. He labored from dawn till dusk, only seeing blue sky on cloudless Sundays. Ratboy learned the underground as well as any miner, and after a harrowing cave-in, decided he'd rather risk running away than go back in the deplorable mines.

So it was that Ratboy started the orphan clan. *Never intended to do any more than survive on my own.* But after King Vardan's new policy on orphan boys, he soon found others needing help. *Lost and scared and crying they came.* With his amiable boyish face and keen survival instincts, he became a magnet for frightened runaways. One by one, his surrogate family grew. But ever since the day he plucked the twins from the river, they'd been his favorites.

"I'll sit with him as long as it takes." Ratboy understood if his friend had any chance at all, time would play a key role. "Jetsam's the closest thing to family I got."

A bruised apple in hand, Ratboy walked to Jetsam's side. "Come on, Jets," he pleaded while offering the fruit. "Ye gotta eat."

Ratboy refused to think about what he'd be forced to do if Jetsam became ill.

Chapter Four

The time Jetsam spent coiled against the unforgiving stone failed to register in minutes or hours. His pain clouded any mental logging of time, as if he sat in limbo, cursed to agonize over his rash behavior that cost him his remaining family.

Nearby, other orphans bustled nervously, arguing in a panic-stricken cacophony.

"Blister, Rooster, and Pike didn't come back this morn," Lil' Pete said.

"That ain't good," replied Biter. "Ye know where they went scavenging?"

"Nay, but I did hear 'em jabberin' about that new hole Jetsam found."

"One with the soddin' troll?"

"Aye—Ratboy warned 'em stay away, but bloody Rooster's got a mind o' his own," Lil' Pete lamented. "And he can't resist explorin' a new tunnel."

"Ain't good at all," repeated Biter.

"Not sure they believed Ratboy's story 'bout the troll anyways," Lil' Pete replied. "Prob'ly just another one o' his tales to scare us outta trouble."

"*Something* killed Flotsam," Biter retorted.

"Aye, but Jetsam ain't said a peep. All we know, coulda been a wolf or even a cave bear—who knows?"

"Bugger," Jetsam mumbled. The chaos of the orphan crisis penetrated Jetsam's fog. His heart sank even deeper when he comprehended the news. A fresh heaping of guilt assailed him. *If I'd have convinced them of the beast, they would've never gone in that hole.* Without hesitation, Jetsam discerned what he must do. As the reality of his friends' absence registered, he understood the clan *was* family. *They're all I have left.*

As he uncoiled his stiff body, aching muscles screamed in resistance. Slowly standing, he stretched in place, his wrinkled clothes clinging to his frame. Dried tear tracks stained his dirty cheeks. With his sling and bag of stones in hand, he acknowledged the weapon's futility against the knuckle-dragger. *But it's all I've got.*

"You tell Ratboy about this?" Jetsam asked the pair.

"Aye—he and Mole left hours ago."

Jetsam realized he might be too late, and that he may be racing to his own death. *Better than wasting away in a cave,* he concluded. *I'm tired of waiting to die.* As his thick blood pumped, adrenaline boosted his resolve, and he vowed to avenge Flotsam.

If I only knew how. He considered his companions. "I'm going after them—they don't know what they're up against."

"We'll go with ye," said Lil' Pete.

"No, stay here. This is bad enough already," Jetsam argued. *I'll not have more blood on my hands.* But his stubborn friends appeared unconvinced. "If anyone comes back before I do, make sure they don't chase after me. None of us should be going in those tunnels. Ever."

"Nay, we're going with ye," retorted Lil' Pete. Biter, however, took a step back.

"You saw what that bloody blaggard did to Flotsam—and he was older and faster than both of you," said Jetsam. "That sodding troll's mean and quick and huge, and if Ratboy and I can't rescue the others, I don't want that fobbing knuckle-dragger to kill the whole clan." Jetsam's voice held an edge the boys had never heard, and his furrowed brow and steely glare told them he meant business.

"We'll stay… and warn the others," Biter said, putting a hand on Lil' Pete's shoulder.

And they did.

Navigating the sewers, Jetsam's senses awakened, shaking off the long inactivity. It felt like years since he and his brother conducted their last nocturnal raid. The townsfolk were fast asleep, their small stone houses dark and quiet. But there would be no scavenging tonight.

Jetsam emerged from the familiar sewers near a stand of alders by the riverbank. He slipped beneath the branches, retracing his steps from that fateful night. The air was cool and moist, the moon hidden behind a thick cloud curtain. The low-hanging mist obscured even the Mirrored Peaks. It took Jetsam a few minutes of travel along the river bank to get his bearings. Once he did, he identified his target.

Jetsam covered the distance adroitly as rain fell. *Sewers'll be wet tonight.* Upon reaching the hole where he escaped the troll, a deep fear overcame him. The bloodthirsty beast's scent and sounds assaulted his memory. His spry body quivered. *For Elvar,* he steeled himself. After a momentary submission to his panic, he gathered his wits and scanned the bank for the discarded lantern. *Nowhere in sight.* After a slight hesitation, he lowered himself back into the earth.

Wish I had that lamp. Without it, he navigated the passage shrouded in blackness. He remembered the tunnel sloping downward for a lengthy run until reaching the only passable intersection. His ears strained to pick up any sound, but were unrewarded. His leather boots slid along the rough stone.

Before long, Jetsam reached the intersection where he and Flotsam deliberated their path. *Wonder what would've happened if I chose the other path,* he lamented. *Maybe Elvar'd still be alive.* Now, another decision beckoned. With only his hushed breath making a sound, Jetsam paused. The corridor to his left sloped downward to the unknown. Ahead lay the tunnel back under the castle, where Flotsam had breached the well shaft. *If they headed that way, they'll have to turn around at the well,* he reasoned. Since he knew where *that* passageway ended, he chose the familiar route. *Either I'll find them along the way, or reach the well and turn back. The logical choice,* he decided, trying to envision what Flotsam would do. And it delayed venturing into uncharted territory.

With his decision delivered, Jetsam headed down the passage where he and Flotsam treaded but days ago. Back toward the well he went, thinking about the troll every step.

And Elvar.

Bent at the knees, he continued along the narrow wormhole. Hands and feet were his senses now, eyes and ears rendered useless by the quiet and the dark. Arms outstretched, he touched each side of the tunnel. Small rocks littered his path and he tried to avoid stumbling on the loose stones. Spiders had already rebuilt the webs he and Flotsam destroyed. Jetsam tore them down again.

A faint scratching trickled from the cavern ahead. His cautious pace slowed even further. Hands extended, his fingertips explored the confined passageway's slippery walls, feeling his way toward danger. With every judicious step, the sound intensified. Then he heard another noise, frightening in its familiarity.

Upon hearing the beastly grunt, Jetsam feared the despicable humpback blocked his path. By its foul stench, he was convinced it was the same creature that killed Flotsam. Frozen in his tracks, sweat coalesced on Jetsam's palms. Instinctively, he retrieved his sling. *What good this'll do, I've no idea.* Even though he possessed keen night vision, he would have to let his nose and ears aim his shot in this blackness.

He wondered if he listened to the gnawing of his comrades' bones.

Jetsam slid forward, hoping for a clue of the troll's activity. *Sounds like the humpback's scraping his claws on the rock.* Ten excruciating steps closer Jetsam moved and, to his amazement, his eyes detected light.

Inching further, he adjusted to the unexpected illumination. He discerned the troglodyte's clawing form at the collapsed tunnel. Bony hands scratched at the stone, pulling out fragments and discarding them in a pile of rubble at its curled feet.

Jetsam spotted the light's source. The lantern he swiped from the guard burned dimly from underneath the rubble. Wedged beneath the broken wall, the dust-covered lamp shone through the surrounding debris.

Someone filled it with oil.

The fact that the troll clawed so intently at the obstructed passage led Jetsam to believe it had something trapped behind the rubble.

Dead or alive?

Barely audible, the faint cries of a boy reached his ears. For better or worse, he'd found his friends.

Watching the hideous troll assault the collapsed tunnel filled Jetsam with dread. Heartened by the fact his friends still lived, he also recognized it may not be for long. *I need to act—and fast.* Jetsam watched the creature's muscled back ripple like bubbling tar. *They're either buried in the cave-in or trapped beyond.* Chiseled arms flailed at the intervening rocks, wafting foul troll scent through the musty air. *It's but a matter of time before the troll clears the passage and devours them.*

Jetsam pulled a sling stone from his belt-bag and brandished his weapon. Creeping closer, he observed the repulsive attacker. Hunched and naked, the troll's dull skin was nearly hairless, except for sporadic wiry bristles. Sinew rippled through its lanky limbs, nary an ounce of fat adorning the spindly frame. *And its odor has a life of its own.* Every step grew more putrid.

Aimed at the grotesque head, Jetsam let his stone fly. Through the stinking air, the whistling rock struck the bald skull. Jetsam heard the thud a split-second before the beast roared in anger. The projectile harmed the troll little, but succeeded as a distraction. The creature pivoted toward Jetsam, mucous-slathered nostrils flaring. Another sling stone struck the troglodyte's right eye, eliciting a harrowing squeal. *That one did damage indeed.*

Furious, the humpback charged Jetsam, who tore off back toward the intersection, away from the blocked passage. Jetsam couldn't help but hear the long-legged troll. Its clawed feet slapped and scratched the stone floor. Fifty feet of tunnel separated Jetsam from the beast. Unencumbered and somewhat familiar with the terrain, Jetsam was confident he could beat the crouching troll. The tall flesh-eater had to hunch in the low tunnels, which slowed it considerably. Yet without looking back, the scraping, grunting, clawing monster drew closer. Jetsam sensed its presence nearing.

Limber legs sprinting, Jetsam's sightless feet hoped to avoid the treacherous debris. His hands reached out, trying to prevent slamming into the stone. As his pursuer gained, Jetsam's confidence wavered. *One misstep and he's on me.* Then Flotsam's fate would be *his.* Jetsam felt the troll's hot breath on the back of his neck. Regret over his decision gnawed at him. He pumped his legs harder.

Then he lost his footing and sprawled hard.

Time accelerated as Jetsam struggled to rise. With the troll gaining, every second was precious. Scraped and bruised on the unforgiving rock, Jetsam regained his feet posthaste and put them to work double-time before the pain set in. In that instant, however, his lead evaporated.

With a whoosh, the troll's huge claw swiped through the musty air, black nails grazing Jetsam's shoulder. The slash wobbled him, but he righted himself on the run. His mind awash with fear, Jetsam pushed forward while bracing for another blow. *I can't outrun it.*

In desperation, he clutched his pouch and tossed his remaining sling stones behind him. The creature grunted and stumbled, its feet slipping on the marbles. The lumbering giant crashed to the tunnel floor, its rubbery skin scraping on the rough surface as it slid to a halt.

Jetsam's relief was short lived.

Undaunted, the troll scrambled up and continued the pursuit. Jetsam prayed the momentary delay would be enough for him to escape. His shoulder stung and throbbed, and the fresh claw marks oozed blood into his shredded tunic.

With every hurried step, Jetsam peered into the blackness for a glimmer of light. No matter how hard he pushed, his aching body lost precious speed. *He's closing again.* A few paces further, Jetsam's outstretched hands could no longer touch both sides of the passage. As the cavern widened, he neared the intersection.

At this pace, he'll catch me before the river bank. Jetsam veered left, downward into the unknown. He dropped to the ground, wrapping his arms over his head as the abomination shambled toward him.

With the troglodyte a step away, Jetsam kicked his legs out in the rushing creature's path. His thin limbs smacked the ankles of the charging beast. In an avalanche of flesh, the knuckle-dragger lurched forward, rolling down the steep wormhole, over and past Jetsam. The painful impact spun and tumbled Jetsam as well, but bought him the time he needed to reestablish his lead.

As he jumped to his feet, Jetsam's bruised shins ached from the collision. Now he scampered up and deliberated. *The time it takes me to swim the moat, run to the well house and scale the shaft, Stinky'll be picking his teeth with their bones,* Jetsam lamented. He forsook the passage leading to the riverbank. *Maybe he'll head for the river,* Jetsam hoped. The brute growled in anger and sniffed the air for Jetsam's scent. The beast clamored back toward the intersection—and Jetsam.

Adrenaline depleted and panting, Jetsam raced for the unknown, abandoning the tunnel back to the Jade. His ears told him the troll chose the familiar route to the river bank. *I've bought some time, but where the sodding gods am I?* Dirty, battered, and exhausted, he was nonetheless safe—for now. *Stinky'll be back soon as he reaches the riverbank.*

Inside the dark cavern, his hands moved across the rock, guiding him. Listening for the troll's return, Jetsam only heard his leather soles shuffling along the stone. He traveled but a short distance in the pitch-black passage before he recognized a familiar sound. Mole's squeaky, panicked voice was discernible. A reliable sidekick, Jetsam was sure Ratboy would have taken Mole with him to find the others. *Why don't I hear Ratboy?* Jetsam followed his ears.

"Mole!" Jetsam shouted. "Mole, it's Jetsam." Mole replied to the call, and Jetsam grew confused. *He sounds quieter now.*

"Mole?"

"Jetsam!" Tilting his head, Jetsam stopped to hone in on the voice. He turned around and backtracked a few steps.

"Keep talking, Mole."

"Jetsam, J-Jetsam," Mole continued chanting his friend's name in a nervous litany.

Sodding gods, where the pus is he? Jetsam took two more steps and the volume decreased. Hands on hips, Jetsam reversed his direction again. This time, a hollow sound echoed beneath his left foot. Jetsam dropped to all fours. He swept his palms along the floor. Feeling rough wood with his fingertips, he groped for the hidden latch. *Another fobbing trap door.* Jetsam blindly cleared the panel of debris, pushing cobbles and rocks aside. He grunted and strained to open the hatch.

With an opposing screech, the door relented as its gravel and dust coating slid toward his feet. Jetsam heard Mole clearly now.

"J-Jetsam… Jetsam… Jetsam… "

"I'm coming!"

Jetsam hustled down a spiral staircase and emerged onto a landing. Far down the tunnel, seeping lantern light provided a dim beacon. While closing the distance, Jetsam heard the troll clawing away on the other side of the debris. *That didn't take long.* Having opened a crack that let the flickering lantern seep through, the carnivore was close now. The beast growled in confusion and rage, and intensified his digging. *He smells me.*

"Jetsam! Help!" Mole cried. Enough light shone through the cracks for Jetsam to see Mole's round face streaked with dirty tears. Mouth agape, immobilized with fear, the skinny boy shook. With his legs trapped by the collapsed rocks, he had soiled himself. On his knees, Ratboy struggled to remove the offending debris. The largest chuck remained wedged in place.

"Gimme a hand with this," Ratboy said, nodding at a heavy shard. Jetsam slid past the trembling Mole and knelt by Ratboy. The air hung thick and still, filled with the stink of troll and Mole's stained trousers.

"Was worried I didn't hear you," Jetsam confessed.

"He's makin' enough racket for the both of us." His head tilted toward Mole, prone on the ground, propped up on his bony elbows.

"Can ye get me out?" Mole squealed in fright, seeing the troll's knotty claws through the open hole.

"Ready?" Ratboy asked Jetsam, who confirmed with a nod. "Pull!"

The grunting duo lifted the rock enough for Mole to squirm free. He scrambled back and Jetsam saw his torn trousers and bloodied shins.

"Can ye stand?" Ratboy asked.

"D-don't think so, I don't," Mole whined.

A clatter of rocks drew Jetsam's attention to the troll. Its rubbery arm broke through the debris and waved mere feet from the lads.

"Try!" Ratboy demanded. Mole complied and shrieked.

"Bloody, stinkin' piss-pail!" he yelled. "It hurts!" Mole flopped to the ground, throwing his head back in pain.

"We'll have to carry him. There's a way out," Jetsam revealed. The two orphans hoisted Mole and began their retreat.

How will we get him up the stairway?

"Did you find the others?" Jetsam asked.

"N-n-nay," Mole stammered. "We got to—" Mole choked on the words and tried again. "Got to a fork and headed this way, we did." The adolescent gasped. Mole took a deep breath, sweat beading on his shiny forehead. "Then, the bloody flesh-eater was on us, it was!" Mole's voice quivered. "Ratboy yanked down a timber to block it and the whole tunnel fell, it did!"

Jetsam and Ratboy made their way through the dark passage, carrying Mole under the arms. Listening for the troll, Jetsam hushed Mole, who continued chatting nervously about nothing at all.

After an interminable journey, Jetsam's backpedaling heel struck a stone, and he landed on his rump. Ratboy and Mole landed on him in a heap. Realizing he found the stairs, Jetsam's fury changed to joy. Even before he returned to his feet, a fearful noise rumbled through the tunnel.

"The troll got through!"

The orphans climbed the stairs three-wide, with Ratboy and Jetsam rubbing their outer shoulders against the stone walls.

Jetsam remained quiet, not wanting to escalate Mole's panic. He understood how fast the humpback could move. *No way we can outrun the troll with a gimpy Mole.* Visions of Elvar's wounds taunted him as he imagined Mole suffering the safe fate. *I'll not leave him behind,* Jetsam promised himself. Elvar's death haunted him. He had no reservations about joining his departed brother. *At least Ratboy could make it out alive.*

When the lads reached the top of the stairs, they hoisted Mole through the trap door. Ratboy and Jetsam scurried behind him. Dragging Mole from the hole, Jetsam had an idea. As he hurried back to the opening, he heard the troll in hot pursuit. With a rattling crash, Jetsam slammed down the hefty trap door. Scrambling to lock the hatch, he found the rotted latch was broken.

"Blast!"

He hesitated as the wheels turned inside his head. Undaunted, he hollered to Ratboy. "Pile all the stones you can find on this door!"

On hands and knees, the boys groped in the dark. There was plenty of rubble in the passageway, and they amassed a pile of rocks on the trap door. *Pray they'll be enough.*

"More, more!" Ratboy shouted. Mole whimpered on the stone floor, pushing the biggest rocks he could find to the sealed aperture. Back and forth Jetsam and Ratboy scampered, rolling everything they found toward the breach.

Like a thunderclap, the troglodyte slapped the door with its massive palms.

The door leapt upward, catapulting rocks off, but didn't swing open. *Thank the gods.* The orphans rushed to push the errant stones back on before the creature struck again. The troll was quicker, and this time, the door lifted even higher. A muscled claw shot through the opening, nicking Jetsam's ankle. Before the humpback could react, the loaded door slammed on its recoiling limb. Squealing in surprise, the monster pulled its arm back. More rocks rolled off the pile.

With no other choice, Jetsam leapt upon the pile of stones, his flat stomach landing on the punishing rubble. Bracing for the oncoming impact, he grasped the rocks, hoping his extra weight would deter the cave-dweller. When the beast struck again, Jetsam's entire body mashed against the rocks. In pain, he shouted to the others.

"Grab two stones and get on!" It took a moment for the command to register. Mole and Ratboy submitted to Jetsam's emerging leadership and complied with his order. Jetsam groaned again as they landed on top of him. Before the troll smashed into the door again, three bodies and two hundredweight of stone rested on the hatch.

The troll hammered the door, flinging its forearms over its head into the impedance. This time, most of the stones beneath them held firm, but Jetsam doubted they could maintain the effort. A few seconds later, the tiring troll struck once more, howling in fury.

Jetsam lost count of how many times the tenacious carnivore flung itself upward into the hinged obstruction. Each battering-ram assault crushed Jetsam's ribs. It was a rough ride for the others as well, although they enjoyed Jetsam's cushioning.

"Mole," Jetsam said. "You've got to crawl out of here. Backtrack to the next intersection, then take the left passage—it leads to the riverbank."

"B-but what about you an' Ratboy?"

"Yeah, what about us?" Ratboy chimed in.

"We're going to buy Mole time, maybe even lead the troll on a goose chase if we have to."

"Sounds good," Ratboy replied, shoving Mole off of him. "Go! Crawl if ye have to, but 'less that leg falls off, I'd run I were ye."

Mole didn't need any more encouragement and fled before the troll struck the underside of the trap door again.

"Don't know how much more of this I can take," Jetsam moaned, bracing for the next blast.

The following onslaught rocked him like an explosion. Jetsam and Ratboy lifted into the air and hovered momentarily before crashing on the unforgiving rocks.

The troll roared in unmistakable enthusiasm.

With the wind knocked out of him, Jetsam tried to suck air back into his burning lungs. Then the earth shook, his ears rang, and rocks rained on top of his prone, aching form.

The trap door was open.

Chapter Five

As fast as it opened, the hatch closed again, slamming on the troll's lumpy head. In the dark, Jetsam couldn't see, nor could he yet breathe. But he heard a clicking, grinding sound, and Ratboy grunting.

"Ratboy?" Jetsam gasped with his first breath.

"Used my knife to lock the hatch." The troll struck the closed door once more and the wedged blade sufficed as a makeshift lock. "Won't hold forever, though," Ratboy said, helping Jetsam to his feet. "Gotta run. Which way?"

"Like to loop back and grab that lantern," Jetsam replied. "Think we can make it?"

"Let's try," Ratboy said, as the troll hammered the door. This time it held.

In the vast cavern, black as pitch, Jetsam aimed for the cave-in.

Hope Stinky's as stubborn as he looks. "Have to hurry," he instructed Ratboy.

After retracing his steps to the cave-in, Jetsam retrieved his lantern without incident. Though dented and scratched, the lamp still burned.

"No sign of the humpback," he said to Ratboy.

"Need to find the others," Ratboy said. "They must've taken the falling path at the fork."

"That means we've got to go past the trap door. Hope your knife holds."

"'Twas a good blade—iron forged."

I pray it was, Jetsam thought.

The two friends arrived at the spot where the three passages converged. Under the dim glow of lantern light, they tiptoed through the passage where they had left the angry troll pounding on the trap door.

"It's quiet," Jetsam whispered.

"The blade held," Ratboy said, pointing at the trap door, still shut.

"Probably gave up," Jetsam said, a touch louder than a whisper. "He may be doubling back through the cave-in. Keep alert."

A furlong past the trap door, the tunnel widened and its wormhole irregularity transformed into a fine-cut square hallway. Textures and colors danced under the glimmering light. The blue granite sparkled with silver specks interwoven with ivory veins, illuminating the dusty hallway with the reflected lantern light.

"This ain't man-made," Ratboy said, slack-jawed.

"How do you know?"

"I worked in the mines 'fore I ran away. Never seen any man cut stone this smooth." He slid his hand across the glassy granite. The years had been cruel to the subterranean tunnel, cracking, heaving, and splitting the rock, but the unmistakable craftsmanship was evident.

"So who carved this stone?"

"Smallfolk," Ratboy said. "The old miners told stories o' the Dwarves, how they built their own city under Dwim-Halloe."

Jetsam's head craned as he examined the hallway. Wide-eyed, the boys continued through the tunnel.

"Look," Ratboy pointed to the remnants of oaken doors that hung rotting and battered. Once a formidable obstruction, the massive doors suffered abuse and neglect for ages. The rusty teeth of a heavy portcullis protruded from a long slit in the ceiling.

"Ratboy!" Jetsam pointed at a radiant blue stone set in the granite.

"Never seen nuthin' like that," Ratboy gushed. Phosphorescent gemstone insets lined the hallway and emitted a dull glow.

"Dwarven lamps?"

"Mebbe," Ratboy replied.

In awe, the lads meandered the sloping passage, their soft hands feeling the carved rock. The footing was excellent, the floor free of debris. Jetsam comprehended he must shake off his sense of wonder and focus his senses to be wary of the troll.

"What happened to the Dwarves?" Jetsam asked.

"Miners said a big quake collapsed their city and they moved on, ages ago," Ratboy said as they walked. The magnificent surroundings lent an authenticity to Ratboy's stories. "Dwarves were here even before Dwim-Halloe. Men came to trade with the smallfolk, then stayed and settled here. *Gwae Gierameth*, they called it."

"Who called what?"

"The smallfolk—'twas their name for the underground city."

Before long, the duo reached another intersection. The sloping floor leveled off, and their slow descent halted. Four corridors met at right angles. With no clue of their lost brethren, Jetsam suggested staying to the right. Their dim lamp radiated but a few paces in front of them.

Debris littered the floor and the walls had collapsed in several places. While trudging down the unforgiving lane, Jetsam heard a faint whisper. He glanced toward Ratboy, who was silent and oblivious to the sound. Wheeling around to check his back, Jetsam's leathered foot slipped on a loose rock and he crashed to the hard floor. When Ratboy stopped to help him up, something in the rubble caught Jetsam's eye. *What's this?*

Jetsam examined a slender tube under the skittish light as Ratboy peered over his shoulder. Jetsam held an ivory cylinder; dusty and scratched, the item was elegant nonetheless.

"It's a case," Jetsam said, pulling off the end to release a rolled parchment. When he unfurled the scroll, his heart stopped.

"What's wrong?" Ratboy asked, noticing Jetsam's shocked countenance. For a moment, Jetsam was silent, staring at the parchment.

"I recognize this seal!" he exclaimed. "It's the same emblem my parents used!" Scrutinizing the symbols and inscriptions on the page, Jetsam cursed himself for not being able to read. His teachings had started just before he was orphaned, and what little he learned was long forgotten. Yet he recognized none of these symbols were from the common alphabet.

"Wonder if it's magic?" Jetsam pondered.

"Magic? Whadda ye know 'bout magic?" Ratboy asked.

"Not much," Jetsam admitted. "But my parents were wizards. I *would have* learned," Jetsam let the words hang.

"Come on," Ratboy nodded toward the cavern ahead. "Still a hungry troll around." *Hope he didn't pick up Mole's trail,* Jetsam prayed. The thought sent a shiver down his back. Jetsam slid the parchment back into its case, slipped the tube into his belt-pouch, and hoisted the lantern.

A dozen steps ahead, they hit a dead end. Walls and ceiling melded into a mass of rubble, making the tunnel impassable. Ratboy and Jetsam scrambled up the debris, poking and prodding for a crack or crevice to sneak through, but none could be found.

"They didn't come this way," Ratboy declared.

With two corridors remaining, the duo backtracked to the intersection.

When they returned to the crossroads, Jetsam wanted to continue ahead, abandoning his right-hand rule. He couldn't explain the feeling, but it sounded as if someone whispered in his ear. "Straight ahead," he repeated aloud, wondering if he was hearing voices.

Twenty paces further, the hallway revealed a series of wooden doors, each opposite the other. Time and neglect had taken its toll on the once magnificent doors. The first one sat open.

Jetsam peeked into a ransacked room of what was once a barracks. Shreds of matting and shards of rustic furniture were all that remained in the chamber. A tall fireplace divided the far wall, ashes and soot spilling out on the floor.

The next several rooms displayed the same signs of prior inhabitancy, but no indication of the lost orphans. They entered the last doorway. The chamber appeared similar to the others, with one exception. A slight illumination emanated from this room.

Jetsam glanced to the hearth, noticing a muted glow cascading off the stonework. The fireplace had collapsed upon itself, leaving a hole in the ceiling. Jetsam crept inside the sooty hearth and peered up the chimney. Fingers of daylight trickled down the blackened shaft.

It's morning. We've been down here longer than I thought. With an opportunity to examine his scroll in the chimney light, Jetsam suggested they rest. Ratboy agreed, and plopped on the dusty floor.

The scroll captivated Jetsam. His gaze wandered over the foreign signs and inscriptions, searching for something familiar, a spark to trigger his memory. Minutes of scrutiny provided no such luck.

"We should keep looking," Ratboy suggested. "That troll's wanderin' around somewhere down here."

"You're right." Jetsam put the scroll away and wondered why he had such a strong urge to search this direction first. The impulse had not led him to his lost companions. He thought of the troll again, and Flotsam. Regret gnawed at him.

For the third time, Jetsam and Ratboy returned to the four-way junction, with one avenue left to explore. They headed down this last hallway and soon faced another intersection. Jetsam began to realize the enormity of their task. With his free hand on his hip, he stared at his boots. The lantern grew heavy in his outstretched arm.

Without moving a step, his free arm shot out and clenched Ratboy's tunic.

"Look," he instructed, pointing at the dusty floor. There, beneath his soles, were smallish footprints, barely perceptible, but fresh. Lantern in hand, Jetsam knelt by the tracks.

"Must be them!" Ratboy proclaimed.

Heartened, they followed the imprints. Tracking the scattered smudges, the youngsters passed several doors, and checked each one to no avail. Then, the faintest of sounds echoed through the hall. Jetsam quickened his pace, forging ahead of Ratboy, brandishing the lantern against the darkness. He half thought he was hearing things again, and didn't speak of it. But this noise emanated from in front of him. Far ahead, he discerned boyish voices. His heart leapt.

"It's them!"

A few hurried steps later, Jetsam recognized the voices.

"Pike!" Ratboy shouted.

"Ratboy!" a chorus replied, followed by joyous whoops.

The five orphans converged in a great hall, illuminated by Jetsam's flickering light. The grand room was expansive, circular with a high vaulted ceiling supported by massive stone columns. Rusty chains hung uselessly from above, their lamps pilfered long ago. The dusty floor tiles swirled in a mosaic. Statues protruded from alcoves circling the vast hall, tickled by the jittery lamplight.

The three lost youths—Blister, Rooster, and Pike— ran toward their comrades.

"Ye clay-brained louts," Ratboy scolded. "I warned ye not ta come down here."

"Couldn't resist," Rooster said. "These are smallfolk ruins!"

"And yet ye burned all yer torches and got yerselves lost," Ratboy countered.

Younger and smaller, Blister and Pike stood alongside Rooster, eyeing him sullenly. All three shared the undernourished frame typical of underbelly boys.

"And there's a troll," Jetsam blurted.

"Really, Jets? A troll?"

"It's what killed Flotsam," Jetsam retorted, with an edge to his voice.

"We were careful. Just like mice we are, and fast as rabbits."

"Knuckle-draggers are faster," Ratboy interjected. "And they don't need ta hear ye; they can smell ye."

"You ever even *seen* a troll, Ratboy?" Rooster challenged.

"Well, no, but I heard plenty o' stories when I worked in the mines."

"*I* saw one," Jetsam hissed.

"Sure it wasn't a cave bear? Or mebbe a wolf?"

"It was a fobbing troll, and you'd have wet your sodding self if you'd seen it."

Before Jetsam could describe the hideous creature, a familiar growl reached his eardrums. His blood changed to ice.

From an archway across the large cavern, the abomination emerged and headed for the boys. Four orphans gasped as Jetsam faced the beast. Out of nowhere, Jetsam again heard an eerie whisper, like a faraway voice inside his own head. He pondered the strange intrusion for but a moment. With no idea where the utterance came from, or why, something prompted him to heed it.

He shouted to his friends.

"Run!"

They were already ahead of him. As the three boys bolted back toward the direction they came from, Ratboy followed.

Jetsam, however, dropped the lantern and fished out a sling stone, then turned to face the lumbering beast.

The creature howled its delight.

Chapter Six

Ratboy watched the backs of the three boys as they retreated from the great hall and the ferocious troll. He never doubted Jetsam was right behind him. Only the absence of light in the corridor made him stop and whirl.

"Blast!" Jetsam had the lantern. "Halt," Ratboy shouted to the youths ahead of him. Their sprint bogged into a frantic shuffle as they made their way along the wall, leading with their hands, searching for the faint glow of a phosphorescent guide stone. *Something's wrong. Horribly wrong.*

"Where's Jetsam?" he asked, knowing the question was moot. A chorus of whispered uncertainty emanated from the three urchins. They ignored his order to stop and snuck further into the dark.

"Stop!" Ratboy called out to the threesome, then turned and raced after the cowards. Six strides later he collided with the pack, huddled together, inching their way sightless through the hall. The charging Ratboy tumbled them like twigs in a windstorm. He grabbed two of his clan members, clutching their tunics.

"We're going back if I have to drag ye!" He stood up, yanking the boys to their feet. "Ye with me?" He shook the lads. "Well?"

A trio of timid affirmations sounded in the musty hallway. In the minute it took them to work their way back, the great room had fallen dark and silent. Jetsam and the troll were gone.

"Where'd he go?" Rooster asked.

Ratboy ground his teeth, ignoring the query. Three doorways entered the gallery; the one Ratboy and Jetsam came through, the one the lost trio entered from, and the one the troglodyte emerged from. Ratboy debated his options. *Either the humpback dragged Jetsam back to its lair, or he escaped through the other passage.* Ratboy figured the troll had terrified the three shaking boys, and they would be useless if they encountered it again.

He ruled out the doorway the knuckle-dragger appeared from. *Would be suicide to head into the unknown with no light.* He reluctantly retreated, suspecting Jetsam must have sacrificed himself to lure the troll away from them. *Knuckle-dragger would have left the lantern if he'd gotten a hold of Jetsam,* Ratboy reassured himself. It was small consolation.

"We gotta get outta here," Ratboy instructed.

"What about Jetsam?" Pike asked. "Can't leave him."

"He lured the troll away so's we could escape," Ratboy explained. "That knuckle-dragger stands between us and him now. We'd be bloody fools ta chase after it." The three lost orphans offered no rebuttal. Ratboy grasped Rooster's arm. "Link up," he instructed. "Follow single-file. Not leavin' anyone else behind." Rooster gripped Pike's hand, who in turn found Blister's outstretched palm.

"We're good," Blister confirmed, squeezing Pike's sweaty hand.

"Now keep yer traps shut and say a prayer ta the Mountain God that Jetsam escapes." The orphan trio obeyed their leader. *I hope Jetsam knows what he's doing,* Ratboy thought. *To do anything else would disrespect his gesture.* He led the way solemnly.

The four urchins arrived at the river bank safely—but with no sign of Jetsam, or the beast. Ratboy maintained a dim hope that his friend would be waiting for them back at the encampment.

He wasn't.

Inside the great Dwarven hall, the troll reacted to Jetsam's scent. *It craves my flesh.* But for the moment, the brute stopped its charge and wavered, head tilted at Jetsam.

Then, despite Jetsam's suicidal bravado, the cave-dweller howled and lunged forward. *Aim for the eye.*

"Blast!"

His sling stone clipped the troll's pointy ear. Jetsam turned tail and sprinted back out of the grand hall, picking up his lantern as he ran. Half of the cavernous room still separated them. Through the tunnels Jetsam dashed, by now able to gauge the monster's closing speed. Nimbly, he sped through the first intersection without hesitation. The troglodyte was gaining. Jetsam didn't have to look back—his sixth sense warned him of impending peril. His leather boots slapped the floor in a steady rhythm.

I'm tired of all this sodding running. From the guards, from the shopkeepers, from the troll; his entire life was spent running away. He longed for an end to it all. Even though he didn't want that end to be death, the specter was near.

I don't fear the Reaper. With Flotsam already on the other side, Jetsam felt comfort in the prospect of joining him. Someday he would be reunited with his twin. He hoped if today was that day, the end would come swiftly. The idea of suffering at the troll's wicked hands frightened him.

When Jetsam reached the second juncture, he again heard the whispering. From deep in his head, the bizarre voice issued an unmistakable instruction. *Right.* Jetsam paused but a moment, and then veered right. With no time to deliberate, he took his eerie guidance at face value.

But the dubious decision gnawed at him.

The troll grunted. *Even Stinky knows I chose a dead end.* A glob of saliva ran down the monster's jutting chin. *Maybe the voice leads me to my death.*

Past four wooden doors raced Jetsam, cutting a quick left through the last portal before the dead end. With one hand, he swung the heavy door closed behind him and locked the latch. The lantern still burned enough to dimly illuminate the ransacked barracks. Jetsam sprinted to the room's center and scanned the chamber. From the crash behind, Jetsam guessed that the knuckle-dragger tore the rotting door from its squealing hinges. *The hearth it is.*

A bloodcurdling squeal leapt from the creature's wet maw as Jetsam clamored into the fireplace. As the troll approached, Jetsam dropped the lantern into the ashes and recoiled inside the sooty chimney.

Nowhere to go but up.

Jetsam reached to the rusty damper and pulled himself up. The fatigued metal failed under his weight and he crashed into the hearth, releasing a cloud of ash. With the troll but steps away, Jetsam leapt to his feet and grasped the smoke shelf through the narrow opening where the damper once sat.

It's too tight!

Squirming upward, pulling with all his arm strength, Jetsam caused the facing of the deteriorated fireplace to give way. As bricks fell, he hoisted himself onto the greasy ledge. The troll tore at the mantle's remainder, trying to expose Jetsam.

Got to get higher.

Jetsam pulled himself up by a handhold inside the flue. The shaft was slippery, and he struggled against sliding down. Desperately, his toes searched for cracks and fissures to cling to.

After a few feet, the futility of his assault became apparent. Despite his best efforts, he could go no farther. The vertical passage was too narrow to climb all the way aboveground. The mysterious voice had directed him toward this chimney, but it was too slick to scale. Staring at the bright distant sunlight, he wondered what he'd gotten himself into.

I must be crazy.

Jetsam hoped he was high enough to avoid the troll's reach. *He can still wait me out,* Jetsam lamented. *Can't stay up here forever.*

The charging troll crashed into the deteriorated chimney. More stones crumbled from the weakened structure. The sheer impact of the creature's bulk shook Jetsam from his perch. As he lost his hold and slipped down the shaft, a terrifying screech burned his ears. Prepared to die, Jetsam fell to the fireplace floor in a heap, eyes closed, curled in a ball. A creosote fog descended upon him.

Jetsam's life flashed before him. In an instant, he witnessed his beloved dead—mother, father, and brother. He anticipated joining them shortly. He only feared the pain.

A rapid heartbeat passed, then two, and finally three. Opening his ash-caked eyes, he saw the wretched troll frozen in place like a desiccated statue, its muscled arms outstretched hovering above him.

The voice saved me! Maybe I'm not crazy after all.

Like a magical poison, the thin rays of sunlight flowing down the chimney petrified the beast. A fine mist emanated from the troll's shriveled skin as every drop of moisture in the lifeless creature evaporated.

Skeptical of the phenomenon's permanency, Jetsam scooted from the fireplace, crawling between the immobile beast's rigid legs. He didn't look back until he reached the doorway. Only then did he steal a glance at the vicious troglodyte. *It hasn't moved an inch.*

Fear receding, Jetsam crept back near the vile statue. With an angry face, he spat on its petrified skin. *For Elvar!*

Filthy and fatigued, Jetsam slogged home, daydreaming about his scroll. A startling chorus of cheers arose in the cavern upon his entrance. Surprise shone on the orphan's pasty faces. *They thought I was dead.* A beaming Ratboy leapt from his mat to hug Jetsam. A coating of soot burst from his ash-laden tunic as Ratboy slapped him on the back.

"Jets! Ye sodding trickster! How the bloody pus did ye shake that knuckle-dragger?"

"Ran like the devil," Jetsam moaned, a crooked grin creeping across his parched lips.

"Drink?" Mole asked, handing Jetsam a full waterskin. Head back and holding the flask with both hands, Jetsam drained the bladder.

"Tell us more 'bout the troll," begged Rooster.

Jetsam wiped his lips with his dirty tunic sleeve, leaving a sooty goatee on his face. Ratboy chuckled and offered him a cleaner rag. As Jetsam cleaned the grime, he debated telling his friends about the strange voice in his head. *Don't want them to think I've lost my mind.*

"Knuckle-dragger chased me into a chimney," he explained, stopping to lick his chapped lips. "I crawled up, and before he could grab me, the sunlight killed him."

"Bullshite!" hollered Rooster. Jetsam's blue eyes narrowed and his fists clenched.

"He's still there, frozen in place, a shriveled corpse." Jetsam snapped. "Go see for yourself."

"Nay!" Ratboy interjected. "We'll not be goin' back there. Where there's one troll, there's bound to be more." Steely-eyed, Ratboy scanned the crowd, making eye contact with each boy. "I'm dead serious. Won't be risking my skin ta save anyone stupid enough ta go down there." He poked Rooster in the sternum. "Ye just got lucky, dung-fer-brains." Rooster swallowed hard and nodded, rubbing his chest where Ratboy stuck him.

"I'm going to sleep," Jetsam declared, glad to exit the spotlight. Rooster patted him on the back.

"Thanks, Jets. Sorry for bein' such an arse," Rooster mumbled. Jetsam forced a smile and strode past.

Exhausted both physically and mentally, Jetsam slept well. In his deep slumber, he dreamed of the scroll and its surely magical powers. Images of Giselle wandering in the garden also entwined in his subconscious visions.

Jetsam awoke focused on his scroll. *I need help from someone who can read.* Although he was doubtful, Jetsam checked with every clan member, to no avail. None of the lads had ever learned to read.

Jetsam flashed back to his dream. He *did* know someone who might be literate. *Giselle!*

He waited for nightfall and prepared for his rendezvous. Jetsam donned a cleaner tunic and breeches, *for Giselle.* His outfit was black, making him nearly invisible at night.

Jetsam had no idea if the girl would be in the garden, but she was his best chance. *Regardless, I need to start scavenging for food again.* He slid the ivory case inside his belt-pouch and headed for the riverbank.

Jetsam avoided swimming to protect the scroll and his shoulder. Despite the change of clothes, his face and hands were still coated in chimney soot. With Giselle in mind, he stopped at the river to wash. His results were somewhat successful. After cleaning up, he 'borrowed' a small skiff and paddled across the moat, staying low and silent.

With the raft stored on the steep bank by the drainage chute, Jetsam again entered the Citadel. The route couldn't help but remind him of his brother. *What a fobbing stupid idea,* he bemoaned. *Sneaking into the castle.*

Ever mindful of the sentry, Jetsam crept cautiously. He again scaled the low garden wall, entering the park near the back. Clouds trapped the day's warmth, blanketing the Citadel with a concealing darkness.

As he snuck through the greenery, he filled his bag with apples. A summer fragrance sweetened the air, tantalizing his nostrils. The garden was quiet, except for crickets. Jetsam dreamed of building a hut in the thick shrubs and living in the garden forever. In his imagination, the girl joined him in his peaceful sanctuary. Jetsam didn't know what love was, but his pounding heart made him wonder if that's what he harbored for Giselle.

The sound of boots on flagstone yanked Jetsam from his daydream. On all fours behind a yew hedge, the heavy footfalls drew closer to him.

Jetsam dropped to the fertile ground, flat on his stomach, and peered below the shrubs. Black leather boots tromped by. Jetsam lay motionless until the guard was long gone. *At least he's made his rounds.*

Alerted by a rustle behind him, he rolled over and sat. Upon glimpsing color through the dark branches, he poked his head above the shrubbery. *Giselle!* Jetsam plucked a hawthorn berry and tossed the red bulb in the girl's direction. The tiny fruit hit her shoulder, and she whirled toward him, her long dress twisting.

Her eyes lit up when Jetsam's head poked from the bushes. She scanned for the sentry, and then advanced toward Jetsam.

"What are you doing here?" she whispered, taking a seat beside him on the soft earth.

"Looking for *you.*" Upon hearing Jetsam's reply, an elegant smile graced her young face. She tried to mask her delight. "Why were you hiding?" Jetsam implored.

"I'm not supposed to be here, either," she answered. "Father found out about your last visit. Forbade me from coming out at night."

"Then how—" Jetsam began to ask.

"Father's too busy to pay attention, and mother is always sad," she replied to his unfinished question. "'Tis easy to sneak away. I love it here." She stopped to squint at the figure in the darkness. "You are Jetsam, are you not?" Now *he* was flattered. He nodded. "Where's your brother?"

Jetsam's expression fell. He tried to force out a response, but none came. Tears filled his eyes, and a fugitive drop fled to his chin.

"Oh, my… oh, my." Aghast at the unspoken tragedy, she stroked his cheek with her soft hand.

"I—he," words failed Jetsam, now choked with emotion.

"He's gone, isn't he?"

Jetsam nodded, eyes down. "Gone forever," he croaked.

"Running from the guards… " she said, a hint of guilt coloring her voice as her words trailed. "There, there." Giselle brushed the stringy hair from his face. They sat together in silence as he breathed heavily, regaining his composure. Her caress was more comforting than he could have ever imagined.

"Wanted to see you again," he confessed quietly, after a long pause.

"I wanted to see you, too."

"Truly?" Jetsam asked in astonishment. She released her radiant smile and nodded.

He flushed with embarrassment and joy.

"I have no friends my age," she admitted. "Well, none that are lads, at least."

Jetsam's next question blurted out. "Can you read?"

"Why, yes, I can."

"Will you read something for *me?*"

"You cannot read?" she asked. Jetsam's gaze fell to the ground.

"No. Had to run away while we were still learning the alphabet."

A flush spread on both their cheeks. Jetsam leaned forward, as if to stand. Her hand guided him back down.

"Of course I'll read for you."

Jetsam relaxed and pulled the case from his belt-bag. Huddled deep in the bushes, he unrolled the scroll. Dim light from a curtain wall torch provided just enough illumination to see the parchment. Jetsam held the scroll for her to see. She reached for the scroll with her long fingers, yet Jetsam tilted the parchment toward his chest.

"I'll hold it," he offered, tightening his grip.

Giselle's mouth dropped. "I must *see* it to *read* it," she snapped.

She's not likely to steal it, Jetsam scolded himself. He titled the scroll back toward her, positioning the document so the torchlight fell on the aged parchment. Giselle's eyes squinted at the poorly-lit script. After a moment of scrutiny, she frowned.

"I know not what this is," she admitted in dismay. "These aren't words I can read."

Jetsam's optimism crashed.

"Do you think it's magic writing?" he questioned.

"Could be, I suppose." She wrinkled her nose. "Where did you find it? Sorcery is *illegal.*"

"Seems everything I do is illegal," he bemoaned. *This was a bad idea. I should get out of here.*

"I know the laws are unfair," she whispered. "The only time my parents talk is to argue about them," she lamented. "I just meant if the scroll is magic, I don't think *anyone* can read it. All the wizards and Elves are gone!"

"I know. My parents were teachers of magic."

"And that's why you had to run away?" Jetsam nodded in reply. "I'm truly sorry," she assured. "More sorry than you will ever know." Her emerald eyes drifted downward. "You must have suffered such a terrible life." She chewed her lip in hesitation. "Tell me what it's like to be an orphan."

"I dunno," he replied self-consciously. "Suppose it's the *opposite* of normal. Sleep in the day and live underground. No parents, no family. Nobody gives us anything—we have to take it."

"How do you eat?" she asked.

"Scavenge and hunt at night. Sometimes we'll catch a hare or squirrel, or even a rat to cook." Jetsam paused as he noticed Giselle's nose wrinkle while she repressed a gag. *I forget nobles don't eat vermin.* "Mostly, its vegetables and scraps, though. And going hungry a lot. It's dangerous to fish the river. The men know all the good fishing holes and are out even after dark." Their eyes met in a moment of awkward silence, and Jetsam continued to break the lull.

"There's other gangs besides ours and we all want the same stuff. So sometimes there's fighting. And sickness," he sighed. "And death." Flotsam's memory stirred him, and he stopped.

They sat quietly for a few minutes. He placed his hand on hers. *Soft and warm.* They both knew it wouldn't last. Then Giselle perked up.

"Do you know any gypsies?"

"Gypsies? Nay," he responded. "Why?"

"I've heard they know all about arcane things like sorcery and the old ways. Do gypsies not live in the underbelly with you?"

"Never seen one."

"I *know* they are in Dwim-Halloe. Father curses them and prattles on how they've no use. Says they should be put to work or driven out. Maybe if you could find one, they could read your scroll."

"Sometimes I see beggars scavenging in the alleys, but I don't know of any gypsies. Guess I'll keep my eyes open."

The conversation was halted by a yelp from close by.

"That's a dog!" Giselle said. A distressed howl echoed. "Sounds hurt," she remarked. "Come, let's see. The sentry shan't return for a while."

Crouched low and stepping lightly, the duo made their way toward the dog. Jetsam stumbled upon the small mutt caught in a rat trap. The bound canine looked up with sad brown eyes, his tan tail wagging.

"He's but a pup!" Jetsam exclaimed.

"Why, 'tis Tramp, the gardener's dog! He's no pup," she said. "He's a terrier bred and trained to keep rats from the garden."

"A trained dog?" Jetsam asked. His familiarity with canines consisted of vicious guard dogs and feral street mutts.

"Of course," Giselle said. "He can hunt and track and sit and stay and all sorts of other things." Jetsam's eyes widened as he returned his attention to the terrier.

Tramp's leg was trapped. The dog whimpered in pain as it struggled to escape. Blood accumulated on the short tan hairs of its hind leg.

Jetsam squatted to free the animal. Upon loosening the trap, the canine squirmed away, bouncing on all fours, limping slightly. As Jetsam let the steel jaws snap shut, Tramp hobbled toward Giselle.

She examined the injury. "Doesn't look bad," she declared. "Just a scrape—probably from struggling." The youngsters petted the furry terrier. It alternated licking each of them, tail wagging all the while. "The old gardener passed away a fortnight ago," Giselle whispered to Jetsam, as if the dog understood. "Tramp's an orphan like you."

Jetsam studied the panting dog. *Wonder if he knows his owner's dead?*

"Think I could keep him?" Jetsam pondered aloud.

"Why not? He looks hungry. We should feed him. Think he likes apples?"

Jetsam dug a chunk of dried squirrel from his pocket and held it toward Tramp. The terrier sniffed intently, and took a step toward the food.

"Go ahead," Jetsam whispered, wiggling the meat. Tramp stretched his neck and gently closed on the treat, taking it from Jetsam and swallowing it with nary a chew. The dog's curly tail wagged.

"He liked *that*," Jetsam said.

"Of course he likes meat! All dogs do," she huffed.

Jetsam raised his eyebrows. *Suppose they do.*

"Come along," she bid with a wave.

Giselle and Jetsam crept toward the orchard, Tramp following behind, now not limping at all. Jetsam picked a low apple and broke it into chunks with his hand. Tramp gulped down every piece. As he finished the last bite, he growled, his narrow tail pointing up.

"The sentry!" Giselle cried. "Must have heard Tramp, too."

Jetsam and Giselle glanced at each other for a moment of indecision. She lurched forward and kissed him. Blood rushed to his startled face as her soft honey lips pressed against his. It was his first kiss, and hers.

When she reluctantly pulled back, his jaw dropped.

"You must flee," she urged, snapping him from his daze. "Worry not, I shan't get in trouble—even if he finds me!"

Jetsam heeded her words. He made his way toward the wall, stealing a final look at Giselle before she disappeared into the knot garden.

Tramp emitted a low warning bark at the yet unseen guard, and then tore after Jetsam.

Chapter Seven

Spindly legs pumping, Jetsam dashed for the garden's outer wall. The canine ran by his side. Tramp gazed at Jetsam, his pink tongue flapping in the night breeze. *He smells the meat in my pocket.* Paws and leather boots thumped the thick green grass. In a moment, they'd reach the garden wall, and Tramp would not jump the six-foot high rampart. *I guess you're coming with me,* Jetsam decided.

Familiar baritone shouts of "halt, knave!" told Jetsam the sentry spotted him again. This time though, his escape path was clear. *Climb the wall and head for the well house.* Once over the stone blocks, the shed sat but a furlong away, hidden amongst noble estates and shade trees. With the terrier along, Jetsam wanted no part of the narrow drainage chute. *Besides, the raft'll be too slow with a guard on my tail,* he decided. *Getting Tramp down the well shaft will be tricky, though.*

As boy and dog pulled up short of the drystone barricade, the closing sentinel shouted obscenities. Tramp spun and growled, baring his white teeth. Jetsam bent and grabbed the terrier by its middle, hoisting the dog upon the ashlar fortification.

"Come on, boy," Jetsam whispered. "That's a battle you don't want to fight."

In the time it took Jetsam to stop and lift Tramp and place him atop the flat stone, the sentry closed the gap. The watchman neared the barricade. *Fobbing rot!* Jetsam swore, accelerating his ascent.

Jetsam scaled the obstruction, as Tramp peered down curiously. With a fluid motion, Jetsam reached the top, swung a leg over, scooped up Tramp and brought his other leg across the wall. With the squirming terrier tucked under his right arm, Jetsam slid off the wall, safely to the other side.

The sentinel arrived at the fortification, waving his short sword like a berserker. Less agile, but taller than Jetsam, the guard pulled himself up and swung a leg atop the barrier. The sentry positioned himself to pounce on Jetsam, then flung himself over the wall.

Jetsam underestimated the dexterity of his pursuer. He never glanced up at the approaching hunter. As the sentinel launched, Tramp snarled. Instinctively, Jetsam sprung from his standstill. The stretching watchman missed him by a foot, landing in a heap as Jetsam and Tramp scampered away.

Luck of the gods, that was close!

Jetsam's long legs reached full speed in a matter of steps. *I'll pull away while he finds his feet.* Then a wail echoed that stopped Jetsam in his tracks. Both he and the dog craned back toward the wall. The upturned guard crumpled awkwardly at the base of the stone blocks, half stuck in a low bush.

The sight brought a sneer to Jetsam's face. He recalled the soldiers who invaded his house and killed his parents. *Message from the king.* Even though those men were the king's elite guards and this was a lowly garden watchman, a surge of sweet revenge coursed through Jetsam. *Serves him right.* Tramp barked once, as if to signal his triumph.

But the sentry howled again and pleaded for help.

"Prithee help, knave!" the cry dripped with desperate agony.

When Jetsam looked closer, he noticed the man had impaled himself on his sword and struggled to lift his inverted form off the wedged blade. The weapon had slipped under the sentinel's short hauberk and imbedded itself in his abdomen.

Jetsam's smile vanished, and his feet slapped to a halt. He lingered for a moment, examining the guard's sweating, scratched visage. No longer a faceless stranger, the man was younger than Jetsam imagined. *Not much older than Ratboy.*

After pondering the suffering watchman for a mere second, Jetsam shrugged and continued toward the drainage chute. *Not my problem,* he decided. Tramp followed.

Four steps later, the guard released another agonizing moan, and Jetsam stopped again. Unfamiliar feelings of guilt crept into his consciousness. With a glance back at the immobile young man, Jetsam determined he could aid his suffering pursuer and still escape unfettered.

Sodding gods.

He sprinted back toward the wall with the terrier at his heels.

"Prithee help me," the guard pleaded, blood gurgling from his mouth. "Bloody skewered meself." The watchman groaned and gagged, grimacing in pain. Jetsam knelt to the hard earth, unsure of how to proceed. He grabbed the guard's legs and twisted him away from the wall, removing his weight from the short blade. Carefully bracing the sentinel's torso, Jetsam slid the weapon from his side, and shivered at all the blood.

Tramp sniffed at it.

Slumped in the grass, the man labored to breathe. His heavy eyes relayed unspoken gratitude as his hands pressed against his abdomen, straining the keep his entrails in place. Then Jetsam heard other noisy guards racing toward him. Understandably, their shouts of anger seemed justified upon spotting him holding the bloody sword, hovering over their fallen comrade.

Stupid me. Thought they might actually be grateful. Upon seeing their enraged faces and comprehending the scene, he figured otherwise. Without another second's delay, Jetsam bolted for the well house, stained short sword still in hand.

He glanced back to see Tramp following at his heels. *Good boy!*

Jetsam couldn't count how many times his long legs had been his salvation. This escape added to the list. He reached his destination ahead of the guards, and slid through the narrow shed doorway. Tramp chased right behind him.

Blast!

A thick slab of granite covered the well.

Sword in hand, Jetsam leaned his back into the stone and pushed.

It budged not a hair.

He dug his heels into the earthen shed floor, flexed his thighs and tried again. The recalcitrant stone's edge cut into his shoulder blades.

Bloody puss-rot. Now what?

Desperate and disgusted, Jetsam shot from the well house with Tramp at his heels. The guards closed to within steps of the duo. Jetsam dodged and darted, cutting every corner to lose the guards. *Could sneak into a house and hide.* He examined the secured estates as he sped by, then glanced back to his pursuer. *Not enough time to break in unseen.* Glancing up at the tall shade trees, he contemplated disappearing in their lofty branches. *They'll just bring out the hounds and find me eventually,* he resigned. *Guess I'll have to find another drainage chute and cross the moat.* "You can swim, right boy?" Oblivious, Tramp chased Jetsam, darting and dodging and nipping at his trousers.

Running beside the sentry-patrolled, torch-lit outer curtain, Jetsam understood he was vulnerable to detection from both ground level and the wall. He cut a sharp corner and swung into a narrow side street.

Jetsam glanced back. *No guards. Yet.* With his speed and zigzagging around structures and hedges, he'd rebuilt a lead.

He slipped the unsheathed sword between the leather strap and his waist. Conscious of the blade, he remembered the watchman's costly mistake, and maneuvered carefully. Jetsam dropped to the cobbles, slid a street drain grate aside, and slithered into the filthy hole. Tramp resisted at first, but relented to Jetsam's tight grip. Upon disappearing into the cubby, Jetsam reached up and dragged the heavy grate back into place. Iron squealed on cobble for but a moment.

Of all the fobbing luck!

As Jetsam recoiled below the street, he realized the narrowing drain chute was much too small for escape. He squirmed and wiggled to no avail.

What now, Elvar?

Jetsam listened to himself pant, and tried to clear his head. *Least I can catch my breath.* Expecting the guards' footsteps any second, the sound of wagon wheels on the stone cobbles startled him. *It's getting closer.* Jetsam peered through the iron grate. Shoed horse hooves clomped above him. As the wagon tongue passed over the grating, the vehicle stopped. Jetsam heard a plop as the horse lightened its load. While the fresh excrement spoiled the night air, Jetsam pushed the heavy grate aside as quietly as possible.

Jetsam popped his scraggly head out and after scanning for guards, tossed Tramp onto the street, clear of the wagon. The dog stared curiously as Jetsam grasped the wagon's underside and pulled himself from the ground. With his legs hooked over the back axle, Jetsam wrapped his forearms around the frame and clung to the wagon's undercarriage.

"Come on, Tramp," he whispered as the horse resumed its pace.

The abandoned dog whimpered in despair, then padded after the stowaway, eyeing the rolling contraption suspiciously.

As the wagon rolled toward the Citadel's circular outer wall, the upside-down orphan watched the elite homes of merchants and nobles pass. As they neared the gatehouse for the moat bridge, a pang of fear stabbed Jetsam. *Tramp won't get across the drawbridge!* He feared the gatekeepers would spot the dog, and detain his furry friend, or worse.

"Tramp," he whispered, "come here!" The brown-eyed terrier tilted his head as he followed the plodding wagon. "Come on," Jetsam urged, realizing the dog wanted no part of the clattering contraption.

The wagon slowed at the gatehouse and Jetsam spotted guard boots walking toward the cart. With his shoulders aching, he fished in his pockets for another morsel. Jetsam waved a dried squirrel liver in Tramp's direction. *Come on, boy.*

Tramp sniffed and slunk toward Jetsam's hand. The moment the cautious dog bit the sliver of meat, Jetsam grabbed him by the scruff and hoisted him on the frame. Tramp squirmed and nipped at Jetsam's wrist, but he held firm as the noisy wagon resumed and rolled across the Jade River.

Once the wagon passed the gatehouse, Jetsam and Tramp dropped to the cobblestones and rolled into a ditch, leaving the wagon master none the wiser. Back in familiar territory, he led the dog to the underbelly and they slept the day away.

"Jetsam?"

Curled at Jetsam's side, Tramp growled and barked at the rude awakening. Ratboy jumped back a step.

"Easy boy," Jetsam said, creeping from his slumber. He sat up from his mat, rubbed his eyes, patted the dog, and tried to focus on Ratboy.

"A dog an' a sword?" Ratboy stood hands on hips, examining Jetsam and his collection in the dim firelight. "Must've had a devil of a night!"

"You could call it that," Jetsam replied and followed it with a yawn. Fire pit smoke stung his nostrils and burned his crusty eyes.

"There's talk in town of a guard murdered in the Citadel."

"Murdered?" Jetsam asked, but continued before Ratboy could respond. "He died, then. Not surprised," Jetsam said somberly, rising from his straw mat. "There was so much blood."

"'Twas ye, wasn't it?" Ratboy asked, staring at the blade.

"I didn't *kill* him, if that's what you're asking."

"But the sword—'tis Dwim-Halloe issue."

"Clumsy sod fell off a wall chasing me. Landed on his blade." Jetsam heaved a weary sigh. "Tried to save him, but when the other guards saw me with the bloody sword… "

"Why'd ye turn back? What'd ye think ye'd do? Yer no healer."

"I don't know. He just… sounded so *tortured.* And he wasn't much older than you."

Ratboy grimaced and scratched his head. "Ye did the right thing, Jets."

"Sure doesn't seem like it now."

"No good deed goes unpunished," Ratboy proclaimed.

"That's what Flotsam always said."

Ratboy nodded at Jetsam, his solemn expression still glued to his face. Jetsam suspected they both shared a quiet moment recalling Elvar.

"And the mutt?" Ratboy asked, eyeing the canine warily.

"Tramp. His owner died. He's with me now."

"Long as he fends fer himself and don't bite me ankles."

Jetsam chuckled and reached to rub Tramp's head. "Feed him and he'll love you."

Ratboy withdrew a piece of cheese from his pocket and tossed it to the terrier. The chunk landed at the dog's feet. Tramp sniffed it once before devouring it. Tongue out and tail wagging, he stared at Ratboy expectantly.

"Guards get a good look at ye?"

"Good enough, I suppose. Least it was dark."

"There'll be a price on yer head," Ratboy predicted.

"We're already fugitives."

"Aye, but they don't hang orphans. Not yet, at least."

I'd rather die than be a slave anyway. He exuded a bit of smug pride that the king himself would want him dead. *First my parents and now me.*

Chapter Eight

The Citadel guards who spotted Jetsam hovering over their dying comrade discerned enough to compile a passable description of the young orphan. A reward was posted for his capture, dead or alive. This description—and the large reward for a mere boy—caught the eye of Yduk Thiern. After pocketing his payment for turning in Weasel and Squirrel, Yduk lingered in the constable's office, examining the other wanted posters. One posting in particular stood out.

Easy pickings, concluded Yduk. *Doubt the little bastard killed a guard, but they're tough on their orphans in this town.* Yduk fingered the parchment bearing Jetsam's description. *Least he ain't an unnatural.* Yduk chuckled to himself. *If he were, they'd probably order him drawn and quartered, then put his little noggin on a spike.*

Jetsam's poster hung alongside others the manhunter examined. Yduk Thiern memorized every bounty that passed beneath his steely eyes. Jetsam shared despicable company, among the likes of burglars, poachers, cutpurses, highway bandits, even a fallen Calderian knight. They were all grown men. *And most of their bounties are smaller than the orphan's!*

Yduk scrutinized the sketch. Long dark hair, read the posting. Thin boy with delicate features. Armed with a watchman's short sword and accompanied by a terrier.

Guess it's time to go talk to the guards.

Yduk spent a few coins at the Citadel barracks before he found one of the guards who saw the orphan the night of the murder. *Time is coin,* he told himself, justifying the meager expenditure. *'Tis but a fraction of what I'll claim when I find this knave.* Yduk waited until his man was off duty, and searched for him in the tavern near the barracks.

A smattering of guards drank and mingled with the handful of prostitutes that made their living off Citadel soldiers. Under the wagon-wheel chandelier, one of the posturing women caught Yduk's wandering eye. *Maybe later,* he thought, letting his greed outweigh his lust. *Been a long time since Calderi.*

Half the tavern's wooden chairs and stools sat empty, yet there were enough thirsty patrons to keep the bartender hopping. Yduk scanned the subdued crowd, searching for a gray-bearded sentry in his early forties. One such man sitting alone at the bar fit that description.

Talking to a gypsy? Yduk eyed the watchman and the old wanderer. *'Tis an odd pair. Surprised they don't run him outta here.* Yduk claimed a spot at the rail next to the chatting men.

"What news of the royal couple?" asked the gypsy.

"King loves his iron," replied the guard. "Got me a new set of armor last week. Who knew the unnaturals' orphans would make such good steel?"

Yduk noticed the gypsy wince.

"'Tis a rough town for orphans," the gypsy commented.

"Aye, that it is." The guard swallowed a gulp of mead, droplets clinging to his graying beard. "King Valin don't let no resources go unexploited."

"Meaning?"

"Orphan lads are put to work in the foundries and mines."

"Just the boys?"

"Aye. Some say it's 'cause the king has a soft spot, his only child a princess."

"You'd think he'd find use for them."

"King's only concerned with the tools o' war. 'Spose he don't see the lasses bein' very good smiths or miners. But the queen uses the girls in the Citadel," the watchmen said. "Washerwomen, maids, serving girls, and whatnot."

"What of the queen?"

"Don't see her much. They say she's sickly, that she never recovered from her father's death."

"That was a long time ago."

"Aye. Guess time don't heal *all* wounds."

Yduk watched the crestfallen gypsy nod and leave the watchman. "Thanks fer the drink," the armored man said to the rover.

Loose lips on this one, thought Yduk. *Might be easier than I expected.* He rolled his shoulders and leaned toward the target. *Rather bribe him than beat him.*

"Yer name Stoddard?"

"Aye."

"So, ye seen the orphan knave what killed the guard?" It was more of a statement than a question. Yduk placed one gloved hand on the bar beside the watchman.

"What's it to ye?" The guard replied, not looking up from his aromatic mead.

"Gonna see justice is served."

"Meanin' ye want the coin." The guard still refused to meet Yduk's gaze.

"Man's gotta eat." *He'll talk to the old gypsy, but not me?*

"Man's got a name?"

Did you ask the gypsy his? "Thiern," Yduk replied. *Maybe they don't tolerate Southlanders up here, either.* "Now tell me 'bout the orphan."

"Mebbe *I'm* interested in collectin' the reward." The bearded man turned his large head toward Yduk, heavy lids weighing his tired eyes. "Little bugger killed one o' me brothers."

"Tell ye what," Yduk said as he tossed two coppers on the worn bar. The coins clinked and rolled on the lacquered wood before falling flat. "Ye seem like a busy man. I'll save ye the trouble and still put coin in yer pocket."

"Hrmph." The bearded watchman looked Yduk in the eye, then glanced at the coins. "'Tis an awful big reward for a bloody runt," the aged soldier postulated. "Might be worth me time."

Yduk recognized where this discussion headed. *'Tis a negotiation now,* he decided. *I can spend a little more and still make plenty.* Two more coppers slipped from his gloved fingers. *Time is coin,* he consoled himself. Yduk moved his unblinking gaze from the guard's dull eyes to the shiny coins and back again. "I can pick 'em up fast as I put 'em down," he said to the slumped soldier, nodding toward his bribe.

"Hrmph." With a deliberate swipe, the four coins disappeared in the guard's three-fingered hand. "Whadda ye want ta know?"

"What'd ye see?"

"Seen a skinny urchin holdin' a bloody blade, standin' over Drewry. Had a tan terrier with him."

"So ye didn't actually see him stab the guard?"

"Didn't need to."

Something doesn't add up, Yduk thought. *A knave killing a guard with his own sword? Unlikely.* But guilt and innocence mattered naught to him. *I don't get paid for solving mysteries.* Regardless of the facts, the guards believed what they believed, and a bounty had been set. *Nothing I can do but collect it.* He pictured the scrawny waif and shook his head.

"What'd this knave look like?"

"Lanky, long dark hair, skinny as a rail. Looked a bit girlish—mebbe ten, twelve summers. Dressed in tatters. Pale as bone, like all them und'orphans."

Yduk himself could be described as an imposing figure, much unlike the boy. Thirty years old, his frame stood lean and muscled. Covered from neck to toe in ebony leather, the only hair on his head was his black mustache that curled into tight braids beneath his jaw.

Yduk ordered an ale from the hovering bartender and pulled up a stool next to the guard.

"Seems I recall Dwim-Halloe being a city known for its unnat—its wizards."

"That was before King Valin outlawed magic, closed the school, and had us chase out the spellcasters."

"You don't sound too upset."

"Nah. Gimme a sharp blade over an Elven incantation any day. King knows weapons and armor build a stronger army than a bunch o' skittish magicians."

Yduk nodded and slugged a mouthful of ale. *Couldn't have said it better myself.*

Yduk's weapons were his most valued possessions. A crossbow rode on his back, but his prized weapon hung at his side. After using the sword for the first time, he christened it "*Regret,*" since anyone unlucky enough to see the blade unsheathed would die with this sentiment.

"So where does one find an orphan in Dwim-Halloe," Yduk asked the guard, now deep into his cups. *Apparently, you find gypsies consorting with watchmen.*

"Nocturnal buggers," the guard replied, licking the accumulated mead from the ends of his mustache. "Sleep underground during the day, and scavenge the town at night."

"Underground, eh?"

"The *runawaifs* live in the underbelly. Little knaves pop out of sewer drains all over town." The guard released a wet belch that offered Yduk a whiff of the tavern's mead. "Beggar's Alley might be a good place ta start. Vagrants and urchins, both lookin' ta beg or steal. Birds of a feather, ye know."

"Beggar's Alley?"

"Can't miss it. Just follow yer nose ta the squalor. And keep a hand on yer coin purse." The guard patted his own, now fatter with four of Yduk's coppers. "But lemme ask ye this," the guard continued. "Ye don't sound like yer from 'round here. Whadda ye really doin' in town? Surely ye ain't here ta chase rogue orphans."

Yduk took another drink of ale, while he pondered a reply. *I was right—these folk* don't *like Southlanders.* He'd been working his way north from the Horned Sea toward Dwim-Halloe for near a year, picking up small bounties along the way. He planned on taking up the trail of the most wanted fugitive in all the Freelands—the murderer of Ulodonn Tygan, Dwim-Halloe's former king. But he found no value in revealing this fact to the guard.

"There's plenty of bounties in the Oxbow Kingdom," he said. "This one looks too good to be true." The sluggish guard nodded. The reward did seem generous for a mere lad, but Yduk understood how vengeful a king can be when one of his own is killed on castle grounds.

"Yer one o' them thinks ye can find the kingslayer, ain't ye?"

Yduk remained silent, arching an eyebrow in response. Even though the reward had gone unclaimed for a decade, Yduk knew he was the man for the job. The new king, Valin Vardan, had increased the bounty every year. Many had searched for the killer, but none had succeeded. *Yet.*

From the time he first heard news of the royal murder in Dwim-Halloe, the tale captivated Yduk. Two hundred leagues north in a fabled city of magic, the assassin had little chance of escaping justice. Yduk Thiern wasn't the only one who entertained those sentiments. With all the Oxbow Kingdom's wealth at his disposal and the need to distance himself from his outlaw brother, the new king would surely find his vile sibling.

But as the years passed and the bounty snowballed, the trail cooled. And the young bounty hunter grew up, finding success along the way, never forgetting about the big fish no one could catch. Seryn Vardan became an obsession for the compulsive Southlander.

"Good luck on that!" the guard grumbled and followed it with a sarcastic chuckle. "The north's littered with the bones o' men thought they could nab the kingslayer."

The failure of others doesn't deter me. I relish a challenge. Yduk learned the hardest tasks paid the best rewards. *Now I've set my sights on the biggest prize of all.*

"Some say the kingslayer's a Grimlord agent who returned to his master," the mead-soaked guard revealed. He paused to finish his mug. With the pewter container on the bar, he nodded toward the barkeep before continuing. "Others have him consortin' with a mountain dragon." The bearded man flapped his arms and chuckled. "Me, I think he's already dead. North of the Oxbows ain't a place where men survive."

Yduk was not convinced the search was futile. *Rumors of dragons and the Grimlord are pure fancy; legends embellished by tellers of tall tales,* he told himself. He understood how fables spread, tumbling farther and farther from the truth.

Coin was not the sole motivator for Yduk, although the gaudy reward would be more than enough to retire. The desire to become a legend drove him. *And the man who brings in this outlaw will indeed be legendary.*

For the time being, however, Yduk couldn't resist snagging such an easy bounty as Jetsam's. Weary of the road, he relished spending a few days in a comfortable inn before continuing into the desolate north. *The extra coin'll let me buy a warm coat for the trip,* he decided. *And mebbe a bunkmate fer the night,* he thought, glancing at the painted lady under the chandelier.

"Thanks for the tip, Stoddard." he told the guard. "Think of anything else might be helpful, I'll make it worth yer while."

"Good luck findin' yer sewer rat," the watchman replied, eyeing his fresh mug.

"Nice diversion, it'll be" Yduk informed the sentry. "Couple days' work, at most," he estimated aloud. "Tromp below, grab the knave by the scruff and drag his bloody ass out."

Yduk startled when he turned to see the old gypsy sitting behind him. *Bugger that old fool. Wonder if there's a bounty on his shriveled hide,* Yduk thought as he left the tavern, glaring at the placid wanderer.

Chapter Nine

That looks like the lad the bounty hunter's searching for, the old gypsy thought, recalling the tavern conversation he'd overheard. *He'll find trouble here if he's not careful.* Rubbing his wrinkled fingers through his gray whiskers, the vagabond watched the urchin wander through Beggar's Alley. *Wonder what he's looking for?*

Beggar's Alley sat in the poorest part of Dwim-Halloe, where even the king's watchmen rarely tread. At this time of night, most of the itinerants slept, wedged under landings or curled up against buildings. A few men surrounded a low fire, murmuring. The smell of cheap wine and feces weighed strong upon the breeze.

Certainly not cutpurses, robbers, and thieves. And most certainly not a decent meal.

The gypsy cringed as the waif approached the men near the fire. *Not them, lad.* Before the rover had a notion of intervening, a bony hand clamped around the boy's arm.

"What ye doin' runt?" the hairy beggar snapped. "Not plannin' on stealin' from us folk, are ye?" Before the urchin could reply, his accuser shook him violently. The orphan squirmed and yanked his arm, but the big hand held firm.

Lifting the waif, the derelict leaned closer, while the boy's toes scraped the urine-stained cobblestone.

His arm's likely to pop from his shoulder, the gypsy feared.

“Mayhaps we’ll see what the runt gots on him?” the drifter replied. With his free arm, the youth grabbed his pouch.

The tramps’ keen eye noticed the reaction.

“Got yerself a pouch, runt?” A second palm clasped over the orphan’s hand and the bag. The large hand tried to pry the purse from the small one, all the while holding the captive in the air. The lanky lad turned from the intruding paw, but the thief twisted him back.

“No!” the youngster shouted in a voice dripping with desperation.

Then the stripling lunged and bit the hairy hand holding his arm. His teeth broke the dirty skin.

With a howl, the angry hoodlum yanked his arm away from the belt-bag and swatted the frightened lad across the face. The boy’s head snapped back, his cheek reddened.

Despite the bite, the rogue’s grip held firm. The waif still dangled in the air.

Once again, the knuckled hand shot for the juvenile’s pouch. Before the thief reached the bag, a solitary voice rang out.

“Put him down!”

Wheeling around, jerking his captive with him, the scraggly drifter turned toward the sound. Cloaked in long tattered robes, his head covered by a draping hood, the gypsy glared.

“Mind yer own business!” the gangly rogue retorted.

“This is no place for open robbery,” the aged vagabond said. “We are scavengers and beggars. We don’t steal from each other!”

“But the knave,” the lanky drifter responded, “he’s *not* one of us!” A tinge of fear crept into his voice. By now, the commotion drew the attention of everyone in the alley. Even the slumbering opened a wary eye to the disturbance.

“Look at him,” demanded the older man. “He *is* one of us. Now put him down, before I run you out. You’re not among common thugs.” The old man’s voice floated in a soothing, hypnotic tone.

The rangy derelict released his grip and slunk away mumbling. As his feet hit the ground, the urchin clutched his pouch.

The timeworn vagrant approached Jetsam. Shambling under his heavy cloak, features shrouded in darkness, the gypsy peered at the boy.

"What in the gods are you doing lad?"

The old man and the young sized each other up. It took three breaths for the youth to respond.

"Looking for a gypsy."

"Gypsy? What for, lad?"

"I want something read for me."

The gypsy ruminated for a moment, his hand rubbing his bearded chin, barely visible in the flickering firelight.

"There's a bounty out for an orphan boy like you. Say he killed a guard."

"Wasn't me," the waif retorted.

He knows more that he's letting on, surmised the rover. "Might be you know this lad, though," the gypsy replied. "Might want to put the word out to your fellows that you'll be getting more attention soon. *Unwanted* attention. Best to lay low for a while."

"And do what? Starve? We've got to be out and about to survive. There's nothing to eat in the sewers."

He's a tough little bugger, the gypsy decided. "I can read," he offered, his curiosity piqued. "What is it you need to know?"

"Are *you* a gypsy?"

"Been called that—and worse. But you can call me Nicu."

"Can you read *magic,* Nicu?"

"Magic, you say? If you can't read, how do you know its magic?"

"I just know."

"Let's have a look then, shall we?" Nicu extended a wrinkled hand, palm high. The orphan leered and reluctantly retrieved a tube from his belt-pouch. As he pulled the elegant case apart and slid out the rolled scroll, Nicu's heart skipped a beat. *Can it be?*

"Don't touch it," the youth warned. He unrolled the scroll and tilted it toward the firelight for the gypsy to see.

"'Tis dark, lad, and I'm old. Move closer to the fire." The waif obliged and Nicu leaned in.

"Why, I'll be!"

"What? What is it?"

Nicu twisted his long beard, his eyes fixated on the parchment.

"What does it say?" demanded the orphan.

"It *is* magic," Nicu replied. *How did he get his hands on this?*

"I *know,*" the waif snapped, "but what's it *say?*"

Nicu rose, releasing his gaze from the scroll. "Where'd you find this?" he asked.

"Never mind where! It's mine. I just want to know what it says."

And I want to know where you found it. "Patience lad," Nicu retorted, rebuking the impertinent boy. "I can't tell what it says, but I recognize the runes as magical. I can also tell you it may make a nice souvenir, but that scroll is of no value to you." *Devil knows, it may not be of value to me anymore, either.*

The boy's expression dropped.

"Tell you what, lad, I might be able to sell that scroll to someone who can use it. Trade you all the silver pieces I have and this gold earring to boot. More than enough to feed your family for months."

Seeing the fire in the boy's eyes, Nicu itched to retract his words.

"I have no family and no use for your stinking coins!" The lad bolted and as his boots slapped the dusty street, he rolled the scroll back into its case and secured it inside his pouch.

Devil's luck. Should have chosen my words more carefully, Nicu lamented.

Jetsam cried himself to sleep that morning, with his disconsolate dog curled by his side. Flotsam visited Jetsam's dream and addressed him by his true name: Eidryn. In the dream, Jetsam again called his brother Elvar. Elvar as he remembered him; healthy, alive, full of life and promise. Not Flotsam. Not the dead boy he'd held in his bloody arms.

The resplendent Elvar spoke, his long hair flowing and shiny, a glint in his bright blue eyes.

"You were rude, Eidryn. You should know better. The gypsy saved your hide *and* your scroll. You need more patience."

Then he disappeared.

Beside his snoring dog, Jetsam woke dejected. He yearned to reunite with Elvar, even if it was but a dream. Reflecting on his brother's words, he realized he was too harsh with the gypsy. *Of all the people I know, this man is the only one able to tell me anything about the scroll.*

After all, the vagabond *did* mention he knew someone who could use the scroll. *And who but a wizard would have use for a magic parchment?* Jetsam resolved to reveal everything to coax more information from the old man. *If I can find a mage, maybe I can learn about my parents,* he theorized. *Maybe the spellcaster can teach me what they couldn't!*

Jetsam planned to return to Beggar's Alley later that evening. This time, he would take Tramp along, both for safety and to let the dog roam aboveground. The terrier had no fondness for cavern life, and Jetsam felt better with the canine by his side.

Still unnerved from last night's encounter, Jetsam also took his short sword. He spent the afternoon fabricating a makeshift sheath out of old rags and strips of wood. An ugly thing, the homemade scabbard would offer some protection for the blade. He fastened the sheath to his belt. Although the sword was short in comparison to a grown man, the blade was equivalent to a long sword for him.

After midnight, Jetsam and his dog ventured up from the sewers. Tramp reveled in the freedom, racing in the deserted back alleys. The terrier scooted along, nipping at Jetsam's heels, goading him into play. Jetsam obliged for a few minutes, tousling the canine and chasing after him. A thin sweat broke across his brow. "Enough," he told his furry companion. "We've work to do."

The evening was warm and humid. A low cloud layer settled over the valley, obscuring the Mirrored Peaks and trapping Dwim-Halloe's characteristic foundry fumes close to the ground. The blacksmith smell hung thick in the air tonight.

Fortunately, Beggar's Alley was right where he left it. Tramp's fur bristled among the collection of vagrants. His black nose sniffed the pungent air.

Jetsam's senses heightened, too. His hand found its way to his sword's hilt. Searching the congregation of outcasts, he hunted for the knowledgeable loner. Jetsam squinted in the darkness, looking for the shabbily-robed stranger among the sleeping vagrants. Drunks and addicts cluttered the curbs. The squalor was oppressive even for an underbelly boy.

But amidst this collection of wretched transients, the mysterious cloaked man was nowhere to be seen. *What was he wearing?* Jetsam tried to recall the man from last night. *Lavender robes and an emerald sash, I think. A gold earring and a green bandana.* With each fruitless second, Jetsam grew more uneasy. *Where are you, Nicu?* He and Tramp traversed the length of Beggar's Alley with no success.

Then, as he prepared to leave, he heard the familiar voice. Wheeling about, he saw the shrouded rover materialize from the shadows of a rickety stairway.

"Back again, lad? Didn't learn your lesson?"

With Tramp steadfast by his side, the contrite Jetsam prepared to address the old man.

"Never thanked you for saving me," he replied. "My apologies for being rude. I lost my temper."

"Quite all right. You were in over your head." The elder crouched to one knee. "Is this your dog?"

"Yeah—Tramp."

The terrier crept toward the gypsy, cautiously wagging. The hooded man scratched the dog's neck.

"What's *your* name, lad?"

"Jetsam."

"Why are you back here? You know it's dangerous."

"I wanted to ask you more about the scroll."

"Why the obsession? Sorcery is outlawed. What do you hope to accomplish?"

"My parents were mages. They were killed by the king's men." The old man's face softened. With quivering voice, Jetsam continued. "I recognized the seal on the scroll from my parents' writings. Hoped it would tell me something about them."

"Aye, the seal," acknowledged Nicu. "I'm afraid the seal's familiar to many. Belonged to Dwim-Halloe's School of Sorcery. Your parents must have had an association with the institution."

"They were teachers there." Jetsam's chin dropped to his chest.

"Sorry, lad. I know you hoped for more. This isn't your parent's scroll. It belonged to another."

"Who? Who'd it belong to?" Jetsam implored. Rubbing his bearded chin, the recluse hesitated in saying any more. After a long pause, he relented.

"Lad, that scroll is dangerous to whoever possesses it. That parchment once belonged to one of the most notorious men in all the Oxbow Kingdom. The man accused of killing King Tygan."

Jetsam's eyes grew wide as saucers. He remembered hearing of the tragedy while still with his parents. At the time he was too young to appreciate the significance of such an event, and had rarely thought of it since.

"I fear dispelling your fantasy, but this scroll will bring danger. Any clue to its previous owner is worth its weight in gold to a bounty hunter." Nicu consoled him. "I'm sorry, lad. Not what you expected."

"It's better than I expected!" Jetsam exclaimed. This reply appeared to stun the old man. "If I can find the assassin," Jetsam explained, "he could teach me about magic, and how he killed a king. Then someday I can avenge my parents."

The vagabond's jaw dropped at the words rolling from Jetsam's mouth. "Such determined hatred at so young an age," Nicu lamented. "Listen, lad, you cannot idolize an assassin. That's no way to think. Murder is never a justifiable solution."

"Why not? King Valin killed my parents. Why should I think King Tygan was any better? Why can a king murder, but not an ordinary man?"

Jetsam watched the man struggle to find an answer. "You *must* tell me of the wizard!" Jetsam entreated, his heart racing with excitement. Nicu still appeared flabbergasted.

"What wizard?" he whispered. "Who said I knew a wizard?"

"Why, you did! Last night, you said you knew someone to buy the scroll!" Jetsam was shouting now, adrenaline pumping. "Why, it's him, isn't it? You know the man who killed the king! Who else would find this valuable?"

"I certainly would," interjected a deep voice from behind them.

Surprised by the intrusion, both Jetsam and the old man spun to face the gravel-throated speaker.

From the shadows appeared a bald man in black leather brandishing a crossbow.

Chapter Ten

With a glance, Jetsam understood the dark figure wanted *him.* The hovering posture, poised crossbow, and determined tone conveyed an unmistakable message. With his ebony cloak and hood, he looked like the Reaper. *Tall, black, and ominous.* Jetsam didn't need a whispering voice to tell him to flee. *I'm a murderer now.*

"Come on, Tramp!"

Launching from his cross-legged position by the fire, Jetsam hit the street running and didn't look back. From the corner of his eye, he glimpsed the old man somehow kick up the fire, sending flames, embers, and smoke into the bounty hunter's agitated face. *Gives me a decent head start.*

Smoke wisps floated from smoldering street fires, blending into the cloudy black sky. Vagrants slumbered in ragged balls, snoring loudly. Others chatted in their sleep. Rats went about their business, oblivious to the filthy humans. And Jetsam ran as fast as he could, terrier at his side.

No pointless shouts of "halt" echoed from this tracker. *He's not as foolish as the guards,* Jetsam deduced, itching to glance back. The silence gnawed at him. *Hope Nicu's all right.*

As Jetsam debated sneaking a peek behind, something zipped past his ear. A split-second later, a *thunk* sounded in front of him.

Fobbing pus-boil! Jetsam saw a quivering crossbow bolt sticking from a barrel. An adrenaline burst increased his breakneck speed.

Tramp kept pace as they scrambled through narrow back alleys separating weather-beaten stone buildings. Even in the poorer sections of Dwim-Halloe, stonework architecture prevailed.

Jetsam knew the streets well enough to avoid the outer rampart. The granite barricade that protected Dwim-Halloe from the north would not be his ally. Instead, he aimed for the tree-lined river, hoping familiar territory may foster his escape.

Got to get underground. It's my only chance.

Furious at the belligerent old man for disrupting his shot, Yduk Thiern searched for the vagrant. "Ye sodding derelict!" he shouted. Waving smoke from his burning eyes, the bounty hunter turned in a circle, without any sign of the cagey vagabond.

Yduk debated chasing him or the boy. *The lad has a hefty price on his head* and *the scroll.* If not for his possible knowledge about the king's assassin, the gypsy was unimportant. *The waif fits the description, and had the sword and the dog. There's no doubt.*

Confused, and not wanting to waste valuable time on the old-timer, Yduk chased after the skinny urchin. *I can always come back to grill the itinerant later. Old drifters are easy to track,* he reminded himself. *And I've got a score to settle with this one.*

Not once did Yduk consider it luck that he stumbled across the boy. He credited the discovery to his instinct and experience. *Made perfect sense to follow the gypsy. Knew grandpa was up to no good.* What Yduk *did* consider lucky was the fact the urchin might have a scroll belonging to the king's assassin. *Now I've two reasons to catch the knave.*

Seryn Vardan. The manhunter repeated the name. *King Tygan's killer and King Valin's brother—what a story,* he mused.

Overhearing the conversation about the scroll filled Yduk with a rush. The possibility of getting his hands on an actual possession of Seryn Vardan's sent his heart pounding. *I'm close.* Running after the waif, Yduk felt young again.

Spotting the fleeing orphan ahead, Yduk decided against risking another arbalest shot. The boy was fast and had a big lead. *If I stop to span and reload, I may lose him.* The fleet quarry cut sharp corners and wove between buildings. Dog by his side, the young fugitive sped off the street and through a vegetable garden. A dozen paces later, the slippery urchin darted into a patch of narrow-crowned trees.

Close behind, Yduk watched every move. *Runs like an antelope,* he thought. Though Jetsam and Tramp were faster, Yduk's legs were longer and, with his sweeping strides, he kept pace, crossbow bouncing on his leathered back.

Across the muddy garden, he tracked the runaway through the thick stand of alders, brushing their long trunks as he raced by. The soft ground sloped toward the river, where the youth jaunted along the banks.

Then he was gone.

Yduk heard no splash, nor saw boy or dog in the river, so he scoured the bank. It took him but a moment to spot the hole where his prey disappeared.

It was a tight fit, but by taking off his crossbow, Yduk slipped through the narrow aperture. When his boots hit the ground, he slipped and slid, dancing a clumsy jig at gravity's behest. Yduk tumbled to the stone floor, smashing his elbow and knee.

"Damn it!"

Regaining his feet, he reached through the hole, grabbed his crossbow and pulled it through the breach, still grumbling about his uncharacteristic spill. Yduk fastened his weapon across his back, then hastily lit a torch. He looked down to see sling stones littering the floor. "That bloody blaggard," he mumbled, kicking the stones from his path.

Fearing he'd lost precious time, Yduk hurried in the only direction he could. Head down, he followed the unseen boy through the low tunnel. His bruised elbow throbbed as he lifted his torch.

At the first fork, Yduk stopped. Lean and fast, he had no doubt he would catch the boy—as long as he chose the right path. Kneeling, he looked for tracks. Fresh prints went each way—they were of no help. Tilting his head, he picked up the sound of distant footfalls from the tunnel sloping downward. Never doubting his judgment, Yduk proceeded in this direction. His torch light soon nipped at the young boy's heels.

Without any light, Jetsam's lead evaporated. *How I wish I'd brought the lantern.* He never imagined he'd be running again through these same unforgiving tunnels. His familiarity with the ancient halls provided but a slight advantage. Jetsam recognized which hallways would trap him into a dead end, but that was all. His eyes strained for the phosphorescent guide stones, which helped his flight, but were not as effective as a lantern. Then Jetsam detected torchlight creeping past his flying feet and on the walls around him.

Devil take you! Jetsam pushed himself harder, trying to outrun the bounty hunter's gaining light. With the abandoned well shaft sealed, Jetsam had to enter the Dwarven ruins, where the familiarity would soon disappear. He knew of no way out, other than the route he was taking in. Jetsam lamented entering the tunnel in the first place, although the arbalest's near miss convinced him he had little option but to seek cover. Pure instinct led him underground.

Jetsam's heart raced. When he fled from the troll down these same dusty hallways, he held a glimmer of hope. His mysterious voice guided him from danger. But now the voice was silent and Jetsam had no plan. Soon Jetsam would dart past the huge chamber where he encountered the knuckle-dragger, and then even familiarity would be lost. *With Elvar gone, I've got no reason to live.* Even Tramp by his side failed to encourage him. The thought of joining his brother on the other side held little fear.

With his lead evaporating, Jetsam charged into the spacious chamber where he once faced the troll. He had a choice to make. *Which way?* Two doorways stood available. He recalled his friends emerging from one and the troglodyte from the other. *I can loop back around,* he thought, recalling that the passage doubled back on itself.

As Jetsam and Tramp dashed across the cavernous dark room, the bounty hunter entered behind them, his flambeau brightening the circular chamber. Shimmering light danced off the smooth marble walls. Granite statues in high alcoves came alive in the fiery glow. Below the vaulted ceiling, three great archways cut into the gallery. Instantly, Jetsam spotted a towering troll blocking his path.

Jetsam nearly lost his water.

Illuminated by the manhunter's rushlight, Jetsam discerned this was not *his* hated troll come back to life, but rather an even larger monstrosity than the one that claimed Flotsam. Jetsam's instinctive reaction of fear and panic retreated under a sudden rush of optimism.

It hasn't spotted us! The deep-set troll eyes wedged under the furrowed brow fixated on the source of light and the man holding it. With long gnarled claws dangling at its side, the troll emitted a sickening howl and charged the startled bounty hunter. The storming abomination intercepted the man in black, who would not reach Jetsam without besting the hungry humpback.

Engrossed beyond common sense, Jetsam watched the muscled humanoid lumber across the dusty marbled mosaic. Holding his ground, the torchbearer withdrew his sword. The dazzling weapon glistened in the light. In a matter of steps, the brute would test the blade.

Tramp's muzzle nudged Jetsam's ankle. Coming to his senses, Jetsam slunk to the doorway opposite the impending confrontation, all the while his head turned toward the showdown. He *had* to know which of the two would be resuming the chase. Jetsam suspected only one would survive.

Or maybe they'll kill each other, he hoped.

Despite his consuming hatred for the creatures, Jetsam pulled for the troll out of self-preservation. He prayed the beast was unaware of his presence. Even if the monster had detected him, Jetsam surmised the carnivore would want to finish the main course before searching for dessert.

As the hairless form closed on the sword-wielder, Jetsam noted the troglodyte towered over the man by at least a foot. Even with the long blade, the human was physically overmatched. By the time the battle started, Jetsam and Tramp reached the arched doorway to the hall beyond. *Hope I can find my way out of here.*

Jetsam moved as far down the corridor as he could, while still maintaining a view of the combat. Hiding in the shadows, he witnessed the confrontation. The troll's stench burned his nostrils while the torch smoke stung his eyes.

Torch in one hand, sword in the other, the bounty hunter held his ground as the troll rushed him. The hulk pulled up beyond the blade's reach, its dim brain acknowledging the weapon. Seconds passed as the combatants scrutinized each other, both wary of striking first.

Faking a charge, the troll jerked in and back, drawing a nervous twitch from the man. The monstrosity growled in anticipation. A second fake saw the blade spasm again. Then the beast made its move—so nimbly, Jetsam figured the man in black would soon be dead.

But the gleaming blade jumped to life, embedding itself in the troll's forearm. For a rapid breath, the two were locked as one, as the bastard sword stuck in the sinewy limb. The Southlander clung to the hilt with one hand, brandishing the flambeau toward the troll's head with the other. With its free arm, the beast swatted the torch from the man's grip. Jetsam sensed the monster was smart enough to recognize it enjoyed an advantage in the dark.

With the brand knocked to the ground, the chamber blackened. In the diminished light, Jetsam barely distinguished silhouettes. If not for the troglodyte's sizable height, Jetsam would have had no clue.

Both hands clenching the sword, the bounty hunter pulled the blade free of the straining arm, while dodging a swing from the creature's other limb. What Jetsam saw next, he couldn't believe.

Unbalanced from its errant lunge, the cave-dweller teetered with naked legs apart, defenses down. Inky blood spurted from the forearm gash. Before the troll reacted, the blade swung around with all the force the Southlander could muster.

The lumpy gray head landed on the floor, next to the sputtering torch. For a few seconds, the headless body remained upright and quivering, then crumpled at the swordsman's feet.

As the bounty hunter bent to retrieve his dying brand, Jetsam sprinted.

"Come on, boy!"

Chapter Eleven

The cavern air loitered stale and musty. Jetsam and Tramp ran through the remnant of an intricate system winding far into the mountain core. While his eyes adjusted to the darkness, Jetsam picked out the phosphorescent hallway markers as he darted from spot to spot. The absence of torchlight encroaching from behind confirmed he enjoyed a decent lead on his pursuer. Tramp followed Jetsam diligently, his nails clicking on the hard floor.

Envisioning the troll's demise, Jetsam shuddered at the strength and skill of the man who chased him. He could hardly believe the tall stranger dispensed with the knuckle-dragger so easily. *No ordinary swordsman—or sword—could have chopped off a troll's head with one swing.* A chill ran down Jetsam's spine as he comprehended the awesome power of the ebony-clad tracker and his frightful weapon.

Escape is my only hope.

As his hand brushed along the stone wall, his thin fingers slid through an occasional bead of water seeping down the granite. Hurrying down the corridors, he also touched several rough wooden doors. *Have to assume they lead to dead ends*.

Jetsam noticed the wall fall from his fingertips and his feet slapped to a stop. *An intersection!* Hurriedly, he mentally mapped his route. *At best, one passage leads to freedom.* He feared the hunter was gaining on him. He *had* to escape these unfamiliar halls as soon as possible.

I don't like my odds.

While debating which direction to go, he once again heard a mysterious whisper. Like the shallow voice of the wind, a barely perceptible word pierced Jetsam's head.

Left, it murmured soft as a summer breeze through willow branches.

Believing the whispering saved him from the troll before, he veered left.

The mystifying voice confounded him though, and his mind reeled to rationalize the phenomenon. *Maybe it's a Dwarven ghost,* he contemplated, thinking of the countless souls who died hopelessly trapped as their world collapsed on them.

At Jetsam's side, the terrier followed every step. The tan fur on Tramp's back stood on end and his black nose twitched in the musty air. Jetsam noticed his companion's diligence. "You won't let him surprise us, will you, boy?"

At the next intersection, Jetsam detected the scent of smoke. He thought of his tracker's torch and froze in panic. The terrier pranced a few steps in front of him, sniffing intently. Inhaling deeper, Jetsam realized it wasn't torch smoke. *It's something putrid and awful.* He contemplated and looked at his dog. "What is it boy? What *is* that stink?"

Tramp stared at him with big brown eyes and tilted his head from left to right, ears pointing. His pink tongue hung out eagerly. Cautiously, Jetsam moved towards the smell. He recalled an old tale, a ghost story the boys told around the fire.

"Trolls regenerate," he mentioned to the dog. "Other than sunlight, only way to kill 'em is with fire. At least that's what they say," he whispered, as if Tramp comprehended. "That would explain the stench, and why Baldy was delayed," he surmised aloud. "And if it's true, it'll lead us out!"

Heartened, Jetsam continued toward the affronting odor's source. His eyes burned and his nostrils stung from the contaminated air. The tunnel grew more noxious than he could imagine, but he treaded on undaunted, more confident than ever that the smoke led to freedom.

Before long, Jetsam and Tramp entered the chamber where man and beast battled a short time ago. The round gallery choked with suffocating fog, but a small flickering cast enough illumination to see. The Dwarven statues leered in the shifting haze, looming from their alcove perches. Jetsam sensed their gemstone eyes upon him.

In the spot where the swordsman felled the beast, a blackened carcass burned and billowed toxic fumes. Until now, Jetsam had thought the worst smell in the world was a *live* troll. The stench of their burning flesh topped that ten times over.

Without delay, he and the terrier backtracked through the venerable halls of Gwae Gierameth toward the river bank. Soon the smoke receded and fresh air revived him. When he and Tramp reached the Jade, Jetsam smiled. *Finally!* All along he doubted if he could elude his tracker, and now he had. Dawn beckoned on the horizon and Jetsam felt as exhausted as the retreating night.

In the back of his mind, a specter of the man in black haunted him.

Fatigued and drained of adrenaline, Jetsam plodded home. His stomach rumbled, but he craved sleep. He imagined curling up on his mat, Tramp by his side. Lucidity abandoned him as he slept-walked the remaining distance. *I could nap right here.* Yet he trudged on.

Home at last, the cavern floor was greasy beneath Jetsam's leather boots. He shuffled on the slick surface, but remained rooted in place on the frictionless plane. Fatigue robbed him of coordination. A nameless fear poked him from behind, like an invisible specter. Jetsam lifted his bony knees and charged into a sprint, yet his legs felt boneless. His eager feet slid out behind him and he lunged face-first onto the coated floor.

Jetsam's hands shot forward, but not fast enough to keep his pointed chin from bouncing on the slippery stone. *That should have hurt.* The mysterious wetness coated his hands and face. He rubbed his undamaged jaw with his shirt sleeve, and in the dim cavern, noticed the dark staining on his palms. He gasped in terror.

Blood!

Jetsam scrambled up, his pupils adjusting to the animated firelight. Nightmarish faces scowled within the flames. The room appeared to spin and distort. He blinked and squinted, not wanting to believe his eyes. Small bodies scattered across the floor.

Wobbling, he again slipped on the traitorous rock. He did an awkward dance, an offering to the fickle gods of balance. His prayer went unanswered as his rubbery feet again failed him. *Can't even stand up.* This time he landed on his rump, but felt no pain. *What's wrong with me?* Blood seeped into his breeches, wicking up his lower limbs. A single sob escaped his trembling lips.

Abandoning his wish to stand, he crawled on hands and knees to the nearest face-down body. With bloody fingers, he turned the small head. Mole's throat was sliced from ear to ear. In horror, Jetsam pulled his sticky hands away from his friend's desecrated head. The lifeless skull fell soundlessly.

Jetsam wept openly, yet his hearing abandoned him as well. Silence deafened him. Fighting the fear, motivated beyond reason, he crawled further. The next body belonged to Ratboy. His head was cut near off.

Cradling the blood-drenched orphan in his lap, Jetsam wailed and cursed, but no sound emanated from this straining mouth. *Am I mute, or deaf?* He screamed silently in defiance. "On the blood of my father, why has this happened?" he mouthed in vain. "Answer me!"

As tears ran down his oval face, he received his reply. It was not the answer he hoped for.

Against the flickering torchlight, Jetsam made out the dark hunter's silhouette.

Jetsam awoke in a sweat. He bolted upright, and his damp head swung around in the impenetrable darkness. He tried to call out, but his voice only squeaked. Then he heard Ratboy speaking, and astonishing relief washed over him.

It had all been a dream. *A horrible dream.*

Panting, Jetsam collapsed back against his straw mattress and exhaled. He was awake, but the stark imagery of his nightmare wasn't so easily shaken. As the recollections of his grisly dream replayed in his mind, he arrived at a sullen conclusion.

It is most certainly a premonition.

Somehow, Jetsam had eluded the bounty hunter in the Dwarven cavern. But he was convinced the relentless pursuer still hunted him. Remembering how the ferocious troll fell at the man's blade, Jetsam recognized staying in Dwim-Halloe made him easy prey. It was only a matter of time before the dark tracker, or an ambitious guard, or another bounty hunter, discovered the orphan hideout. *Then everyone's in peril.*

Jetsam reached a quick decision. His comrades were the only family he had left. *I'll not jeopardize their safety.* He would leave his surrogate home once and for all. *The magic scroll and the manhunter's appearance are signs.* Destiny pushed him to seek out the sorcerer who owned the parchment, and chase the path of his birthright. *No turning back.*

Jetsam tossed off his thin blanket and rose to his unsteady feet. The price of his decision sank in. *I'll be on my own for the first time.* His parents and dear brother had been torn from him, and now his friends faced the same peril. Jetsam would have to leave Ratboy, Mole, and the rest, likely forever. *And Giselle.* The possibility of never seeing her again stung as well.

In truth, he understood the odds were not in his favor. He had no experience on his own. Surviving alone, without his twin or the clan's companionship, was a disheartening thought. Death crept closer and closer. *If nothing else, I'll lead the Reaper far from my friends.*

Jetsam pulled on his boots. He began to appreciate the cramped, musty cavern that had been his home for so long. *After today, this dim, dank hole will be but a memory.* His thin hand pulled the flat stone covering his cubby, and he retrieved his possessions. Jetsam placed his few spare clothes, fur-lined coat, sleeping mat, shoddy gloves, lantern, oil flask, apples from the garden, bowl and spoon, knife, and a chunk of hard cheese on the blanket. He rolled his belongings into a pack, securing it with rope strands. He fastened his short sword and pouch to his belt. In went his sling, a hand full of stones, flint, steel, and tinder, and his treasured scroll. *That's all I have to my name.*

As he fastened the blanket into a makeshift backpack, the reality of his choice nagged him. *Where will I go?* He'd heard only rumors of where the rogue sorcerer had fled. *If bounty hunters can't find him, how will I?* Jetsam resigned himself to wandering the rest of his days searching for the enigmatic warlock.

But that wasn't his sole worry. More disconcerting thoughts crept into his head. *If I sneak away, will that stop Baldy from raiding the sewers?* Jetsam mulled over this dilemma. He wanted to lead the tracker far from his friends, yet still ensure an unfettered escape. His head began to ache. Minutes since making his momentous decision, he was already awash in doubt. *I must speak with Ratboy.*

Jetsam understood it would be cowardly to slip away without telling his friend. *Yet Ratboy won't make it easy—he'll do everything in his power to convince me to stay.* It was not a conversation Jetsam relished, and as Ratboy rambled in, it arrived before he was ready.

"What're ye doing?" Ratboy asked, staring at Jetsam's packed belongings. The orphan startled Jetsam, and he stammered before spitting out the hard truth. Ratboy trembled as the dreaded words tumbled from Jetsam's mouth.

"Zounds! Ye'll *not* be leaving! Only a simpkin would strike out on his own."

"I've no choice. Baldy's coming for me. He'll swat you aside like flies if he doesn't slit your throats first," Jetsam exclaimed. "I'm a caged bird bringing danger to the rest of you."

"We can take care of ourselves!" Ratboy retorted. "He doesn't know the underbelly like we do. We'll move our camp, keep out of his way."

"You don't know what he's like. He's no slow-footed guard. He slashed down that troll like a stack of hay. He'll kill us *all.*"

"He's just a man. I'll kill *him* first."

"That'll just bring more." Jetsam shook his head and changed the subject. *I should have snuck away.* "I'll think about it," Jetsam stated, "but first, tell me what you know about the man who killed the king."

"What the devil do ye want to know about *him?*"

"I have his scroll—the old man said so. In exchange for it, I want him to tell me about my parents and teach me spell casting."

"Yer crazy for sure," Ratboy declared, shaking his tangled head. "Ye know there may be no truth in those stories. The man's probably dead and gone. Ye'll only be chasin' a ghost and catchin' yer death."

"Ghost or flesh, I'll chase him either way. I'm dead if I stay."

"And deader if ye go."

They looked wordlessly at each other, waiting on the deadlock. The moment grew painful. Finally, after a drawn-out sigh, the older boy broke the stalemate.

"I'll tell ye what I know," Ratboy offered reluctantly. Jetsam knew Ratboy had listened to the stories of Seryn Vardan during his time as a miner. The shabby youth let out a deep sigh and started his tale. "He's old by now—almost old as his *brother* King Valin. Maybe thirty. They say after killin' King Tygan, he fled north to the mountains, or the badlands beyond—into the Grimlord's realm. Too far away and treacherous for the king's men to hunt." Ratboy paused, a worried look on his face. "That's what I've heard anyways. I ain't no expert."

"Then that's where I'll go. I need to flee the king's men as well. After all, I'm a wanted murderer too!"

Ratboy hung his head in disgust. "The North ain't like the sewers. Gets deathly cold and windy. Storms like the devil, with snow piled higher than yer head."

Jetsam's determined expression didn't waver. Ratboy tried harder. "The badlands are barren—no fruit or game. If ye don't freeze, ye'll starve." Ratboy extended his hands, pleading. "Head south. Forget yer wizard and aim for low ground and better weather."

"That's *exactly* where they'll think I went. My bounty'll be posted in every town. It'll be worse than living here, always running from the guards, running from everybody," Jetsam lamented. "I'll head north, and find a cubbyhole to stay warm, and I'll be fine. If not, at least I won't die running."

"Then I'm going with ye," Ratboy announced.

Jetsam anticipated this response. As much as he wished his best friend could join him, Jetsam had to refuse. *I'll not lead him to his death. Besides, the underbelly is where Ratboy belongs. It's his home. He has responsibilities.*

"You can't come with me. The younger ones need you," Jetsam pleaded, half hoping Ratboy wouldn't listen. "Even with me gone, things will be tougher down here. They think one of us killed a guard, and that means life for everyone will be harder."

"Rooster can take me place. I'm going *with* ye."

"Rooster? He's no replacement for you. They boys need *you*—you're like a father to them." Jetsam wondered why he opposed Ratboy. *In truth, I'd relish his companionship.* Yet, Elvar's death tugged at him. Depriving the orphans of Ratboy's leadership could prove catastrophic.

"There'll be more than just Baldy looking to claim my bounty," Jetsam stated. "You may have to move camp anyway. Stay here and keep the lads safe. I can't have more blood on my hands." Ratboy ground his teeth.

"We'll move the camp first, and then leave together," Ratboy countered.

"It won't be that easy. Without you, those boys are lost. You've got to stay."

Ratboy shook his head in defiance. Tears welled in his brown eyes. "Going *with* ye," he repeated, his voice a notch higher.

"You must stay," Jetsam replied, his tone soothing. "You're their leader. They look up to you. You keep them safe. This is where you belong." The words rang true. Ratboy hung his head.

He knows I'm right, Jetsam suspected. "You can't join me," he reiterated, "but you *can* help me. I need to lure Baldy out of Dwim-Halloe without giving myself away. I don't want him to learn I've left by scouring every inch of the underbelly. Then you'll all be doomed."

Ratboy scratched his scalp as he mulled over this request. He offered no quick response.

"Need to lead him on a false trail, keep him out of the sewers. Has to be obvious I've left for good."

Ratboy chewed his lip, a strained expression darkening his cherubic face. "Got naught," he admitted with a shrug.

"We've got to come up with *something,*" Jetsam demanded.

Close as brothers, the two orphans deliberated, rethinking their old pranks and scams, trying to put together a plan. They'd orchestrated elaborate diversions before, foiling slow-witted peasants and merchants to steal their necessities. But this was different.

This is life or death.

Then Jetsam's face lit up, illuminated by the perfect scheme. "I've got it!"

Jetsam understood there was no time to waste. *The bounty hunter won't be delayed for long. He's likely searching the underbelly already.* Jetsam urged Ratboy to keep his departure secret. Yet as Jetsam prepared to leave, a few of his closest friends collected to bid him farewell. Ratboy leaked the news to a handful of the older orphans, those that knew Jetsam the longest, and truly understood his sacrifice.

Tears welled in Ratboy's eyes as he presented his friend a parting gift.

"Take these boots. Good as new, and'll keep the wet out better'n those ragged things o' yours. Can always steal me another pair before winter." Jetsam tried to refuse, but Ratboy wouldn't hear of it. Knowing the boots would come in handy, Jetsam relented and thanked his friend.

Following Ratboy's lead, Mole gave Jetsam a small, but thick, blanket. "It'll get cold out, it will," he replied. "Besides, ye and Flotsam stole it for me a few winters ago. Time to have it back, it is." Jetsam remembered pilfering the blanket for his friend, and accepted the gift graciously.

After Mole, other clan members presented Jetsam with gifts for his travels. A cape and hood from Blister, a tunic from Pike, a paring knife from Rooster, dried meat from Biter, and a pot from

Lil' Pete were added to his stock. The generous outpouring warmed his heart, making it even harder to leave. *I'll miss them.*

Jetsam decided to leave under cover of darkness, so with Ratboy's much-needed help, he spent the rest of the day constructing a small skiff. Mole pitched in, scavenging a few planks and strapping them together. The lightweight dinghy was just big enough to carry Jetsam, his pack, and Tramp.

Looking at his home for probably the last time, a sour melancholy washed over Jetsam. *For so long, I hated these dank, dirty, caverns.* But now, he hated to leave their familiar security. They had become the only refuge he had, too barren and unforgiving for any but the truly desperate.

Jetsam took one last teary-eyed look at his homely home and family of outcasts, and then he was off. Ratboy and Mole followed him out, carrying the skiff. They would escort him from the sewers and run interference for their friend. Ratboy sent out a pack of scouts to look out for any sign of the bounty hunter. *Don't want any surprises spoiling my escape.*

Jetsam had one final stop before leaving the underground. He and his two escorts made their way to the catacombs where they laid his twin to rest. Rot and decay tainted the air. The musty caverns frightened Mole and Ratboy. Of the many emotions Jetsam experienced, fear wasn't one of them. *The dead don't scare me. The dead are my family.*

While Mole and Ratboy waited for him outside the dreaded catacombs, Jetsam went to the hole where his brother was buried. His parents were somewhere down here, too, although their location would be forever unknown to him.

The guilt of Elvar's death weighed heavy on Jetsam. *If only we'd never snuck into that garden. If only I'd listened to Elvar. If only it wasn't a crime to be an orphan.*

If only.

Jetsam placed his hand against his brother's tomb. *So many questions left unanswered. So much potential left unfulfilled.*

"Why, oh, why, did you have to leave me?" Jetsam questioned.

Isolation and regret bombarded him.

Jetsam forced himself to remember the good times. *Playing in our home as small boys. Raiding the market district after dark. Tricking the other orphans, pretending to be each other for days on end.* A renegade tear and a reluctant smile met at the bottom of his cheek.

"Time to say goodbye," Jetsam whispered. He was leaving his family for good.

"Mother, Father, Brother," he murmured into the quiet darkness, "I shall honor you." With a sharp-edged stone, he scratched the rock sealing his brother's tomb. The letter 'F' Ratboy had left to mark the tomb became an 'E.' "In death you were Flotsam," Jetsam whispered, "but in memory, you shall forever be Elvar."

Red-eyed and sniffling, he joined his fidgeting friends and they headed for the surface. Jetsam's escape plan would lead him back inside the castle one last time. With the abandoned well sealed off, he had to cross the moat to get inside the castle walls. Ratboy and Mole escorted him to the moat's edge. Now the goodbye was even harder.

Jetsam embraced Mole first, leaving the hardest parting for last.

"Fare thee well," wished Mole.

"Keep an eye on him," Jetsam instructed, nodding toward Ratboy. "Up to you to keep him sound."

"Give 'em bloody hell," croaked Ratboy, tackling Jetsam with a bear-hug, trying in vain to hold back his tears. Jetsam was almost too choked up to speak.

"You've been a brother to me," Jetsam said. "Take care of the lads."

Then Jetsam and Tramp slipped onto the wobbly raft. *Barely seaworthy, but it'll suffice.* Jetsam pushed off to the calm water and waved solemnly to his friends. *Suspect I'll never see them again.*

With a makeshift paddle, Jetsam guided his unsteady craft across the moat. The bank was steep and his legs got wet as he dismounted and pulled the skiff from the water. He wedged it upright, and then picked up Tramp.

Jetsam crept along the slim ledge at the base of the castle wall. He docked near the drainage chute he'd utilized for entry before. Holding Tramp tightly, Jetsam wiggled his way through the hole, and minutes later, stood inside the castle walls. With no time to spare, he headed for the garden. *If I can't find Giselle, my plan's foiled.*

Fragrant and still, the garden was the same as before. Jetsam's senses were on edge, for the ever-present sentry was about. Jetsam presumed the patrol had been fortified since the *incident,* and likely increased the frequencies of their rounds. He hoped the girl still made *her* nightly visit.

Afraid Tramp would inadvertently give him away, Jetsam carried the dog. Staying against the outer wall, Jetsam crouched behind the hedges. He tiptoed around the garden's perimeter, looking for movement. The partial moon hovered above, providing natural light. Jetsam noticed additional torches mounted along the curtain wall. The torchlight made the garden much brighter than before. *That's both good and bad.* He'd be able to spot Giselle or the watch more easily, but he was also more visible. So far, nothing moved besides blossoming branches in the light summer breeze.

Before he covered half the garden's boundary, he spotted a guard. Back against the stone, Jetsam sunk below a yew hedge. Tramp kept quiet, much to his relief. After the armed sentry passed, Jetsam continued his search.

Treading the garden's edge was safer, but proved harder to view the park's interior. Thick branches and tall hedges blocked his view as he peered for Giselle. By the time he circled the spacious garden, Jetsam discerned he would have to breach the interior for any chance of success.

Relying on memory, he navigated for the location where he had met the girl previously. He moved slowly, staying off the paths and crawling through the bushes. Branches pulled and tugged at his limbs, while thorns bit his pale skin. Jetsam heard more movement. *Just the sodding guard.*

Tramp released a murmuring growl. Jetsam hushed the dog, and slipped his hand around Tramp's snout. The terrier jerked free and nipped Jetsam's finger. No blood was drawn, but Jetsam received the message.

Blast! Don't touch the nose, I guess.

Jetsam dropped low into a thick flower bed. Deep in the blossoms, the potent fragrances tickled his nostrils. Twisting his slender nose, he fought back a sneeze. Clenching his teeth, he feared it would give him away. He rubbed his tunic sleeve on his nose to dispel the sprouting sneeze. So far, it was a stalemate. The footsteps faded. Jetsam relaxed, and the sneeze escaped while his defenses were down.

The sneeze wasn't loud, but it echoed more than Jetsam hoped. His heart pounded as he tried to sink lower in the grass. Noise came from behind him.

Tramp barked at the intrusion. *Sodding rot!*

Before Jetsam decided to run or reach for his sword, a voice halted him.

"Jetsam? Is it you?" the sweet voice whispered. A smile overtook Jetsam's nervous face. He spit out a feeble reply. He caught his breath as Giselle extended a hand to help him from the flower bed.

"How'd you find me?" he asked as she pulled him to his feet.

"Please, take not offense," she answered, "but I caught a whiff of you and Tramp on the breeze." Jetsam's face reddened. "Don't feel bad," she offered. "I have a very good nose. And I heard you sneeze."

Giselle petted Tramp's head. His tail wagged against Jetsam's stomach. He set the dog down, and it pranced around Giselle, standing on its hind legs, its front paws patting her satin thighs.

With a smile, she stroked Tramp's soft fur. "Sit, sit," she said. The terrier obeyed. The girl looked at Jetsam, her face turning grim. "I cannot believe you are back. They will *hang* you if caught!" She viewed him through pleading green eyes.

"I *didn't* kill him," Jetsam blurted.

"I believe you."

I wonder if she truly does? He longed to hug her, yet feared breaking the fragile spell. *I'm pushing my luck.*

"I'm leaving and I'll never see you again," he whispered. She pulled away, a sorrowful expression on her fragile face. Tears filled her eyes, and Jetsam felt terrible. *Never meant to make her cry.* "I need your help," he beseeched. "Tell the guards I was mean and you hate me. Tell them I stole a bunch of apples and took a raft down the river. Tell them I'm fleeing south. *Tell them.*"

"But why? Why should I say those awful things?"

"Because I'm fleeing *north.*"

"But the North is a terrible place," she replied, wiping her emerald eyes. "Why *not* head south?"

"South is where they'll expect me to go. Only a shandy fool would head north."

"You are no fool," she countered.

"I have a plan. I'm going to find the scroll's owner." Jetsam wanted to tell her more. He wanted to sit and talk and hold her hand. He wanted her to say everything would be fine. He wanted to taste her sweet lips. But familiar footsteps on the garden path foretold his leave.

Before Giselle could utter a warning, Jetsam bent down to scoop up Tramp. When he stood up, Giselle's crestfallen face hovered before him. She kissed him full and hard on the lips.

He wished he never had to leave.

It pained him to pull away from her tender touch. With a final glance, he stared into her eyes, sensing it would be the last time. He peered down the path toward the footsteps.

"Tell him," he nodded. "Tell him now." Then, he was off. Heart aching with grief, his wiry legs launched him on his way.

Teary-eyed and distraught, Giselle strode toward the guard as Jetsam instructed.

I hope she's a good liar.

Chapter Twelve

For the first time in his life, Jetsam ventured outside the protective walls of Dwim-Halloe. Tramp by his side, Jetsam floated beneath the starry skies. All his possessions were contained in his pouch or in the sack slung across his shoulder. He let the current carry them downstream, southward toward Dwim-Halloe's outer wall. Their little skiff made nary a wake.

Bending branches clawed at them as they rode the river. The stone bridges spanning the Jade were lifeless. Dots of torchlight from the final granite wall loomed on the horizon. The river ran underneath Dwim-Halloe's perimeter walls north to south.

As long as no guards see us, we should make it.

Jetsam rarely ventured this far south. The townhouses dwindled near the outer walls. He typically foraged in the dense part of town, with narrow alleys and plenty of hiding places. *Hope the watchmen have their attentions focused elsewhere.*

As they floated nearer the last rampart, Jetsam scanned the top of the wall and adjoining bastions. He detected two sleepy guards high atop the fortification. They faced southward, looking down the sloping mountainside. Ahead lay three low archways in the stone wall, assembled for the river's passing. Iron bars embedded deep into the riverbed pierced the Jade across the openings.

Uh-oh. Upon seeing the bars, Jetsam reached for his oar. Splashing the plank into the water, he tried to slow the craft. As the iron barricade neared, he realized they were traveling much faster than he imagined. *The current's smooth but strong.*

Jetsam worked the paddle to no avail. He dropped the oar, grabbed Tramp and his belongings, and braced for the collision. A narrow space separated the stanchions, and the skiff would not slip through. A second before crashing, Jetsam twisted his body sideways and aimed for the gap between the shafts. Holding Tramp at his hip, he ducked low and leaned forward.

Jetsam's shoulder clipped one of the iron bars as he launched into the river. Splashing into the cool Jade, he was lucky to escape with a bruise. Tramp hit the water beside him, dog-paddling and tongue wagging.

So much for floating a league down river.

Jetsam assumed the bounty hunter would eventually find the makeshift raft, and the farther downstream the better. Now his skiff was wedged against the iron grating. Fighting to stay afloat, Jetsam acclimated to the frigid river. Tramp paddled alongside, little paws pumping. *Might as well stick to the plan as best I can.* Jetsam and his belongings were drenched, so he floated downstream until the torchlight on the rampart faded from view.

The swift water soon chilled him. Observing the slick dog, he suspected Tramp was freezing, too. Spotting a shallow inlet gleaming in the moonlight, they swam toward the calmer cove. Dripping wet and shivering, the pair tromped through the sedges until firm ground held their feet. *Guess we'll head northwest, since Ratboy said the fugitive assassin fled that way.*

Fearful of the bounty hunter, Jetsam wanted to journey as far as he could before sleeping. The river bank was thick with trees, and Jetsam discovered movement through a dark, unfamiliar forest was slower than anticipated. The terrain climbed steeply from the river, which hindered him even more.

Daylight unveiled the majestic evergreens blanketing the mountainside. Woodpeckers tapped out a staccato rhythm while nuthatches and chickadees chirped to usher in the morn. Sunlight cut the fog, leaving the forest floor moist and humid. Warm rays filtered through the lush branches and fleeting mist, painting the environs with a blend of light and shadow.

Winding their way northward, Jetsam and Tramp traversed gullies and ravines, ridges and slopes, all under a conifer cover. They strode on a brown needle floor, accumulating for ages on the furrowed mountainside. The footing was tolerable, and the higher they hiked, the more the pines thinned and shrunk, turning to patchy scrub. By afternoon, they neared the top of the tree line, and could see the western Mirrored Peak looming before them. Jetsam stayed under the lanky evergreens to avoid being spotted from afar on the naked face.

By mid-afternoon, the journey's pain set in. His knees, ankles, and feet throbbed. His back ached from his heavy, wet pack. Still he trudged on, motivated by fear of the tracker. The pair covered five leagues that day, before setting up camp along an outcropping. The summer air was still warm, and a long day in the sun and wind dried Jetsam's belongings, so he resisted starting a fire. He ate stale bread and moldy cheese from his pack, shared it with Tramp, and fell asleep under the stars.

His restful slumber was short-lived.

Jetsam awoke with a start to the sound of a howling wolf. Darkness still covered the land as the wild dog bayed at the moon. Jetsam was certain he heard meaty paws circling on the needled ground. He grabbed his sword and unsheathed the blade.

Tramp growled in response and surprised Jetsam. The canine's ferocious snarl rivaled that of any dog three times his size. Announcing his presence with authority, the terrier barked. With tail up and fur on end, Tramp's feet scraped the ground like a bull ready to charge. His white teeth shone in the sallow moonlight.

The wolf sounds moved farther away. Tramp continued to bark and growl until silence again reigned. Although the dog never left his side, Jetsam rested uneasily the remainder of the night. The slightest sound prompted his inflamed imagination. With every rustle, he envisioned gruesome beasts crawling toward him. Spiders, snakes, wolves, goblins, trolls—all crouching beyond the next bush, waiting for him to doze off. *A night never lasted longer.* He felt four years old.

Somehow, dawn arrived without further incident. The colorful sunrise was a glorious spectacle. Pink and crimson streaks rose over the mountain tops like billowing ribbons. Achy and sore, the first morning proved harsher than Jetsam anticipated. *I need to adjust to a full-time life above ground.* Tramp, however, was in his glory. *He won't miss the underbelly at all.* After a dry and tasteless breakfast, the duo resumed their trek.

Jetsam concluded crossing the rocky spine was his best strategy. *Ratboy said the king's assassin was rumored to dwell north of the Oxbow peaks.* Jetsam wanted to put the arduous mountains between himself and Dwim-Halloe. The hard part would be finding a place to cross. He surveyed the jagged peaks as far as he could see, yet no pass appeared suitable. The height of the snow-capped range dipped to the west, so he proceeded in this direction. North of him, the rocky slopes looked too daunting to scale.

Jetsam and Tramp chased the sun all day, remaining beneath the timberline. The footing was softer under the trees, and the thick branches screened the beating rays and buffered the escalating wind. The highland terrain was easier going than the barren, rocky slopes above the pines.

From atop a stony escarpment, Jetsam spotted his first bear in the valley below. Even at a distance, the dark animal was fierce and commanding. Tramp released a low growl, but Jetsam hushed the nervous terrier and stood in awe of the black bear. Mesmerized, he watched for several minutes before it disappeared into the woods below. Jetsam realized how small and vulnerable he was in this vast wilderness.

I've seen no break in the peaks that looks possible to cross. The closer he got to each low spot on the horizon, the more daunting it appeared. He wondered how he'd manage to traverse the range. He didn't want to backtrack to the Serpentine Pass, fearing discovery or capture on the thoroughfare. *Or even worse, running into Baldy.*

Exhaustion came before sunset, and Jetsam's pace slowed as he searched for a suitable spot to spend the night. Ominous clouds rolled in by late afternoon, darkening the mountainside and cooling the air. Soon, thunder heads blackened the sky. Gentle rain began to fall, and then intensified to a downpour. Lightning danced on the horizon and a thunderclap shook the evergreens to their roots. The wind gathered momentum.

Tramp trembled and whimpered at the sound of thunder, and Jetsam yearned for cover. The rain soaked him deep while lightning pranced closer on skeleton legs. He had no sewer to scamper to, no cavern to shelter him from the storm's wrath, no blaze to warm him and dry his wet clothes. He and Tramp had only the trees and each other. They were discouraged and exposed.

Hunched over, with rain dripping off his nose, Jetsam trudged on, peering through the prickling rainfall for cover. He noticed a small hollow in the base of an ancient tree. As he approached, he spied a nest on the ground. Four baby birds bawled with wide open beaks.

They'll surely die down here. He picked up the nest cradling the four siblings. "Where's your mother? Looking for you up in the tree?"

Jetsam, his pungent wet dog, and four nestlings sheltered in the alcove to ride out the storm. The venerable tree protected them from the rain and he held the baby birds close to keep them warm. Jetsam and the whimpering terrier watched nature's light show and ate a bit of cheese as the thunder rolled. Before the storm passed, they all drifted off to sleep. Harried dreams of nature's fury tormented Jetsam throughout the night.

Tramp woke Jetsam with a nervous yelp. As Jetsam's eyes adjusted to the morning light, he gasped at the hazy form standing before them.

"*Heth ille gweathrym val-nivore?*" the silhouette asked in a voice like a zephyr. Jetsam comprehended none of the angelic-sounding language, and his sleepy vision couldn't yet discern her shadowy features.

"What kind of gnome dares to defile my tree and steal my babes?" demanded the stern female voice, this time in a tongue he understood. Jetsam sat up and rubbed his eyes. They reluctantly adjusted to the daylight.

Standing before him was a willowy woman—or the ghost of one. Tall and thin, her luminescent skin shone pale lime. Clad in a short gown of leaf and foliage, the ethereal being swayed barefoot on a sunbeam. Her glistening hair was the color of pine needles and cascaded across her shoulders and down her back. The tresses billowed and flowed, though not a breeze stirred in the branches. Her timeless face brimmed with both wisdom and innocence. She retrieved the nest, calming the frantic birds.

Speechless, Jetsam offered no response. She spoke again, her tone harmonious, yet forceful. "Why have you intruded into my home?"

"I—I'm sorry," blurted Jetsam, Tramp trembling at his side. "I mean no harm; I only sought shelter. The wind knocked this nest to the ground, so I took it out of the rain."

"What sort of gnome are you? I've never seen a fox like that."

"I'm just a boy, m'lady, not a gnome. And this is my dog, Tramp."

"A boy? You radiate a magic aura like a wizard in disguise. What would a boy be doing in my hills? Speak true, or I shall smite thee, powerful as you might be." She raised her arms high and wide, and grew menacing despite her beauty. Jetsam cowered before her.

He felt compelled to tell her everything, whether of his own will or some enchantment of hers, he never knew. As he gazed into her emerald eyes, the words poured from his lips. He told her of his lost family and his flight from home. He narrated encounters with Baldy and the trolls, of Giselle and the garden. As he described the serene lush park, her stern face softened. He continued, speaking of rescuing Tramp, his search for the reclusive mage, and his desire to find the truth about his parents and himself. He revealed everything.

"You speak of things I know not," she replied after his unintentionally long-winded tale. "But I sense truth in your heart and a kindness to nature's creatures." Her sparkling eyes returned to Jetsam. "You have suffered great misfortune, but I fear you are in store for more. These highlands are no place for you. The wilderness is unforgiving, and surviving will test your mettle."

Jetsam's apprehensiveness waned. Transfixed by this wonder, he hung on her every word. Tramp calmed as well, his ears perked.

"But I pity you," she continued, "and none shall say I am cold-hearted, so I offer you assistance, little though it may be. First, step into the sunlight. Let me have a fair look at you." Jetsam did as he was told, grabbing his sack and ushering Tramp along. He stood before the mistress of the wood, not as nervous as before.

"The help I can offer is twofold," she stated. "Firstly, I bestow an offering to let you pass unharmed through *Sylallian;* my woodland." She strode past him toward the gigantic pine. Her feet made no sound as they tread upon the crisp needles. Her arm stretched into the hollow, and retrieved a strange necklace. With her slender fingers, she lifted the string and placed it over his head. The gift was woven of delicate ivy threaded through an assortment of dried nuts and berries.

"None of nature's creatures will harm you whilst you tread in these mountains, as long as you bring them no harm. Be forewarned," she said, "although you will be safe from wolf and bear and mountain lion and the like, this shan't protect you from creatures of unnatural origin, like ogres and goblins and trolls. Of these beasts I can offer only advice—flee at first sight."

"Thank you, m'lady." Jetsam bowed.

"Know this as well," she advised, "when hunger takes you, any berries and nuts matching those on this necklace can be eaten. And if a berry tempts you that does not match one around your neck, be wary, for it will make you ill."

Jetsam nodded.

"Secondly, I know something of the one which you seek."

Jetsam's eyes grew wide. "Truly? You know of the wizard?"

"I know of him, though he passed through here but once, years ago. The trees tell me he lives in the mountains still, but not on this side of the peaks. He resides in the Northland, but where exactly, I know not. To cross the peaks is treacherous, and I would counsel you against it."

"Pardon, m'lady, but I've no other choice. I'm homeless and on the run. It's my only hope."

"Then I shall help as best I can. There is a pass not far from here that holds the best chance for crossing to the Northland. Be forewarned, the North holds more danger than my woods. The unnatural creatures I spoke of are rare in these parts, but wander freely in the *Kierawaith.* You will need much luck to escape harm."

"Thank you again, m'lady. I'm forever in your debt." Again he bowed, his hair falling across his face. With a swift hand, he corralled the locks.

Jetsam and Tramp followed the woman through the woods. She moved effortlessly across the forest floor, and they hustled to keep up. Along a dry creek bed she led, to the edge of the shrinking trees, where only the barren mountainside separated them from the peaks.

"This is as far as I go. We are at the edge of my realm. Past the heath and scrub, only rock stands betwixt you and the North," she replied, stretching her arms toward the steepening slopes. "No such beauty will you find once across the peaks. Trees still grow there, but not as vibrant as here, for in the Kierawaith, their days are waning." A hint of sadness crept into her voice. Jetsam couldn't help but feel melancholy.

"Beyond the mountains and balding foothills lie the badlands," she continued. "Treeless wastelands and fetid marshes stretch ever northward until ice coats the barren land. After that, the white blanket stretches to the top of the world." She uttered the words with visible disgust. "Pray your journey doesn't take you that far." Jetsam looked upon her with awe. She reminded him somehow of his mother, and he regretted taking her leave.

"Summer is short in the Kierawaith, and autumn surrenders quickly to winter. Find this man you seek before the snows come, or you will see not spring," she warned. "But daylight shan't wait for you, so I shall delay you no longer. Follow this furrow as it winds upward." She pointed a willowy hand north. "Cliffs rise on both sides and the way will grow ever steeper, but hold true the path. By sundown, it will lead you across the peaks. Then you are beyond even my help."

"If I may be so bold," Jetsam entreated, "may I ask a question before I leave?"

"Ask as you may."

"Are you an elf?" he inquired, "and if so, what name should I remember you by?"

"I am not an elf, though 'tis humorous *you* should think so. Nay, I am a forest nymph, and the weald is my realm. You may remember me as *Illyassa,* though never speak it aloud. Go now whilst the day is still young."

A tear came to Jetsam's eye as he stepped reluctantly from the conifer shadows. He began his hike up the hollow, and glanced back one last time. Tramp wavered halfway between him and the dryad, looking to and fro.

"You, too, little fox," she prompted, waving her lithe hand at the small dog. Tramp gave a tiny whine, and trotted up the hill after Jetsam.

Their climb consumed the day, as the thinning air and gusting wind tested their lungs. The dwarf shrubs now stood behind them, and only the occasional heather or bilberry peeked out from behind a sheltered crag.

By late afternoon, the duo neared the ridge of the Oxbow Mountains, or as close to them as their path would go. Towering peaks rose like mighty sentinels on both sides of him as he marched along the narrow crevasse.

Although the summits dominated his view to the left and right, the world sprawled out before him and behind. To the south, beyond the heath and scrub, emerald land fanned out like a lush blanket. North, however, was a stark contrast. The mountain's tree line and foothills were patched with darker evergreens and foliage, and further north, the land changed to hazy gray and brown. It was a bleaker picture than even the dryad could paint.

The first week in the Kierawaith proved the hardest. Nuts and berries were rarer than in Sylallian. The wind blew sharper and colder, while the clouds rode lower and shed rain more often. Fauna was sparse. Replacing the songbirds were dark birds of prey—vultures, harriers, hawks, and falcons circled ominously. Jetsam suspected they eyed his small companion. *And wolves howl every night.* Even with his warding necklace, Jetsam shuddered at their predatory sound.

Unaccustomed to being without his brother and his friends, Jetsam treasured his furry companion. Alone in the wilderness, he talked to Tramp more and more. The terrier responded as best he could—with yips and barks.

So far, Jetsam resisted lighting a campfire, for fear of discovery. He shivered through the high-altitude nights, the warm dog curled beside him. With each passing day, the night grew longer as summer tiptoed away.

Strenuous activity and sparse food took a toll on Jetsam. Already thin, he began to look gaunt. The pace he set for himself was nearly impossible to maintain. Finally, Tramp broke the routine. The dog caught a squirrel and returned proudly, the dead form drooping from his mouth. He dropped the prize at Jetsam's feet, staring up with tail and tongue wagging. Jetsam couldn't resist the treat.

"Tonight we'll make a fire."

Beside the crackling flames, Jetsam ate his first hot meal in over a week.

Once below the timberline, they covered less and less ground each day. Jetsam felt safer under the towering trees, although not as safe as he did on the mountain's south side. The northern conifers didn't age as well as their southern brethren. It seemed the northern evergreens lived a harsher life, spending more days under cloudy skies than embracing the sun's caress.

Under these somber trees, Jetsam and Tramp devoted several hours a day to finding food. The terrier was a natural. Bred for ratting, the dog adapted to catching squirrels and coneys. Jetsam's sling shot skill also proved valuable, and the pair usually enjoyed meat for dinner.

Every day since fleeing Dwim-Halloe, Jetsam scoured the skies for signs of a campfire, but as yet had seen none. Though a fire wasn't necessary, he guessed the tracker was not so desperate as his prey. "Maybe we lost Baldy after all," he told the dog.

Chapter Thirteen

Rapping on the door started low and timid, hours before sunrise inside the dark Dwim-Halloe inn. Candles had been out since midnight. Slumber permeated the two-story establishment. Still, one man knocked, louder with every stroke as his pounding went unanswered. He wore crimson and cream with a short sword by his side.

When the door finally opened, the nervous guard notified Yduk Thiern of the orphan's escape. The sleepy bounty hunter asked him how he knew for sure, demanding the details. The guard complied, repeating Giselle's lies word for word, strengthening them with repetition. Satisfied with the twitchy watchman's response, Yduk gruffly sent him on his way, handing him an extra coin before shutting the door.

Scratching his stubbly chin, Yduk debated his choices aloud. A strange habit, this talking to himself, but he rather enjoyed the sound of his own deep voice. Murmuring his thoughts was one of his few eccentric indulgences.

"So the lad headed south, did he? Prob'ly could nab him in a day or two if I hurried." Yduk paced half-dressed in the middle of his austere room and reconsidered. "Smarter than most lads, I'll give him that. Maybe'd take a week, no more." He ambled to the window and appraised the starry sky. His big hands opened the sash and the night breeze slipped in.

"'Tis a generous reward for a knave," he said. "But I didn't come to catch a minnow. Nay, I'm here for the whale—Seryn Vardan." He shuffled to his bed and sat down. The bed squealed in objection.

"But then there's that scroll," he muttered. "Might be the minnow's scroll leads me to the whale." Yduk rose and strolled to the chest, where his gear spent the night. The warped floor boards creaked beneath him.

After fumbling with a lantern, he ignited a small flame. In the flickering light, the room looked even more squalid. Luxury was not a necessity for Yduk Thiern.

He opened the chest and inspected his leather and weapons. "'Tis a spell scroll, not a map. And the word of a crazy gypsy trying to impress a knave." Pausing for a heartbeat, he held the lantern and watched the light dance on the wall. "For the life o' me, I can't see what I'd do with that scroll, even if 'twas Seryn Vardan's."

Yduk closed the chest, put out the lamp, and crawled back into bed.

"No more distractions," Yduk stated, pulling the blanket over him. "I'm headin' north at dawn. Kingslayer's my target, orphan be damned."

A month since he left his underbelly home, Jetsam had been a quick study of the outdoors. His pale skin took on more color and his hair was as long as it had ever been. Jetsam had taken to tying the brown locks in a ponytail that hung halfway down his back.

By now, he'd assumed the bounty hunter had given up on him. *My bounty can't be that large.* Sensing the hunter's skill, Jetsam figured if he *had* tracked him, he would've been caught weeks ago.

Jetsam also realized the enormity of his task in finding his fellow fugitive. The vastness of the outdoors was more than he ever imagined. His entire life spent within the confines of a walled city, he never dreamed how far the horizon stretched. *Only been a month,* he told himself. "I have all my days to find him," he affirmed to Tramp.

Which is why his heart raced the day he spotted his first wisp of smoke in the blue sky.

Jetsam stared at the sooty vapor floating to the heavens. The fire burned somewhere to the northeast, in the direction of the Serpentine Pass.

He doubted the campfire belonged to the enigmatic sorcerer. *May not even be a camp fire,* he reminded himself. He waffled back and forth over aiming for the smoke. *I could reach the fire site before morning.* Being the only smoke he'd seen in a month, he decided to appease his curiosity. "Might be him, you never know," he told Tramp.

Jetsam was confident of his stealth. He spent his whole life honing it, and felt secure he could spy on the encampment without being detected. *Then I'll decide whether to approach.* Jetsam and terrier changed direction and headed for the smoke. The closer he got, the more Jetsam's anticipation heightened. *Will I know a wizard by looking at one? What if he truly is evil?*

Pine cones bounced off his boot tips as he made his way east, deeper into the northern timberline. Beneath the conifers' thick branches, he lost sight of the smoke. The prodigious trees blocked out all but slivers of sunlight to the forest floor. To hold his course, he climbed high ridges to see beyond the trees and track the gray wisp.

Tramp kept pace near Jetsam's side, black nose sniffing the air. The dog zigzagged between the trees, soon moving ahead, although in the same general direction. *He smells something.*

Soon, the sparse rays of sunlight disappeared, and the duo plodded in darkness. Beneath this evergreen canopy, the moon was no help. Jetsam considered lighting his lantern, but that would ruin his chance of approaching undetected. They continued in the dark, slow but sure.

Without warning, the horizon brightened before them as they cleared a bluff. Both he and the dog stopped.

"Tramp," Jetsam whispered while motioning with his hand. The terrier trotted to his side. Not sure how the canine would react upon seeing another person, Jetsam picked up the dog. By now, Tramp was accustomed to the ride. He licked Jetsam's chin.

Fire light splintered through the maze of pines as Jetsam inched toward the flames. Wet wood crackled and spit. He worked his way closer tree by tree, keeping the trunks between him and the fire. At one hundred yards, he was sure he saw a camp site. At half that, he was certain there was only one camper. At thirty yards, he heard a voice.

"What in the world are you doing, Jetsam?"

He squinted into the fire light. Astonished, he made out the old gypsy from Beggar's Alley. *Nicu?* Jetsam stood up, amazed the rover spotted him. "Good eyes for an old man," he mumbled to Tramp. "Good eyes for *any* man," he corrected himself.

"Well, don't just stand there, come by the fire."

Tramp squirmed at the old man's voice, his tail wagging against Jetsam's chest. Jetsam set the terrier down, and the canine scampered to the elderly vagabond. *He's cooking meat.* The wanderer petted the dog as it licked him.

"Have a seat," the loner offered, motioning to the other end of the log. Jetsam complied.

"So you *are* the one who killed the guard?" Nicu asked.

"I didn't kill him," Jetsam snapped. "I was trying to *help* him. Serves me right."

"No good deed goes unpunished," Nicu replied.

Like Elvar used to say, Jetsam recalled, wishing the words came from his brother, not this old man.

"Didn't figure you a murderer."

"How'd you know about it, anyway?"

"Word gets around, lad. Guess I don't need to ask why you're this far north."

"I'll find that wizard someday," Jetsam boasted. "What are you doing up here? I thought only criminals came north of the Oxbows."

"To some, I am a criminal. The king doesn't take kindly to gypsies."

"Or orphans," Jetsam interjected.

"Aye, or orphans." The old man chuckled wistfully. "I'm meeting a caravan further down the pass. Gypsies like to stay as far from Dwim-Halloe as they can. Valin will tolerate a handful of us sleeping in his gutters, but a whole clan is certain to bring out the Royal Guard."

Jetsam scrutinized the old man. He had no horse, and carried his possessions in a pack. His pale hand rotated a skimpy skewer of meat over the fire. *Smells delicious.*

"Lad, things are going to get tougher up here once winter rolls in. In a few months, this mountain will try to cover you up. Not too late to head south before the cold sets in."

"I can take care of myself," Jetsam retorted. "I *will* find the wizard."

"Why so determined, lad? What do you think this man has to give you?"

"He can tell me about magic. Teach me what my parents were supposed to. If not for the king, I'd be an apprentice right now. Me and my twin brother. But he's gone, too, just like my parents. So this wizard's my last chance."

"Last chance? You're only a lad. Dwim-Halloe's but one city in a wide world. Head south, learn a trade, live your life."

Jetsam just shook his head. "Tell me more of this wizard assassin."

"He was born the second and last son to Duke Daelis Vardan."

"The last son? The Duke had only two boys?"

"The duchess died after birthing… Seryn. 'Tis said father and brother never forgave him."

"Wasn't *his* fault."

"No, it wasn't, yet the blame fell with him, right or wrong."

"Life's not fair."

"You may be right, lad. Life is a tricky thing to understand," Nicu said. "And so is wizardry."

"What do *you* know about magic?" Jetsam quizzed.

"I know some. Gypsies know a little of everything."

"Tell me what you know, then. Please."

The cloaked man leaned back on his log and lit his pipe. "Magic is everywhere. Just like the air, you can't see it, but it's there. Like a mole breathing underground or a fish breathing underwater, magic's like that. The trick is knowing how to use it."

With his elbow planted on his knee, Jetsam held his chin in his cupped hand.

"Magic is much older than mankind. The elder races have an affinity for it. Dwarves and Elves sense magic like you and I feel heat and cold. That's why their craftsmanship's so renowned. They detect magic in the stone as if they 'see' it. Elves are the same way, only they craft spells and enchantments. Dwarves never mastered spell casting, and Elves never crafted nature's materials so deftly. But both have something man never will.

Jetsam craned closer. Nicu waited a beat before resuming.

"But through the centuries, man learned from them. Skilled humans can take raw materials mined by the Dwarves and craft items almost as good. If the metal's strong with magic, the very best human hands can craft nearly as fine as the smallfolk."

"What of the Elves?" Jetsam implored. Taking a deep puff from his pipe, the wanderer exhaled the white smoke in a curly wisp. The rich aroma reminded Jetsam of his father.

"The Elves taught man how to tap into magic. And the races mixed. Humans and Elves married and bred, and elf blood mingled with man, passing on more of the ability. Although the average human will never have near the affinity for wizardry an elf does, a few men have become as great a sorcerer as any elf. And some men may look nothing like an elf, and still have Elven blood in their veins.

"When man learned spell casting, there came both good and bad. Much was accomplished for the benefit of all. However, corruptness also allowed sorcery to be used for dark means. And over the centuries, black magic has become nearly as prevalent as the pure wizardry passed on from the Elves.

"So that is man's challenge in learning magic. To pursue good, not evil. And a youngster such as you, so filled with anger and hate, has little chance of hanging on to the good."

These words disheartened Jetsam. "Why does magic have to be good or evil?" he asked. "You say the air's like magic, but it's neither good nor bad."

The old man smiled. "Good point, lad. The difference is, as man learned to use magic of the earth, he also tapped into the

Beyond. Magic's not restrained to this world alone. It connects the quick and the dead. And the dead outnumber the quick by more than you could imagine.

"So when a man learns the art, he draws into the spirit world. And depending on how the magic is used, the sorcerer becomes aligned with forces he draws upon. Good begets good. Evil begets evil. Magic is rarely used without one of the two.

"The pull is strong either way, but once a path is taken, 'tis hard turning back. If a man uses sorcery for wickedness, bit by bit, his wizardry turns dark, and he's no longer just of this earth, but of the spirit world. Once that happens, the natural laws of this earth no longer bind him."

Jetsam detected a seriousness in the man's tone that made him take note. Nicu paused, as if he'd said too much. But after a moment, he proceeded.

"There is one who walks this earth that is completely of the Darkness. He is called the Grimlord."

Tramp sniffed the air and growled, jarring Jetsam from his trance.

"What's wrong, buddy boy?"

The terrier glanced at Jetsam then released a shrill bark.

"Something's out there."

Chapter Fourteen

For a moment in the Kierawaith foothills only crickets, crackling flames, and the growl of a small dog defied the silence. Nocturnal predators crept silently, veering clear of the revealing fire light. Treetops tickled the muffling clouds drifting across the ebony heavens. And three men in varying stages of life stood quiet.

Jetsam tightened his grip on his sword. Nicu let the long pipe go slack in his bearded mouth. And the bald man steadied his crossbow as he cleared his throat.

Baldy! Followed me all this way? I can't believe it.

"So ye've fallen in me lap again, aye, knave? Can't look a gift horse in the mouth, can I?" Venom dripped from the tracker's gravelly voice. The speaker stepped out of the shadows. Flickering light reflected off his lacquered leather and shiny pate. Jetsam eyed the hand-and-a-half sword hanging sheathed at his side. He recalled the troll's gruesome head flopping to the ground. *Troll's bane.* A shiver scampered down his spine.

"Both of ye, face down in the dirt." At the bounty hunter's command, Jetsam observed the gypsy's pained expression.

He's not after you, Nicu.

As if reading Jetsam's mind, the tracker continued. "Worry not old-timer, I'm only taking the lad."

The devil you are!

Neither the gypsy nor Jetsam complied with the tracker's directive. They didn't move at all. Tramp continued to growl.

"On the ground! Now!" Taking a commanding step forward, the Southlander thrust the crossbow toward them. His forceful voice shook Jetsam from his stupor, and he prepared to drop. The old man remained still. Tramp, however, leapt to action.

Jetsam saw the tracker glance at the charging terrier. *No!* Yduk dismissed the dog with a grunt, but the split-second distraction animated the old rover.

"Run, lad!" Nicu shouted, raising his hands. With his pack still strapped to his back, Jetsam obeyed. He bolted opposite the bounty hunter, darting for the nearest pine trunk.

"Come on, Tramp!"

Yduk hoisted the arbalest and Tramp lunged, sinking his teeth into the man's calf. The dog failed to penetrate the tough leather, but as the tracker kicked away the growling assailant, his shot went awry.

The bolt grazed Jetsam's thigh, tearing his worn breeches and the skin beneath. Jetsam felt the bite, but didn't slow a bit. *Come on, Tramp.* Adrenalin numbed the pain faster than the blood soaked into his torn trousers. His mind went blank as his survival instinct took over.

"Damn ye flea-bitten mongrel!" Yduk swore at the dog while spanning his weapon and loading another quarrel. The terrier, undeterred by the kick, barked and charged again. This time, Yduk caught the canine square in the ribs with his boot. The dog yelped as he took flight. The terrier landed in a heap near the fire, at the old man's feet. Dirt covered the canine's tan fur, his small form unmoving.

Yduk straightened and aimed at the boy disappearing into the thick woods. Yduk cursed himself for letting his temper interfere. *Little mutt won't do me no harm.* He fired and, upon hearing the bolt impact in a tree trunk, knew he missed.

"No matter," he said, knowing full well he'd find the urchin. In the wild, he could track the runaway for days without losing the trail. *I'm stronger, smarter, and faster.* Of this Yduk was sure.

Capture's inevitable. The reward meant nothing now—catching the youngster was a matter of pride and a test of his skill. *A difficult prey's the sweetest catch.*

Yduk had no interest in the dog or the vagabond. He loaded another quarrel in his spanned crossbow and started after the boy. Yduk didn't notice the vagrant, but he heard the single unintelligible word escaping the gypsy's lips.

"*Tarihn-eviera.*"

Two steps into a full sprint, underbrush tugged at the bounty hunter's boots. His left foot caught behind him and he fell forward on the firm ground, landing with a thump and a grunt. The arbalest landed in front of him.

Catching his breath, it struck him as odd that he tripped—he was always sure-footed. Yduk tried to jump up, but his legs tangled and he flopped to the ground again. Flat on his stomach, he kicked to no avail, entwined in the thick scrub. Yduk reached for his sword to hack away the vines, then glanced suspiciously at the old man.

"Damn thee, unnatural!"

An odd sensation compelled Yduk to suspect a spell had been cast on him—it wasn't the first time. Determined to survive this attack, Yduk rolled over, picking up his crossbow for a shot at the old man. The tracker saw the gypsy finish casting his second spell before exhaustion washed over him.

Devil take ye, old man.

Yduk's arms grew too weary to even lift the arbalest, much less aim it. The fight left him as the animated foliage strapped him to the earth. Then his eyelids crashed down, sucking him toward a magical slumber.

Instinctively, his hand landed on the hilt of his sword, Regret. Drawing from the magic embedded in the Dwarven-forged steel, the bounty hunter resisted the incantation. Still unable to move his arms or legs, he did manage to open his leaded eyelids. His icy orbs met the mage with a determined glare.

You'll not finish me, unnatural.

Then, the conjurer picked up the fallen canine and vanished into the darkness, while Yduk waited for the spell to wear off. If possible, Yduk's hatred of the arcane art grew even stronger.

Prone in the underbrush, the embedded memories of his childhood taunted him. His peasant father was felled by his landlord's magic. Widowed and penniless, his grieving mother fell victim to the lusting mage's charm. As young Yduk watched helplessly, this mage became his stepfather. *He surely ensorcelled her.* The mage acquired the object of his desire, and Yduk became a necessary evil. Suffering repeated abuse by his unnatural stepfather, Yduk developed a bottomless hatred that strengthened with age, just like the vulnerable Thiern boy matured into an imposing man.

You just added yerself to my list, old man, Yduk swore. *Every unnatural's worth at least a few coins. And you, I'd do for free.*

Jetsam heard Tramp's anguished yelp and longed to return to his companion. *That dog's braver than me.* But Jetsam knew his only chance, however slim, was to run. *My lone defense, as always.*

Jetsam sped through the black forest. *Stay behind the trunks.* Branches flogged him as he raced into the unknown. A warm wetness seeped down his leg and his thigh throbbed, but he didn't dare stop. *Stopping means death—or worse.* Fear swept him away as fast as his long legs would carry him. *I'd rather die than go back to the mines.* He suspected he ran in vain—that his pursuer was but steps behind, aiming to put a quarrel in his back. Listening for footsteps behind him, he heard nothing besides his own panting breath and crunching boots.

Jetsam couldn't help but sense things were going to get worse before they got better—if they got better at all. He remembered Elvar's old saying, 'It's always darkest before the dawn.' *I could use a little dawn right now.* But he didn't expect it. His sinking feeling was multiplied by the fact he ran alone. *Tramp, where are you?*

Though Jetsam heard Tramp squeal, he expected the dog to catch up any minute. But as he ran further and further from the camp, he doubted Tramp followed at all. *He should have been at my heels by now.* Jetsam feared more for his dog than himself. Losing Tramp brought on the familiar agony of abandonment. *I'm destined to be a loner,* he lamented. *Maybe I am better off dead.*

His legs tired and he stumbled into a ravine. His limber feet lost footing and he tumbled head first to the unforgiving ground. As he barrel-rolled to the bottom, the rough forest floor gnawed his tender skin.

Puffing and sweating, part of him begged to just stay still. *Lie and wait for Baldy to catch up and cleave my skull from my shoulders.* Jetsam recalled the tracker beheading the troll in Gwae Gierameth. *Surely a quick death.* Jetsam wearied of running. His flight seemed endless, and pointless, and he could finish it all by waiting in the dirt, counting the stars till his time came.

But he couldn't let it end that way. *I can't give up.*

Jetsam struggled to his unsteady feet. His bruised and scraped body ached with fatigue. He knew he couldn't go on forever, but feared anything less wouldn't be far enough. Jetsam debated climbing a tree, but decided against the risk. *I'd rather be shot in the back than be trapped up a tree.*

Sprinting as fast as his battered body could, preoccupied with his lost dog, averting trees and roots and rocks and logs, Jetsam never saw the cliff's edge. His feet were treading air before he realized he ran out of ground.

It took but a second to land. Pain stabbed up his plant foot before he tumbled into the water. Then he sunk below the icy surface.

Racing through the black weald, he forgot about the *Gaalf* River. He and Tramp had discovered its meandering path previously, but as the river snaked through the wooded foothills, Jetsam frequently lost track of its course. Thunderstorms the previous night had the wide river running swift.

Thoroughly disoriented, Jetsam flailed underwater. Entrained air inside his pack kept him afloat momentarily, and he pulled his head above the dark ripples. Strong and fast ran the current, and try as he might, he couldn't maneuver toward a bank. Gasping for air, he went along for the ride. *My bloody nickname's a curse.*

His shivering limbs numbed, except for his throbbing ankle and thigh. *I must get out soon.* Kicking in the frigid stream, he couldn't feel bottom. He *did* feel stabbing pain in his ankle.

The current moved him swiftly and the water grew rougher. He resolved to cling to the next rock or log he smacked into. Struggling to look forward, he peered into the darkness. Turbulent water splashed in his eyes, blinding him. Then he heard the roar.

The sound baffled him for a moment, before he discerned where he was headed. He didn't need eyes to tell him a waterfall was fast approaching. There was no time to worry or react. Again he catapulted into space, wet and weightless.

Then everything went black.

Chapter Fifteen

Reluctant daylight crept into the Kierawaith. Cast in shadows, Yduk Thiern slumped disheartened at the ledge. The Gaalf River gurgled in the gorge below. The ancient waterway had stolen his prize and robbed him of a fresh trail. Looking at the white water, the bounty hunter guessed the boy was dead.

Now Yduk had a decision to make; track the winding river through the rocky foothills in search of a small corpse, or continue northwest, looking for Seryn Vardan. His pride demanded him to find the runaway, dead or alive. His common sense told him tracking the river would be slow and arduous.

But the lad's so close, and pays a pretty purse.

Yduk shook his head. *My target's the king's assassin—not some slippery orphan.* Yduk had investigated the tales of the kingslayer's flight after King Tygan's death. The stories of fellow bounty hunters who had searched and failed recorded in his brain. The locations where other hunters had last been seen—never to return—were also remembered. Yduk memorized maps of trails and rivers covering the Oxbows. He studied mountain ecologies, looking for inhabitable areas. He absorbed endless tales and rumors in countless taverns. *Yet none pointed me in the same direction.*

So all these facts and more Yduk logged into his conscious mind, only to let his subconscious sort them out and guide him.

Now he had to rely on rational thought to make his decision. To the northwest lay the rougher terrain of the Kierawaith, more typical for caves where an outlaw may take up residence. *I'm still too near the Serpentine Pass for any fugitive to hide out.*

As he wavered back and forth between continuing northwest or following the river, Yduk considered the boy. *He searches for Seryn Vardan as well, and* is *a resourceful little bugger.* Yduk understood the waif possessed the scroll, and somehow acquired the aid of the mysterious old conjurer. Yduk did not discount the power of the unnatural. He recognized there existed forces he could never understand, but respected nonetheless. *Dead or alive, the lad might be the best lead I have to finding Seryn Vardan.*

With a shrug, he started north along the banks of the Gaalf. He would have the boy once and for all, and the magic scroll as well. *The scroll may be the key.*

Jetsam awoke next to a roaring fire. *Tramp?* Feeling pain shooting up his leg, his spirits plummeted. His clothes were dry and stiff, like his body. His head ached and he felt nauseated. He recalled the old gypsy and Tramp's yelp, and tried to sit up to look for his dog. The effort proved a struggle and he relented. *He's not here.*

Glancing to his feet, Jetsam spotted his torn and bloodied trousers. Then he noticed his short sword and pack were *gone.* Grasping his pouch at his side, he realized his precious scroll was still safe. Rolling away from the fire to have a look around, he met the gaze of a tall armored man hovering over him.

It was *not* the bounty hunter.

"Awake ye are," proclaimed a masculine voice.

Jetsam viewed the man, dressed in steely plate mail. *Big* and *shiny.* A surcoat of blue and silver covered his gleaming cuirass. *Thank the gods it's not crimson and cream.* The radiant armor ran all the way to his boots, with matching cuisses and greaves. His brown hair hung long and a scraggly beard and mustache hid most of his pockmarked face. *He's an ugly sod.* The man leaned down toward the drowned rat. Jetsam smelled his foul breath. *And he stinks.*

"Didn't know if ye was ever goin' to wake. Been out since we found ye." The man scrutinized Jetsam. Apparently satisfied, he continued. "Time to answer some questions, methinks." Jetsam nodded wearily. Only now did he remember the river. *That waterfall banged me up good.* He was surprised to be alive, although not altogether grateful. Jetsam noticed horses and three other men near the fire. They all watched him.

"What's yer name, knave?"

"Jetsam."

"What're ye doin' up in the weald, *Jetsam?*"

Jetsam remained silent, debating his answer. *What should I say?* The towering brute had little patience. He raised the back of his hand and in a flash, struck Jetsam across the cheek. "Well?" Jetsam couldn't come up with any lie better than the truth.

"I'm a runaway," he blurted as his cheek turned rosy-red.

"From where?"

"Dwim-Halloe. I'm an orphan."

"Where'd ye get yon wound on yer leg?"

No delay from Jetsam this time. "A crossbow."

"I can *see* 'tis from a garrock. I ain't daft. *Who* shot ye?"

"Bounty hunter, probably. There's a reward for orphans at the Citadel."

"I highly doubt there's much reward for yer scrawny hide. Can't see a bounty hunter making a living off chasin' orphans through the Kierawaith." The men behind him chortled. "Must be more'n that to the story. Spit it out, knave, afore ye get another taste o' me hand." More chuckling from beyond. "Hold yer cackling, ye witches," he scolded, turning back to his comrades around the fire.

"They think I killed a man," Jetsam indicated. Now the men roared.

"So we've caught ourselves a *murderer!* Perchance yon Citadel ain't such a tough place after all?"

Jetsam bit his tongue while they reveled in his misery. *If only the castle guards thought it was this funny.* When they quieted down, the adolescent spoke again. "I didn't kill anyone," he avowed.

"Knave, ye must take me for a shandy simpkin to think I'd figure ye a murderer. Good for a laugh, ye are, that I'll grant ye." The armored man amused himself. "Well, rogue or runaway, ye're in no shape for these woods." He stood up, hands on hips. "As much as I'd like to toss ye back in the drink, I'm honor-bound to see to yer safety. 'Tis me duty as a *knight.* Sir Prentice Imoor of Calderi am I. Pleased to meet me, ye are." He chuckled at himself, but the others had stopped laughing.

A knight who slaps boys, Jetsam thought.

"Ye'll travel with us until we decide what to do with ye," he declared. "We're not turnin' back on yer account." Spinning away from Jetsam, he barked an order. "Get him some food. Thin as a twig, he is."

The youngest man fed Jetsam bread and cheese. As he sat up for the meal, pain stabbed his ankle. At best, it was badly sprained. *I can't even push off with it, much less try to stand.* Jetsam ate the food, mulling over his situation. *Wish Tramp was here.*

Finishing his meager meal, he sat quietly as the men ate and talked around the fire. Scrutinizing them, Jetsam could only make out dark silhouettes against the flame, tall and lean. He tried to eavesdrop, but their mumbling and the crackling fire made it difficult.

Relenting to fatigue, he stretched to remove his boots. His right shoe resisted. The swollen ankle throbbed in pain as he pulled on the boot. Jetsam nearly wet himself when he gazed up to see someone hovering over him with a hunting knife.

"Have ta cut it off," the man nodded toward Jetsam's foot. Jetsam's eyes shot wide while his jaw fell slack.

"The boot—not the foot," the man snapped.

Of course. Jetsam flushed and stuck out his foot.

The man took a knee and grabbed the injured leg. Jetsam winced as the redhead proceeded to cut. He felt the cold blade brush his swollen calf. The pressure and motion ignited pain. *Just leave the sodding thing on.* Jetsam gritted his teeth and fought the urge to squirm.

Through watering eyes, Jetsam examined the man to distract himself. Wearing brown leather armor similar to the bounty hunter's—though not as stunning—the man's cheeks were shaved, yet a ring of red whiskers encircled his mouth. A leather coif covered his head and neck, extending to the reinforced gorget across his broad shoulders.

With much effort, the man cut enough of Jetsam's wet boot to release the foot. Even in the firelight, the ankle looked ugly. Jetsam's leg had swollen from his toes halfway to his knee and bruised nearly as far, streaked with purple, crimson, and yellow. His head pounded and despite his pain, exhaustion pushed him and into a restless sleep.

"Thanks," he mumbled as the man walked away with a nod.

Morning came without warning. Jetsam was hoisted on their pack horse, a dour beast of burden, carrying the bulk of the supplies. *Seem prepared for their journey, wherever it may be.* Among the packs, Jetsam spotted *his* sack, and breathed a sigh of relief. The outline of his sword poked against the material. Jetsam didn't mention his belongings to anyone. Just knowing they were packed on a horse brought him comfort.

They spent the day riding west, Jetsam bouncing painfully the entire way. The terrain was uneven and rocky, with towering pines obstructing their path. Movement and noises played tricks on Jetsam's mind, as every motion and rustle on the hillside led him to hope for Tramp's appearance. The recollection of the terrier's anguished yelp haunted Jetsam and the day proved pure torture. His whole body was bruised and sore, some parts more than others. Jetsam's head was groggy and he struggled to keep his breakfast down. And visions of an injured terrier tormented him.

Jetsam did learn more about his "benefactors," however, via overhearing their conversations. With the exception of a few words from the squire, none spoke to him all day. *And I dare not speak myself.* His puffy cheek was still sore.

The young man beside Jetsam was Sir Prentice's squire, who rode a svelte chestnut mare. The other two men were not knights, but accompanied the Calderian on his quest. *None but the knight wear mail.*

Sir Prentice rode in front on a muscular gelding. The ebony destrier rippled in the morning sunlight. Dressed in full armor, the knight wore his visored burgonet and an arming sword, dirk, and kite shield at his side. The shield's heraldry was unfamiliar to Jetsam. *Not an Oxbow coat of arms that I've ever seen. Though how many would that be?* This kite displayed a wide set of royal blue wings sporting the head of a roaring lion, set against a silver field. Sir Prentice's sheathed sword beheld a glistening azure pommel matching the winged lion. *Altogether, he appears quite formidable.*

Behind their leader rode the man who freed Jetsam from his boot. He was armed with a two-handed sword and a hazelwood long bow, both strapped behind him. The sheathed dagger he'd used to cut the leather also hung from his belt, below the small of his back. His brown gelding was smaller and less chiseled than the knight's, but still rode like a healthy animal.

The third man wore a dark navy hood and matching long cloak, his face well hidden, although from what Jetsam could see, he looked the oldest of the lot. A gnarled staff hung at his side. *I see no other weapons on the man.* His gray mount was smallish and thin, but kept pace with the others and had an easy gait.

Side-by-side, Jetsam and the squire brought up the rear.

They camped again that night under the soaring evergreens. Before starting his chores, the young man wrapped Jetsam's ankle and changed the bandage on his thigh. He applied an odd ointment to the trauma. Jetsam found the astringent odor unusual. *And it stings!*

"Watch and learn, knave," Sir Prentice instructed Jetsam. "Ain't no free ride. Tomorrow, ye help Kandris with chores. Even if ye have to bounce on one foot." *So Kandris is the squire,* Jetsam thought. The young man looked no older than seventeen and was lanky but strong.

Jetsam detested the knight's tone, but suspected his situation wasn't that dire. *Without them, I may have died.* As it was, he couldn't walk, and was grateful for the meals. Jetsam's eyes followed the squire, as he set up camp, started a fire, cooked dinner, tended the knight's mail, and fed and rubbed down the horses.

Sir Prentice introduced Jetsam to the other two men at dinner. "Enthran Ashvar this is," the knight offered, waving his hand toward the oldest party member. Jetsam glimpsed his clean-shaven face beneath the hood. "And Lohon Threll that is," he motioned to the quiet redhead in brown leather who cut Jetsam's boot. "But think not ye can address them by name, knave," the knight warned. Both men mumbled half-hearted greetings in Jetsam's general direction.

Jetsam sat near the fire with them as they talked openly in his presence. He surmised they'd been traveling northwest for over a week. *They're not from Dwim-Halloe, and maybe not even from the Oxbow Kingdom.* They ate their food and talked of maps and trails.

Sir Prentice was clearly the leader, but based on the arguing during the meal, Jetsam figured the other two were not mere lackeys. There was a general disinterest in the knight's haughty rambling. Neither Lohon nor Enthran even pretended to have an abundance of respect for the egotistical warrior. Each had a strong opinion about the direction of travel and their ultimate destination, and none of the three opinions coincided much at all. They settled naught before they left the fire, and soon all slumbered, except for the watch.

Wonder what they're looking for, or where they're headed? Jetsam dared not ask. *Might they be searching for the fugitive assassin, too?* Contemplating this possibility, he thought it unlikely. From the little he'd heard about knights, they were not in the business of bounty hunting. But Sir Prentice didn't live up to Jetsam's fairy-tale expectations for a knight, either. He was not nearly as handsome, polite, or noble as the knights from the stories his mother read. Reality fell short of Jetsam's imagination.

Discouraged, he stretched out and tried to find sleep. Wide awake, looking at stars through a canopy of pine needles, he envisioned the bounty hunter. *With this injury, I can't outrun Baldy.* Jetsam wondered if he was being followed, and if Baldy would dare steal him right out from under the Calderian. *And what of Tramp?* His thoughts beat back slumber for a good hour before relenting.

The next day produced the same routine, and Jetsam spied no sign of his lost dog. The party moved on horseback through the wooded foothills and did not find whatever they searched for. Sir Prentice led the pack on a winding path westward into the setting sun.

That evening, Kandris didn't need to remind Jetsam he expected assistance. Moving about as little as possible, he helped make the fire, prepare food, and clean up afterwards. He even bounced around on one foot. The ankle was still too tender and swollen to support him.

Squire Kandris came short of thanking him, but he offered a backhanded compliment. "At least yer not dead weight."

When no one was looking, Jetsam managed to discard a few scraps of meat into the brush in hope of Tramp finding the food. *If he's anywhere near, he'll smell it.* Yet Jetsam feared he may never see the terrier again. Before relenting to slumber, Jetsam sewed his torn breeches, and then fished around for a sturdy stick to use as a makeshift cane.

And in the morning Jetsam's arbalest wound looked better. His ankle, however, was another story. Despite the men's assurances, he worried about the injury. *Never had pain like this before.* "I pray it's not broken."

"'Tis but a sprain," assured Kandris.

The men managed to speak a few more words to him, although he kept his responses short and polite. Kandris tolerated him the most. *As well he should—I'm sharing his fobbing chores.*

Jetsam still didn't trust the men, and feared them discovering his scroll. *Until I learn exactly where they're going, I won't reveal any more than I have to.* Sir Prentice was undoubtedly convinced he was a liar, but certainly not the first he had met, and definitely not the last. *He's too wrapped up in his own quest to care anything about me.*

By now, Jetsam was bored out of his skull during the day while they journeyed ever westward. He tried to keep his mind off his missing dog and underbelly friends by focusing on the mountainside's beauty. Sometimes he lost himself staring at the blue sky through the thick pine ceiling, following a hawk's majestic flight high above.

Mostly, he fretted over his injured ankle. The wound on his thigh continued to heal and his various bruises were fading, but the ankle still betrayed his health. *Wonder if I'll get a chance to run away before they reach their destination—wherever it is.* He had a sinking feeling that once his leg healed, Sir Prentice would want to keep him along as an extra hand. This much had already been implied. The knight had justification in thinking this way, since he *did* save Jetsam's life. Jetsam, however, had no intention of becoming squire to a squire. *Soon as I'm surefooted, I'll find a way to be on my own again.*

That evening, after Jetsam completed his chores, he edged closer to the fire to eat his own meal. Sir Prentice and the others were deep in discussion, their dinners long since finished. Jetsam could tell they were planning an attack strategy. Talk of enchanted arrows and a magic amulet intrigued him. *And a scroll!* Voices peaked and waned with the wind. He inched closer, trying to hear more.

Then he heard the words that dropped his jaw.

"*That,*" Sir Prentice declared, "is how we'll kill the dragon!"

Chapter Sixteen

Jetsam could hold back no longer. Hearing of their intent to slay a dragon, his youthful exuberance broke free.

"A *dragon?*"

"Aye, knave, a *dragon.* And I remember speaking to ye not."

"Pardon, m'lord."

Fear and excitement danced in Jetsam's eyes. The knight pandered to Jetsam's enthusiasm.

"'Tis what knights do—vanquish dragons. Scourge upon the land, they are," Sir Prentice exclaimed. "From leagues away, this wyrm was seen flying in these mountains. Entirely too far south for any such beast to roam. One o' the Grimlord's minions, no doubt spreading his vile scourge. No place for dragons south o' the badlands—or anywhere for that matter!"

Jetsam offered his attention to the knight like a shiny gift.

"As a Knight of Calderi, I'm honor-bound to destroy this foul beast." Jetsam heard a muffled groan from Lohon. Sir Prentice ignored the noise and continued. "On good authority this creature's lair is somewhere deep within the heart o' this range. Find it, we will."

"*My* good authority," Lohon mumbled.

Jetsam couldn't believe his ears. He remembered tales of dragons, but never entirely believed they were real. *'Tis too fantastic.* Hundreds of questions rattled in his head, but he hesitated in being so bold as to speak again. The knight halted his deliberations.

"Ye've heard enough, knave. Nightmares ye'll be having, and I shan't have ye crying like a wee babe. Off to sleep." He waved his hand and returned to his comrades, paying Jetsam no further heed.

Jetsam crawled to bed, but was far from slumber. His mind raced with anxiety. He tried to picture a dragon. His only reference points were childhood fairy tales and orphan ghost stories. *Fierce and terrible, I expect.* Breathing fire and flapping immense scaly wings, with a long snaky tail and huge clawed feet—that's how his mind molded the wyrm. *Wonder if I'll actually get to* see *a dragon.* Curiosity outweighed his fear, and he prayed he'd witness such a sight.

The evening unfurled cool and clear, and Jetsam curled tight in his blanket as visions of ferocious dragons ran through his head. Everyone slept except him. Even Enthran Ashvar, who was on watch, snored loudly. Looking at the hooded man, Jetsam's nostrils twitched. The scent fluttered on the soft night breeze for only a moment, but his hairs stood on end.

Fear swept over Jetsam. He tried to tell himself he was imagining things. But he would never in all his life forget *that* smell. The rank, putrid odor burned into his memory. Jetsam was accustomed to the sickly-sweet aroma of dirty boys, but this stink was like no other. He inhaled a confirming whiff, and gagged on the pungent stench. The noxious scent left no doubt that a knuckle-dragger lurked nearby.

For a moment Jetsam froze, hoping the creature had passed by, or was too timid to attack a party of men. Then he smelled the foulness stronger than before. He crawled from his bedroll toward Enthran, grabbing him by the ankle.

The cloaked man awoke with a start, and kicked away Jetsam's hand. "What the devil are ye doing, knave?"

Jetsam's voice squeaked as he tried to whisper his urgent warning.

"Speak up, knave. Can't hear ye." Enthran grew more perturbed, sitting straight and glaring at Jetsam.

"Troll! I smell a troll!"

"Trolls! Knew they shouldn't a told ye about the dragon," Enthran scoffed. "'Tis a bad dream, knave. Go back to sleep."

"No!" Jetsam protested. A vision of wounded Elvar flashed before him. "I've smelled them before. There's one here now. I swear it."

Before Jetsam uttered another word, a wiry arm swatted Enthran in the back, launching him forward. The man rolled over Jetsam, both of them now yelling at the top of their lungs.

Jetsam scrambled toward the fire, shouting for help. But he didn't hear Enthran anymore. When he glanced back, he gasped in terror. *Three* trolls were pummeling the man, rolled up in a ball, hands over his hooded head. The dim-witted creatures jostled with each other as each tried to position itself over the fallen prey.

Jetsam witnessed one of the beasts examining him. The drooling troll left Enthran to his companions and lurched toward Jetsam. *I'm a lame duck!*

As the carnivore lunged, Jetsam dove to the ground and rolled out of the way, putting the fire between himself and the monster. His injured ankle punished him for the effort, sending waves of shocking pain up his leg.

Before the beast circled the fire, Sir Prentice and Lohon rose to their feet. The knight brandished his shield and sword, while his armor sat on the ground. Lohon wielded a gleaming blade as well. In a flash, both men leapt to action, attacking the fearless humpbacks with fury. Lohon intercepted the creature eyeing Jetsam.

Squire Kandris followed.

On hands and knees, Jetsam watched in awe as the thin steel danced in the firelight. *Stay near the fire.* Scrambling in the dirt, he hugged the searing flames while maneuvering to keep the blaze between him and the raiders.

The trio of sharp swords attacked the cave-dwellers' rubbery skin, yet the creatures yielded not. *Their hides protect them from all but the most precise hit.* The beasts swung long sinewy arms in sweeping arcs, knocking away nearly every blow without a scratch. But as long as the troglodytes defended themselves, their offensive was deterred.

Even though the three men held their own, they were not as effective as the bounty hunter in dispatching the beasts. Sir Prentice appeared to be the only one with the upper hand. His swordplay was graceful and deadly, while Lohon and Kandris resorted to hacking like lumbermen. *They all look tired.* The growling trolls looked hungry.

In all the commotion, Enthran crawled along the ground, avoiding the trolls' legs. Jetsam wanted to help, but his short sword was packed well out of his reach, and his throbbing ankle kept him immobile. *What can I do?* Jetsam recognized he had little chance against a troll, and the dawn was still hours away. He grabbed the wet end of a burning log, and brandished it before him as a last defense.

A ghastly shriek rang out. Turning toward the unearthly sound, Jetsam saw Sir Prentice's arming sword buried deep in the side of a troglodyte. The raider fell dead beneath the withdrawing blade.

A heartbeat later, Squire Kandris left his sword idle a moment too long, and a mighty swipe separated him from the ground. The young man landed steps from Jetsam. Blood poured from the laceration. *His flesh is cleaved shoulder to shoulder!*

A troll spied the vulnerable Jetsam. The grunting creature abandoned the downed squire and leapt at its new target. With cavernous mouth open wide, the knobby head shot toward Jetsam.

On his knees with the flames licking his arms, Jetsam stuck his red-hot log square in the carnivore's toothy maw. *Bite this!* Glowing ashes exploded in the creature's face. The monstrosity screeched in surprise and recoiled.

Before the troll regrouped, a bright flash burst from the darkness. The mountainside transformed to white as all form and shadow disappeared. Like staring at the sun, the astounding glare blinded Jetsam. Eyes stinging, he snapped shut his lids and waved the burning stick in front of him. Even with eyes closed, the powerful light seeped through.

Before he could panic, the brightness faded. With vision still blurred, Jetsam heard another humpback squeal in pain. As his sight adjusted to the returning darkness, he made out two forms swinging at a crouching troll. A second later, the beast fell. With three swift blows, Sir Prentice hacked off its lumpy head.

Jetsam recognized the attacker he had poked in the mouth—or at least its skull—sitting several paces from its body, a few bright ashes still glowing in its maw.

Seeing all three trolls dead, Jetsam breathed a relieved sigh.

Enthran raced to aid the fallen squire. Kandris bled from the shoulder, a hideous gash opened by the sharp claws.

"Knave! Grab yon head," Sir Prentice shouted. Jetsam gawked at the knight, dumbfounded. "Throw that noggin in the fire," the man commanded. "These beasts can only be killed with fire or sunlight." He lumbered toward the campfire with a severed head of his own.

Jetsam obeyed, crawling over to the decapitated monster's grotesque skull. The head felt heavy—too heavy to lift. On hands and knees, he dragged the hefty skull through the dirt and rolled it into the flames, where it was soon joined by the third and final head. Orange tongues licked and bit the greasy skin.

The stench of burning troll flesh sickened Jetsam. *Gonna be ill.* He couldn't crawl from the fire fast enough, and regurgitated his dinner. His whole body trembled.

After vomiting, Jetsam crawled several more yards away, and sat with his back to the base of a huge pine. The smell was still atrocious, but bearable at this distance. Lohon and the knight lit the three trolls' headless bodies on fire as well. The oily hide burned steadily as the carcasses withered away.

As Jetsam's adrenaline receded, he wondered about the activities that transpired. *Where did that blinding flash come from?* Surely it stunned the trolls, for Jetsam knew their hatred of light. The moaning squire distracted Jetsam from further deliberation. Now, both Sir Prentice and Lohon hovered over him as Enthran tended to his wound. What Jetsam saw next, he could scarcely believe.

Enthran Ashvar moved his fingers and hands in the strangest fashion as he wove peculiar gestures over the squire's injury. His dusty cloak billowed as his thin arms swung beneath it. Foreign words tumbled low from his lips. Rousing a buried memory, the motions somehow reminded Jetsam of his father. Jetsam suspected Enthran was casting a spell. *What else could it be?*

His suspicions were strengthened when the squire regained his feet. *A wound that severe couldn't be overcome so quickly!* Kandris didn't stay upright for long, though. Visibly shaken and white as an eggshell, he returned to bed, gingerly setting himself down. Enthran conducted the same strange ritual over Lohon's forearm, which had also been sliced. After that, the three men talked amongst themselves until the last carcass had burned.

Jetsam stayed by the tree until Enthran came and ushered him back to his bedroll near the fire. The troll flesh crisped and curled, and the brisk mountain wind flushed away the horrible stench. Jetsam wondered if Enthran had indeed healed the others, and if so, why hadn't he cured *his* leg.

Jetsam tried to spit out an impatient question, but the weary man hushed him. Battered and bruised, the mage was in no mood to chat. Jetsam slept in fits and spurts the rest of the night. Fear, suspicion, and mistrust gnawed at him. As far as he knew, Sir Prentice kept a careful watch until dawn.

With the first fingers of sunlight, Jetsam awoke to stern voices. The Calderian spoke the loudest.

"By the devil, Ashvar, the lad tried to rouse ye! I know ye failed at yer watch," the knight scolded. "If not for the knave, we'd be troll dung. 'Tis bad enough ye fell asleep, but tryin' to take credit for our rescue's near enough for me to send ye packing! If not fer ye spells, ye'd be worthless." He spun away from the admonished sorcerer, and before Jetsam could pretend he still slept, Sir Prentice caught his gaze. Jetsam averted his blue eyes from the knight's fiery stare. For the first time, he experienced a tinge of respect for the man.

"Pretend not yer asleep, knave. There's work to be done," he hollered at Jetsam as he strode past. "With me squire wounded, there's a heavier burden for ye."

Jetsam completed his chores as efficiently as possible, hopping around on his good leg, using his makeshift cane as much as possible. This was not a morning to test the patience of Sir Prentice. After last night, Jetsam wasn't the only one who held a bolstered opinion of the surly knight.

Mountain air flowed crisp and clean through the low branches. The clearing was soon free of the party's gear and only the fire pit and troll ashes remained as a testament to last night's fury. Squire Kandris wore bandages under his tunic and moved cautiously. Whatever boon Enthran bestowed last night, it did not completely restore the young man. But Jetsam was convinced the spell casting saved his life.

Once the horses were loaded, Sir Prentice called an audience.

"Too close a call that was," he declared, stating the obvious, although eliciting no snickering from Lohon. "Failing to keep watch will no longer be tolerated. More danger is afoot from here on." Enthran Ashvar's hooded head hung low. A solemn look covered Lohon Threll's grizzled face. "We'll talk no more of this carelessness, but keep it close in our minds if our lives we value." The tall man's voice softened as he continued.

"A silver lining or two there may be," he spoke, pausing for dramatic effect. "Where there are trolls, there are caverns, for none of their kind dwells aboveground. And where there are caverns, we shall find the wyrm. We draw close—I sense it. We'll search for the entrance to these caves and follow them till we meet the scaly beast.

"Last night revealed a thing or two. Our runaway proved himself more worthy than I could have imagined. Time's come for him to take on added responsibility—and not just in housekeeping." The towering knight looked Jetsam square in the eye. He didn't flinch.

"We'll teach ye to wield a sword and shoot a crossbow. Even gimpy, having ye know how to stab and shoot might come in handy. For all of us.

"And Enthran here confided he sensed a spark o' magic in ye." Jetsam's eyes lit up. He couldn't believe what he heard. *Did he say what I think he said?* The knight continued his speech, disrupting Jetsam's thought.

"Last night proved the value of a spellcaster—when he's *awake,*" Sir Prentice jabbed. "For even a simple *sunblink* spell can stun a troll long enough to lop off its head." For the first time that morning, the knight smiled a toothy grin, crooked as it was. "So as a punishment for our sleepy wizard, and a reward for our alert knave, Ashvar shall begin instructing ye in casting a basic spell. Then we'll see if ye truly do have magic in ye!"

Chapter Seventeen

Yduk Thiern spent the day tracking the Gaalf River downstream. The meandering waterway bled the Kierawaith of meltwater as it snaked through the patchy foothills. Cutting a turbulent path through the rocky terrain, the river ran all the way to the badlands, draining into the vast swampland north of the Oxbows.

Yduk crossed the Gaalf back and forth several times, whenever a shallow stretch presented itself. Even then, fording this swift river was treacherous. His ebony mount held steady. *So far, no signs of the boy.* Yduk suspected when he did find a clue, it would be a small dead body. Either way, he made his decision to follow the waif, and would see it through.

Upon the moist river bank he identified tracks that astounded him. *Well rub me raw!* There was no mistaking the man-sized boot prints beside a boyish hand print. Smeared blood on an adjacent rock painted a picture for Yduk.

"Will wonders never cease?" he mumbled aloud.

Yduk followed the boot prints up the bank. *More than one man.* The imprints led him to trampled underbrush rife with horseshoe tracks. After that discovery, the tracking came easy. Men on horseback paved an obvious trail. *They did naught to conceal their path.* The bounty hunter spotted their campfire the day after he took up the chase.

The following morning, he surveyed the party from afar, using his spyglass to observe from behind a high bluff.

"What, pray tell, is a man in plate mail doing up here?" he quizzed himself. "If I didn't know better, I'd guess he's a knight." A dim spark of recollection kindled in the back of his mind.

That evening, Yduk crept near their camp site. The tracker doubted the men would object to handing the youth over if he *was* noticed, but he didn't want to relinquish his advantage yet. Clad in his black leather, with Regret hanging by his side, he slipped from trunk to trunk, keeping his tall frame concealed behind the thick pines. He approached close enough to overhear the conversation and observe the hobbled waif.

Little bugger's not in bad shape, considering all he's been through.

After the armored man proclaimed he was hunting a dragon, Yduk stifled a laugh. That provided all the information the he needed, and he snuck back to his own camp. *Hunting a wyrm! Maybe there is something to those rumors of Seryn Vardan consorting with dragons.*

When the ravenous trolls approached the campsite from the opposite direction, Yduk heard the caterwaul from his hidden camp. By the time first blood was drawn, the stealthy tracker watched the melee with rapt attention. *Only one of 'em is a true swordsman,* he decided. When Kandris suffered his chest wound, Yduk grimaced. *I know how hard those blaggards hit.*

Then Yduk saw the old man cast a spell and white-wash the hillside. *Another unnatural!*

Yduk spied on the party until they ignited the corpses. He shook his head. *They need more practice if they intend to face a fire-breather.* The stench of burning troll fresh sent Yduk creeping back to his camp once more.

The troll stink forced Yduk to sleep with his blanket covering his face. *I may be letting me imagination run wild,* he pondered, coughing at the troll odor. *But methinks that armored brute is the fallen knight Prentice Imoor.* Yduk recalled the wanted poster at Dwim-Halloe. *He wears the blue-winged lion—the Calderi coat of arms—but not rightly so any longer.* He rolled over and buried his face in the crook of his arm. *Must fancy he can reclaim his honor with a dragon head.*

Yduk's mind danced with wild theories, evading a much-needed slumber. *Why else would they be traipsing so far from civilization?* Over the years, he'd seen men with a price on their head perform all sorts of outrageous acts. *A desperate ploy for a desperate man,* Yduk decided. *If they truly find a wyrm in these hills, 'tis a mess I would surely like to clean up after.* Yduk chuckled through the moist wool covering his mouth. *By the time this is over, I'll need a herd of steeds to carry back me bounty!*

Silence reigned among the dragon hunters, with the previous evening's troll terror still fresh in their minds. The sun kept well hidden, coating the Kierawaith in somber gray. With a thick layer of clouds between them and the sun, seeing a foolhardy troll shambling in this oppressed daylight would have been little surprise.

"Trolls venture not far from their caves," Sir Prentice preached. "No more'n a few hours roam at best, for even the most daring flesh-eater wouldn't risk racing the dawn. But fast they are, and can cover much ground in that time."

As the squire rode beside, Jetsam's mind wandered. While the men scoured the hillside for troll caves, Jetsam looked for Tramp. *Hope you're all right, buddy boy.* Every rustle or movement in the brush drew Jetsam's eye, yet he recognized the chance of it being his dog was next to none. Jetsam tried to take his mind off the terrier by daydreaming of learning sorcery and casting spells. *I pray they keep their word.*

"Mind yer steed, knave!" Kandris scolded, as Jetsam's horse lagged and veered away from the group. His words caught the ear of Sir Prentice, who offered additional rebuking from the front.

"Pay attention, knave. If ye can't guide a horse, I doubt ye'll be much good at casting spells."

Whether intended or not, the knight struck a nerve in Jetsam. He would do nothing to hurt his chances at learning the art, so he paid heed.

By late afternoon, Lohon Threll commenced mumbling about the futility of the search, offering his own ideas about finding dragons and heading toward higher peaks. "'Tis too dry and rocky to pick up a trail. A whole bloody day riding in circles. And for what?" he griped.

"Try riding with a bloody scar across yer whole chest," Kandris mumbled, loud enough for only Jetsam to hear. "Sure, Ashvar cast a healing spell, but it still hurts like the devil. 'Twas his fault for falling asleep on watch, the useless fool."

Why complain to me? Jetsam thought. *Because you don't have the backbone to speak to the wizard's face, perchance?*

As for the dowdy sorcerer, Enthran Ashvar kept quiet and carried a sullen look about him. Only Sir Prentice remained steadfast, ever vigilant in his quest.

"We don't find this dragon soon, winter's gonna trap us up here," Lohon continued. "Then we'll need the wyrm to keep us warm."

"We get stuck in the mountains after snowfall, ye'll be the first one we eat," Kandris taunted, looking at Jetsam with hungry eyes.

Jetsam shuddered at the thought.

The crimson sun slipped behind the Oxbow peaks, and yet the troll cave eluded them. Spirits sank low among the group, though Jetsam's rock-bottom morale perked up with the prospect of learning wizardry, even from the lackluster Enthran.

Jetsam set camp, doing most of the work on his good leg. *I wonder why the spellcaster can heal troll wounds, but not my injured ankle?* Bouncing around on one foot, it nagged him, and left him bitter and distrustful. He feared asking though, since Sir Prentice riled so easily.

Jetsam bit his tongue while cooking, waiting for some mention of his training. Disgruntled murmuring about the fruitless day monopolized the dinner conversation. Jetsam sat patiently until the four men finished eating, and then devoured his own portion. When no one was looking, he tossed a chuck of meat into the bushes. *For Tramp.* He started his cleanup chores before swallowing his last bite.

"Forget not, ye're to start learnin' the knave a few tricks," Sir Prentice reminded Enthran. The mage mumbled a dour acknowledgment as he sat next to Jetsam.

"Well, knave, 'tis time to see what ye've got," Enthran said. "I can sense power about thee, but that doesn't mean ye've got the knack to tap into it. We'll start with the basics, and mayhaps someday ye'll startle a few trolls."

A dry sponge waiting for a drop of water, Jetsam ignored the condescending tone. He hung on every word the rusty wizard coughed out.

"Using sorcery is like using yer muscles. Ye can but run so far, or lift so much, before ye're exhausted. Same with spell casting. Ye've got only so much in ye, and when spent, 'tis gone 'til resting."

Jetsam nodded, taking in the lesson. *Get to the good stuff.*

"And just like a boy can't run as far or lift as much as a man, neither can a whelp conjure as much as a seasoned caster. Like anything else, with more practice, the stronger ye get."

Jetsam's impatience bubbled like a cauldron. *Less talk, more action old man,* he thought. Yet the wizard rambled on.

"There's magic in everything—the air, the ground, trees, fire. Ye've got to feel it inside and draw from the world around. That, and memorize the Elven incantations. With the exact motions and gestures, of course." Enthran snickered. "And if yer pea brain can handle all that—and ye don't accidentally kill yerself—ye'll be casting spells."

Wonder if Elvish is the language inscribed on my scroll? The parchment was still tucked in his pouch, sitting unread while he traipsed through the mountains with these dragon hunters. He tried not to get impatient. The warlock stared at him.

"Paying attention, knave? Magic shan't just explode from yer arse!"

"Yes, m'lord."

"Let's see if ye've got the feel." The mage fished his pale hand inside his cloak. Opening his palm, he revealed two small stones, a gray chalcedony and a black opal. "Take one in each hand," he instructed. "Now, close yer eyes and feel the gems, sense the magic."

They feel like stones. Jetsam squeezed them harder, rolling them inside his clenched fists with his fingertips.

"Which one is magic?" Enthran asked.

Jetsam grew nervous. They felt the same. *I'm failing the test.*

"Well?" inquired the sorcerer.

Jetsam's heart fluttered, his adrenaline flowing. He glanced at Enthran, looking impatiently at him.

Relax.

Jetsam heard a voice. It wasn't Enthran, or anyone else in the camp. The words came from inside his head. It was *the* voice.

Relax and breathe, it said.

Although Jetsam couldn't fathom the whispering intrusion, he trusted it. Whether it was a product of his imagination, or an outside influence, it didn't matter. He obeyed.

Palms down, Jetsam extended his arms. His thin limbs floated in the air, his head back, eyes closed.

"Can't tell, can ye?" Enthran goaded. Jetsam opened his eyes to the spellcaster.

"The black one," he blurted, knowing he was right before Enthran could open his mouth. The wizard's eyebrows rose.

"Pretty good for a first try. Ye may have magic in ye, but harnessing it's another trick."

The mystifying voice fled as quickly as it came, but it had shown Jetsam the light. Enthran had him try other objects. A few more gems, a ring, a dagger, and an ornate amulet. He correctly identified the magic, or lack of, in each one, especially the glimmering talisman. *This one is the most powerful by far.* Enthran only let him touch the amulet, keeping it in his grip the whole time. Even so, Jetsam felt the potency within. It almost frightened him.

"What is this?" he asked.

"It's enchanted. That's all ye need to know." Enthran stashed the amulet in his robe.

It's for the dragon, Jetsam guessed, recalling their hushed voices by the fireside.

"Enough for tonight," the wizard pronounced. Jetsam couldn't hold his tongue.

"But I want to cast a spell."

"Ha! Just like a boy. Ye've taken a first step, but there are miles to go. Keep that opal with ye. Get used to sensing its aura. Tomorrow night I'll teach ye an incantation to memorize."

"But—"

"Test my patience not!" he scolded, a fire growing in his eyes. Enthran's demeanor changed quickly, and Jetsam wisely relented.

Gazing at the slivered moon through the thick branches, Jetsam realized how much of the evening had slipped away. Kandris and Sir Prentice already slept, while Lohon Threll sat tight-lipped against a tree, whittling away the first watch.

The following day disappeared much like the previous. Countless leagues northwest of Dwim-Halloe, the mounted troupe plodded through the Kierawaith's high stony foothills. An oppressive sky again loomed overhead. A stiff breeze blew the crisp mountain air into the rider's faces. Though it was late summer, at this altitude and without sun, the temperature felt chilly.

Tempers ran short as the search dragged on. Lohon Threll grumbled openly, and even the sullen Enthran Ashvar released snide comments about their leader's ability. Most sounds from Squire Kandris' mouth were moans and groans as the bouncy ride pained his mending wound. Sick of the constant complaining, Sir Prentice barked at the bunch more than once.

"A barrel o' weak-kneed, whiny milk maids," he lamented.

To Jetsam the day seemed interminable. Fanciful daydreams of spell casting competed with a wistful longing for his dog. He hung to the consolation that nightfall brought another lesson with the irritable wizard.

For the second day, darkness fell before finding any sign of a troll breach.

"This is pointless," Lohon whined, sitting cross-legged by the campfire. "We'll not pick up a trail now. The terrain's against us, and yer no tracker."

"And what good are ye?" the knight shot back. "Thought trackin' might be something ye'd be good at. Guess I was wrong."

"We must have missed the caves by now. This wandering will be the end of us."

"Yer free to leave, Threll, if'n that's what ye want."

Jetsam spied Lohon bite his lip, then fall silent.

Once Jetsam served dinner, the men ate quietly, ignoring each other the rest of the evening.

After his chores, Jetsam plopped down next to the warlock, eager for his next session. The cantankerous mage again lacked any fleck of enthusiasm for his task, but started the lesson regardless.

"Tonight, practice motions and gestures. Not until they are flawless will I teach the chant to release the spell. For the slightest err in speech or gesture can bring about dangerous consequences."

I'll not be casting a spell tonight. Despite this disappointing revelation, Jetsam awaited further instruction.

"The differences between calling for a flash of light and calling for lightning are subtle. Last thing a conjurer wants is to hit himself. So pay heed, knave. I shan't have my skin risked with childish blunders." Jetsam studied the sorcerer, absorbing his every word.

The mage rose above Jetsam and, with bony arms and hands, cut a swift pattern in the air. He stopped, glared, and repeated the motions, slower this time.

"Now try."

Jetsam imitated Enthran as best he could.

"Like this," the spellcaster corrected, grabbing Jetsam's elbow and moving him like a rag doll. "Again."

This performance of the eager student and impatient teacher continued for an hour, as the sorcerer scrutinized his every move, harping on his execution, delivery, and speed. Jetsam's arms fatigued and his ears grew as tired of Enthran's barking as they were of Kandris' whining. Finally, the mage had enough.

"Keep practicing. I'm going to sleep," he declared. "And mind the black opal. Repeat the motions while thinking of it. Train yer mind to find its power while yer hands move. Let yer arms bridge the air and stone."

Despite Enthran's irascibility, Jetsam was full of zeal. *I'm one step closer.* Sitting near the lapping fire, he practiced under the black sky until his shoulders ached. Lohon sat nearby, waiting for his watch to end, carving a stick and shaking his head at the relentless youth. Everyone else slept soundly.

The following morning, despite his aching arms and tender ankle, Jetsam awoke with anticipation. *Only fifteen hours 'till my next lesson.*

For the third consecutive day, the group followed Sir Prentice Imoor through the rocky foothills. Rips in the clouds let beams of sun sneak through, periodically brightening the forest floor and the group's mood.

Flowing vigorously, the Gaalf River blocked their way. Citing trolls' distaste for water, the Calderian reversed the troupe, directing their path in a looping half-circle, until they again encountered the snaking river several leagues south. Spotting the white water, they curved back north, still without seeing any caves.

All the while the group tromped through the hilly woods, Jetsam kept a keen eye for any sign of the fugitive mage's residence. Truly, he had no idea what to look for, but he suspected a campfire or a cave or shack would be a good omen. In the days they spent roaming the mountainside, he saw none of these. Jetsam felt as aimless as the others, and wondered how long Sir Prentice had led this futile dragon hunt.

How I wish Tramp was with me, sniffing out a trail, leading me in the right direction. Jetsam imagined Tramp alone and hurt in the wilderness, and tears flooded his eyes. *I've Illyassa's necklace and the company of men, but Tramp's all by himself against bears and wolves and worse.* He prayed the dog wasn't dead, and tried not to think of it.

Since the troll attack, Jetsam had not caught the scent of any more knuckle-draggers. Even though they searched for the trolls' cave, he was glad he hadn't smelled their foul odor again. He wondered why the group refrained from asking him about his knack for smelling the beasts. *They probably never believed me in the first place. Just a stupid servant boy,* he thought, *too lame to run away on my own.*

No caves or holes revealed themselves that long day. Sir Prentice consulted Lohon several times on directional decisions. Despite their apparent reconciliation and cooperative navigational efforts, they labored in vain.

At least Lohon shot game for dinner.

With twilight closing in, Lohon spotted something on the hillside.

"Over there," he shouted to Sir Prentice. "Those trees are charred." Lohon dismounted and crouched. Jetsam stayed on his horse. With his throbbing ankle, every dismount proved treacherous. Yet he discerned the scorched pines bubbling sap from their blackened branches.

"These needles are burned," Lohon reported, dumping a handful back on the ground and turning toward the knight.

"'Tis dragon fire," Sir Prentice replied. "Look, you can follow its path." He pointed toward the start of the scarring. "It started high, and curves down to the ground."

"Can't think of what else would've left a path like that," Lohon agreed.

"Wizard?" Sir Prentice asked.

"A fire spell could do it, if there's another mage out here," Enthran said. "Even then, 'tis a powerful blast. Other than that, I'd say dragon, too."

"Lots of broken branches," Lohon commented. "Dragon wings could snap off limbs like that. Some aren't even burned."

That's a big swath, thought Jetsam, trying to imagine a dragon swooping down to snatch up a troll.

Lohon rubbed his red chin while his gaze followed the trail of destruction.

"Bet the wyrm ate our trolls," Lohon surmised. "We won't ever pick up the trail to their lair now." Jetsam sniffed the air, and found the telltale scent of troll lingering. *Knuckle-draggers* were *here. Could it really have been a dragon?*

"Getting dark," Sir Prentice said. "Let's make camp. We're *close.*"

Jetsam again hobbled through his campsite chores, discouraged over his still-ailing ankle. He suspected the damage was worse than a simple sprain. He feared he'd fractured a bone or torn a muscle. *Never had an injury like this.* Anticipation of his next lesson with Enthran lessened the pain. He hoped this night he'd cast his first spell. The wizard, however, entertained other ideas.

"All right, lad, let's see yer gestures." Jetsam obeyed and performed the achy-armed motions. "Not bad," he replied. "Not bad at all." Jetsam tried not to smile, but a sly grin escaped nonetheless.

"Listen, for this is most important." At these words, Jetsam held his breath. "Tonight, I'm going to teach the Elven chant triggering the sunblink spell." Jetsam's heart leapt. "But," the sorcerer continued, "under no circumstances repeat the chant while making the gestures." Just as quickly, his heart sank.

"If I catch ye trying to cast before ye're ready, the training's over for good," Enthran warned. "And ye'll get a whipping like ye've ne'er had—if ye don't kill yerself first." Hovering over Jetsam, the mage's words rang menacing and grim.

"There's more danger in casting a spell than just getting the wrong effect. For when *some* spells are cast, a door is opened to the Beyond," the conjurer whispered solemnly. "Magic isn't confined just to this world—it reaches the spirit world as well," he stated, sounding like the old gypsy. "If the wrong words or gestures are used, the gate between worlds can swing wide enough to let a spirit pass, or a demon in!" Enthran shuddered at his own words, and Jetsam perceived it was not just an act for his benefit.

"Listen close, knave, and watch my lips. This is a language ye've never used, and it shan't come easy to thee." Slowly, the scruffy warlock let loose the words of the Old Tongue.

"*Av-kier epira gwedath.*"

He repeated them, and then directed Jetsam to try. His first attempt didn't satisfy the mage, nor the second. The ancient Elven words tumbled again and again from Jetsam's mouth. His teacher critiqued his intonation and pronunciation. Enthran's pasty white fingers squeezed his cheeks to make the words come out right.

"Again," he ordered. This repetitive litany unraveled like the previous sessions, Jetsam growing tired of the sorcerer's insistence on perfection, yet following instructions as best he could.

In Jetsam's mind, he spoke the words exactly as Enthran said, but the teacher remained displeased. *Wondered when I'll finally be allowed to cast my first spell?* He felt more than ready. Thinking ahead, Jetsam planned on asking to learn a healing spell next. *Then I'll mend my ankle and leave this motley collection forever.*

But even as he hatched this plan, a tinge of regret stung him. After all, the crotchety wizard *was* teaching him sorcery—what Jetsam always wanted. And he was in safer company than being all alone. *It could be much worse.*

Heated words from the campsite halted his wandering mind and rote repetition. *Sir Prentice and Lohon are at it again.*

"Three days we've done it yer way! What has yer wanderin' got us? Bloody naught!" Lohon's voice was shrill.

"Pray tell then, this grand scheme ye've got in yer empty noggin," Sir Prentice goaded. "For I've had enough o' yer fool-headed whining and am ready to see yer plan fall flat!"

"Finally!" Lohon retorted. "'Tis nonsense to search for trog holes when the flesh-eaters will come to us!"

Chapter Eighteen

No one liked the sound of Lohon's plan. *Especially Kandris, I bet,* Jetsam thought. The squire's last troll encounter left a lifelong reminder, or would, when the ugly wound finally scarred over. *He fears trolls like nothing else, and fails to hide it. Can't say I blame him, though.* Jetsam couldn't hear the word *troll* without thinking about his brother.

Voices tore Jetsam from him painful daydream. The group listened to the redhead, for they all wearied of searching. *That's all they complain about. As if finding this troll cave is their only chance at locating the dragon.* Jetsam wearied of the arguing. But more so, he tired of Kandris' mumbling objections. *Kandris is but a squire—his opinion matters naught. He'll overcome his fear, or find a new occupation,* Jetsam suspected. *Sir Prentice will not retain a craven squire.*

Lohon sat by the fire, a gleam in his eye as he explained his scheme. His fingers kept busy rubbing his rusty goatee. "We'll set a trap. Lure the bloody beasts to us, then chase 'em back to their hole. With the element of surprise, we'll knife through 'em like butter."

The group maintained silence, granting him that courtesy at least. Undaunted, Lohon continued. "On the morrow, I'll ride into the foothills and hunt a deer. We'll use the carcass as bait and lure the knuckle-draggers to us!"

“And when naught show up, we’ll eat venison for dinner!” Sir Prentice laughed at himself.

“Mark me words, knight,” Lohon rebutted, “fresh meat will bring out the trogs.”

“Aye, but how many?” Enthran asked. “We had our hands full with three. Twice that, even with surprise on our side, may be too many.”

“We had our hands full, thanks to yer snoring,” Lohon snapped. “This time I expect we’ll *all* be awake!”

“You could use the *artifacts*,” Kandris interjected.

“*Those* are for the dragon,” Sir Prentice snapped. “If we waste ‘em on trolls, we’ve nothing for the wyrm.” His furious glare shriveled the squire. “We’ll stick to *my plan.*” The knight removed his attention from the squire and addressed Lohon. “Besides, humpbacks rarely travel in packs o’ more’n four or five,” he added, sounding to Jetsam like he endorsed Lohon’s scheme. “If ye catch game tomorrow, we’ll make camp and sit tight through the day. Come back empty-handed, and ‘tis back to my way.”

“A day off the horse will do me good,” mumbled Kandris. *And I can keep practicing,* thought Jetsam.

The following morning dawned with autumn clouds clustering the mountainside. A harsh wind bent treetops and swayed branches as strong gusts funneled through the limbs to the forest floor. Embers spit and jumped from the crackling campfire.

By the time Jetsam awoke, Lohon was gone. Without prodding, Jetsam undertook his morning chores. Kandris’ injury relieved him of all duties, and while Jetsam picked up the brunt of the work, Sir Prentice cleaned and oiled his own armor and weapons. He didn’t yet trust Jetsam with that important task.

After eating, the Calderian donned his silver mail, readied his mount, and resumed his search alone. However, the knight remained within a horn’s blast of the campsite.

The wizard wandered the hillside collecting herbs to brew a tonic for the injured squire. He roamed the woods, poking and prodding the foliage, scavenging bits here and there, lamenting the lack of growth on these destitute hills. Eventually, the sorcerer strolled out of Jetsam’s earshot.

Just me and sleepyhead now, he thought, glancing at the snoozing squire. *Guess I'll practice my magic.* Jetsam routinely practiced his spell components, but never simultaneously. He feared upsetting the mage, and despite his overwhelming desire to cast his first incantation, resisted the urge. *But no one's around,* he contemplated. *Who would see?*

Jetsam scrutinized Kandris Bayen, still curled beneath his blanket. *He'll sleep all day if I let him.* Jetsam hobbled away from the camp site, standing outside the squire's line of sight. *I've practiced enough,* Jetsam decided. *Time to see what I've learned.*

Jetsam inhaled deeply and began reciting the phrase.

Fob it! He started moving his hands a beat too late, and cut the spell in midstream. *Don't think so much.* He rubbed his fingers across his moist palms. *Maybe I should wait,* he deliberated. *I've learned so much already, if Enthran finds out, he'll be through with me.*

Jetsam rolled his shoulders and cracked his knuckles. *Sod it, I can't wait any longer.*

Without another thought, he started both spell components on time.

Or so he thought.

A blinding flash enveloped him with a heat that singed his brows. His eyes clamped shut from the burning light. A moment later, everything went black. Jetsam wobbled on one leg before tumbling to the ground. His compromised ankle made him pay for the fall.

Fobbing, bloody, pus-boil!

Opening his stinging eyes, Jetsam saw only darkness.

I'm blind?

"What the devil was that?" Kandris croaked.

Frightened to tears, Jetsam couldn't spit out a response.

"Knave? Was that ye?"

Jetsam heard Kandris' crunching footsteps. "'Twas nothing," he shouted in a strained tone that foretold the opposite.

"What'd ye do?" Kandris' voice was close now. Jetsam suspected the squire hovered over him, but he kept his head down. *Now I've done it.*

"Nothing, I said. Go back to sleep, rest your injury."

"Cast a spell, didn't ye?" Jetsam could hear the smirk in Kandris' voice. "Won't Enthran be surprised?"

"Don't tell him!" Jetsam blurted, his breathing labored.

"So ye don't deny it?"

You sodding fool. Tears streamed across Jetsam's cheeks. He blinked and blinked and blinked again. *Nothing.* Sitting with his knees to his chest, he buried his head. "Leave me alone!"

"Hurt yourself, didn't ye?" Kandris waited for a response but received none. "Fine, sit here and cry. I *will* go back to sleep." And with that, Kandris left Jetsam to his misery.

With every ounce of will power Jetsam possessed, he stifled his sobs. *I can't walk and I can't see. May as well be bloody dead.*

Planted on the unforgiving ground, time crawled as Jetsam sat and waited. He turned his head from side to side, up and down, rubbed his eyes and blinked till his lids were dry. *What am I to do?*

Then he heard the wizard's voice.

"Knave! Give me a hand. I've a potion ta brew."

Now what do I do?

"The waif seems to have hurt himself," Kandris interjected. "But he doesn't want *my* help."

"Hurt himself? How?" Enthran asked.

Don't say it.

"He tried to cast a spell."

You stinking bloody skunk! Jetsam waited for the wizard's reply, but only heard footsteps approaching.

"Thought I saw a flash," Enthran mumbled, now standing over Jetsam. "Finally cast a sunblink, did ye?"

Jetsam only nodded.

"Surprised it took ye this long."

He's not yelling at me?

"What's wrong with ye, knave?"

"I can't see." Tears and snot flowed freely now as Jetsam convulsed.

"Let me have a look." Jetsam felt the mage's rough hands grasp his cheeks. "Open yer eyes." Jetsam complied, yet naught but inky black greeted him.

"Told ye not ta cast a spell," Enthran scolded. "See what happens when ye don't listen?"

Jetsam nodded.

"A wounded squire and a blind gimp," Enthran mused. "Guess I'll have ta cook dinner."

Jetsam sobbed.

"Easy, lad," Enthran soothed. "I only jest. Yer blindness is but temporary."

Jetsam felt as if the weight of the Citadel had been lifted from atop him.

"Temporary?"

"Pretty sure," Enthran replied. "If it don't come back in a few hours, I'll cast a spell ta fix ye."

"Could," Jetsam started, while wiping his cheeks, "could you please cast it now?"

"S'pose I could, but not sure if that'd help ye learn yer lesson. Few hours o' blindness seems a proper reminder ta heed yer master."

Jetsam heard Enthran stroll away. He thought he noticed the blackness had changed to a dark gray. *Or am I imagining it?*

"Ah, sod it," Enthran blurted. "I need ye ta help me mix this elixir for the squire." Jetsam heard an Elven chant, and as much as he tried to memorize the phrase, the words spilled from the mage too quickly.

Then daylight stabbed at Jetsam as he closed his eyes against the wonderful intruding glare. "Thank you!"

Fed with Gaalf water, Enthran's concoction boiled over the camp fire, filling the air with a stringent aroma. Bits of marigold, juniper, and sorrel were added to the bubbling pot. Jetsam's nostrils wrinkled at the potent scent, while his blurry eyes burned. The hardy elixir fascinated him, and he watched Enthran dote over the steaming kettle. Before long, it was ready.

Kandris swallowed the first hot sip. "Tastes like piss!"

"Surprised ye know what *that* tastes like," Enthran said. "Keep drinking."

Bet it tastes as bad as it smells. Still, Jetsam wished he could have a swallow to aid his ankle, but he dared not ask. *I know the answer anyway,* he anguished.

Enthran admonished the squeamish squire, and Kandris finished the potion. Jetsam took the pot to clean it, hoping to salvage a few drops for himself, but there were none to be had. *So much for that,* he thought. *At least I can see.*

No results of the tonic appeared immediately, although Jetsam surmised Enthran knew what he was doing. Kandris appeared not so convinced. *He still harbors a grudge over the failed watch.*

Soon the sun rolled west, reddening as it neared the peaks. Voluminous gray clouds had gathered throughout the day, their undersides now turning crimson. Sir Prentice returned unsuccessful, and had little to say about his efforts. Everyone knew well enough to stay clear of the cantankerous knight. He arrived hungry as well as surly. *Please don't tell him about the spell,* Jetsam prayed.

Jetsam hopped to work, assembling a meal. Kandris lazily rubbed down the knight's sweaty black gelding. Enthran and the knight talked briefly, low and beyond Jetsam's earshot.

Absent still was Lohon Threll.

The foursome consumed their meal in relative silence. Jetsam hoped Lohon would come back empty-handed. *Never is too soon to see another troll.* He figured his luck with the beasts ran thin.

The meal finished, and Jetsam resumed his chores. He had grown somewhat mobile with his damaged ankle, covering enough ground to get by. After dinner, talk turned to Lohon.

"We ought to sleep before he returns," Sir Prentice suggested to Enthran. "If the Hunting God smiled on him, we might be up all night waiting for trolls."

Unlike the southern Sylallian, wildlife was not abundant in the Kierawaith foothills, especially on the north face, where the Grimlord's realm loomed in the distance.

Enthran sullenly nodded. The knight continued. "Kandris, ye and the knave keep awake while the wizard and I rest."

After drinking Enthran's restorative, Kandris had been more groggy than ever, so the main responsibility for the watch fell upon

Jetsam. It was the first time they tasked him with this duty, even indirectly. He felt a bit of pride.

The forest lay still in the late afternoon. A rare bird or squirrel occasionally broke the silence, but no other creature stirred. Jetsam enjoyed the quiet while watching the ribbed clouds absorb the sunset's colors. After his bout with sightlessness, the colors seemed richer than ever. Thick bands of red and magenta striped the sky above the silhouettes of the pines. After his years in the sewers, he marveled at nature's canvass.

While twilight overtook the sky, Jetsam recognized the far off sound of hoof beats. The pounding neared, so he roused Sir Prentice and Enthran. A moment later, the others picked up on the sound as well. Each checked their weapon, although the rider was most surely Lohon Threll. In the gloaming, however, there was no telling for certain until he was upon them.

The leather-clad rider trotted up, a mountain goat slung across his gelding. A knowing smirk creased the redhead's bearded face. "Aye," he called out, "best get moving if we want to set the trap tonight."

With daylight already gone, the party enacted the plan. They packed camp and loaded the horses.

"Here, knave," Lohon said, holding Jetsam's short sword toward him grip-first. "If nothing else, ye can stab one in the eye if it gets too close."

"Thanks," Jetsam replied, as Lohon walked away.

The five rode back toward the Gaalf, reaching the surging water shortly. Lohon left a trail of goat blood for the trolls to sniff out. At the river, the party rode their horses through a shallow spot to the other side. Even then, fording proved tenuous, since the Gaalf flowed swiftly and touched the horses' bellies. The dead goat was left on the opposite bank.

"Remember," Lohon instructed, "the idea isn't to kill them all, just thin the herd, then trail 'em to their bloody hole."

The Gaalf ran wide at the shallow crossing, but by climbing a pine, Lohon attained a decent view across the water. He had set the carcass in an opening near the bank where filtered moonlight provided illumination.

The horses were tied to pines far back off the river, behind a stand of thick brush. Lohon didn't want the mounts anywhere near the action, or within sight, sound, or smell of the carcass.

Still on his mare, Jetsam's exceptional night vision gave him a fair view of the trap, despite the distance. He didn't want to miss the show, but he didn't want to be caught in the fray, either. His heart thumped in his narrow chest.

The distant moon drifted across the starry heavens and midnight came and went. Crickets, a hoot owl, and the occasional howling wolf provided the evening's concerto. Jetsam's excitement waned and changed to boredom. He rested against his horse's neck, petting the chestnut's mane. Sir Prentice and Enthran sat on the hard ground. Squire Kandris slept on his bedroll, too weary for the wait. *Only Lohon remains steadfast.* Head-high up a conifer, the redhead waited for his plan to unfold.

While whittling away the dismal hours, Jetsam thought of Giselle. He remembered her golden hair, her lively eyes, her tender lips. His heart leapt at the memory of her kiss. It brought a redness to his shallow cheeks. *How I wish I could see her again.* And Ratboy, and the others.

And Tramp. *Poor Tramp.*

Sitting on his steed, looking at Sir Prentice, Enthran, and Kandris on the ground, and Lohon in a tree, Jetsam considered riding off and leaving the men for good. *I need to find Tramp and the mage—and being on horseback would help.* He patted the horse's thick neck. *It'd be a huge risk, stealing their horse,* he thought. *And if they caught me, there'd be hell to pay.* Still, the possibility tempted him.

The hitch is I'd abandon my magic training—if there's even to be any more of that, after today. That sole silver lining proved difficult to relinquish. Enthran had proved gracious, and not nearly the tyrant Jetsam had feared after botching his spell. *I'd be gambling away my dream. I can endure a little longer.*

Just then something caught his eye. He was certain he detected movement near the trap. A dark shape came into view. He rubbed his eyes in disbelief, while his horse startled and stomped.

The swaggering silhouette was thick and stocky—and huge! This monstrosity was neither a prodigious man nor a fat troll. With a humanoid form, the creature towered over seven feet. Jetsam whistled the signal to Lohon, but he'd already seen the beast. The rogue slithered down the evergreen and raised his longbow.

"Ogre!" Lohon whispered at Sir Prentice. The knight jumped to his feet with crossbow in hand. A moment later, an arrow flew from Lohon's bow. The Calderian launched a quarrel right behind. Jetsam's hand tightened on the grip of his sword.

A guttural growl exploded from the brawny ogre as the missiles pierced its hide. The brute dropped the goat carcass and moved toward the river, clutching a massive club. Effortlessly, the ogre pulled an arrow free from its chest and discarded it to the ground. Then once more Jetsam heard the snap and twang of Lohon's bow. Sir Prentice was still spanning his arbalest.

The bald ogre roared again as an arrow hit home, yet still it rambled forward. Lohon's third missile veered into the darkness, while the knight's second quarrel found dirt.

Approaching the riverbank, the abomination stepped full into the moonlight. Jetsam saw the behemoth clad in fur, bare armed and legged, with an arrow protruding from its thigh and a quarrel in its shoulder. *The creature looks undaunted.*

Lohon loaded and fired as the muscled ogre sloshed into the water. The archer hit the beast in the midsection, but the tough hide resisted the arrow's bite, and it glanced away. Sir Prentice slapped another bolt in his arbalest. Lohon's fifth arrow broke against the ogre's cudgel.

Then Jetsam heard the unmistakable mumbling of the ancient Elven tongue, although the words were not to the sunblink spell.

Simultaneous with the ogre's thunderous roar, a lightning bolt crackled through the pines and across the illuminated Gaalf. A splash of warm air crossed Jetsam's face. The charge struck the ogre in the chest and tailed off into the trees beyond. Jetsam turned to see Enthran Ashvar, his arms outstretched, staff in hand.

The ogre fell with a thump on the bank. For a moment, no one moved. A second later, Lohon Threll dashed for the river. "Come on," he shouted to the knight, "he's *ruining* everything!"

Sir Prentice slung his crossbow over his back, picked up his shield, and unsheathed his blade. "Blasted fool!" the knight groaned, following behind Lohon. The riverbank was slick, with wet rocks and slippery roots to turn a misstep into a fall. Jetsam, Enthran, and Kandris held their ground.

Lohon splashed through the chilly water, the knight lagging by several steps. Stopping at the fallen beast, Lohon appeared distressed. He tried to roll the body into the river, but four hundred pounds of dead weight proved too much. Sir Prentice caught up. "What are ye doing man?" the flabbergasted knight demanded.

"Knuckle-draggers will know 'tis a bloody trap if they see a dead ogre," Lohon snapped.

Jetsam screamed a warning, but it rang too late. Still on its back, the ogre swung its burly arms, catching both Lohon and Sir Prentice in the ankles.

Both men lurched backward and splashed into the frigid Gaalf, as the muscular ogre regained its feet and roared.

The panicked horses had heard enough. The steeds struggled against their tethers, neighing and shrieking, making an unearthly ruckus. *Calm down!* Jetsam's horse reared and sent him to the ground in a heap, inflaming his injured leg with searing pain. An achy Jetsam rolled free of the dangerous hooves, collecting twigs and needles in his long hair. His nostrils twitched at an offending odor.

Smells like dung and vomit!

Chapter Nineteen

Silvery moonlight danced on the turbulent river. The calm air defied the conflict at hand and the towering pines stood still. A moment after Jetsam smelled the putrid stench floating across the water, he spied the lanky forms in the pale lunar glow. He scrambled to his feet. Four hunched bodies strode toward the river, beckoned by the ogre's call. Jetsam watched in horror.

Lohon Threll struggled to stand, as the swift current tugged at him. Sir Prentice's weighty armor anchored him to the slimy bottom, his upper torso jutting above surface. Downstream with the flowing river went their luck.

Salivating at their human prey, the trolls stopped at the riverbank, seemingly reluctant to enter the Gaalf. *Guess they don't like water, either.*

Riveted in place, Jetsam heard a simultaneous gasp from Enthran and Kandris as the sinewy hand of the now upright ogre reached down to the fallen knight. Sir Prentice struggled to roll away, but the ogre grabbed his arm. The monster's broad hand wrapped around the knight's armored biceps.

With an effortless yank, the muscled beast jerked Sir Prentice from the river and tossed him like a potato sack toward the bank. The disoriented knight landed at the humpbacks' feet, plate mail clanging. His loaded arbalest tumbled free and fired an errant quarrel at the moon. The shiny warrior *did* manage to hold on to his sword and shield.

Jetsam broke from his stupor at the sound of Enthran Ashvar's voice. The mage was preparing another spell. Jetsam loaded his sling. Far downstream, he saw Lohon regain his feet and ready an arrow.

Before Jetsam could fire, the river flashed with blinding light. *Enthran released his sunblink.* Dim moonlight became a fond memory. The trolls shrieked and even the ogre grunted in startled dismay. The horses' cacophony escalated as they stomped and bumped and reared and snorted, testing the strength of their tethers.

Jetsam's lidded pupils were two clenched fists. *The light burns through my eyelids!* Then the glare faded as quickly as it came.

Nearly a minute passed before his sight adjusted. When it did, he saw Sir Prentice had rolled free of the bewildered trolls and stood battle-ready, arming sword in hand.

The stunned trolls took even longer to recover. By the time their eyes regained focus, Sir Prentice had slain one of the creatures and hacked off its lumpy head. As the misshaped skull rolled into the rushing river, the other three beasts set upon the knight. They jabbered in an angry language of grunts and snorts. The swordsman parried furiously, steel on skin, trying to keep the clawing arms at bay.

Jetsam watched the ogre standing in the river and took aim at its protruding brow. With a flick, Jetsam slung a stone. *Got him!* Despite sprouting a trickle of blood on its pale skin, the creature barely flinched. An arrow from Lohon's bow produced scarcely more reaction, hitting the brute square in its hide-covered chest. In defiance, the ogre roared. The monster locked on Enthran and started across the water, ignoring the archer down river.

Jetsam slung another stone as the ogre reached midstream. His shot missed completely, as did Lohon's. With a sigh, the sorcerer fell silent and a ribbon of fire leapt from his outstretched hands. Lighting the forest in an orange flash, the fiery bolt aimed for the lumbering creature. Flames engulfed the approaching ogre, and the beast flailed in agony at the conflagration. The scorching wizardry burnt its leathery flesh and ignited its hide armor. An ear-piercing howl left its toothy maw.

Even before the conjured flames receded, the ogre dropped to its knees and flopped face first into the Gaalf. A blast of steam rose from the cooked monstrosity as the river hissed. The beast rolled, splashing all over, trying to cool its blistering flesh. Adding insult to injury, Jetsam bounced another stone off its smoldering skull.

Lohon headed toward the fallen ogre. The current pulled at his water-filled boots as he struggled upstream. Before he reached the quasi-giant, the recalcitrant monster rose again and trudged to the bank. Its deep-set eyes locked on Enthran Ashvar.

The stoic mage remained in place, speaking in the Elven tongue and moving his hands to the spell's rhythm. Jetsam marveled at the impressive display, and a hint of jealousy poked him. Another spear of flame erupted from the conjurer's fingertips. This time, the ogre covered its face and leaned behind a thick trunk. The flaming bolt struck the evergreen. Fiery tendrils zipped around the burnt tree, biting the cringing monster as bubbling sap oozed from the blackened bark. The ogre's wet skin and soaked hide resisted the blazing attack. *If the ogre would have suffered the spell while dry,* Jetsam guessed, *he would have been cooked.* But as the flames faded, the beast charged with renewed vigor.

Enthran broke and ran for the horses.

No, thought Jetsam. *Don't lead him this way!* The ogre stamped its bulky foot to the ground and howled like a devil's wolf. Enthran's dapple-gray broke free and bolted. Shoulders drooping, the spurned wizard watched his mare disappear.

Without word or warning, Kandris Bayen raced after Enthran's frightened animal. Jetsam flashed a disapproving look. *This is no time to retrieve a startled mount. And you'll never catch it.* Jetsam saw fear in the squire's eyes, and realized the trolls had unmanned him.

Abandoned, Enthran faced the ogre, raising his staff in defiance. Mimicking the tiny wizard, the scorched humanoid lifted its gnarled club.

"Cast another!" Jetsam screamed.

"No time," the mage lamented.

Across the water, Sir Prentice fought valiantly, but lost ground. A wily troll caught the knight's shield and tore it from his grasp. The rubbery assailant sent the kite shield spinning into a tree trunk. The trolls made an evil noise that was surely laughter. With both hands, the Calderian clenched his sword and kept swinging.

The three cave-dwellers closed on the tiring knight. They clawed and batted at him, ever wary of his perilous blade. Each time the knight jabbed a troll, another swatted him from behind. As Jetsam glanced across the mighty Gaalf, it seemed the troglodytes were toying with the man. *Cats with a mouse.*

Sir Prentice lurched forward, the tip of his blade striking the resilient skin of a troll's torso. After an imperceptible hesitation, the sharp blade pierced the rubbery hide and the blade slid through the narrow abdomen.

The skewered troll crumpled in agony, clutching at the weapon while gasping for breath. With both hands, Sir Prentice pulled his blade from the coiled carcass, but the troll flesh clung to the steel. In the extra second it took the knight to free his sword, another humpback landed a balled fist against the side of his head.

The knight's visored helm rang like a bell and he tumbled to the ground next to his bleeding victim. Two trolls screeched in delight.

Head on a swivel, Jetsam swung back to the ogre. Fear gripped him as he watched his comrades' undoing. *They're being dismantled before my eyes.* He contemplated running away, escaping his possessive benefactors, leaving them to die. But part of him couldn't flee. *Not yet.*

Within two steps of Enthran, the ogre swung its club, aiming at the stoic sorcerer's hooded pate. As the weapon descended, Enthran clutched his staff with both hands, holding it above his head like a cross bar.

With all his strength, Jetsam slung another stone at the assailant, and in the process, lost his balance. Before hitting the ground, he witnessed his projectile striking the ogre's monumental jawbone. The shot jolted the beast for but a second, but that was all Enthran needed.

Darting aside, the agile conjurer dodged the wicked blow. Wide as a tree trunk, the ogre's club glanced off Enthran's hardwood staff and came crashing down. Without hesitating, the ogre pivoted, and with a roundhouse swing, brought the club around. The knotted weapon peeled a strip of sod from the earth.

Jetsam broke his fall with his hands and lifted his head to see the ogre's club whistling toward the wizard. This time, Enthran wasn't quick enough. The cudgel caught his knee as he leapt away. The blow spun the sorcerer to the ground, his cloak twisting around his prone form. With a long stride, the ogre hovered over the fallen mage. Both hands clasping the club, it hoisted the wood above its head.

Jetsam tried to cry out a warning, but his breath was gone.

Poked and cooked, the damaged ogre inhaled, nostrils flaring, as it prepared to land the death blow. A glint of steel reflected in the moonlight, and Jetsam spotted Lohon Threll.

With a leap and a bound, Lohon sprung from the shadows. Hands wrapped around his great sword, he planted the gleaming blade in the ogre's flank. Lurching forward, the swordsman buried his weapon to the hilt, and then twisted with all his might.

Sharp steel protruding through its abdomen, the ogre screamed. Still raised above its head, the weighty club slid from its hands. Both ogre and cudgel fell to the earth. As the beast toppled, Lohon lost his grip, and his blade went with the behemoth. As the sword slipped through Lohon's gloved fingers, the ogre's club crashed down on his head, knocking the senses from him.

Now, the only creatures standing are horses and trolls.

Helm dented, Sir Prentice writhed on the ground. With renewed vigor, the humpbacked duo assaulted the fallen knight. The foul carnivores pried his cherished sword away and flung it into the hungry Gaalf.

Unarmed, dazed, and disoriented, the knight covered his head with his forearms as the abominations clawed and beat at him. Black talons scratched between his plates, ripping his arming doublet and rending his skin. He tried to crawl to the water, but they corralled and kicked at him with long bony feet.

Still on all fours, Jetsam regained his bearings and observed the relentless assault on the knight. Lohon sprawled unconscious beside the lifeless ogre, while the groggy sorcerer lay buried beneath it.

Staggering to his feet, Jetsam deliberated fleeing. *With a horse under me, I could save my own life.* But in the confusion, he feared mounting a horse would be impossible. Yards apart, Jetsam eyed the frantic mounts and doubted his chances.

Escape's not an option, he decided. *I can't let these men be slaughtered, at least not without trying to help.* Jetsam steadied and took a deep breath. *Can't go worse than last time,* he told himself. Standing still, Jetsam cleared his mind and clenched his eyes shut. He repeated the Elven words in his head, then began. Like a volcano inside him, the power erupted from his core. Sweat dripped from his pores as his body heated. Hands moving in rhythm, he trembled as he spoke the words.

"*Av-kier epira gwedath.*"

Then the world disappeared.

Chapter Twenty

Within the dense woods, the darkness of deep night vanished without a trace. Like a snowy field on a sunny winter morn, the brightness was blinding and instantaneous. Soaring pines and the starry sky washed out in this sea of white. Every eyelid snapped shut, and even then the light displayed the intensity of the midday sun.

Jetsam's own eyes burned from his short glimpse into the powerful glare. He heard the tormented trolls' unmistakable squealing. Three seconds passed, then four. Jetsam waited for his spell to fade, but the stinging brightness lingered. The troll screeching sounded farther away.

A moan and a gasp rang out, and Jetsam recognized Enthran's voice. After a dozen tense heartbeats, darkness returned as abruptly as it left. Weak and dizzy, Jetsam cautiously opened his eyes. The world was fuzzy and distorted, standing still. He detected no sign of the humpbacks. Seeing dancing spots, Jetsam slumped to the hard earth.

He closed his eyes again and rested his heavy head in his sweaty palms. The confused voices of his comrades rang out. Sir Prentice, Lohon, and Enthran all called for aid, but received none. Then Squire Kandris cried out in fear and astonishment.

"Ye gods! Where are ye?" Three weary voices answered the squire. Jetsam didn't reply to the craven. His senses started failing as he listened to the Calderian splashing through the water. The knight cursed the foul beasts for throwing his sword in the river.

Then Jetsam blacked out.

Jetsam awoke with a start. Enthran was shaking his shoulder. The world was still dark, and Jetsam's vision remained blurred. He saw a fire across the river and smelled the awful stench of burning troll flesh.

"Come on, boy, get on the horse," Enthran ordered. With the wizard's help, Jetsam did as told. *They must have got the ogre off him,* he thought. Sure enough, he saw the huge corpse face-down in the brush. *Finally dead?*

Turning from the fallen monstrosity, the dazed youth mounted behind Kandris Bayen, who took the reins.

"Where we going?" he asked the squire.

"After the last flesh-eater," Kandris answered. "Two ran off after Ashvar's incantation, and the one Sir Prentice killed is burning. But the fourth is bloodied and moving slow. Master Threll is ahead tracking it as we speak."

"That was *my* spell," Jetsam retorted.

Kandris roared in laughter. "That must have been some knock on the noggin," he exclaimed, still chuckling. "Even from a distance, it looked as if the sun burst from the ground. Didn't know the old tooth had it in him! No wonder the knuckler-draggers ran. Must of thought dawn came early today!"

Jetsam fumed, but he kept his mouth shut. He felt too spent to argue with the squire anyway. *How would he know who cast the spell? Chicken-liver jumped at the first chance to flee.*

The group rode in single file, spaced well apart. When Jetsam opened his eyes, he could barely make out the back of Enthran's horse, although he knew Lohon and Sir Prentice rode ahead. The night sky lightened as dawn approached. Then Jetsam sniffed a familiar scent.

The troll's near! Jetsam now hoped they would find the troll cave. The prospect of seeing a dragon was impossible to resist. He didn't give the men much chance to survive, but he coveted a glimpse of the wyrm.

As they rode on, Jetsam noticed the smell dissipating. His brow furrowed. *We're heading in the wrong direction!* "We must turn back," he informed the squire.

"Ye're delirious, knave." Kandris dismissed him coldly. "Shut up. We're in enough trouble."

Incensed, Jetsam yanked the back of Kandris' tunic. "*I* cast the spell and *I* can smell a troll a mile away. Now halt!" Before the flabbergasted squire could reply, Jetsam shouted at the top of his lungs. "Master Enthran, the troll's this way. Turn back!"

"Now ye've done it, knave," Kandris scolded. "The knight'll have our arses!"

The squire's jaw dropped when the troupe turned around and headed back. Sir Prentice and Lohon appeared in the distance. The pair were battered and bloody, but the Calderian had his recovered sword by his side and a determined look on his face. Lohon mirrored the knight's conviction.

"Ye'd best be right, knave," Sir Prentice warned, "or I'll whip yer bloody hide."

"This way," Jetsam indicated, wondering if *anyone* realized he'd saved them all. Lohon and the knight rode up to Jetsam, and the horses galloped three abreast, with Enthran bringing up the rear.

As they headed south, Jetsam again picked up the scent. A minute later, Lohon found the trail, and soon all could smell the wounded troll's foul stink. In less than a furlong, they spotted the beast on the horizon. The troll responded to their approach, and with dawn growing near, picked up its pace. The monstrosity hunched noticeably, and the party closed the gap.

"Hold yer fire. It's got to lead us to the lair," Sir Prentice instructed.

Jetsam observed the wicked creature from a distance. Remarkably, the farther the beast traveled, the less injured it appeared. Once doubled over, the troglodyte was now almost as upright as humpbacks get. Everything he had heard about their healing capabilities proved true, and then some. The troll lumbered diligently, paying no heed to its pursuers. Still, no cave was in sight.

Just then, the first rays of daybreak rose above the peaks. As if time stood still, the troll stopped dead in its tracks.

It would never move again.

"Blast!" Lohon roared. "We were so bloody close!" They rode up to the still beast. Lashing out in anger, Lohon struck the abomination with his sword hilt, knocking its shriveled head to the ground.

"We'll stop here," Sir Prentice ordered. "Some rest we need. In a few hours when the sun's up, we'll search again."

These words relieved Jetsam. He felt ill since casting the spell. He grabbed his bedroll from the chestnut and slid to the ground. He didn't care if he was supposed to help set camp—he fell asleep in seconds.

Hours later, he awoke to hushed voices and bright daylight. The sound of his name caught his ear. With eyes closed, he kept still, but strained to eavesdrop on the quiet conversation.

"The lad's drained," Enthran Ashvar whispered. "Doesn't know how to restrain himself yet, and everything poured out of him."

"Methinks ten boys his size shouldn't have been able to cast a spell like that," Sir Prentice responded.

"Aye, it runs strong in the lad," the mage agreed. "I sensed it in him, but that outburst surprised even me. He asked to learn the heal spell. I'm sure he wants to mend his leg."

"Nay," the knight retorted. "Ye'll not teach him that. I shan't have him runnin' away afore we're through with 'im. Now more'n ever, he's a valuable asset."

"And he'll need sorcery to repair that leg anytime anon. The bone is surely broken."

"Tell him the ankle must mend on its own," the knight insisted. "Wizardry can't fix everything."

Jetsam's blood boiled. He bit his tongue and kept his eyes clamped shut, waiting for the anger to pass. *Curse their ungrateful souls,* he thought. *This is their gratitude for saving their miserable lives?*

"Hush," Lohon Threll scolded. "The knave's brighter than ye think. Keep yappin' and he'll surely overhear. Then he'll be pissin' in yer mead."

"The lad'll be out for hours," Enthran guaranteed.

Jetsam begged to differ, but played opossum nonetheless. He conceded the sorcerer was partially correct, and soon fell back asleep, despite his best efforts.

Jetsam dreamed of his parents, shadowy figures, yet unmistakably his mother and father. Elvar was there too, and they sat together on a warm summer night, casting spells to make colors dance on the wind. Thunder heads rolled in with lightning and driving rain. The show ended, and so did the dream.

When he awoke, the sun was high overhead. He yearned for his dream world where his family was whole again. The reality of his circumstances set in, and more than ever he missed Tramp, Ratboy, and Giselle.

Despite his melancholy, he felt better physically. His vision still suffered the effects of his conjuration, but it seemed much improved. Beside him lay a well-crafted wooden crutch. *Looks like Lohon's handiwork.* He gladly abandoned his crude cane and accepted the offering without a word.

Kandris called to him with a bite to eat. Jetsam grabbed the crutch and used it to stand. With his surrogate leg, he hobbled to the campfire. *Sure beats that old stick!*

"They found the trog den this morning," the squire proclaimed. "Just over the next ridge."

Sir Prentice, Lohon, and Enthran returned with a plan. Each man bore the scars of last night's debacle. "Ye'll stay put and mind the horses," the battle-worn knight instructed Kandris and Jetsam. "We'll trod in and investigate. Likely several knuckle-draggers await us," he stated without a hint of fear. "We'll advance during the daylight. If we're forced to fall back, they shan't follow us into the sun. The beasts have twice gotten the best of us. Retribution is at hand."

Time crawled as Jetsam and Kandris guarded the camp. An occasional hawk broke the silence, but for the most part, the dark forest bit its tongue. The quiet added to the tension, as every distant sound was met with a quick glance from the duo. With the others gone, the two young men posed little challenge to any wandering creature.

The sun inched across the heavens and its bright rays trickled down the lanky conifers, providing a warm day. Jetsam killed time by checking through his belongings. He didn't trust anyone in the party, and inspected his possessions daily. Other than his secret scroll, he owned little of value, except maybe his short sword. But these men all had better weapons than his anyway. *Besides, the blade's too small for a dragon hunter,* he rationalized with a smirk.

Small-talk came at a premium, and Jetsam and Kandris conversed sparingly. Jetsam sensed animosity from the squire, and returned the same. *I've outdone him on more than one occasion, and mastered his daily chores, even on one leg.*

Still, Jetsam helped the young man dress his wound, and was amazed at how well the gash was healing. Jetsam remembered the torn flesh after the troll's swipe and wondered if Kandris would live. Now Jetsam wondered why the squire didn't reclaim some of his mundane duties. *Everyone takes advantage of me.*

Seeing Enthran's healing power first hand, Jetsam longed to learn the spell that repaired the ripped flesh. He knew there *had* to be sorcery that could heal a torn muscle or a fractured bone.

Finished with every task he could think of, Jetsam sat against a tree and scanned the mountainside. The daystar slid toward the jagged western peaks, growing ever redder. A slight breeze picked up, cooling the temperate air. Foliage on the southern hills thrived full and lush, but on the north, greenery was sparse. The dwarf birch and junipers were fragile and twisted. Even the timberline grew denser to the south, and the sun kept on better terms with the clouds.

As Jetsam's eyes wandered the horizon, a trail of smoke gripped his gaze. The gray stream originated a few furlongs away. A moment of panic struck him before his nostrils detected the now common scent of ignited troll flesh. This could mean none other than success for the threesome.

"Look," he said to Kandris, "they're burning trolls!" A concerned look covered the squire's face. "How do ye know it's trogs?"

"Can't you smell it?"

Kandris wrinkled his nose and took a whiff. "Aye, of course. Most foul and putrid stench," he replied unconvincingly.

"We should start a campfire. Surely they return," Jetsam declared.

"Aye," agreed Kandris, "To yer tasks."

Before the frowning boy started dinner, the three men returned. Long-faced with slumped shoulders, they bore no additional outward injuries.

"I smelled the trogs," Kandris shouted. "What number did ye vanquish?" A long silence greeted him.

"Two from last night and three others met their death this day," confirmed a fatigued Lohon.

"Aye, fierce beasts indeed," offered Sir Prentice, "but nay match for a righteous blade and well-placed incantation. We found no other but those. But snaky are the caverns and many branches are left to scout." The knight dumped his dented silver helm and shield on the ground. "Near be the dragon, though. I feel it in me bones."

"On the morrow I shall cast a divination," stated Enthran, "which shall reveal to me if the beast does indeed lie beneath this mountain." The exhausted spellcaster sat by the fire.

Jetsam's curiosity piqued. He plopped down next to the weary mage. "Master," he petitioned, "why haven't you cast the spell to find the dragon before now?"

Enthran let out a long condescending sigh. "Because, lad, the spell is taxing and has a limited range." The sorcerer glared into Jetsam's eyes. "If I concentrate long and hard, I can sense powerful magic within a few leagues, no more. And then I'm spent for the day." Enthran's face tightened as he sat up. "But if that firedrake's in those caverns, I'll know it. Wyrms are full of magical power."

That night, Jetsam counted the glittering constellations in the endless heavens. Anticipation of the dragon filled his heart with wonder. He resolved to watch the wizard cast the divination. Jetsam convinced himself if he heard the words and studied the gestures closely, he could learn *without* the mage's tutelage.

Then I can use the spell to find Tramp. And Seryn Vardan.

When dawn broke, Jetsam received a pleasant surprise.

"Come on, knave," Enthran goaded. "I'm going to prepare the incantation. Might as well watch and learn." With a twisted smirk, the sorcerer leered at Jetsam. "Ye certainly mastered yer first spell!"

The teacher strode from the camp. He answered Jetsam's unspoken question. "I must have silence, out of earshot of louts and horses." With the aid of his new crutch, Jetsam followed, although the warlock didn't wait for him.

Enthran sauntered a furlong under the ageless evergreens until reaching a narrow ridge. Jetsam tagged along as best he could, the man moving further in front. The terrain proved challenging, but determination kept Jetsam going.

The mage marched to a small terrace, stopping near a massive boulder. Before long, Jetsam caught up. Tired from the effort, he set down his crutch and plopped to the hard earth. Highland silence enveloped them. A soundless harrier cut invisible seams in the cream sky.

The chant started low, almost inaudible as Jetsam concentrated on the foreign words. *Slow down.* They spewed forth too fast and unintelligible to comprehend. Enthran's voice rose, his hands waving, fingers dancing. Arms outstretched, the sorcerer dropped to his knees, head down, eyes shut. He uttered not another word.

Jetsam watched awestruck, not daring to speak. Enthran knelt in open-armed supplication. Not a muscle moved as minutes passed. Afraid to blink, Jetsam held his breath.

Then the wizard's head twitched, but that was all. The sun climbed higher in the pale sky, and Jetsam grew anxious. A long sigh ushered from the mage's lungs and he fell forward on all fours. On hands and knees, the man raised his covered head. His haggard face shone white as the moon.

"I found the dragon!"

Chapter Twenty-One

Enthran Ashvar rushed off without another word, his dark cloak billowing as he strode away. Jetsam followed at a safer pace. His wrist ached from the crutch and the wood bit his arm pit. As the sorcerer disappeared over a ridge, Jetsam again envisioned escaping. With the crutch already a burden, he knew he must have two good legs to even have a prayer of getting away. *And where would I flee?* He had no idea how far the river carried him from Tramp and Nicu, and the days spent searching for the troll cave confounded his sense of distance.

With a long sigh, he headed back to camp.

When he returned, the others were gone, save Squire Kandris.

"They've left to scout," the young man informed him. "The wizard had a vision and they follow it."

"You mean they're going to fight the dragon right *now?*"

"Nay, lad," the squire replied scornfully. "They're looking for the passageway the wizard saw in his mind. It was of Dwarven craft, lying deeper than the rough-hewn troll holes. Certainly, we are near *Asigonn.*"

"What's that?"

"Ye know not ye're history, do ye?" Kandris asked in a patronizing tone. "Asigonn's a Dwarven city. Legends tell of an evil wyrm routing the stout folk and chasing them from their home. We'll have our hands full with that beast."

Jetsam almost laughed at the squire's use of the word 'we.' Nevertheless, he bit his tongue.

He and Kandris again spent the day together. Tending and mending and cleaning, they spoke briefly. Polite courtesies and small talk dominated their sparse conversations.

"I'm supposed to teach ye the crossbow today," Kandris mentioned after the young men finished their camp chores. "Don't know how he expects ye to span the bow on one leg." Kandris examined Jetsam and his crutch. "Guess ye can watch me."

Kandris demonstrated by placing the weapon's stirrup on the ground and anchoring it with his foot. "Draw the string back like this," he demonstrated for Jetsam, pulling up and over the nut. "Doubt yer strong enough for that," Kandris chided. "Then load the bolt in the groove, like this." He pulled a garrock from his quiver and slid it into place. "Then ye aim." The squire raised the crossbow to his shoulder. "Lean yer face across the deck and line up the bolt clip with the arrow." Kandris lifted his head to check on Jetsam. "See that dead pine over there? Just pull the trigger."

With a click and a snap, the squire fired at the tree, grazing its dead bark. "Close enough. Now ye try. I'll span the bow for ye."

"I can do it," Jetsam replied, holding out his free hand for the weapon.

"Suit yerself," Kandris snarled. "Just don't blame me when ye get hurt."

Jetsam hobbled to a nearby stump and plopped down on it. Stretching out his good leg, he slipped the crossbow stirrup over his boot and drew the string. Grunting and grimacing, he pulled the string over the nock. *That* was *hard—almost fell off the log!*

"Same tree," Jetsam said, then aimed and fired. His bolt buried in the dirt at the base of the tree. *Easier to learn than a sling, I'll admit. And more deadly.*

"Not bad," Kandris admitted. "Yer on line—just raise yer aim a bit. Here, try another."

Jetsam practiced several more shots before Kandris called it quits. *'Cause I'm a better shot than him already.*

"Sir Prentice tasked me with teaching ye how to use your blade, as well," Kandris said. "We can't practice footwork, but I can show ye how to grip, guard, cut, and strike. Grab your little sword."

Brandishing his blade, Kandris demonstrated stance, steps, and pivots for Jetsam, explaining techniques as the knight taught him. *Not bad,* Jetsam thought of the squire's demonstration. *Too bad you forgot to use it against the trolls.*

Kandris trained Jetsam until their arms were sore and evening beckoned. *I've got the knack of it,* Jetsam decided, trying to convince himself this one-legged practice held some value. Dusk came and went and they ate their dinner without the men.

Brooding darkness chased away the last remnants of sunset, and Kandris told Jetsam to get some sleep. "I'll keep watch 'till they return. Keep yer blade close at hand."

Sleep proved elusive for Jetsam as he envisioned the toothy dragon dining on the flesh of the three men. *Wonder what I'd do if they were indeed dead?* Slumber overtook him before he solved his own riddle. He endured strange and troublesome dreams.

Upon awaking, Jetsam heard the trio conversing. *They're not dead after all!* One eye open, he turned his head toward the noise. They huddled several yards from camp, barely visible by the campfire's flickering. Squire Kandris wasn't included in the discussion. *Must be important,* Jetsam concluded.

The urge to eavesdrop overcame him, but they stood too far away to hear anything but muffled mumbling. He slipped from his bedroll. Jetsam crouched behind the low brush and crept closer. He could almost make out their words.

"Get up, knave!" Lohon Threll shouted. Jetsam froze in fear. "Aye, boy! I'm talking to ye. Come hither," commanded the redhead. "Yer bloody ears must be burning."

Jetsam hopped over to the congregation. Sir Prentice addressed him solemnly.

"A vision of the winged beast the wizard has seen, and we searched deep beyond the troll warrens for the caverns he saw. But from what we could tell, when the Dwarves escaped the dragon, they sealed off the tunnels as they fled.

"Problem is, the smallfolk designed the gates to barricade themselves in their central fortress as they fell back from a perimeter attack. But since the damned dragon attacked the heart of Asigonn, instead of sealing themselves in, they locked themselves out."

"Why would they do that?" Kandris blurted.

"Probably to stop the wyrm from blowin' fire at their backs." Sire Prentice explained, giving his squire a cockeyed glance. "Try as we might, we couldn't breach any of the passageways. The stone blockades are impenetrable. Yet other than climbin' in the roof breach straight into the wyrm's maw, it's the only way into the great hall, save one." The knight's eyes burned deep into Jetsam.

"My scrying showed airways cut in the rocks above," Enthran explained, "leading to the central chambers inside the fortified barriers. The rub is, the passages are too narrow for any *man* to fit through. Even Kandris," he admitted.

"But not too narrow for a skinny *lad!*" Sir Prentice piped in.

Jetsam swallowed hard. He didn't need to hear the rest—the gauntlet had been thrown down. Sir Prentice continued anyway.

"We're asking ye to sneak down the passage and release the blocked portals from the inside, so we can get to the creature."

Lohon interrupted the knight. "I know Dwarven craft. These 'doors' have a mechanism to unlock from the inside. There'll be a lever that opens the passage like the legs of a two-bit wench."

"The lad knows naught of cheap whores, ye rogue," Sir Prentice scolded. "And watch yer tongue, fer if ye interrupt me again, I may just yank it out." Lohon clenched his whiskered jaw, but gave no reply to the admonishing knight.

While Sir Prentice and Lohon shared an icy glare, Enthran spoke. "The danger, lad, is that I cannot foretell how close the airway comes to the wyrm lair. Ye may tread very near to the beast itself before finding the entryway." Jetsam shuddered, and was already convinced there was no way they could make him go down that passage.

"We plan on rewarding ye for the deed," the knight promised. "If ye agree, the wizard will try to heal yer leg. It takes strong sorcery to mend bones, and it'll drain him sorely, but if ye'll take on the task, it will be done."

The offer took Jetsam off guard. *Heal my leg?* The deal became more tempting.

"If ye help us, we'll share a bit o' the loot and ask that ye travel south with us to me Freelord's castle, where I'll present the proof of conquest.

"Enthran seems to think ye've got the makings of a wizard—with the proper instruction of course—and is willing to bring ye along in the art. But only if ye agree to the plan. Consider it a test of yer loyalty."

He's asking my permission? Jetsam almost agreed on the spot, but the gypsy's words rang in his head.

Nicu said dragons were not a foul scourge, but a venerable race steeped in magic. These words conflicted with the bloodthirsty vigor in which the Calderian pursued the creature. He'd never trusted these men before, but their promises lured him.

Jetsam thought of his desire to learn more about his parents. Heading south with the knight would end his quest. *And what of the price on my head? Will these men not turn me over to the fist bounty hunter that recognizes me?* Returning to civilization would have its risks.

Jetsam contemplated the consequences of refusal. *Would be dangerous to say no.* With Kandris mending, his value to the group decreased. *If they left me lame in the woods, I'd surely die.* And that was probably the best scenario.

"I'll do it."

"'Tis what we wanted to hear, lad. We'll make an adventurer out of you yet," proclaimed Sir Prentice. "The vent breach sits high upon a rocky slope, and two legs will be needed for the climb. Can ye heal him now?"

Why'd they wait till now? Jetsam wondered. *Didn't want me to run off, I bet.*

"Sit down, boy," the sorcerer instructed. Jetsam obliged, his ears focused on the impending chant. Enthran commenced the incantation, and Jetsam watched and listened. The spell was longer than the others he'd heard. He waited for his ankle to feel better, but nothing happened.

Then the conjurer changed his cadence, and a deep burning started in the marrow of Jetsam's leg. His blood ran like lava, damaged ankle throbbing while the magic surged through him. He gritted his teeth, amazed at the power he was witnessing.

"'Tis done!" Enthran declared with a flourish. "Go ahead, boy," he ordered, "stand!" Again, Jetsam followed instruction, cautiously putting his weight on the injured foot. His blood still ran hot, but the tingling subsided.

He did it!

Standing on both feet for the first time in days, Jetsam experienced no pain at all. His leg muscles were weak from being unused, but other than that, he felt fine.

"Thank you kindly, m'lord." Jetsam bowed his head.

"Overdue it not," Enthran warned. "The sorcery worked, but there's still healing to be done."

"Yes, m'lord." Jetsam limped just a little—and only for show. The ankle felt healed, but if the wizard believed he wasn't at full strength, then Jetsam saw no reason to let them think otherwise.

"Here, lad." Lohon tossed Jetsam his boot, neatly stitched with leather strips where Lohon had cut the boot from Jetsam's swollen foot.

"Get some rest," Sir Prentice bellowed. "Tomorrow, we assault the firedrake!"

Jetsam could scarcely sleep. *With my leg healed, I could escape at first chance.* He had no intention of opening the locked doors. *I plan on fleeing long before risking my neck. Now I need the opportunity.* With each man taking turns guarding the camp, it wouldn't come before dawn.

The morning sun crept over the scarlet peaks, pouring daylight onto the mountainside. Birds chirped high in the pinewood branches, harkening the dawn. A bustle surrounded camp. Squire Kandris hurried about his chores. Unlike previous mornings, Jetsam had not been roused for his daily tasks. Uncharacteristically, the knight allowed him to sleep. *Apparently, my decision elevated me above the squire.* One look from the fuming Kandris told him his guess was true.

Kandris packed the horses while Lohon and the Calderian prepared their tools of war. Armor was repaired, swords sharpened. Bows were tweaked and enchanted arrows and bolts were readied. A solemn silence shrouded the preparations. With no weapons of his own, Enthran sat off by himself, deep in meditation.

"Wake up, lad," Sir Prentice chimed. "We ascend on the hour." Jetsam donned his short sword and loaded his most valuable possessions in his belt-bag. The pouch was bursting.

His lantern, bedroll, and spare clothes would stay on the horse, and hopefully, rejoin him later, though he had no idea how. *I'll have to abandon them if given the chance to escape.* This discouraged him, but his mind was set. He wore his long coat, afraid to leave that precious item. Despite the sun, the mountain air felt chilly, and he expected wearing the garment would raise no suspicion.

With the camp packed and horses loaded, the party embarked on their trek. The terrain steepened and the tall conifers thinned. Soon they climbed above the timberline, through the scrub, until the mighty Oxbow peaks loomed before them, unobstructed by the evergreens. Jetsam saw the small maw of the troll cave.

Sir Prentice and Lohon dismounted and unsheathed their blades. They disappeared into the hole without a word of explanation. Enthran rode his dapple-gray to the breach, but held steady upon his mount. Jetsam was left to wonder what would happen next.

Little time passed before Jetsam recognized the unmistakable shriek of a troll. His heart skipped a beat and his ears pricked, but he heard no further sound. Soon, the two men emerged from the cave. Sir Prentice clutched a large sack. Lohon dragged out the disfigured remains of a small troll—captured, bludgeoned, and bound yesterday—which he promptly set afire.

"Squire, ye'll stay with the horses," the knight instructed as the carcass caught flame. "Tend the fire and make sure the beast burns to a crisp. We'll proceed from here on foot." He turned to Jetsam. "'Tis time, lad."

Jetsam followed the knight, rogue, and mage as they climbed a rocky incline. The morning sun burned bright on the gray stones, but did little to warm the high mountain wind. The toothy peaks loomed above, ever vigilant. Only sparse shrub called this land home. They ascended slowly while the footing grew more unstable. Even though Jetsam's leg felt healed, the climb challenged him.

"There it is!" Enthran gasped. The vent was no larger than the drainage chute Jetsam used to infiltrate the castle wall. Even for his narrow frame, it looked a tight fit.

"Here, lad, take this sack. When ye shimmy down the chute, drape yerself with the troll hide." Jetsam gawked slack-jawed at the knight. *Troll hide?*

Noticing his bewildered expression, Sir Prentice offered an explanation. "Dragons possess an exceptional sense of smell," he explained. "This troll skin will mask yer scent, so the wyrm shan't make ye fer a tasty morsel."

Jetsam shuddered at the idea of wearing a troll carcass. He told himself he wouldn't do it. *I'd rather be eaten by the dragon!*

Sir Prentice fastened the sack of troll flesh to Jetsam's good ankle with a rope.

"Work to the south, lad," Enthran directed. "Don't get turned around in the passageways."

"Ye'll need yer lantern too," Lohon replied, producing Jetsam's lamp. Jetsam fumed that Lohon would retrieve the item from his pack without asking. He wondered when the rogue rifled through his belongings. *Probably the very first day.* The decision to keep his precious scroll in his belt-pouch seemed wise.

At least now I don't have to leave the lantern behind when I escape, he rationalized.

Lohon lit a flame on the wick and tied the glowing lantern to the sack of troll hide. He lowered the lamp and sack down the hole until the rope pulled taught on Jetsam's ankle. Then the redhead fastened a rope around the youngster's narrow waist.

"Time to go," Sir Prentice urged. "Soon as yer in, we'll head back down and meet ye at the door. Give two sharp tugs when ye reach bottom. May the gods smile upon ye!"

With that, Jetsam crouched down and slipped into the hole. The men above lowered him in. The exploit reminded him of slithering down the abandoned well inside the castle. Jetsam inched down, watching the sunlight above shrink into a white dot. The lantern flickered like a firefly beneath him. Rough-hewn rock bit his skin, and his hands and clothes were covered with greasy creosote.

Jetsam deliberated escaping, knowing once he gave the signal, the men would soon be underground awaiting his arrival. The uncertainty of the whole affair would give him a good head start, for they would wait hours, if not more, for him to open a passageway. He considered doubling back and stealing a horse, but thought better of it. *My two good legs are all I need. Besides, feeding myself will be hard enough without adding a horse.*

Jetsam decided to head back up. *This is far enough.* He braced himself inside the chute and tugged twice on the rope around his waist—the signal he had reached bottom. The cord went slack and slithered down and around him. *Now my safety net's gone.* He waited a few minutes until he was sure they had left. Then he began his ascent.

The slippery passage entertained other ideas. Every foot he crawled up, he slipped back another two. For several minutes he struggled against the uncooperative shaft, until he was out of breath. The sack and lantern anchored him in place. Ascending didn't *appear* difficult, but doing it proved impossible. It felt like his body fought his very wishes.

Now, there was no turning back. *However I manage to escape, up the hole won't be the way.*

After holding still for a minute to catch his breath, he resumed the descent. By now, the sack grew heavy and the rope burned his ankle. And he no longer enjoyed the luxury of being secured from above.

Jetsam's muscles ached and his hands and knees rubbed raw. He feared losing his hold altogether and dropping like a stone, remembering the fear in his heart when he thought Elvar fell down the Citadel well.

As his mind wandered to better times, the tension on his leg relented. *The sack hit bottom!*

Jetsam inched down. In the darkness, his foot dangled in a void. The tunnel ended. Hovering above an unknown landing, he paused, one leg swinging in the musty air, while the rest of his body clung to the end of the chute. Pulling on the slack rope, he guessed the floor sat less than a fathom beyond his outstretched leg.

Craning his neck, he tried to spot the lantern below, but it had either gone out, or landed under the sack. Darkness pervaded. Jetsam took a deep breath. *Don't want to turn another ankle.* Like a rock, he dropped from the shaft.

He plopped on the sack of troll hide and tumbled onto the stone floor. Fortunately, he missed the lantern—and didn't twist anything.

Jetsam retrieved his flint, steel, and tinder and fumbled in the dark to kindle the lantern. As light spread, he observed he sat inside a large room. Wood and debris littered the dusty floor, and hovering stone gargoyles eyed him from each corner.

Jetsam walked into the chamber's center. He intended to leave the troll skin in the fireplace, but something made him turn back. *You don't need that sodding hide.* Kneeling, he opened the sack. A foul slap of troll stink assaulted his nostrils. *Just leave the fobbing thing.* He tried to turn away, but his body refused.

That black-magic blaggard cast a spell on me! Now Jetsam understood why the healing spell ran so long, and why the men seemed so ready to trust him. *They didn't trust me after all—they didn't have to. That's why I couldn't climb back up!* Even as he realized his predicament, his possessed hands grasped the oily troll skin. Sparse, wiry hairs protruded from the awful pelt.

Against his will, his own arms donned the flap of hide like a cape. The knight had wound a cord through the flesh, and Jetsam fastened it about his neck. *What am I doing?* The stench was overwhelming.

He regurgitated his breakfast on the stone floor.

No more than a puppet on a string, Jetsam relinquished control to the dominant spell. *Until I tried crawling back up the vent, I'd done exactly as directed, and didn't notice the spell.* But now he was keenly aware of the wizard's mastery and felt powerless.

Lantern in hand, he surveyed the fine marble room as he marched toward the door. He tried to stop and admire the glistening stone, to regain his composure, but his feet tromped on. The thick door squeaked open with a soft push, and led to a wide hallway.

Musty air and cobwebs met Jetsam past the doorway. He cleared the silky strings with a wave and proceeded southward. A strange sensation captured his attention. The reeking troll hide on his back felt *alive!* The flesh rippled and vibrated. *I don't believe it.* This flap of skin was growing, even though it was stripped from the rest of the body, now ashes on the mountainside. Jetsam surmised this skin would eventually regenerate into a full-grown troll.

More than ever he longed to tear the stinking carcass from his back and light it afire. His wishes, however, were ignored by his limbs. Jetsam could almost see the puppet strings moving his arms and legs. He discerned the sorcerer scrutinizing the passageway through his own blue eyes. The sensations of the spellcaster's possession felt sinister. *This must be the black magic Nicu warned me of,* Jetsam lamented.

As he rounded a corner, traipsing across the stone floor, he grew despondent. Several closed doors passed by, barely noticeable in the dim light, their outlines leaving nary a trace against the deep blue marble walls.

Then, without warning, his feet stopped in front of a huge obstruction. The slab sealed the passageway. Seamless and unyielding from the outside, the magic-infused stone stood stronger than any portcullis or castle wall. Inside its flanking watch-post alcove, Jetsam spied a lever.

His possessed right hand shot out and pulled the steel bar. With a stone-on-stone scraping, the stubborn rock swung open.

On the other side, Jetsam saw the hated threesome waiting with greedy grins.

At least it's done, Jetsam thought. *Now I can shed this damnable hide.* Reading his mind, the sorcerer spoke in a deep raspy drone. Jetsam wasn't even sure if the words came from Enthran's mouth, or if they just rang inside his head.

"Now, thee shall find the wyrm!"

Chapter Twenty-Two

Smoke from the burning troll carcass made the party easy to spot. The thick gray strand coiled to the heavens. A lone vulture circled above the smoldering remains.

From the timberline's cover, Yduk studied the group climbing the rocky slopes. *One in armor, another in leather, and the third in a robe, all following a boy in a long coat.* The same boy Yduk knew all too well. *A slippery, resilient, confounding boy.* More trouble than he was worth, but now a deep thorn in the bounty hunter's pride.

The urchin and men reached a narrow shelf and halted their ascent. Moments passed as the men worked diligently near the boy. Yduk saw a lantern, rope, and sack.

As the orphan vanished down a hole, the tracker gasped. After lowering him in, the three men headed back down. Yduk stood dumbfounded for a moment.

"They've found Asigonn!"

Yduk Thiern waited for the party to disappear into the cave before he approached. A single young man guarded the horses at the entrance. "Time for action," Yduk announced to no one but himself.

Kandris Bayen never knew what hit him.

Yduk bound and gagged the unconscious squire and slung him over the back of a horse. Then the tracker led the five steeds into the forest and harnessed them alongside his mount. "If any of yer comrades do make it out alive," he told the insensible squire, "they shan't be riding away!"

Fully armed, Yduk entered the troll cave in pursuit of the wyrm hunters. He lit his lantern, then unsheathed Regret. The golden lantern light frolicked on the shiny steel. Typical for a troll encampment, the entrance caverns were rough-hewn. Hollow bones and fetid dung littered the floor. Yduk examined the footprints. *Signs of battle are obvious.*

Yduk crept through the low caverns. As he moved deeper into the mountainside, the trail grew easier to follow. Boot prints became visible on the soiled cave bottom. After winding through a furlong of snaking tunnels, Yduk came upon a sloping passage. Debris was strewn about the opening, as if the trolls tried to seal the breach. Crouching low, he entered the slim gap.

This looks different from the troll caverns. The stone walls were cut smooth. Yduk recognized the unmistakable Dwarven touch. "Asigonn," he whispered. Creeping, he lowered his lantern light. The angling tunnel leveled off and stretched higher and wider. He detected feint flickering torchlight far down the hall, and extinguished his lantern. A wide smile crossed his mustached lips.

His black leather boots stole like cat's paws down the long corridor. As Yduk closed to within a furlong of the end, he made out the forms of the knight, mage, and rogue, standing as dark silhouettes in the dancing rushlight. Planted inside a huge doorway, they peered down the passage before them.

Upon further scrutiny, Yduk noticed the knight and rogue fidgeting anxiously, while the sorcerer remained still as stone. A picture formed in the bounty hunter's mind, and he almost pitied the runaway. *He's surely in over his head. Four against one hardly seems fair.* He fingered his oily mustache, thinking of the slippery orphan. *He's a resilient little bugger, that's for sure. Maybe I'll take him in alive,* Yduk pondered. *Once I get paid, I don't care what happens to him.* The bounty hunter cracked a smile. *The squirt'll probably escape from wherever they send him anyway.*

In the darkness, Yduk waited for the game to play out.

Jetsam's heart sank when the spellcaster proclaimed his next task. Now he comprehended their plot in all its sinister glory. *They'll march me through the tunnels right to the dragon's lair.* Then the conniving sorcerer would survey the scene through Jetsam's eyes, thereby gaining the advantage of familiarity as well as surprise. *A cowardly plan.*

Despite his dismay, he turned and headed off to find the ancient beast. *Truly, I have no choice.* His head clouded in confusion while his legs chose the warlock's path. The vile sorcery brewed a powerful stew in his mind. Jetsam wondered if it would have been better to stay in Dwim-Halloe, playing cat and mouse until the bounty hunter caught him or tired of the chase. It seemed a poor choice, but better than his current dire straits.

So this is how it ends, he thought. *I'll be no more than a human sacrifice for their greed.* Despite the wizard's control, tears welled in his blue eyes. *Elvar will be waiting for me,* he tried to console himself. *And mother, and father. And Tramp.* The thought of his little dog dead forced a sob from his lips.

Fight it, came a voice from deep in Jetsam's head. He blocked out the words in abject terror, fearing Enthran was instructing him to attack the dragon as a diversion. *Not yet, not yet,* Jetsam objected in vain.

Lantern in hand, he soldiered on, unaware of the hallowed corridors he navigated. The ancient marble rose in sweeping arches, coated with dust and spider webs. Stern busts of Dwarven heroes guarded each portal, looking down with gemstone eyes. Onward Jetsam strode, through the long hall, under pointed archways, around corners, and up and down wide stone stairs.

Jetsam lost track of time and direction, mentally exhausted by the meddling wizard's innermost invasion. His mind was too foggy to fight the possession. Then Jetsam halted in the musty passage. *What now?* Charred debris and guano covered the floor. Thousands of sleeping bats clung to the arched ceiling. *This stinks nearly as bad as troll flesh.* Veined marble walls were coated in black crusty soot.

Without direction, Jetsam doused the lantern at Enthran Ashvar's control. *Who needs to see? My eyes are not my own anyway.*

Fight it! the inner voice commanded again. Jetsam paid no heed. His body already operated without his will. When the sorcerer wanted him to draw his sword or fire his sling, he doubted he'd have any warning, or recourse.

In the dark, with the wiggling, stinking troll flesh clinging to his back, Jetsam crept forward, eyes adjusting to the blackness. A faint light flowed down the corridor before him. His feet planted in bat dung, Jetsam sensed a rumbling beneath his soles. *The mountain itself stirs.*

Approaching the glow, he hunched closer to the ground. A dim archway appeared at the hall's end and the dull light emanated from beyond. A cold sweat seeped from his pores. *I doubt the black-magic blaggard is controlling that.*

Within sight of the soaring archway, Jetsam dropped to his hands and knees without any consent of his own. He cursed the damnable wizard as his palms and fingers squished in the guano. Like a mouse, he crawled along the coated granite floor.

Reaching the portal to the room beyond, Jetsam saw the doorway led to a debris-strewn balcony, high above a yet-unseen room. The gallery encompassed the room's perimeter, with an ornate stone railing bordering the edge. Even in the dim light and rampant shadows, the architecture displayed battle scars.

The curved rafters were blackened and a gaping hole punctured the vaulted ceiling as fingers of sunlight cast a pale illumination into the room below. Black soot coated the marble ceiling and balcony. Chunks of stone were missing from the balustrade and the heads and arms of several colossal statues had been dislocated.

The rumbling beneath Jetsam's hands and knees increased and his nostrils filled with the scent of brimstone. With fear and wonder, he crept unwilling toward the terrace rail.

Fight the black magic, said a voice again, clearer than before. Jetsam halted, bolstered with a new resolve. It was *the* voice! The whisper again echoed in his head, weaker now, fading away.

Jetsam concentrated to make out the words. *You're stronger than him. Use your power to expel his.* As if spent, the voice withered into silence.

Hope renewed, Jetsam was now convinced the whispering came from a spiritual guardian, and not his own imagination. For once, he felt *lucky*. But only for a second.

Taking a calming breath, he closed his eyes and reached deep inside, groping for the power he experienced when casting the sunblink spell. Like a shining jewel at the bottom of a deep pool, the strength was there—just out of reach. *Enthran's too strong,* he lamented. He felt himself crawling forward.

Then Jetsam experienced a surge of strength that shook the binding tendrils. *What was that? Does Enthran weaken?* Concentrating fiercely, Jetsam swam within himself, searching for his elusive magic essence. He redoubled his concentration. As the mage marched him on hands and knees toward the balcony rail, he felt a waiver in the sorcerer's mental grip. *His power wanes.*

With new resolve, his mind focused against Enthran's will. The wicked presence ran like ice through his young veins, resisting the uprising. Jetsam trembled as his body grew cold. But like a wakened fury, his own magic stirred. *I've got a second wind.* A flickering flame fed with oil, the energy within him surged. The chill reluctantly abated. He warmed and began to sweat.

An epic struggle ensued in his mind, yet his body inched forward. Entwined in a waking nightmare, he battled for sole possession of his will. Deep within, he felt the wizard's frigid touch, but unlike before, the strangling tendrils faltered. *As if someone's helping me.*

Concentrating on the vile intrusion, he shut his mind from the mental infestation. He pulsed with a force heretofore unknown. Like a body expelling a fever, Jetsam felt Enthran's influence beaten back, and vanquished altogether. The enemy was ousted.

I'm free!

Exhausted and panting, Jetsam wiped his dung-covered hands on the troll carcass, and then slid the disgusting skin from his back. Emancipation from that sickly entity heartened him. The hide slithered to the dirty stone floor, growing imperceptibly to regain its gruesome form.

Still on hands and knees, Jetsam rested a moment while debating his course of action. His returning freedom of choice brought little relief. He suspected the confounded sorcerer and the rest were now making their way toward him. *Retreat through the passages I entered from would be dangerous at best.*

The balcony ran to his left and right around the huge room, but without standing, Jetsam couldn't see another exit. With the very floor rumbling strangely, he feared raising his head above the stone rail for a peek. He shuddered at what he might see.

After a moment of reflection, Jetsam realized he had little choice. He crawled to his right, hoping to find another doorway before encircling the cluttered gallery. His boyish curiosity begged him to sneak to the edge and look through the stone balusters to the great hall below. Fear kept him from giving in.

Before he reached the first corner, a deep voice resonated from the room below.

"What are you looking for?" the rich throaty voice thundered. Jetsam gasped in surprise, then crawled to the granite rail. He poked his long nose over the terrace edge, his neck craning and blue eyes peering below.

Jetsam recoiled in terror, landing on his rump and smacking his head on the stone floor.

Chapter Twenty-Three

Boredom taunted Yduk Thiern as he watched the three men linger by the sealed passageway. The knight and rogue idled restlessly, shifting their weight from leg to leg. Covered head bowed, the unnatural held still and motionless. Yduk itched for the impending fireworks.

As if shot with an arrow, the inert mage leapt from his trance, arms flailing in the air. *Now we're getting somewhere,* Yduk thought.

From his distant post, the tracker heard the sounds of raised voices. The formerly still men were animated now, pointing and waving. *They're panicked.* Eyes wide, Yduk inched closer, listening intently. The echoing words bounced like marbles down the hall.

"The spell is broken, the knave is free," bemoaned Enthran.

Ha! Yduk thought. *I should've known.*

"Did ye see the wyrm?" beseeched Sir Prentice.

"I saw it not, but close it was. That is certain."

"Then in haste we must go," proclaimed the knight.

"And rush to our deaths?" blurted Lohon. "This plan is undone. Without knowing where the beast sits, how can we guarantee our approach? 'Tis bloody folly to continue," he declared.

A look of pure disgust filled the knight's bearded face.

"'Tis no time for cowardice. Ye shall accompany us as planned, or I shall smite ye where ye stand," roared Sir Prentice. "The decision is yers. Choose now!"

Yduk could not hear the sullen rogue's quiet reply, but by his submissive posture, the bounty hunter suspected he agreed to the knight's demand. *This is getting good,* Yduk thought. Seemingly satisfied with Lohon's compliance, the plated warrior turned to the mage.

"Have ye the amulet and scroll?"

The cloaked man nodded, retrieving a stunning talisman from inside his robe. A bright crystal hung from a glimmering gold necklace. *That's gotta be worth a pretty coin.* The unnatural pulled back his hood and placed the amulet over his head.

"And ye, dissident," the knight said toward Lohon, "I pray ye aren't unmanned. Remember, the enchanted arrows will do the work for ye. Just give 'em flight and they'll find the mark."

The scolded rogue withdrew one of the said arrows and readied his long bow. Sir Prentice spanned and loaded his arbalest. Stepping in front, the knight led as the trio crept down the passage.

Yduk trailed at a safe distance, just close enough to see their fading torchlight. He followed them down spacious hallways, under arched doorways, up and down staircases, and finally, to a grand corridor, where they stopped. A nervous excitement bubbled inside him.

Again, he heard the knight's Calderian drawl.

"'Tis time for the scroll," he instructed the wizard. Enthran withdrew a case and unrolled a parchment. The unnatural held it before him in the flickering rushlight. Then, the conjurer began to read. Elven words rolled off his tongue.

Amused, Yduk gazed intently. *More goodies?* Then his jaw dropped.

Into thin air, the three men vanished. Even their torchlight ceased.

"Blast!" Yduk whispered to himself. He halted, listening for their footsteps. Certain they were not retreating, he moved cautiously. *Invisible or not, I shan't spot 'em in this blackness.*

He stopped again upon feeling the floor rumble beneath his boots. *The devil was that?* His gloved hand gripped Regret's hilt. "Far enough," he whispered.

Jetsam's eyes blinked in wonder at the fantastic sight before him. Frigid fear shivered his skin, but he couldn't tear himself away.

"A troll wouldn't be so foolish," the deep voice declared, "as to intrude upon my lair."

The dragon *had* smelled him.

Dumbstruck, Jetsam watched the wyrm's mouth form words. The beast stood several fathoms below, in the center of Asigonn's great hall. The ancient room was immense, but the venerable hall's grandeur paled in comparison to the creature residing within.

Standing on two muscular hind legs, the green dragon's massive talons scratched the stone floor. On each side of its spiny back, wings folded against its scaly sides, and a pair of smaller legs protruded from where wings met body. A long slender neck raised its head to Jetsam's level. Two slim horns curved above the beast's pointed ears and flowing crest, while its deep-set eyes shone like fire-lit emeralds.

"You shall answer my questions, little one." The dragon spoke through a long snout, nostrils flaring above a mouth of razor teeth. Two prominent fangs jutted from this dreadful maw, sharper than any blade Jetsam had ever seen.

Paralyzed with awe and fear, Jetsam nodded. An aura of magic radiated from the behemoth like nothing he'd experienced before. *If my death comes today,* he thought, *it shall be by the greatest creature to walk the earth. I'm but an insect by compare.*

"Truer sentiments I have never known," said the dragon. "'Tis a shame one so perceptive should be so careless." The voice sounded like low thunder rolling over the mountains, shaking branch and bush along the way.

"Tell me, little gremlin, why you have been so foolhardy as to venture here? Surely, 'tis a grand place to die, but certainly very far from your home."

Jetsam cleared his throat to speak. Meekly he answered the talking beast. "It wasn't of my will, m'lord, that I came into your hallowed home."

"M'lord? I'm no lord, nor am I a drake," the dragon hissed. "I've birthed eggs, hatched *dragonlings*, and raised them to adulthood. Be glad there are none here, fore you would not have made it thus far were eggs or young in my care."

"My humble apology for the mistake *and* unintentional intrusion."

"If not your will to intrude, than whose? And why come hidden under the taint of troll hide if not intending to deceive me?"

"I had no desire to wear the putrid flesh," Jetsam replied with trembling voice. "Rather, a wizard cast a spell to bind me to his will. It's only under such persuasion that I dared enter."

"And yet, I have freed you from this burden."

"That was *you?*"

"Fell magic shall not intrude upon my lair, no matter how cleverly disguised. I do not permit it."

"Why did you help *me?*"

"You wear the mark of the mountain dryad, which heralds strange friends indeed," noted the queen lizard, spotting Illyassa's necklace. "Although from *me,* it will protect you not. But I do sense a fair bit of magic in you. Are you a sorcerer in disguise, trying to appear as a wee lad to lull me into carelessness with tall tales?"

"Nay, m'lady, I'm no wizard, and speak no lies. I'm a mere boy who's cast but a single spell." The dragon raised a scaly eyebrow at this, and Jetsam debated revealing more. He concluded his hope lied in the great wyrm's mercy. "If I may, m'lady," Jetsam beseeched, "three men lurk behind me, plotting to strike you down, for one is a knight claiming he is honor-bound to the task."

With that, the dragon bellowed in laughter. Fine sparks and pipe-smoke spurted from her nostrils and the roar shook the walls. "Those that send a lad first would think themselves able to slay me? Bring on the fools! I shall enjoy a delicacy tonight!" And the dragon roared again.

Before her laughter died, the sound of snapping bows filled the air, and Jetsam heard Enthran Ashvar's unmistakable chanting. Jetsam turned in a circle, looking about, but saw no one.

An arrow embedded in the dragon's long neck, finding a soft spot between the hard scales. A crossbow bolt followed, aimed for an eye, but didn't bite. Missing the crystalline orb, the projectile pierced a pointy ear. The beast hissed in anger, its head scanning the room for the unseen intruders.

The invisible onslaught continued unabated.

Another arrow struck the dragon's neck, though failed to penetrate the scaly hide. A third enchanted missile tasted dragon flesh, and another followed. A second quarrel flew at an emerald eye. Before the proud victim could retaliate, a bolt of searing blue lightning exploded into its green skin.

Jetsam watched the surprised dragon claw at the arrow in its neck and shudder from the lightning charge. It flicked the needle off and bellowed in anger. The dragon unleashed a jet of raging flames from its gaping maw.

Fire poured forth in a long stream as the dragon scorched the balcony. She started at the doorway where Jetsam entered, and proceeded to the left, blasting her fiery stream along the terraced perimeter.

I'm in its path!

Without thought or rationale, Jetsam leapt to his feet and sprinted. Heat closed behind him as the wyrm blast circled the balcony. Ahead, the doorway still smoldered, residual fiery fingers flicking the grimy stone. Hungry flames lapped at his racing legs. *I won't reach the exit.*

In a last desperate effort, Jetsam dove to the floor and wrapped himself in the troll hide, still lying where he left it, yet untouched by the fire.

No sooner than he pulled the fetid carcass over himself and rolled into a ball, a wave on searing heat passed above him. Scorching his skin, the troll flesh melted. In agonizing pain, Jetsam flung off the burning hide and jumped to his feet. The dragon fire had passed, and now the entire gallery smoldered. *But I'm not burned!*

Jetsam brushed himself off, and although his skin stung, he did not blister. Now a charred remnant of its former self, the troll hide burnt to a crisp at his feet. *The hideous cloak saved me—for now.*

Jetsam gazed upon the dragon; angry, confused, and bleeding. A thin layer of smoke hovered around the beast, courtesy of the potent lightning burst. Down into the deep room Jetsam peered. *Where are they?* Still he detected no sign of the three men. And yet, two more projectiles breached the dragon's vulnerable underside. Then a second crackle echoed in the cavernous hall. Another electric bolt surged into the raging wyrm.

Jetsam stood transfixed by the awe-inspiring lightning. *But how?* he wondered. *His magic is stronger now than it was against the trolls.* Jetsam ground his molars. *And to hide three men from the eyes of a dragon is strong conjuring indeed.*

More fire discharged from the emerald wyrm. Pointing its narrow head toward the floor, it cut a circle of flame around its bulk. And as the blast shot forth, the beast flapped its enormous wings, creating a whirling firestorm in the great hall.

Jetsam leapt back from the stone rail, throwing his arms over his ducking head. Acrid fumes stung his eyes. Waves of heat and billows of green-gray smoke rose to the vaulted ceiling and poured into the atmosphere from the high breach. Now Jetsam suspected the ceiling hole was the dragon's doing during the attack on Asigonn so long ago.

On the flame-licked walls below the terrace, long-dormant torches erupted into flame, casting light on the spacious great hall. The hibernating brands illuminated the room, revealing the magnificent architecture. The dragon's blazing barrage lasted a dozen beats of Jetsam's racing heart. Spitting its last bit of flame, the green wyrm howled in pain and glory.

For a moment, all was quiet. Bloodied but not broken, the dragon scanned the floor. With a flutter of its gigantic wings, the wyrm rose into the air. The dragon's long spiked tail cracked like a whip, and Jetsam heard a man scream.

Lohon?

Again Jetsam moved toward the balustrade, unable to resist the battle below. What he saw astounded him.

Although the attackers remained invisible, smoke and flames flickered from their transparent silhouettes. *Her flames exposed them!* One of the smoking forms lay crumpled on the stone, rendered legless by the dragon's tail.

Before the wyrm could strike again, a third stream of blue lightning shot from the invisible mage. The animated bolt stuck the beast square in the chest and coiled around her long neck, climbing like an electric snake to her furious green head. The dragon's shocked form fell back to the marble with a thunderclap.

The azure bolt danced long enough for Jetsam's keen eye to trace it to the root.

Of course—the amulet!

Jetsam spied the dragon's gaze follow the lightning to its source. *Enthran's given himself away.* Jetsam heard the wizard's voice utter an unintelligible phrase. *He's commanding the amulet.* Yet no charge came forth. *Is the talisman spent, or broken, or both?*

The crumpled dragon raised its proud head and spit a ball of fire at the lightning source. Wyrm spittle exploded in a blinding flash, crackling with heat. For a moment, all was still.

Jetsam could scarcely breathe.

When the smoke cleared, Jetsam saw the charred remains of Enthran Ashvar, burnt to a crisp, skin blackened not unlike the charred troll hide. The once-powerful amulet hung around his neck, melting into the cooked flesh. Jetsam spotted the knight and rogue materialize upon the wizard's death.

Lohon Threll *had* been the tail strike's victim. His body was rent in three by the vicious lashing. Leather armor cooked and split, his severed legs spilled onto the smooth marble. With stumps for thighs, Lohon's burned face contorted in agony.

"*Bloody,*" Jetsam mumbled.

Lohon intercepted Jetsam's sympathetic glance, and mouthed the word '*run.*'

I can't, Jetsam replied with his eyes.

With that, the archer gritted his bloody teeth, lifted his scorched bow, and nocked a steaming arrow.

Before Jetsam could scream '*no!*' the spiked tip of the dragon's wing punctured Lohon's breastplate, impaling the man before his final arrow took flight. With a shake that lifted Lohon from the floor, the dragon shed the corpse from its wing.

Sir Prentice Imoor now stood alone.

"For honor," he cried, charging with his sword held high. With a flick of its other wing, the wyrm knocked the knight to his knees, spinning him across the floor.

Jetsam waited for another blast of flame, but none came. *Has she none left?* Instead, her emerald head shot toward the felled knight, ivory teeth gleaming.

Sir Prentice raised his scorched shield in defense. The dragon struck with fury, impaling the shield on a lengthy fang. The knight, however, rolled from the bite unscathed. Rearing its angry head, the wyrm chewed the shield and spit the crumpled metal back at the resolute warrior.

Sir Prentice dodged the projectile, and raising his blade with both hands, charged again.

No longer able to fly or breathe fire, the dragon returned to its wings for defense. This time, the knight sidestepped the assault and bounced his blade off the tough hide. The hard scales resisted the sting of his fine sword.

Like a cobra, the dragon struck. With no shield, the sharp teeth tore into the knight's armor. As the lizard recoiled, the man's shiny left pauldron remained in the wyrm's maw.

Blood flowed from the knight's bare arm, his mail gusset under-sleeve shredded by the dragon's incisors. Jetsam was certain he saw the toothy beast grin. *She enjoys the challenge.* Watching in awe, Jetsam was unable to decide which side to root for. *None might leave this battle alive.* The shock of seeing Enthran and Lohon dead had yet to sink in.

Staggered and torn, Sir Prentice Imoor wavered, as if pondering retreat. Jetsam understood that was no option. *If the knight turns his back, he's surely dead.*

Regaining composure, the swordsman attacked. His good arm hoisted his blade as he advanced. Teeth bared, the dragon lunged at the charging warrior. Catching the knight in its pointy maw, the embattled wyrm lifted him by the torso.

The dragon tossed the knight into space. Sir Prentice spun into the air above the wyrm's head.

She's toying with him—like a cat with a mouse!

Before the knight started his descent, the dragon snatched him from the sky. In a flash, half of Sir Prentice disappeared into the toothy maw. Jetsam witnessed the knight's protruding legs kicking violently.

Then, with the warrior clenched in its jaws, the dragon lurched to the side and fell crashing to the floor. Sir Prentice slipped free and tumbled across the hard stone. His silvery cuirass was pierced with teeth marks.

Where's his blade? Glancing at the dragon, Jetsam found the knight's sword. With a final desperate thrust, the Calderian buried the blade hilt-deep in the dragon's maw. Just below the beast's jutting jaw bone, Jetsam spied steel poking through a gap between the ancient beast's scales.

Neither man nor beast moved. Jetsam watched the gruesome scene unblinking, his mouth agape. *They're both dead!*

Then, to his surprise, Jetsam spotted movement on the cavern floor.

Sir Prentice!

Slowly, the knight rose to his feet. Unsteadily, he staggered to the wyrm. Pausing over the breathless head, he bent down, and with his unbloodied hand, reached inside the open mouth to grasp his sword's hilt. With a valiant heave, he pulled the stained blade from the prone dragon's maw. The creature didn't twitch.

The champion lifted his sword again, ready to claim his proof of conquest. Jetsam's jaw dropped, shocked that the vile knight defeated the magnificent beast.

Jetsam couldn't stand to see the wyrm defiled, and as Sir Prentice readied to carve, Jetsam turned away. Averting his gaze, he heard an unmistakable baritone.

Baldy!

Chapter Twenty-Four

"Halt, Imoor," Yduk Thiern shouted. The commanding voice echoed in the huge chamber. From Jetsam's spying perch on the terrace, he could see Sir Prentice, but not the other. Sword in hand, the battered knight wheeled to face the bounty hunter. "There's a price on yer head and I'm here to claim it. Now drop yer blade!"

"How dare ye besmirch my moment of glory?" asked the bleeding Calderian, still standing by the fallen dragon. "This wyrm will be my retribution and prove my honor. To the likes of *thee* I'll not surrender," Sir Prentice shot back, his voice strained and wearied.

"*Yer honor* is what's besmirched, courtesy of defiling a Duke's daughter," the Southlander revealed. "An effort worthy of death for one of *the Order.* The bounty pays dead or alive. I'm only giving ye this chance because I'm not a cold-blooded killer."

"Then a fate worse than the dragon's ye'll suffer," the knight threatened, shaking his bloodied arming sword.

"Ye had yer chance, now prepare to meet Regret." The bald man in black leather gripped the legendary blade with both hands and marched across the hall.

Sir Prentice held his ground, brandishing his own sword, while blood ran down his arm and dripped from his exposed elbow. His helmeted head glanced right and left, surveying the cluttered battle field.

Jetsam slunk low, peering over the balcony edge just far enough to view the impending combat.

As Yduk closed, Sir Prentice backpedaled. The two men grew closer, Yduk measuring his opponent. The Calderian already weathered the blistering dragon fire, and bled from his wounds. Jetsam realized this couldn't bode well for the knight.

Selecting his footing, Sir Prentice took his stance. Regret sliced the air. Swords engaged and clash of exquisite steel echoed in the stone hall. Yduk cut while the knight parried. The swordplay began in earnest.

Jetsam stared intently, knowing another of his foes would soon fall.

Neither sword drew blood in the first onslaught. Jetsam studied the duelists. *Baldy's like a maestro waving a baton,* he thought. The knight moved like a seamstress, practiced and precise, offering feints and beats to assess his opponent. The leathered swordsman attacked and the plated knight used his ingrained techniques to ward off Regret's sting.

Jetsam saw the tracker maintained the upper hand. *If Sir Prentice was at full strength, the advantage may have been his.* As it was, Yduk toyed with the knight, feinting and cutting in tempo, draining his stamina as his very lifeblood ran into his gauntlet.

The Southlander scored the first hit, and the second, only nicking Sir Prentice, yet setting the tone. The assault forced the weakening knight into a more aggressive style. He attacked from counter, acknowledging his opponent was too skilled to leave himself open for an easy *coup de main.*

Gleaming blades clanged again and locked at the hilt. Both men crashed into each other, and for a moment, their faces were inches apart. With a grunt, the Calderian shoved the bounty hunter back, throwing him off balance for but a second.

The knight backpedaled to a stairway against the wall opposite Jetsam. He climbed three steps and turned to his attacker, postured low, ready to defend from higher ground. *Like Kandris said,* Jetsam recalled.

Again the manhunter engaged, but the knight's elevation bought him time. *Still, he'll bleed out before Baldy tires,* Jetsam suspected. Steel sang, and Yduk gained ground, pushing ever closer to the knight. Sir Prentice backpedaled, and now both men fought on the staircase.

This maneuvering would eventually lead them to the gallery and reveal Jetsam's position. Despite longing to see the finish, he inched backward toward the door. Whomever won, he did not want them to follow him. *Especially not the tracker.*

Jetsam crept off the balcony and down the charred hallway. He jogged through the corridor until the great hall's light faded. Upon reaching his first intersection, confusion overwhelmed him. *I can't recall the path I took from the locked portal.* The spellcaster had truly chosen his footsteps, and the entire journey seemed a bad dream.

Jetsam guessed and turned left. Soon, he reached a flight of stairs, and another intersection, and then another. In no time at all, he felt hopelessly lost. With no other choice, Jetsam pressed on. At the end of a long corridor, he came upon another stone door, closed and blocking his passage. *I don't want to backtrack.* Jetsam scrutinized the door. *Similar to the other.* With a tug of a lever, the massive stone rolled open.

Beyond lay the flickering dragon chamber. *I've come full circle!*

Jetsam froze like a troll in sunlight. His blue eyes peered into the grand hall. The dragon, wizard, and thief still lay motionless on the floor. High on the balcony, the ebony-clad tracker darted through the same portal Jetsam passed under minutes ago.

Luckily, he didn't spot me.

Jetsam crept through the doorway to glimpse a view of the staircase. Halfway up, the body of Sir Prentice Imoor slumped on the narrow stairs, an arm dangling through the stone balusters. Blood puddled on the steps and dripped from his fingertips to the cold floor.

Then Jetsam heard a voice that stopped his heart.

It was the dragon.

"Little gnome? Is that you?" The prodigious nostrils twitched, but the voice sounded a shadow of its former commanding self. Jetsam's tongue stayed still.

"I can smell you, tiny elf. Be not afraid, I shan't—nor cannot—hurt you now. Step into my vision."

With a flood of compassion, Jetsam minced toward the dragon. The fallen wyrm was immense. Mouth wide, Jetsam tiptoed close enough to touch the shiny green scales, but dared not. He paused before the prone head. Its emerald eyes were the size of melons, but they moved not. Rather, the dragon's gaze pointed straight ahead, and Jetsam stepped into it.

"They're all dead now," Jetsam whispered, "save one, but he hunts me, not you."

"All men hunt dragons, 'tis but a matter of time and opportunity."

"Are you hurt badly?"

"I was careless with your hunters, and I paid the price."

"They had a magic amulet," Jetsam replied.

"Hush," the dragon said softly, "I'm gravely wounded. Leave me to die in peace."

"You cannot die! There must be some way I can help."

"Do you know healing incantations?"

"No, I'm afraid not. The wizard taught me but one spell."

"Then I am doomed, as I deserve."

"What of the fugitive wizard from Dwim-Halloe? They say he dwells in these parts. Do you know of him?"

"The fugitive?" A glimmer flickered in the wyrm's cloudy orb. "Ah, the hermit, perchance. Indeed that one *could* help. As he did aid me once before." The wyrm paused to suck in a breath of cavern air. Jetsam listened to the pain in the creature's effort. "But I have not seen that one in a long time."

"He is who I search for," Jetsam confessed. "If you help me find him, I will beseech him to aid you."

The massive beast closed its lids and murmured. Jetsam waited until the wyrm lifted its heavy lids but a crack.

"I do recall his lair laying several leagues from here, but I only spied it from high above."

"Where is it?"

"Where indeed? By nature, a hermit is reclusive. Let me think a moment. Pain clouds my memory."

The mountains are vast, Jetsam lamented. *How will I find this man, if even the great wyrm knows not where he lives?*

"I will show you. Lay your hands upon my brow."

Jetsam glanced at his dirty palms before placing them on the dragon's trembling scales. *She's warm!*

"Close your eyes and clear your mind," the wyrm instructed.

Jetsam shuddered as he felt a familiar magic pulse emanate from the dragon. *She did break the wizard's possession!* The surge planted a vision in his mind's eye.

The foothills, Jetsam realized. *A creek bed, sitting in the shadows of a two-pointed peak. And a cave—I see it! But where?*

"To the west," the dragon revealed. "Sadly, more than that, I cannot recall."

"West it is," Jetsam replied, his voice tinged with uncertainty.

"Find him and bring him here with most haste. Time is of the essence!"

Jetsam appraised the hole in the cupola roof. *Don't think I can climb out through that.* His gaze fell to the dragon.

"How do I find my way out of these tunnels?"

Jetsam nodded and listened as the wyrm proceeded to direct him from the maze-like corridors. *Pray I can remember all that.*

"The mountains are dangerous," warned the dragon. "You have a blade, but no armor. Behind me are chests of Dwarven mail. Find a hauberk and wear it well. You mustn't fail!" With that, the dragon's voice fell silent and its emerald eyes closed.

Jetsam did as told. The oaken chests were charred and covered with soot, still smoldering from the lightning and dragon fire. But their contents were well-preserved, filled with jewelry and gems, axes and swords, armor and helms.

He sorted through the rare mail. Even the smallest armor was large enough for his narrow frame. He donned a shirt of glistening ringed mail, then tugged his coat over the hauberk to disguise his advantage. *Much lighter than it appears.* He swaggered in the sturdy armor.

With the dragon's memory etched in his mind, Jetsam left the great hall posthaste.

The fallen knight had given Yduk Thiern more of a fight than he expected. *Never underestimate a man who's killed a dragon. Even if he's nearly dead himself.* But eventually the knight wearied and slipped on the stairs. When he faltered, Yduk lunged beneath his wearied parry. Regret then finally found its mark, piercing the knight's fatigued cuirass and releasing the Calderian from his earthly shackles.

Yduk took the knight's engraved arming sword as proof for his bounty, and then sauntered up the stairs. *Now the waif.* As Yduk surveyed the balcony and room below, he spied the charred remains of the troll carcass. He jogged across the stone terrace to where the burned hide lay.

So that's what they gave the boy! A vile stink to cover his scent! Yduk raced from the gallery down the corridor. *That poor bastard.*

A faint voice from the great hall below stopped him in his tracks.

It cannot be! Yduk turned and slunk back to the balcony. Hunched on all fours, he peered over the edge. He could hardly believe his eyes.

The dragon lives!

And none other than the boy trembled before him. *That bloody indestructible urchin. Looks like he's made another friend.* Yduk strained to hear the wyrm's hoarse words as they echoed through the great hall, floating on the smoky air. Upon hearing of the hermit, he nearly laughed aloud. His greasy black mustache stretched atop an ear-to-ear grin.

Well, I'll be damned; the rumors of Seryn Vardan consorting with a dragon were true!

The wyrm's voice weakened and Yduk could only make out the occasional word.

He watched the youngster leave the room, then leapt to his feet and sped to the stairs. Down the narrow descent and over his crumpled foe, the bounty hunter reached the floor. The dragon didn't stir. Yduk hesitated a moment, as if considering finishing the beast himself. Shaking his head, he circled the wyrm, avoiding its gaze. He passed through the stone portal and continued after the boy.

"A dragon that can speak is still a dangerous foe," he mumbled to reassure himself. *Besides, I can't risk losing the knave* and *Seryn Vardan. The dragon will die without the sorcerer's help anyway. And I can claim its bounty when it's dead.*

Chapter Twenty-Five

Jetsam tiptoed through the corridors of Asigonn. The sulfuric smell of dragon breath bit at his watering eyes. His lantern was lit high enough to see a fathom in front of him. *Baldy's somewhere ahead. Don't want to give myself away, or worse yet, run up the back of him.*

Jetsam paid close attention to the dragon's directions. As wondrous and extraordinary as these legendary halls were, Jetsam had no desire to get lost again. But more pressing, he was certain that finally he would meet the infamous wizard Seryn Vardan. *Then I'll show him the scroll and learn about my parents.* Wild fantasies ran through Jetsam's head while navigating the smoky passages.

After several turns and stairways, he reached the stone door where he let his captors in only hours ago. From the familiar portal, Jetsam navigated the gnarled troll tunnels and within the hour breathed fresh air.

Immediately, he met with despair.

"They're gone!" Jetsam gasped, seeing no sign of the horses or Kandris Bayen. With the mounts went Jetsam's pack and possessions. *Fobbing coward ran off again!*

After fuming for a moment, he admitted he would have done the same had his comrades all been slain. Nevertheless, Jetsam wondered how Kandris knew, for he expected the squire to wait at least twice as long before giving up. *Cowardice is the patient man's enemy.*

As the sun rode a bed of ivory clouds, Jetsam resigned himself to traveling on foot. He hurried across the mountainside until well past sundown. Nightfall slowed his pace and fatigue begged him to indulge in a quick nap. *Keep going,* he urged himself. *The wyrm is dying.*

Jetsam covered two leagues of rugged terrain before dawn crept in, coloring the jutting peaks as he journeyed westward. He hung along the timberline where the footing was kinder. The long shadows provided him cover throughout the day.

Soon he spotted the landmark from the dragon's implanted vision—a double-edged peak jutting like a knife with a broken tip. "Dwim-Dwaeroch, the dragon called it." His heart danced with anticipation and his feet moved faster. Beyond the peak, the wyrm's image painted a slope to the north, downhill into the pines. *From there, I'm on my own.*

Jetsam's long legs covered the last league of mountain terrain nimbly. As the daystar moved toward the high ridge, Jetsam found himself north of Dwim-Dwaeroch. With a deep breath, he scrambled down the rocky slope into the black forest's waiting arms.

Now I need to find the creek bed. He hunted for the stream the better part of an hour, to no avail. Gazing through the towering conifers, he saw the blue sky darkening. Soon the forest would be pitch black. *I'll never find it in the dark.*

His heart pounding, Jetsam heard the blood rush behind his ear drums. *And something else?* He swung around to the direction of the sound. *Was that a yelp? Sounded like a dog.* Jetsam tried to temper his enthusiasm, but he couldn't help but think of Tramp. His ears pricked at a growl and he crept toward the noise.

"Tramp?" he whispered, and listened intently. But the sound vanished.

Visions of his trusty sidekick in his head, Jetsam listened for another minute, but heard no more. Finally, he shook off the noise. His concern settled on the task at hand. *Find the wizard's cave, before it's too late.*

Jetsam took three steps and he heard the noise again. *Claws clicking on rock.*

"Tramp?"

Jetsam jogged toward the sound and the breeze tickled his nose. *Smells like dog.* Crouching beneath low branches, Jetsam spotted movement from the corner of his eye. *Or did I?* The thick forest shadows surrounded him and played tricks on his vision. *Am I imagining things?*

"Tramp?"

Beneath his feet, the ground sloped downward. As he descended the gully through the grabbing underbrush, he heard trickling water. *The creek bed?* His heart skipped a beat as he moved faster. The forest floor fell away and soon he stood in water. Following his instinct, Jetsam moved along the rocky bank.

I know I saw something that time.

Jetsam moved a pine branch with his hand to clear his line of sight and peered toward the sound.

That's not a dog!

Jetsam spied the back of a small hunched creature, standing on two legs and prying a boulder with a spear. *What the sodding gods is that?*

Before he could stand up, something jabbed him from behind. Jetsam wheeled about as a wooden switch stung his shoulder.

Two beady red eyes stared at him and the sharp stick jabbed into his ribs. His Dwarven mail laughed it off, and he grasped his sword.

Blade in hand, Jetsam focused on a second creature, growling and snorting at him, waving its staff-spear at his head. Before he could focus on his attacker, the sharp wood bit into his thigh. *Pus!* This time it drew blood.

In the shadows, he glimpsed the rod coming again. Both hands on the hilt, he swung his blade around and split the spear in two. The foul-breathed creature shrieked in surprise.

Too small for trolls.

The other pointy-eared beast lunged at Jetsam from behind. His spear struck Jetsam square in the back. The resilient chain armor resisted the blow, but the impact knocked him off balance and he fell forward into a pine trunk.

With a shattered weapon, the first attacker charged at Jetsam, claws bared and aiming for his eyes. In a purely defensive move, Jetsam swung the short sword in front of him. The leaping skulker impaled itself upon the blade, the thin steel poking through its armpit and out the back of its shoulder.

The squirming creature pulled the sword to the ground. Before Jetsam could extract the weapon from the assailant, the other red-eye gouged him in the leg again. This time the wooden spike went deeper, and Jetsam yelped at the stabbing pain.

Fobbing dog-men!

Jetsam yanked his bloody sword from the crumpled creature. He swiveled to face the other attacker. Whimpering like a whipped cur, the injured foe scampered away.

Into the fray stepped the second mongrel.

Wood met steel as Jetsam parried the first thrust.

Only good thing I learned from Kandris.

His opponent displayed none of the technique the squire had taught Jetsam. White-knuckled hands gripping his blade, Jetsam deflected the creature's second awkward lunge.

A lot harder than practice, Jetsam lamented, sweat breaking on his brow. *Or stick-fighting with orphan boys.*

Grunting feverishly, the attacker drove hard and Jetsam's blade missed the spear. For the third time, the weapon hit the Dwarven mail. With the creature's full force behind it, the spear snapped in two, as Jetsam bounced back into the tree.

Sodding devil!

Before the assailant could recoil, Jetsam buried his blade in the back of its neck. *For Elvar!* The skulker fell face-first on the stony ground. Without remorse, Jetsam dispatched the hairless creature with a second cleave.

The other attacker was nowhere in sight.

And don't come back!

Jetsam's heart raced and the reality of his kill registered. Death was no stranger to him. He'd hunted wild game, witnessed dying men and boys, held his dead brother, and pulled the sword from the expiring sentry, but this felt different. *They were almost human-like.* He felt proud and powerful, and yet felt like crying, all at the same time.

Pull yourself together—it's just lack of sleep. Jetsam inhaled deeply and trembled. *It was me or them.*

He slumped to the ground, staring at the dead creature as it bled out. *It does smell like wet dog. Ratboy told stories of all sorts of creatures,* Jetsam recalled. *Baby trolls?* He shook his head. *Nothing like knuckle-draggers.* Recalling ghost stories by the campfire, he pondered another creature from Ratboy's lore. *Were they goblins, I wonder?*

Swallowing hard, Jetsam regained his feet. *No time to sit around.* He scanned the area for the other creature, but the forest stayed silent. *Wonder what it was clawing at?* Jetsam approached the spot where he spied the first creature. *Food?* Overhung by a sagging awning of roots and moss, sat a solid boulder wedged against the creek bank. Shrouded in shadows, the rock was barely perceptible. *Could this be it? Sure looked like that little bugger was trying to get inside.*

Apprehension overcame Jetsam and his mouth felt numb. *Should I knock, or shout? I don't want to barge in unannounced, especially on a sorcerer who has reason to fear the uninvited guest.* Pondering his next action, he paused; all the while hoping the wizard would somehow sense his presence and beckon him in. *Maybe it's not a cave at all.*

Jetsam leaned close to the rock, looking for seeps of light from the cave beyond. *No cracks at all.* He placed his ear to the stone, hoping to hear movement within. Silence reigned.

Now Jetsam feared this wasn't the cave at all, or that the mage wasn't here, or had even moved on. An anxious panic set upon him. He spat out a glob of saliva.

"Hello," he said, barely above a whisper. Nervously, he cleared his throat and tried again, louder. "M'lord?"

No reply.

With the hilt of his sword, he knocked on the stone. *This racket couldn't be ignored,* he thought. Yet, no response came.

Jetsam had no other choice. With a fervent effort, he tried to roll the formidable boulder. He strained and pushed and pulled, grunting and grimacing all the while. The stone resisted his every attempt. Panting and sweating, he stepped back from the recalcitrant obstruction.

That creature was trying to move this boulder for a reason.

He took a breath and assessed his situation. *Got to get inside.* Examining the boulder, he ran his narrow fingers around the edges. They discovered a small gap. With his bare hands he dug and pried at the hole, able to squeeze four fingers inside the fissure. He found no pressure plates or triggers. *This is a plain rock.*

In desperation, Jetsam jabbed his sword blade at the hole. *Won't fit.* He bent down and picked up the long half of a broken staff-spear.

Effortlessly, the narrow shaft slid into the cavity. Jetsam pulled back on the staff, but nothing happened. Then he pushed the lever upward, and the stone inched forward.

Jetsam nearly burst with joy.

Using what was left of his tapped strength, Jetsam pushed the lever until the stone moved enough to reveal an opening. *A hole, black as night.* Leaning in, he heard no sound at all.

"Please, m'lord, forgive the intrusion. I come with a plea from the emerald wyrm!"

No one replied from the darkness or stirred within. *The cavern's empty.* Jetsam's hopes fell.

Hands trembling, he lit his lantern and peered into the cave. A few paces past the entrance, a narrow passage sloped upward. An unlit torch set in a stand against the wall. Wishing to conserve his lamp oil, he grabbed the brand and ignited it. Not wanting any more surprises, he let the boulder roll in to close the opening. *I pray I'm not sealing my doom.*

Much like the troll caverns, the passage looked rough and natural, and very different from the smooth carving of the Dwarven walls. The air was musty and humid, and the sound of dripping water echoed beyond. Straight ahead, the narrow tunnel rose.

Jetsam trudged up the slope and saw a sprawling cavern beyond. High above, glistening stalactites hung from the domed cavern. Flat-topped stalagmites reached up from below. A few lengthy formations touched in the middle, creating thin-centered columns. Toward the back, a trickling stream ran along a wall of irregular crystal.

But man's touch was evident in this natural void. The furnishings seemed plain and crude for a sorcerer. *But not for a fugitive,* rationalized Jetsam. A mossy bed rested in an alcove, with a bear-skin blanket sprawled across it. Jetsam remembered the black bear he saw in the Sylallian, and gained an instant respect for any man who could fell such a mighty animal. *If he can kill a king, I wager he can kill a bear.*

More furs hung from a crudely-fashioned rack. In the room's center sat a small fire pit, with cooking utensils stacked nearby. Against one wall leaned a cord of wood and an axe, while a hanger of dried herbs, roots, and plants hung on another wall. A rough-hewn table and stool had been fashioned from stumps. Several fat, stubby candles stood unlit about the room. A few stone jugs held creek water and dried nuts and berries.

But what the cavern did not hold was what concerned Jetsam the most. *The mage is not here.*

Tired and hungry, Jetsam resigned himself to wait. With much trepidation, he took some clean cloth to bandage his wounds. The crude spears left him with a pair of nasty punctures.

He lit a modest fire in the pit and swiped a handful of nuts from the stone jug. Plopping down on the plush bearskin, he tried to stay awake. *Those nuts aren't sitting well.* Despite his anticipation of the mage's return and the throbbing in his leg, he soon fell asleep.

When he awoke, the fire contained only embers. *Bloody pus-boil!* Sweat drenched his clothes as they stuck to his thin frame. As he climbed from the bed and rose to his feet, his legs wobbled. *These ugly wounds sure ache.*

Jetsam threw kindling on the coals to illuminate the cave. The sorcerer had not returned, and Jetsam had no idea how long he slept.

Jetsam rushed to the sealed door and in his haste, dizziness assailed him. *I don't feel so good.* He held a clammy hand to his forehead. *I'm feverish.* He glanced at his leg wounds again. *Filthy goblins.*

Utilizing his makeshift lever, he rolled the boulder out. Exiting the cave, Jetsam fell to his knees and vomited. Sunlight trickled to the gully floor. *Slept longer than I should have.* Dawn was an hour past, and vultures picked at the goblin carcass. The sight made him wretch again. *Time's running out. I can't afford to be sick.*

Jetsam was now confounded. *The dragon needs aid posthaste, and I can't wait forever for the mage to return.* With much regret, Jetsam scoured the cave and rummaged through the belongings, looking for salves or bandages for the wyrm. *Hope there aren't any traps or wards.* If the sorcerer couldn't heal the magnificent beast, Jetsam would have to do it himself. *How I wish I could have learned the healing spell from Enthran.*

Jetsam discovered parchment and quills, along with crushed-berry pigment. A pair of boots, a robe, and other clothes were folded in a small chest. Several knives, two swords, a long bow, and a suit of leather armor were stored behind the furs. *The inhabitant of this cave must have contact with the outside world,* he thought. *Wonder if these goods are the spoils of unlucky bounty hunters?*

Still searching, he uncovered several crude jars filled with pungent pastes and jellies. *Maybe one's a healing salve.* Thinking of the two wounds on his thigh, he decided to experiment. *Too bad they're not labeled,* Jetsam thought. *Not that I could read them anyway.* Jetsam opened a jar and the rank odor assailed him. Before he could cap the container, his empty stomach convulsed in dry heaves. *That was a bad idea.*

After suffering through the abdominal cramps, Jetsam timidly sniffed more jars, without opening them, this time. *That one smells like rotten potatoes. We'll leave it alone.*

The next jar he grabbed exhibited an astringent odor. *Like the balm Enthran used on the squire.* And like Enthran's stones, he detected a faint aura of magic radiating from the vessel.

Jetsam dropped his dirty breeches and dabbed a bit of the ointment on the gash. Grimacing in pain, he pulled his coated finger away as the application stung his open flesh. *Mistake for sure!*

But as he was about to swear off his test, a soothing relief pulsed through the wound.

Agape, he gawked at his red puncture. *It's healing!* He smeared more ointment on both lacerations, and withstood the stinging. *Feels better already.* Biting his lip, he examined his ugly leg. *Now I know what to take for the wyrm!*

Jetsam found three more jars of the healing ointment. He stuffed them all into his pouch, and then took the robe to use for bandaging. He refilled his flask and dropped two handfuls of dried nuts and berries into his pocket. With the long journey ahead, he couldn't ignore his hunger. *If I could only keep it down.*

With quill and ink, he scribbled a crude drawing of a bleeding dragon on the parchment, hoping the wizard could guess the rest. *Looks like a fobbing shingled vulture.* Jetsam regretted being unable to read and write. With much resignation, he left the cave with the "borrowed" items. It would prove a tiring day to reach the dragon before nightfall. *And now I've got the chills.*

As Jetsam retraced his path along the mountainside, the sun bled a diluted light through a thin veneer of gray clouds. *Feel worse with every step.* The somber atmosphere further depressed him. His failure to find the mage dismayed him, and he feared he would fail at saving the dragon as well.

Chapter Twenty-Six

Stinking mongrel ran right past me, Yduk Thiern observed. *Guess I'll follow him.* Since the first two goblins failed to finish off the lad, Yduk decided a pack of vengeful eye-biters would only be a distraction. *Last thing I want is some hungry dog-men interrupting my vigil.*

Yduk tracked the fleeing goblin Jetsam had maimed back to its hovel, where he found the rest of the pack. *Three more little buggers.* Yduk spied their snouts twitching. *And now they've smelled me.*

Yduk finished the injured goblin with a crossbow shot before the others spotted him. He unsheathed Regret as the trio charged him. *Watch out for the spears,* he reminded himself. *They coat 'em with wolfsbane.* Yduk dodged and parried the first flurry of attacks, then struck down another dog-man. *Two to go.* Stepping over the corpse, Yduk approached the wavering attackers. *Get 'em before they run.* A precise thrust mortally wounded the third creature and Yduk finished the final goblin with a slash to the back as it turned and ran.

No more interruptions.

Being this close to Seryn Vardan, Yduk now cared little about the boy. *His reward's but a trifle compared to the king's assassin.* Still, losing the waif to the skulkers would have left a sour taste in his mouth. *I hate losing.*

Like Jetsam, Yduk was equally dismayed at the absence of Seryn Vardan. Yduk was certain, like the boy, that the cave belonged to the fugitive. *Now I just have to find him.* He spent the entire night outside the cavern with no sign of the unnatural. Now the sun was up and his patience wore thin.

Quiet as a shadow, Yduk watched the adolescent hop over the dead goblin and start on his way. Yduk waited until the youngster treaded far down the dry gully, then he entered the unnatural's cave himself. A silent darkness enshrouded the cavity.

"I'm sure it's empty," he mumbled, "but I'm not falling for any tricks." He lit a torch and looked around. Empty it was, and now the manhunter had a decision to make. *Follow the knave or sit here and wait?* He sat on a carved stump inside the cave. Yduk noticed the furs. He strolled to the rack and poked around.

How about that? he mused, pushing the pelts aside to reveal the armor and weapons. "Not the trappings of an unnatural," he muttered. "Must *not* be the first bounty hunter to get this far."

Yduk saw the parchment on the table and Jetsam's drawing. *So he's going back to the fire-spitter, eh? That seals it.* Yduk took a piece of the parchment and sketched out a map. He would not leave the location of this hideout to memory alone. Satisfied with his drawing, he curled it up and stuck it in his pouch.

"Ye stay here," he told Jetsam's dragon sketch, "and send that unnatural right back to me!" With that, he was off. But not before grabbing a handful of the dried nuts.

Yduk sealed the cave, leaving no trace, and picked up the urchin's trail.

Time to kill two birds with one stone. Or maybe three, he hoped, thinking of the dragon.

Jetsam backtracked along the Kierawaith's foothills. His wounded thigh ached and burned, but he dared not use more salve on himself. *The dragon will need every drop. Even then, this might not be enough.* His empty stomach churned while his head pounded. *Food and sleep will cure that, once the dragon is safe.*

The ashen sky concealed the sun as it struggled west into the sharp wind. Jetsam headed east, the yellow orb at his back, separated by a thick layer of clouds. Visions of vengeful goblins occupied his mind.

Darkness raced him to the troll cave, and he won by a hair. The gray heavens changed to starless black as Jetsam entered the tunnels leading to the dragon. A few steps onto the smooth dust-covered stone floor, he heard a strange noise. Far down the wide corridor, he hearkened the clicking of nails on marble. Recalling goblin claws scratching on the creek bed, he drew his sword and doused his lantern.

Hope there's only one.

Jetsam backtracked, hoping to avoid confrontation. *I'm so weak and tired, this sword feels heavy as a maul.* Despite Jetsam's retreat, the sounds grew closer. *Sounds like two of them. Wonder if they caught my scent?* He stepped into a narrow corridor. Without light, he fumbled in blackness and slowed to a crawl.

And yet they follow.

Jetsam wiped his clammy forehead with his forearm and walked face-first into a dead end.

Sodding gods.

He turned to face his pursuers.

Guess I make a stand. The grip of his sword felt slippery in his hand. He placed the lantern down and grasped the blade with both shaky hands. Lightness bled from around the corner and then the full glare blinded him. *Here they come.* Squinting at the brightness, Jetsam swung his sword.

He cut nothing but air.

Dizzy and off-balance, Jetsam's lead foot slipped and he lunged forward. A vision of the impaled castle guard flashed through his mind as he tossed the blade aside a moment before crashing to the floor.

As the blade clanged away, Jetsam sprawled face-first on the cold stone. *So tired.*

Before he could lift himself from the unforgiving rock, claws scratched his cheek.

Small claws?

And a warm wet tongue.

"Tramp?"

The gypsy's lantern revealed the terrier, pawing and licking Jetsam's face.

"Oh, Tramp, I can't believe it's you!" Jetsam bubbled, rubbing the dog's short-haired head.

Looking healthy as ever, tail wagging and tongue flapping, the terrier pranced over and around Jetsam. "I missed you, buddy boy!" Jetsam sat up and hugged the dog. Tramp licked at Jetsam's face.

"I cursed the dog when it tore off, but he seems a smarter creature than me," replied Nicu.

"What are *you* doing *here?*" asked Jetsam.

"I found a strange note on my table. It almost looked like a wounded dragon."

"Indeed it was!" Jetsam gasped. *Yet you are not the wizard.* Despite his joyful reunion, painful exhaustion assailed him. He tried to continue, but lightheaded and heart racing, he couldn't form the words. His vision blurred and he slumped on his side.

"Lad?"

"The dragon needs help," Jetsam whispered, his hand grasping for his borrowed salves. Before his clammy hand found his pouch, Jetsam blacked out.

When he awoke, Jetsam found himself wrapped in a musty Dwarven blanket, reclining in the dragon's grand hall. Tramp sat by his side. *I feel much better.* Then he heard the familiar chant of an Elven incantation. Sitting up, he spotted a man standing near the injured wyrm.

Who's that? Jetsam scrutinized the spellcaster. Tall and lean with a brown pony-tail, the bearded man looked near thirty. *And where's Nicu?*

While the mage finished his spell, Jetsam watched the wyrm. *The dragon looks dead.*

His spell completed, the wizard turned toward Jetsam. "Ah, you're awake! How do you feel?"

"Better, I think. But what of the dragon? Is she dead?"

"I think not, though she needs rest. I pray my healing spells will aid her recovery."

"Then you," Jetsam stuttered, "*you* are the wizard from the grotto?"

"I am he. The one whose belongings you helped yourself to."

Dismay swept over Jetsam. "M'lord, I'm so sorry. I thought only of the dragon."

"Easy, lad, I'm only jesting. I know you had good intentions."

A hundred questions raced through Jetsam's head, but before he could utter one, the man continued.

"I'm spent. We shall all rest here for a while." The man took a seat next to Jetsam, who entertained many questions—and much trepidation. But his boyish curiosity beat back the fear.

"Are you the fugitive who killed King Tygan?"

The man glared at Jetsam with steely eyes. "'Tis true I'm the fugitive, but I didn't murder the king," he responded somberly.

Jetsam wanted to believe the man, but he held a sliver of suspicion. *Yet I understand how easy it is to be falsely accused.* He wondered if the mage *was* truly evil, and the dragon as well. *After all, he's a wanted assassin, and the wyrm slaughtered a clan of Dwarves.* Good and evil blurred. Jetsam could find little virtue in the bounty hunter or the unfortunate dragon hunters. *Yet both acted under the guise of righteousness.*

"Begging your pardon, m'lord, but where's the gypsy?"

"As you can imagine," Seryn Vardan professed, "it's in my best interest to appear much different from what I am."

Jetsam scratched his chin. *My brain's still foggy.* Yet the man's implication was clear.

"So *you* were Nicu?" The mage nodded. "Amazing," mumbled Jetsam. *Truly, he is a powerful wizard.* "If I may be so bold, m'lord, another question?"

"Go ahead, lad. But understand you need rest. Your wounds fester and look poisoned."

Jetsam's hand shot to his thigh. *Poisoned?* The punctures still throbbed; painfully tender and sensitive to the touch.

"What happened to you, lad?"

Jetsam recounted his tale, from the dragon hunters and their ill-fated attack to his battle outside the wizard's cave.

“Those were goblins,” Seryn explained. “They oft poison their spears with wolfsbane.”

“Will I die?”

“I think you’re out of the woods,” Seryn replied. “I cast a spell on you as well, and the poison’s effect appears to wane. You’re a strong lad.”

“Thank you m’lord. I do feel better.”

“We’ll stay here tonight and travel by first light. The dragon and I are on good terms, but she isn’t one to endure guests. And your departed companions may have routed the trolls for now, but there are more about. An empty cave is a rare thing in these hills, and won’t stay as such for long. But you had a query for me?”

“Before I ask, I must thank you, m’lord, for taking care of my dog.” Tramp barked once, as if in agreement.

“The dark one’s boot did much damage to your companion. Try as he might, he was in no shape to chase after you. My healing touch worked quite well on him however.” Seryn patted the dog’s head. “I shall miss his companionship.” A look of genuine affection crossed the man’s visage. While the reverse aging unveiled ruggedly handsome features, his bearded face still brimmed with the maturity that comes with a lifetime of experience. “On with your question. Then we must rest.”

“You speak as if you know the dragon. Do you truly?”

“There’s no way to answer without being long winded,” the sorcerer sighed. “But I shall tell you, so you may think better of her, and maybe grow weary of my voice, and find slumber soon.” Seryn folded his slender hands in his lap. His long polished staff rested by his side.

“I met Drahkang-roth when I was fleeing from false accusations. One night, I saw the most marvelous spectacle on the horizon. Never had I seen the sky so full of color and rage. I moved toward the light, longing to find the source of this barrage. Soon I made out the forms of two wyrms engaged in an aerial battle.”

Jetsam’s lithe hand rubbed Tramp behind the ears. The furry terrier rolled on his back, four paws in the air. The pacified canine paid no heed to the wizard’s story telling.

"It seemed impossible that these mighty warriors would notice me. And, truly, they did not. The smaller beast was deep emerald. The other was ebony, only visible against the night sky when flashes reflected off its scale.

"I then suspected where I was and what I witnessed. Legend told of a black dragon that ousted the Dwarven clan of *Guran Gwehaar*. Asigonn's location was lost to legend, but rumored to have been in the Kierawaith. The black lizard I observed could be no other than *Aht-ir Aht-ir*. The emerald wyrm, however, was a mystery."

Jetsam listened intently, while his hand tired of petting Tramp. No matter, the dog snored by his side. *Probably dreaming of chasing coneys.*

"Before the time of man, and even Dwarves and Elves, dragons ruled the earth. But like every other race, conflict arose within them. Wars came and the beasts fought amongst themselves. Eventually, attrition took its toll and their numbers decreased.

"Elves appeared in the world, garnering little notice from the wyrms. Soon came Dwarves, and finally, man. When the first wyrm fell by the hand of man, the dragons finally took notice of the two-legged races. Their coexistence has been acrimonious ever since." The wizard leaned back to stretch, taking a deep breath. Jetsam sat on edge, soaking up every word. Tramp twitched, his legs jerking in dreamy pursuit.

"At first, the two wyrms appeared evenly matched, but soon I saw the ebony wyrm held the advantage. That's when I made the decision that changed my life. For reasons I never quite understood, I entered the fray on behalf of the emerald wyrm. It may have been a death wish, but I perceived that if I could turn the tide, I'd have the emerald wyrm's gratitude. And believe me, the number of men who have *ever* been in the good grace of a dragon are far less than the days in a week.

"So I cast my spell, catching the black lizard off guard. Although I felt the heat of its breath that night, I kept casting and the emerald dragon kept attacking. Finally, the ebony wyrm crashed to the earth, never to rise again."

Jetsam gasped, slack-jawed as the wizard paused to retrieve his pipe. Jetsam waited as the mage fiddled with the item. Finally, Seryn inhaled a deep breath, then blew out an aromatic wisp. Tramp opened his eyes, his short nap over.

"Drahkang-roth was gravely wounded. We sought refuge in the great hall where the ebony dragon had lived. I tended our wounds and healed the majestic beast. And she told me of her lineage and of the history of dragons that I have repeated for you tonight."

"But why were they fighting?" Jetsam asked.

"Drahkang-roth once lived inside the mountain the Dwarves eventually claimed as home. Because dragons live so long, they have lairs all over the world and spend years traveling amongst them. In Drahkang-roth's absence, the Dwarves found this vast cavern, then sealed the gap where she flew in, and built a city around it. Years later, Aht-ir Aht-ir discovered this wonderful cavity filled with the tiny folk, and decided to claim it for himself.

"The smallfolk put up a valiant struggle, but were vanquished in the end. Guran Gwehaar fell, and the clan's spirit died with him. The survivors fled Asigonn in disarray."

A wet tongue on his wrist distracted Jetsam. He scratched the dog's belly and focused on the sorcerer's tale. Tramp released an appreciative snort.

"Years later, when Drahkang-roth returned, not only had her cavern endured a renovation courtesy of the Dwarves, but it now housed an ancient black dragon. Aht-ir Aht-ir had no intention of relinquishing his lair, and came at Drahkang-roth with a fury. Only minutes later did I stumble across their fiery path.

"Once Drahkang-roth healed, I took my leave. Although we reached a cautious peace, no wyrm could ever share a lair with a human. And someday men would come hunting her, just as they would come for me. We kept an eye on each other, for it was in our mutual interest to keep our lairs secret from the rest of the world."

Taking another deep puff from his long pipe, Seryn gazed upon Jetsam, curled up fast asleep with his dog beside him.

Chapter Twenty-Seven

Wondrous as it was, Seryn's story lulled Jetsam to sleep. With slumber, however, came dreams, or rather this evening, nightmares. Tossing and turning, he suffered an onslaught of frightening memories. He enjoyed no pleasant dreams of Giselle or his orphan brothers this night. In the space of the short rest, Jetsam relived his parents' death and his brother's. Trolls, guards, ogres, and goblins chased him relentlessly. Sir Prentice and his cronies lived and breathed again, tormenting him even worse than in life. And the daunting bounty hunter materialized as well, forever on his trail, drawing ever closer. The gleaming silver sword sliced toward him.

Jetsam awoke with a gasp, covered in sweat. Seryn Vardan gently shook his shoulder.

"No wonder your dreams trouble you so, with the tales I told," the mage said. "I fear I have dire news."

"The dragon?"

"Afraid so."

"She's dead?"

"No, but neither has she recovered. Her injuries were greater than I feared and she slips closer to death."

"I have salves from your cave, still in my pack."

"If they'd work, I would've used them, but they're not cures for a dragon."

"Then there's nothing you can do?"

"I'm afraid I've done all I can, and it was not quite enough." The mage let the words hang.

"Then she will die?" Jetsam waited for a response as the man deliberated, grinding his teeth.

"There's one more chance, slim though it is," Seryn revealed. "But it involves risk on your part."

"What must I do?"

"You responded well to my healing spell, and I sensed a strong magic presence within you."

"Tell me what to do, and I shall."

"If I can tap into your magic, combined with mine, it may be enough to pull the dragon from the brink."

"Then do it, with my blessing."

"Lad, this is a dangerous spell. Once I open the conduit, magic will siphon to the dragon, only stopping when she's healed."

"What does that mean?"

"It means you risk your life in allowing me to do this."

"I would've died from the poison if not for you, wouldn't I?"

"It is possible, yes, but you owe me nothing for the favor."

Jetsam swallowed hard and bit his lip. His lithe fingers roamed absentmindedly through Tramp's warm fur. "Could this kill you as well?"

"It is possible, though you'd be at greater risk, as I'd be using you as a reservoir."

"I'd die first."

"I'm afraid so."

"The dragon freed me from Enthran's mind spell. I'd have likely died if not for that."

"'Tis a dangerous thing I suggest. I shall not risk one life for another."

"I'm not afraid of death. Everyone I love is on the other side." Jetsam watched the man waver. The wizard's face betrayed conflicted emotions. *What say you, Elvar? Is it time for me to join you?* Jetsam hoped for an answer from the voice, yet none came.

"You truly understand the risk? I shall do my best to protect you, but that may not be enough."

"I'll do it if you promise me one thing."

"Whatever you ask."

"If I die, promise that you'll not sacrifice yourself, and that you'll take care of Tramp."

A sound burst from the wizard that sounded like the half-breed of a chuckle and a sob.

"Of course, of course. I promise."

"Then do what you must."

"Take my hand and stand with me by the wyrm." Jetsam offered his hand and Seryn took it, helping him to his feet. As they approached the dragon, Jetsam trembled. *Elvar, what have I done?*

"Stand still and clear your mind," Seryn instructed. "Breathe deep and lean on me for support should you need it." The wizard waited a moment for Jetsam to comply. "Ready?"

"Ready," said Jetsam.

"Then we begin."

Jetsam did as told and cleared every thought from his mind. As Seryn started the incantation, Jetsam noticed perspiration between their entwined palms. *He's as nervous as I. But don't think,* Jetsam admonished himself.

As the wizard chanted, Jetsam experienced the familiar intrusion of a foreign presence. Like Enthran Ashvar before him, Seryn Vardan now occupied a part of Jetsam. *Don't fight it.* A magic wind blew through his core, sucking a part of him away. *It has begun.*

Jetsam's heartbeat slowed. *Breathe deep,* he told himself as his lungs expanded. *So far so good,* Jetsam assured himself, yet he felt drained, akin to when he cast his sunblink spell. Seryn's grip tightened and Jetsam realized the wizard was holding him upright. *How much longer?*

First his feet went numb as he hung from Seryn's arm. His legs followed shortly thereafter. Dropping to his knees, Jetsam struggled to remain conscious. *And yet the dragon doesn't stir.*

Seryn's chanting drifted and echoed as Jetsam's head spun. His breath ran shallow and his heart slowed to a crawl. *Dizzy.*

The world disappeared in a blinding light.

Elvar?

Hold on.
So dizzy.
'Tis not yet your time.
Elvar? Is that you?
Go back.

Jetsam awoke with Seryn Vardan rocking his shoulder. *Again?* His head pounded and the gentle motion stirred his nausea. *Was it a dream?* His memories of the healing spell hung vague and blurred. *I still feel poisoned,* he thought.

"Jetsam?"

Through the slits of his heavy lids, Jetsam spied the wizard through blurry eyes. The man hovered over him, concern draping his weary face. "Wher'm I?" Jetsam mumbled.

"Can you sit up?"

Jetsam ignored the question. "The dragon?"

"I live," said a rumbling voice.

It worked! Jetsam closed his eyes and fell back asleep.

"Have a bite of food." Awakened by the delicious smell, the ravenous Jetsam took the dried meat and devoured it. *He's a much better cook than me.* Tramp gnawed on a bone at Jetsam's feet, while a small smokeless fire burned in the hearth.

Drahkang-roth rested flat on her stomach, her wide eyes glistening.

"How do you feel?" Seryn asked.

"Better now," he replied with a mouth full of meat.

"I'd prefer to let you rest, but I fear we are in danger here," the sorcerer confessed. "The dragon spoke of one who's been inside these caves. One who still lives. The bounty hunter, no doubt. He searches for us *both.*"

"Baldy?"

Seryn chuckled. "Yes, that one. With all of us weakened, it would be dire if he discovered us here. We must leave posthaste."

Jetsam stared at the wyrm. "We can't leave her alone. I'm sure she'd fetch a bounty, too."

"I'll be safe once you seal off the entrance you opened for the hunters," Drahkang-roth said.

Of course! We can seal them behind us, just like the Dwarves.

"Are you well enough to walk?" Seryn asked.

"Only one way to find out." Jetsam rose to his feet. Though light-headed and wobbly, he felt strong enough to walk. *I think.*

"Then ready yourself. Dawn beckons, and we must be off before sunrise. I want to leave under cover of darkness."

After wolfing down another chunk of meat, Jetsam donned his worn leather boots, Dwarven hauberk, belt-pouch, long coat, backpack, and sword.

Then he remembered the scroll.

"M'lord, is this then your scroll?" he asked, producing the slender case.

"It is indeed," Seryn replied. "But keep it for now," he instructed. "You've been a vigilant guardian thus far. We'll discuss it later. But now we must go."

By lantern light, the trio snuck through the hallowed entry halls of Asigonn, all the while wary of the bounty hunter. Jetsam noticed Seryn led them down a different path that led to a hidden door. The tall wizard crouched to slip through the portal. Jetsam followed into a low snaking tunnel. The cloaked man crept ahead. *He's afraid of an ambush,* Jetsam suspected. His sleepy eyes peered into the darkness, but perceived nothing. After a minute of inspection, Seryn waved him on.

Jetsam, the wizard, and canine slipped from the cavern. Dawn lurked beyond the horizon. Clouds hung as low as the peaks, blocking out the starlight. Fingers of mist dangled from the sunken clouds, tickling the hillside. A crisp scent filled the air. The temporary absence of trolls did wonders for the surroundings. A pervasive silence shrouded the hills.

Jetsam noticed Seryn scanning the area, and did the same. Like a stairway cluttered with broken glass, the jagged mountainside rose before them, sharp peaks piercing the gray ceiling. Below them, the slope softened as the rolling folds bled into the receding evergreens. Naught stirred among these daunting rocks and ancient conifers as far as Jetsam could see. The languid daybreak and floating mist limited vision, however, and he used his ears and intuition as much as his sight. Satisfied, they moved on, heading for the sorcerer's grotto.

"We must go quickly and quietly," Seryn warned, speaking just above a whisper. "Healing the wyrm drained me and I'm vulnerable. I'm not intimate with Asigonn's tunnels and fear if we linger, we'll be trapped like mice. We'll be safer at my grotto, and most able to defend ourselves, if need be."

Lightly they stepped, Jetsam and Tramp side by side following the cloaked man. Seryn raised a finger to his lips, petitioning for silence. With a quiet Elven phrase, the mage appeared old again. *Amazing,* Jetsam thought, hardly believing his eyes. His hood far over his grayed head, the wizard tiptoed. His shrouded form nearly disappeared into the mist. Jetsam marveled at his mastery of the art. He itched to learn.

Under the retreating darkness, they traveled in the open, forsaking the timberline cover below. Jetsam felt naked beneath the changing sky. He grew accustomed to traversing between the sturdy trunks, below their canopy of needles. Jetsam took comfort in the wizard's presence, though. Not since his parents were alive had he experienced a safety like this. Jetsam hoped Seryn Vardan would live up to his lofty expectations. *I've so many more questions to ask.*

Dawn broke with the gradual lightening of the cloudy skies and the dissipation of the mist. Jetsam observed their path aimed for a spotty stand of conifers less than a league off. As the creeping daylight seeped across the mountainside, the monochromatic world was cast in shades of gray.

The trio had hiked less than a furlong along a steep ridge before Tramp growled. *He smells something.* Stiff-furred, Tramp barked once before a loud snap echoed across the hillside.

Jetsam recognized the dreadful sound, and his heart stopped. Tramp let out a distressed howl.

A crossbow bolt embedded in the mage's shoulder.

With a voiceless gasp, Seryn dropped to one knee. Jetsam glanced toward the direction of the shot, but saw naught. The wizard struggled to his feet and wheeled toward the sniper as well.

Before Jetsam's keen eyes could spot the assailant, a second quarrel ripped into Seryn's torso. Agony etched on his face.

Gripping his staff, the sorcerer crumpled to his knees and then slumped to the ground. Off balance, he slid down a steep embankment, several yards from Jetsam, before stopping his descent with the butt of his staff.

"No!" Jetsam screamed futilely. Tramp barked wildly, circling Jetsam.

With a leap and a bound, Yduk Thiern emerged from his hole, thirty paces up the mountainside. Dust from his hiding spot covered his black leather and bald head. Even his mustache turned gray, blending him with the rocky environs.

Sprinting, the Southlander covered ground swiftly, brandishing Regret.

Jetsam unsheathed his sword, but the man headed for the sorcerer.

The sodding devil.

Seryn began feebly chanting a spell, but the bounty hunter sprang upon him. The blade sliced the air as the wounded mage struggled to his knees. With a desperate lunge, he stuck out his staff in defense.

Regret struck the splendid oaken rod and bit into the wood. Yduk yanked on the blade lodged in Seryn's staff. With a mighty effort, the manhunter tore the seasoned oak from the sorcerer's grasp, and with a quick flick, sent the freed rod flying.

Stripped of his staff, Seryn lost his balance and slid further down the slope. Before the tracker took another step toward the wizard, he reared back like a startled horse.

Jetsam had charged the man from behind and pierced his tough buckskin with the tip of his sword. The bounty hunter cursed in pain and swiveled to face his young foe. *I got him good,* Jetsam thought. Jetsam thrust again, stabbing the man above the knee. *Like Kandris taught me.*

Tramp charged as well, white teeth bared. The canine's big brown eyes locked on Yduk's black boots. The terrier shot for the man's legs, but his teeth failed to take hold, and he slid away harmlessly.

"Bloody urchin," Yduk grumbled as he brought Regret down with full force upon Jetsam. Their blades met, and the impact sent the short sword spiraling from Jetsam's grip. Empty hands stinging, he wobbled defenseless before the hunter as his blade bounced across the stony ground.

Fobbing pus-boil, he's strong!

Yduk loosed Regret again. Jetsam tried to dodge the second blow, but the steel crashed hard against his back.

Jetsam rolled down the rocky embankment, stopping yards from the injured mage.

Tramp growled and charged again. Yduk kicked him away like a beggar's hand. Into the dust the dog tumbled.

The tracker descended the treacherous incline toward the fallen duo. "Now I'll put an end to ye, spellcaster." Jetsam noticed the wizard's glare, but Seryn offered no retribution.

Sliding down the slope, one hand to the dusty rock, Yduk glared at Jetsam.

"No man ought have survived that blow, much less a boy!"

The ferocious strike cut through Jetsam's long coat, bruised his ribs, and knocked the wind from him, but his Dwarven ring mail defended his skin from the sharp steel. No blood was drawn.

Jetsam chanted the ancient words as fast as they could pour from his lips.

Av-kier epira gwedath!

On treacherous footing, the bounty hunter hurried to within striking distance of Jetsam. Regret was raised above his head, but before the blade could seek Jetsam's neck, a piercing flash splashed across the hillside.

Sightless and gasping for breath, Jetsam rolled away. *I did it!* The bounty hunter's blade hit rock.

"Devil take you, knave!" Yduk shouted.

He's surely blinded, too!

Jetsam heard Tramp charging toward the unmoving tracker. *No, Tramp.* With a ferocious bark, Tramp launched and bit into the man's calf.

"Damnable mutt!" Yduk roared, bringing Regret around blindly. With his blurry eyes still burning, Jetsam saw the blade but nick the agile dog. *A direct hit would have cleaved him in two.* As it was, the blow cut the terrier deep, and with a yelp, sent him rolling down the incline. But not before Tramp tasted the tracker's blood.

From the Elven words starting below him, Jetsam realized Seryn attempted to release a spell. *Does he have any magic left?* As the tenuous words commenced, the bounty hunter sheathed his blade and pulled his arbalest from his back. *His sight's coming back. Or he's aiming by sound.*

Either way, Yduk was too fast for the weakened mage.

A third bolt struck the sorcerer in the chest, and he tumbled down the hill, dropping several fathoms before hitting his head on a jutting stone.

He moved no more.

With horror, Jetsam watched the wizard's abrupt stop, and saw Tramp motionless and bleeding. Jetsam was breathless, empty-handed, crippled with pain, and had cast his only spell.

The bounty hunter loaded another quarrel and aimed at Jetsam. With no recourse, Jetsam curled into a ball.

Finally, the end, he thought. *Elvar, prepare my way.*

With a *thunk,* the bolt hit him in the back and ricocheted down the hillside. Jetsam felt like he'd been kicked by a mule, but the projectile didn't break his skin.

"Damnable Dwarven armor!" Yduk swore. "Then I shall cleave yer head and take it in a sack for my bounty!"

Regret again saw daylight. Jetsam tried to gain his feet, but the blow to his back left his legs numb and sluggish. He crawled in vain as the tracker neared. Jetsam sobbed and closed his eyes.

My nightmare's coming true.

Chapter Twenty-Eight

A swirling wind blew up and the clouds over the Kierawaith darkened. Dawn rolled back to the East. An eerie silence painted the landscape with wide strokes. Death rode in on its black stallion, quieting the world and frightening the sun.

Prepared to die, Jetsam waited on the barren hillside for the shining blade to sever his head. With his blue eyes closed tight, he didn't notice the darkness descend upon the mountainside. Curled in a ball, he didn't feel the wind. He lamented his fate and wondered who would take care of Tramp when he was gone. *My time is up.*

He prayed his family would be waiting on the other side.

It's always darkest before the dawn.

Then he felt the impact.

But instead of a steel blade, a wave of heat splashed across his body like breakers on the rocks. A shrill cry shattered the silence and echoed off the slopes. The bounty hunter screamed in pain, and Jetsam's nostrils filled with brimstone.

Raising his weary head, Jetsam saw flames dancing behind him. The tracker was covered in frolicking fire, his cape ignited and burning. His black leather baked, cooking him like a lobster. His sword and crossbow fell steaming to the earth as the man batted the fiery tongues with both hands.

No clouds had gathered, nor wind blustered. Rather, the wounded dragon had taken flight, and its enormous wings stirred the air and separated the daylight from the mountainside as if a furious storm had blown in.

For Yduk Thiern, indeed it had.

The wyrm swooped low toward the ridge, kicking dust and flame and smoke into the air. Jetsam shielded his eyes as the monstrous flying beast glided toward the burning man.

Before Yduk could drop to the dusty ground, the dragon's razor-sharp teeth pierced his scorched armor. Clamping hard on the man's torso, the dragon picked him off the hillside. Bones and crisp leather cracked like twigs.

The sound *almost* made Jetsam ill.

Emerald wings flapping, the fire-breather rose into the air. Dust devils leapt from the ground beneath the expansive wings. The bounty hunter rode along, clenched in the wyrm's maw.

With a desperate final maneuver, Yduk grasped his dagger. Ribs broken, gasping in pain, he swung his arm in a wide arc, burying his dirk in the dragon's left eye. Writhing in agony, the wyrm crashed into the barren hillside. Dagger in hand, the Southlander rolled free of the lizard's maw and forced himself upright.

With the bounty hunter standing in the dragon's blind spot, the wyrm didn't see the man charge. Dirk raised, face grimaced, Yduk hopped on the dragon's snout, and aimed for the other eye.

Before the startled dragon could react, a sling stone hit the bounty hunter square in the face, breaking his crooked nose and releasing a fountain of blood over his chin. Jetsam's shot provided all the time Drahkang-roth needed to shake Yduk loose. Before Jetsam could fire another stone, the dragon snapped the bounty hunter's bleeding head clean from his shoulders.

The voice in Jetsam's head murmured *It is done.*

Jetsam glanced at the dragon in disbelief. *She's still not well.* Seryn had healed the wyrm enough for flight, but the gruesome scars of battle still shown fresh on its hide. *Now she's lost an eye.*

Temporarily abandoning the wounded wyrm, Jetsam scrambled down the slope to Seryn and Tramp, both injured and unmoving. Tears welled as he slid down the loose embankment.

He reached his fallen comrades and hovered dumbfounded above them. Both the man and dog lay bleeding and unconscious.

Jetsam again stared death in the face. And again, the Reaper held the advantage. Jetsam was burdened with the familiar torture of watching dear ones die. With the sorcerer's passing, Jetsam would lose all hope. The memories of his parents faded against his will. His one chance to reclaim his heritage lay dying at his feet. In desperation, he turned again to the wincing dragon.

"Please," he begged, "can't you help?"

"I'm not a healer, little one," the emerald creature bemoaned. "The man has saved me twice, yet I am unable to return the favor. I would defend him to the death, but alas, my razor claws and fiery breath can do naught to tend his wounds."

"Nor am I a healer," lamented Jetsam, kneeling to pick up Tramp. "I was never able to learn the healing spell. I cannot even cure a tiny dog." Tears streamed from his bloodshot eyes, streaking his dusty cheeks. With a lump in his throat, he lifted Tramp gently and rocked the whimpering canine in his arms.

Jetsam began to sob. *What can I do? I wish I had—*

Jetsam dropped to his knees and carefully set the dog on the ground. Shaking his head, he retrieved the borrowed ointments from his pouch. *I almost forgot about these!*

"Don't worry, boy, I'll fix you up good in a minute!" Leaving the panting canine, Jetsam crawled to the crumpled wizard, again transformed to his younger self. Jetsam leaned close to the man's pained face. Dirt and sweat covered his anguished visage. A faint breath seeped from Seryn's dusty nostrils. Three quarrels protruded from his cloaked form. *One's dangerously near his heart.*

"Remove the garrocks, tiny healer," instructed the dragon, her voice bearing the tone of renewed hope. With a reluctant force, Jetsam withdrew the bolt from the mage's shoulder. A sickly feeling swept across him as he felt flesh pull against the retracting missile.

Seryn convulsed in agony.

With his narrow fingers, Jetsam tore the cloak open to expose the trauma. He spread a layer of ointment over the puncture, and then removed the second projectile from below his ribs. This bloody quarrel hadn't embedded as deep, but opened a wide slice.

Jetsam emptied the first jar and opened another, liberally covering both wounds. The final bolt frightened him. *I fear I'll kill him.* With shaking hands, he gently pulled on the missile, trying not to turn the tip against the sorcerer's heart. The shaft resisted the pull. *Sodding rot.* The quarrel lodged against a rib. Seryn's prone form quivered in pain as sweat ran from his pores.

Jetsam took a deep breath and tried again. *Steady and smooth.* He angled the projectile and pulled firmly. Coated in blood, the final bolt slid free. With a sigh of relief, Jetsam applied more salve.

Seryn remained unconscious, and Jetsam lifted his head from the rock he'd struck. Seryn's hair was soaked with blood. Jetsam's lithe hand dripped with the crimson wetness. He used the second vial and some of the third on the wizard, but saved enough for Tramp.

Jetsam bandaged the warlock and covered his motionless form with his coat, shading his ashen face from the beating sun. There was nothing more he could do, so he returned to Tramp. Jetsam brushed the short fur from the fresh gash and applied the remaining ointment. Then he wrapped the dog's belly.

Seryn said this salve wouldn't work on the dragon. Otherwise, I'd try to save her eye.

Tired, sore, and covered in the blood of others, Jetsam sat back on the steep hillside. His Dwarven armor shimmered like a rippling lake at sunset. Once more, he looked to the perched dragon for instruction.

"Now, we wait," the wyrm replied to the unspoken question.

Jetsam closed his weary eyes and the morning sun's brightness warmed his lids. He opened his blue orbs to see the gray clouds retreating, revealing a rare and marvelous day on the north face.

Like a grandiose statue, Drahkang-roth sat unmoving, watching over Jetsam and his fallen comrades. Bird nor beast dared venture within the sight of the giant winged lizard. *Yet she is weak as well,* Jetsam understood.

Soon, Tramp snored at Jetsam's feet. Seryn remained still and silent, but breathing nonetheless. The climbing daystar warmed Jetsam, and slumber tempted him. Before long, he slipped into the land of dreams.

"Wake up, lad!"

Jetsam heard the words as part of his dream, and they stirred him. He heard them again and his subconscious tried to ignore their urging. The third call snapped him from his satisfying slumber.

He shook off the cobwebs and gasped in surprise at his waker.

Still lying on the ground, but propped on his elbows, wide awake, was Seryn Vardan.

He lives!

Dusty, torn, and bloody, the mage looked like the ghost of a horrible death.

"Fetch my staff, will you, lad?" he asked meekly. With every breath, he winced in pain.

With a wide grin and a loss for words, Jetsam nodded.

"Careful, now," Seryn croaked. "Watch your step."

Agile as a mountain goat, Jetsam retrieved the dusty staff. It rested on the rocks a few steps down the slope from the enfeebled mage. Sliding down the embankment, Jetsam glimpsed the bright sun. Already it had reached its pinnacle, and now started its descent. *I slept the morning away.*

Jetsam found the staff at the bottom of the ridge. As his hands grasped the wood, he experienced a pulse of magic like none before. *It's even stronger than Enthran's amulet!* With awe and wonder, he cradled the potent staff and returned to the reclined sorcerer.

The long polished rod bore a notch where the bounty hunter's sword bit into it, but other than that, looked no worse for wear. Jetsam handed Seryn his priceless possession. The mage clutched the shaft with shaky hands. Instantly, calm spread over the man.

Seryn sat with staff in hand and began to chant. Jetsam studied his deep concentration. The wizard's eyes remained closed as he mumbled the familiar but indecipherable Elven words. His pained expression gave way to a look of quiet resolve.

Jetsam left Seryn to his healing meditation. Tramp napped soundly, curled beneath the warming sun. The green dragon continued her stoic watch, seemingly in bottomless circumspection. Her regal hide glistened, the emerald scales shiny as polished brass.

Jetsam scanned the mountainside. Refreshing sunlight glittered on the bare stones and rocks. Dust from the tumultuous morning had settled, and only Seryn's gentle murmuring and Tramp's soft snoring resisted total quiet. Jetsam shivered at the Kierawaith's vast bleakness. This high up, there were no trees or scrub, no branches for bird or squirrel, no flowers or bees, not even tufts of grass between the rocks. His attention was drawn to a sparkling object. Waiting for the mage to regain his strength, he meandered toward the gleam.

Baldy's sword! Fine patterned etchings were inlaid on the diamond-hard steel. Soft ebony leather wrapped the grip, with a gold pommel finishing the hilt. *It's much longer than my blade.* Jetsam wondered if he could even lift the impressive weapon. He bent down to the orphaned sword. With his first touch, he sensed the magic ingrained in the precious weapon. Like Enthran's amulet and Seryn's staff, the gold and silver sword contained an inherent power.

Lifting the blade, Jetsam marveled at how light it was. *Not any heavier than my little sword.* He wiped the steel across his thigh, leaving a trail of dust on his already-stained breeches, but revealing the blade's gleaming splendor. He held it aloft in the sunlight, and it shone blinding white.

"An excellent weapon indeed," spoke the dragon from her lofty perch. "It should be yours. You've earned it. I have your staff as well," professed the wyrm. Jetsam looked at the dragon, perplexed by her words.

"My staff?" he questioned.

"The wizard's before you," the dragon stated. "But since it resisted my fire, and you summoned me, I thought a morning flight was in order. Only to stretch my wings of course."

The dragon's words vexed Jetsam. *Did the wyrm say I summoned her?* Jetsam was certain he misunderstood. But he noticed his former teacher's staff protruding like a twig from the wyrm's prodigious claws.

"I sensed the power within you," replied Drahkang-roth, "but even I underestimated your capabilities. 'Tis strong magic indeed to rouse me with whispering words from so far away. I have no use for the staff, and you did act on my behalf to warn of the attackers and then find the healer. 'Tis fortunate indeed that I heeded your call, for my assistance was most beneficial."

"Begging your pardon, great one, but I didn't summon you."

"It certainly was *your* voice," retorted the dragon. "Worry not, little one. 'Twas bold indeed to call me, but I am glad you did. I wanted not to lose my healer for good."

"I assure you, I didn't call," Jetsam humbly insisted. "But I've also heard a voice inside *my* head. One which has guided me in time of need. Maybe the same voice, though I don't know where it comes from or understand why. Till now, I was half afraid it was but my imagination."

Overhearing the conversation, Seryn broke from his meditation. "You said it was the lad's voice," the mage stated to the dragon. "And yet, you insist it wasn't you," he said to Jetsam. "Although you claim to hear voices, too. Interesting indeed." Both Jetsam and Drahkang-roth stared at Seryn with curiosity.

"Back at my campfire, you told me of your twin's passing. It's been said that when one twin dies, his spirit is bound to the other until they're joined again in the Beyond. I'd venture your dear brother is a very strong ghost indeed!"

Jetsam gasped at this statement, and in his heart felt the mage was right. *Elvar, it was always you!*

"I can find no other explanation for how Drahkang-roth heard *your* voice urging her to save us. And it would explain the voice you hear as well. For I believe you speak the truth in saying you did not summon her. You have many talents, I can attest to that, but you surely cannot summon a dragon!"

Drahkang-roth laughed at this. *She realized she overestimated me,* Jetsam suspected.

"Indeed, for if the powerful Seryn Vardan cannot rouse me, how could this little one? But a spirit from the other side can act in forceful ways. And the voice sent me not to you wizard, rather to the boy," clarified Drahkang-roth.

Jetsam beamed, recalling how the strangely familiar voice had saved him several times since Elvar's death. The words he heard before the dragon rescued him rang in his head. *It's always darkest before the dawn.* "That's Elvar's saying," Jetsam mumbled, only half astonished. It comforted him to know his twin was still with him, even if only as a spirit. *I could ask for no better guardian angel.* Deep inside, part of him felt whole again. He nearly burst with joy.

"I'm afraid I won't be able to travel far today, or maybe even tomorrow," lamented Seryn. "I must take lodging once again inside Asigonn, with your leave, Great Wyrm."

"As much as you are welcome to heal within the halls of Asigonn, I suggest another solution," said the winged beast. "I offer to carry you back to your grotto. It would be a quick and painless trip."

Jetsam arched his brown eyebrows as the mage pondered.

"I shall take you up on the gracious proffer. I have no appetite for trolls or any other vile creature roaming those halls." Seryn, now standing, albeit timidly, glanced at Jetsam.

"And what of you? Your pursuer is dead, and you're free to go where you please."

"I came searching for you, m'lord. I would beg of you to take me on as servant and apprentice. Most surely I would earn my keep. I'm a hard worker, and good hunter, and the dryad showed me the berries and nuts to eat, and—"

"Enough, lad! I consent. We outcasts must stick together! But there's one condition," Seryn decreed.

"Anything, m'lord," Jetsam responded.

"You must take my word that I didn't kill the king, and furthermore, you shall not regard his assassination in high esteem. Rather, vow to abhor such acts and retribution of such by like actions. I realize you've been greatly wronged and suffered much misfortune, but a life of vengeance will lead only to evil."

The words struck a chord with Jetsam. His experience since leaving the underbelly told him the wizard spoke true. *I feel it in my heart.* "You have my word, m'lord."

"Then take the rod the dragon offers you. Every spellcaster needs a good staff." Jetsam hiked up to the mighty wyrm and accepted her generosity, thinking it a gift as much from Elvar as from Drahkang-roth. Caressing the smooth wood, he wiped it clean of soot and dust. *It's fine and powerful indeed.*

"Here, you'll need these." While Jetsam was fetching and admiring his staff, Seryn retrieved the belt and sheath from the headless bounty hunter. "That sword needs a true scabbard," he replied, nodding to Regret, which Jetsam had set down to handle the staff.

Jetsam wiped Yduk Thiern's blood off the leather belt and fastened it about his waist. He lifted the grand blade and slid it into its exquisite sheath. *I'll grow into it.* Jetsam kept his old sword as well, and for the time being, the two blades dangled clumsily from his narrow waist.

With that, they were off. Jetsam lifted his wounded dog and carried him in his arms. The dragon then crouched so Seryn and Jetsam could climb on her back. With nary a rumble, the emerald wings flapped. In a swirl of dust, Drahkang-roth lifted her passengers from the earth.

Jetsam gasped as he rose gracefully to the heavens. The view stole his breath. He marveled at the spectacular Oxbow range, stretching east and west as far as his eye could see. Jetsam gazed south to the jagged peaks. Blue sky gave them a magnificence all their own. Northward, the rocky terrain dipped into a sea of green. Like hair on a balding head, the evergreens struggled to cover the highlands, but the harsh environ left the forestation thin and spotty. Off in the far distance, the trees faded altogether, and the blue sky blurred into dirty gray, darkening until the ashen lands and cloudy skies were indistinguishable.

"I saw horses," the dragon said, "off to the northeast, under the pines."

Jetsam peered in that direction. He detected the slightest of movements far below, well hidden by layers of branches. But he knew the horses belonged to the dragon hunters. "They are the steeds of my captors, or former companions, if you will."

"Shall we stop and see?" asked Drahkang-roth.

Seryn answered affirmatively, and agile as an eagle, the wyrm swooped down, landing softly at the edge of the sprawling timberline. Leaving Tramp to rest with Drahkang-roth, Seryn and Jetsam strolled into the woods. Once again, Seryn transformed into an old man, gray and stooped.

A furlong into the conifers, Jetsam observed the headless petrified troll, and beyond, five horses tied to trunks—the mounts of the tracker and the dragon hunters. And he saw Kandris Bayen bound and gagged.

Seryn released the young squire and informed him of the demise of his companions. Kandris sat in stunned silence at the news, a crestfallen look coating his face.

Jetsam collected his possessions from the horse, and peered questioningly at Seryn.

"As much as I'd like a hearty steed, I'm afraid we cannot take the horses," he declared to Jetsam. "I've no place to keep them nor food to feed them. They'd only attract attention we don't want." Jetsam nodded as he slung his sack across his shoulder. "Take the bounty hunter's possessions," instructed Seryn. "He shan't need them again."

"And as for you, young squire, take this herd of yours back south to whence you came and return richer and wiser. Count yourself lucky to be alive, for you have sided with evil, and yet been granted a second chance. Be warned, though, never again tread in the Oxbow Mountains, or speak of what you've seen here, or I guarantee your fate will be not so fortunate."

Kandris Bayen nodded.

"Take this blade as a symbol of our pact, lest you forget what you've learned." The mage held out Sir Prentice's arming sword. Yduk Thiern had stowed it among his belongings.

As Kandris accepted the blade, Seryn uttered a few words in the Elvish tongue and cast a binding spell on him, to help keep the agreement.

Jetsam and Seryn left the astonished squire and were soon airborne again. From their lofty height, they saw Kandris and his five horses moving southeast toward Dwim-Halloe and back to the Southlands.

Well before nightfall, Drahkang-roth landed at the edge of the forest near Seryn's grotto. They bid farewell to the ancient wyrm and watched her disappear into the darkening sky. As they sauntered through the woods and up the dry creek bed, Jetsam was bursting with questions. *I've so many to ask.* Finally, the dam broke from his youthful enthusiasm.

"If you will, m'lord," he said, "tell me of my parents, and the scroll, and of the king, and the real assassin, and how you were wrongly accused, and—"

"Patience, lad, all in due time," said Seryn, smiling gently. "You can stop running. You're home."

###

To be continued in
Mirrors & Mist
Book II of
The Oxbow Kingdom Trilogy

Glossary

Aht-ir Aht-ir [**aht**-eer aht-**eer**] - An ancient ebony dragon who attacked and routed the Dwarves of Asigonn. It is rumored that after defeating the Dwarves, the great wyrm made his lair in Asigonn's Great Hall.

Asigonn - An ancient Dwarven city, long abandoned. Legends tell of an evil dragon routing the Dwarves and chasing them from their subterranean home.

Av-kier epira gwedath - An Elven phrase that, along with the proper focus and gesture, releases the sunblink spell. This incantation instantly floods the area around the caster with a blinding white light.

Biter - An underbelly orphan boy who gives Jetsam bread and dried meat.

Blister - An underbelly orphan boy, Blister is one of the three youths who get lost in Gwae Gierameth. He also gives Jetsam a cape and hood as a gift.

Calderi [kal-**der**-ee] - The next large city on the Serpentine Pass south of Dwim-Halloe.

Citadel, The - The central castle of Dwim-Halloe, which houses the Granite Palace; the residence of the Oxbow King. The Citadel proper consists of a moated, double-walled castle, with north and south gate houses. The Jade River has been routed to encircle the Citadel, serving as its moat as it flows southward. The castle sits atop a revetted motte, to withstand the eroding surges of the Jade.

The circular outer castle wall contains 12 towers, spaced like numbers on a clock. The outer curtain has a barbican with a drawbridged gate house on both its north and south sides. These defensive structures provide the only entrances across the Jade into the castle. Within the outer curtain lies the rectangular inner curtain. The higher inner wall surrounds the Oxbow King's Granite

Palace and has four prominent guard towers at each corner, with gate houses on the east and west walls. If one were to look down from the Mirrored Peaks, the Citadel's curtains would appear as a small rectangle inside a circle.

Drahkang-roth - The rumored name of an emerald dragon.

Dwim-Dwaeroch [dwim **dwey**-räk] - A famous Oxbow Mountain landmark in the Kierawaith, west of the Dwarven ruins of Asigonn. Dwim-Dwaeroch is the Dwarven name of a double-edged mountain peak that juts like a knife with a broken tip.

Dwim-Halloe [dwim **hal**-oh] - The capital city of the Oxbow Kingdom, located midway along the Serpentine Pass through the Oxbow Mountains, in a fertile valley near the Jade River. Named in the days when a Dwarven king ruled beneath the city while a human king ruled above, Dwim-Halloe is Old Tongue for *City of Two Kings*, although it had long been misinterpreted as *Vale of the Twins*, in reference to the Mirrored Peaks.

To leave Dwim-Halloe means weeks of travel south, until the foothills recede into the fertile flatlands of the Freelords, where hospitable settlements can be found. Journeying north from Dwim-Halloe is treacherous. Beyond the Citadel, past the Mirrored Peaks and down the north slopes, the Grimlord's barren badlands encroach on the evergreen-covered foothills. Only the heartiest of hunters, outlaws, and hermits live north of the Oxbow range. Strategically, Dwim-Halloe is the first defense against the malevolent inhabitants north of the Oxbow Mountains.

The city of Dwim-Halloe is protected by the Mirrored Peaks to the east and west, and massive stone ramparts which extend completely across the pass north and south of town, intersecting the steep mountain faces rising on each side of the valley. At its lofty elevation, Dwim-Halloe sits near the top of the Oxbow Mountain timberline, at an elevation of approximately 6,000 feet. North of the city, the terrain rises above the evergreens, providing an unobstructed view for leagues. To the south, the Serpentine Pass winds lower into the green foothills. These natural features make

Dwim-Halloe a crucial military defense point for the southern Freelords in protecting their border from any northern threat.

Major buildings in Dwim-Halloe include The Citadel, the city's royal fortification, and The Granite Palace, a double-walled castle that resides inside The Citadel. Dwim-Halloe's general populace lives outside The Citadel's outer curtain, but are still protected by Dwim-Halloe's boundary ramparts.

Eidryn Lothyrn [**ahyd**-rin **loh**-thrin] - The birth name of Flotsam's brother, Jetsam.

Elvar Lothyrn - The birth name of Jetsam's brother, Flotsam.

Enthran Ashvar - A clean-shaven, surly wizard, typically seen wearing a hooded cloak and holding a hardwood staff.

Fathom - A distance of 6 feet or approximately 1.8 meters, predominantly used to measure the depth of water.

Flotsam - The underbelly orphans' nickname for Elvar Lothyrn.

Furlong - A distance equal to 220 yards or approximately 604 meters.

Gaalf River [gahf riv-er] - The meandering waterway bleeds the Kierawaith of meltwater as it snakes northward. Cutting a turbulent path through the rocky foothills, the river runs all the way to the Badlands, draining into the vast desolate swampland north of the Oxbow Mountains.

Giselle - A green-eyed, blond-haired girl who lives in The Citadel.

Granite Palace, The - The palace of the Oxbow King sits in The Citadel in Dwim-Halloe. The Granite Palace consists of several buildings; The Grand Hall, Lesser Hall, the Keep, chapel, royal storehouse, and the now-vacant wizard's tower. In the center of the royal grounds sits the royal inner bailey.

Guran Gwehaar - The name of the late Dwarven king whose clan once resided in Asigonn, but was ousted from their subterranean home by an evil dragon, after the wyrm felled their king in battle.

Gwae Gierameth [gwey **geer** ah meth] - The ruins of the Dwarven mountain stronghold beneath Dwim-Halloe. The underground Dwarven city was built hundreds of years ago, before mankind inhabited in the Serpentine Pass. The Dwarves mined the Oxbow mountains for precious metal and stone.

In the year 899, an earthquake devastated Gwae Gierameth and caused innumerable fatalities. Although the quake caused severe damage to Dwim-Halloe, the destruction paled in comparison to the havoc wreaked in the Dwarven stronghold. As the mountains heaved and shook, even the exceptional subterranean architecture crumbled and collapsed, killing thousands of unsuspecting Dwarves, thus ending the reign of Gwae Gierameth.

Rather than attempt the impossible task of rebuilding their ravaged city, the surviving Dwarves moved on. Further west they migrated, deeper into the Oxbow range, away from the painful memories etched inside the mountain's core.

Jade River - This large river is formed north of Dwim-Halloe, at the confluence of three mountain streams fed by the meltwaters of the Mirrored Peaks. Near the Dwim-Halloe, the Jade is still small, but expands in width and depth as the Oxbow watershed feeds it on its southward journey to the Horned Sea. The Jade River runs through barred cutholes at the base of the north and south outer walls of Dwim-Halloe, flowing southward around The Citadel.

Jetsam - The underbelly orphans' nickname for Eidryn Lothyrn.

Kandris Bayen - The squire of Sir Prentice Imoor of Calderi.

Kierawaith [**kier** ah weyth] - The region of the Oxbow Mountain foothills on the northern face of the mountain range, located northwest of Dwim-Halloe and the Serpentine Pass. The Kierawaith is noted for its rough terrain and harsh environment, especially in comparison to the foothills on the southern face of the Oxbows. The Gaalf River runs through the middle of the Kierawaith and drains the region's meltwaters into the fetid marshes of the Badlands.

League - A distance equal to three miles or approximately 4.8 kilometers.

Lil' Pete - An underbelly orphan boy who gives Jetsam cooking gear as a gift.

Lohon Threll - A quiet, grizzled red-headed man with a suit of dark leather armor.

Mirrored Peaks - The near-identical mountain summits sit on each side of the Serpentine Pass, near the midpoint of the Oxbow Mountains. The snow-capped peaks rise sharply above the timberline near the city of Dwim-Halloe. The peaks are similar in shape, size, and height, rising nearly 12,000 feet above sea level.

Mole - A skinny, squeaky-voiced underbelly orphan boy who gives Jetsam a blanket. The long-haired Mole is 14 years old.

Oxbow Mountains - This range crosses the continent of Tythania, separating the northern part of the continent from the larger southern portion. From the northwestern coast of Tythania, the Oxbow rises out of the sea from a series of jutting islands and curves southeast to its southernmost point, mid-continent, near the Serpentine Pass. From there, the Oxbow begins to curve northeast, eventually disappearing into the ocean on the northeast edge of Tythania. From end to end, the Oxbow roams nearly 2,000 miles, spanning the entire width of the continent. The mountains can be divided into three principal sections; the Northwestern Oxbow, the Southern oxbow, and the Northeastern Oxbow. The Northeastern Oxbow contains the range's highest point, Devil's Peak, rising

15,000 feet above sea level. The Oxbow is widest in the Northwest, stretching nearly 160 miles, and ranges to about 90 miles at its narrowest region near the Mirrored Peaks.

Pike - An underbelly orphan boy, Pike is one of the three youths who get lost in Gwae Gierameth. He also gives Jetsam a tunic as a gift.

Ratboy - A brown-eyed underbelly orphan boy, Ratboy has tangled, end-curled, sandy hair. Ratboy unofficially founded the underbelly orphans and is its senior member and father-figure to the younger orphan boys.

Rooster - An underbelly orphan boy, Rooster is one of the three youths who get lost in Gwae Gierameth. He also gives Jetsam a paring knife as a gift.

Serpentine Pass - The snaking mountain path cuts a curving, thirty-league, north-south swath through the midpoint of the Oxbow Mountains. The pass is the major route between Tythania's hostile northern quarter and its loosely-allied southern lands, being the only horse-accessible crossing near Dwim-Halloe for hundreds of miles.

At Dwim-Halloe, the Serpentine Pass spans nearly two miles at its widest part. At its northern and southern narrow points, walls span east to west, connecting to the rocky slopes of the Mirrored Peaks. Each wall has a large, two-towered gatehouse, providing entrance to the northern and southern portions of the town. Bastions are set near each end of each wall, alongside the peak slopes. These walls provide Dwim-Halloe's first line of defense.

Sir Prentice Imoor - A Calderian Knight who wears full armor, a visored burgonet and an arming sword, dirk, and kite shield at his side.

Squirrel - One of the older underbelly orphans, Squirrel is a tall blond lad who fled Dwim-Halloe with Weasel.

Sylallian - The region of the Oxbow Mountain foothills on the southern face of the mountain range, located west of Dwim-Halloe and the Serpentine Pass. The Sylallian is noted for its green, alpine environment, especially in comparison to the foothills on the northern face of the Oxbows. The Sylallian has long been rumored to be an enchanted forest.

Tythania - The continent where Dwim-Halloe and the Oxbow Mountains are located. The events of Crimson & Cream take place entirely within Tythania.

Ulodonn Tygan [**Yoo**-loh-don **Tahy**-gin] - The previous Oxbow King, who was assassinated in the year 1004. King Ulodonn Tygan was followed by the current king; Valin Vardan.

Underbelly - Four distinct components comprise Dwim-Halloe's underground; storm sewers, abandoned mines, catacombs, and the Dwarven ruins. Filled with unknown dangers and bolstered by generations of terrifying fables, these unmapped wormholes were avoided by all but the truly desperate. The storm sewers serve as a makeshift home for the orphan clans, and are nicknamed the "underbelly." Before King Valin took the throne, there were no orphan clans in the Citadel's underbelly. But the thwarted wizardry rebellion orphaned many children. Those brave enough to escape underground banded together in any of several gangs to survive.

Hewn by the Dwarves centuries ago, the subterranean conduits were cut to harness the fury of the Oxbow Mountain thaws. Humans expanded these sewers in later times to channel storm waters away from the walled town and Citadel. Connected to the surface throughout Dwim-Halloe, the sewer drains provide the orphans access into town.

The abandoned mines had also been carved by the Dwarves. In search of resources for their craftsmen, the Dwarven miners hollowed out meticulous, complex passages in the mountain. Long ago tapped of their mineral riches, these tunnels sat dormant for ages. Dwim-Halloe's active mines now rest south of the city, excavated by men and boys, and separated in distance and spirit from the winding tunnels carved so long ago.

Centuries after the Dwarves, the catacombs were placed by the humans, transforming stretches of the uppermost mine shafts into the final resting place for Dwim-Halloe's departed. Sitting in a narrow mountain pass, land was sparse around Dwim-Halloe. Precious farmland could not be sacrificed for burial grounds. So to rest their deceased, the humans ventured meekly into the abandoned underground, carving crypts and alcoves into the former Dwarven mines to house their beloved dead.

Little is known of the former Dwarven city that now laid in ruin, buried deep in the mountain beneath tons of shifted rock. A savage earthquake left little of the stronghold intact, including the tunnels to the surface. Townsfolk passed on stories from generation to generation hailing the glories of this underground fortress, where few men had tread, before or after the deadly quake.

Unnatural - A term used to describe otherworldly or magically-influenced creatures, such as spirits, undead, and ghosts, as well as trolls, ogres, goblins and the like. It is also a slang derogatory term for one who uses magic, such as wizards, mages, and spellcasters.

Weasel - An underbelly orphan boy who fled Dwim Halloe. Rail-thin with long black hair, Weasel also sports an adolescent beard.

Yduk Thiern [**Ee**-dook Theern] - A bounty hunter from the southern part of Tythania.

Acknowledgements

Thank you to everyone who helped and supported me on this long journey, especially my wife Regina and my mother Barb.

R. J. Blain toiled as my editor and helped me mold an unwieldy hot mess into something readable. Her insight and guidance were invaluable to my development as a writer.

A big thank you to my dedicated beta readers who helped me polish the manuscript and evict the gremlins; Jennifer, Lee, Gary, Dominique, Anne, Matt, Tony, and Barb.

In addition, I'd like to thank the many friends from Saturday Scenes on Google Plus for sharing their suggestions with me, and finally, you, dear reader, for giving this book a chance. I hope you enjoyed it. If you would be so generous as to leave a rating or review, I would sincerely appreciate it.

About the Author

C. M. Skiera currently lives in Southern California, a long way from Michigan, where he grew up, graduated from Michigan State University, and started a career as an environmental engineer. He and his wife are devoted dog-lovers who share their home with rescue dogs. Crimson & Cream is C. M. Skiera's debut epic fantasy novel. He started writing Crimson & Cream in 1999, and after many twists and turns, the ebook was published in 2012.

Introducing an excerpt from
Mirrors & Mist
Book II of The Oxbow Kingdom Trilogy:

Prologue

"You impressed Princess Ioma, I presume?" Duke Daelis Vardan asked his son Valin.

"Of course." A game bird sat on the table with a loaf of wheat-flour bread. Valin broke off the end piece as he continued. "'Twas easy to see she was taken with me."

Seryn bristled at his sibling's misplaced bravado. *Liar.* Seryn bit his itching tongue. *The princess is right—this will get complicated. And ugly.*

"Excellent," replied Daelis, reaching for the fowl. "'Tis time Tygan narrowed the field. The Calderian relics may as well go home." He tore off a chunk of meat and continued while chewing. "Same for those fisher lords. Can you imagine, a sailor prince from Ost, or one of those *lakeling* lords wearing the crown?"

"Did you gain audience with King Tygan?" Valin asked.

"On the morrow, we'll meet to discuss the advantages our family brings to his southern interests. And I'll remind him of the depth of our coffers. 'Twas never a king that didn't fret about his treasury." A smug look on his face, the duke slid a slice of roast quail into his grinning maw. "Princess Ioma is a handsome lass. She'll make a fine wife."

"Even Seryn was smitten," Valin said. "Had a dance for himself." Valin's gray eyes burned through Seryn.

His ire from last night's confrontation diminished naught, Seryn feared.

"Campaigning on your brother's behalf, I hope," Daelis said.

Prepared for a fatherly reproach, Seryn fancied himself fortunate to get off with a disapproving glance. *Must be my lucky day.*

"M'lady is free to do as she chooses. She *is* a princess, after all."

Daelis narrowed his eyes, his thick white brows weighing them down.

"Do not shame each other," he warned. "For the shame will be on our house." Duke Vardan leaned forward, his frigid gaze reaching out to Seryn. "'Tis no game. Your brother can be king."

Seryn glanced at his plate and breathed deeply. *She deserves better.* The terse look on his face did little to hide his inner turmoil. *And I shall see that she gets it.*

"When will you see her again?" the duke inquired of his eldest.

"I'll call on her this eve," Valin replied.

"You've not sent a message yet?" Daelis frowned. "The princess is in high demand. She'll not sit idle awaiting your beckon." Daelis glanced at his unfinished plate, then at Valin's. "Get dressed. We'll go to the palace posthaste." Duke Vardan rose like steam from a boiling pot. Daelis hovered over his sons, as Valin shoved a final bite into his mouth. "The game's afoot. I'll not lose a step to those oafs. Now, move!"

Valin rushed off still chewing and Daelis followed. With his own plate empty, Seryn picked a bit of bread off Valin's and retreated to the library. He dozed with a book in his lap, dreaming of Ioma and his scheming family.

Seryn was surprised when a messenger returned but an hour later. Still groggy from his nap, he broke the wax seal, while the housekeeper peered over his shoulder. *How about that? She accepted my invitation to meet this very day!* Still in his morning robe, a rush of urgency surged through Seryn. "Alma, what should I wear?" he asked the housekeeper.

"We shall find something handsome," she replied. "And ye best take yer note," she nodded at the table. "Don't want ta leave *that* around for yer brother."

He smiled and raised his eyebrows, tucking the parchment in his pocket.

"Come," he said to her, "I must dress."

Alma followed Seryn upstairs and extracted an appropriate outfit. Seryn donned the clothes and bounded down the stairs before a glowing Alma could appreciate her handiwork. Through the window, he spotted her watching as he left. He waved a grateful goodbye.

Walking to the Granite Palace, butterflies danced on lightning inside his nervous chest. *I'd half expected an outright refusal.* Seryn entered the green palace grounds, sauntering across the royal bailey. *Alma chose well,* he thought, light and cool in his luxurious fabrics. Just past the lesser hall stood the tower where Dwim-Halloe's lord high wizard dwelled. In his wildest dreams, Seryn imagined someday, after paying his dues in service to the king, he might be considered a worthy appointment for the position. *I wonder,* he mused, *could I be both king and lord high wizard?* He chuckled to himself. *One pipedream at a time.*

Princess Ioma Tygan met Seryn at the Great Hall's front doors.

"M'lady, you look truly radiant this day."

"Thank you, Lord Vardan—you are too kind."

"Shall we stroll the garden, my princess?"

"That would be lovely. The hyssops are in bloom." Seryn wasn't interested in the purple-spiked flowers, or anything else besides the princess.

Ioma grabbed his arm. "I know a shortcut." She led him to an unassuming postern door behind the Great Hall. He followed her through the small doorway, and they snuck beneath the castle wall. The narrow tunnel left him to walk behind her, hunched to avoid rapping his skull. Trailing the princess, close to her backside in the confined space, Seryn's heart fluttered. *Don't even think it,* he admonished himself. They exited the curtain wall through another gate buried in ivy, into the walled garden.

Squinting in the sunlight, Ioma led Seryn to a whitestone bench outside the orchard, where they sat next to a bubbling fountain.

From within his tunic, Seryn extracted an ornate folding fan. "For you, m'lady." The colorful design mimicked peacock feathers. Wide-eyed and smiling, Ioma took the gift.

"Why, 'tis lovely! Thank you, Lord Vardan," she said, fanning herself. "Truly, you should not have troubled so."

"'Tis no trouble, m'lady, for next time the heat takes you, I may not be ready with a spell, so the fan must suffice."

"You certainly are the family jester." She mimicked his pose.

"Were you not roaring at Valin's witty repartee?" He faced her with a grin. Side-by-side on a bench, the free-spirited pair sat oblivious to the world.

"Your brother's a serious man, full of ambition." She feigned a pout.

"He is indeed. Yet, I can be serious as well, though, ambition is not my master."

"There's no disguising last night's purpose. Father intends I wed, and each one of my suitors surely has ambitions beyond winning my heart."

"I daresay, I must disagree with you, m'lady."

"Lord Vardan, you cannot dance with a princess without thinking of the throne." She leaned toward him as she spoke.

"'Tis true, Your Majesty, but, I confess, I was not even supposed to dance with you."

She stared at him, perplexed. "Lady Darksparrow scribed your name without your intent? How presumptuous!" Ioma halted and put her fists to her hips, elbows pointing wide. "I must have a word with my gentlewoman." The corners of her mouth curled to release a mischievous smirk. "Though, I can't fault her taste."

Seryn flushed. "You jest, yet, 'tis true," he replied. "My father and brother conspired for Valin to dance with you twice, after I excused myself due to a sudden queasiness. But, I knew I would not relinquish my chance."

"You flatter me, Lord Vardan. I fear your ensorcelling skills may be at work yet again."

"The truth holds a magic all its own, m'lady."

Her lithe hand floated towards his, grasped it, and squeezed.

"I fear you do not know what you're getting yourself into."

"'Tis half the fun." He tightened his grip in return.

"Father and Lord Nargul scheme to find me an advantageous match, with little care for my own wishes."

"I've not proposed *yet*, m'lady." She blushed and giggled. Her fingers felt soft and warm in his grasp. *Am I squeezing too hard?* He released his grip a bit, only to feel hers tighten. *Relax,* he told himself, taking a deep breath. *Enjoy the scenery.* Seryn realized his hands were sweating, which turned out to be the least of his problems.

"Now more so than ever, I feel like the prize sow at the farmer's auction."

Seryn chuckled at the imagery. "You are no closer to a sow than I am a toad."

"Rib-bit," she said, her mouth curling upward. "You know what I mean." She flashed him an acknowledging smile. "I spend my days being courted and wooed by Tythania's nobles. Two Calderian lords are staying in the lesser hall. I fear they shall not leave till I'm wed." She chewed her lip in consternation before continuing. "And the fish-lords. Charming as longshoremen, those three. Oh, and lest I forget, the swaggering Dwim-Halloe blue-bloods. A dozen, if I count you among them."

"Please do, m'lady—though I do bleed red." His response elicited a royal chuckle that blended with the garden sounds of buzzing bees and rustling leaves.

"And this is after father and Lord Nargul culled the herd considerably."

"The politics of royal matchmaking. Do they hear your opinions at all?"

"I fear not. Certainly not Lord Nargul, and I further suspect he is no admirer of yours."

"Shocking—he was most hospitable while ignoring me at the harvest ball."

"Your sarcasm betrays you, Lord Vardan. Yet, it amuses me."

Seryn leaned toward the princess, placing his mischievous grin next to her ear.

"I shall tell you a secret, but you must keep it close," Seryn teased. "I suspect Lord Nargul is infatuated with my brother."

"Observant of you," she replied, inching closer to him, their shoulders rubbing. "He's made it clear that your sibling's his preferred choice."

Larks chirped in the branches above them, yet even as the princess sat hand-in-hand with him, Seryn felt only the sudden heaviness of disappointment.

"And what does her majesty think of this Valin Vardan?"

"I deem him charming and handsome." She smiled as Seryn failed to hide his chagrin. "Nearly as much as his younger brother."

"You toy with my emotions, m'lady."

"As you do with mine, Lord Vardan. If only we didn't suffer this pressure of my betrothal hanging over us. The thought of it is oppressive."

"And yet, 'tis the reason we are here now, so I cannot begrudge it."

"Though the year of mourning is passed, I still miss Mother terribly. If she were here, she'd navigate this chaos. Father needs her guidance."

"He still retains the counsel of a very wise daughter."

"A daughter he's grown deaf to, and is all too eager to marry off." Their knees touching, Ioma placed her free hand on his thigh. Seryn wiped his palm on his breeches and placed his hand atop hers. He could feel her pulse. *Her heart beats as fast as mine.*

"So, tell me of these other suitors—do they treat you well?"

"Oh, most certainly. Everyone is on their finest behavior when under the king's scrutiny. 'Tis what makes it so difficult—I see them only with their best foot forward. The Calderians are polished and polite—charming even. But they are both so *old*."

"I saw some local men my age dancing with you. Did they not impress?"

"'Tis *all* they tried to do—impress me. Success eluded them, however," she said with a wink.

And what am I doing? Seryn wondered. *Naught but trying to impress.* He unleashed a confident smile in spite of himself. "Good to hear it," he said, "for jealousy nips at me when you're entertaining the others." He instantly regretted admitting jealousy, but the words flew away, irretrievable.

"Seems like an occupation, really. Going through the motions until one or the other makes a gaffe serious enough for father to dismiss him." She waved her hand, mimicking the disapproving king.

"Being royalty sounds arduous, Your Majesty."

"'Twill not resolve itself today, so I shall enjoy my time with you and deal with the morrow when it comes."

For Seryn, the time *had* come. He leaned in and kissed Ioma softly. She floated into his embrace. The sun failed to match the heat of her lips.

Within the Vardan library, books covered the maple-shelved walls from floor to ceiling. The study breathed an aroma of candle wax, hardwood, and parchment. *This is my favorite room.*

"Seryn!" The comforting spell vanished. Seryn recognized the tone in his brother's voice. *He knows.*

"'Tis gone on long enough," Valin said. Fists balled, he planted himself in front of Seryn. His face a steely mask of determination, Valin reeked of the practice yard.

"What, exactly, do you speak of?" Seryn hoped it was other than what he feared. His brother's bulging neck veins told him it was not.

"This is your sole warning ere I take this to Father and Lord Nargul." His unblinking eyes burrowed into Seryn. "I *forbid* you to see her again."

Seryn held his tongue and comprehended Valin's consuming desire for the throne. He suspected his brother *was* fond of Ioma. Yet, it mattered not, for at that moment, he knew in his soul he *loved* Ioma. *I fear this will break him.*

"I'm sorry, brother. But I'm an adult, and Ioma's a princess. We'll not take orders from you."

Valin stabbed his rigid finger in Seryn's chest. "You've no right," Valin said. "I'm the eldest! 'Tis my birthright to take the throne."

Seryn chose his next words carefully, but doubted it mattered. "You speak as if the princess has no say in the matter."

"Little does she—for *she* serves the king. And the king's right hand favors me for the crown." Valin leaned in closer, and Seryn detected wine on his breath.

Seryn inched back from his brother's uncomfortable closeness. The enormity of the situation sank in. *I'm courting for a kingdom.* His mind churned as he scrambled for the words to respond. Though they had drifted far apart, guilt still crept from the corners of his mind. *He'll never forgive me.*

"Your selfish dalliances will not ruin this family," Valin said. "Release her from your hypnotic ensorcelling."

Seryn stood stunned. "You think I cast a spell on her?" *What kind of monster does he take me for?* Seryn's shoulders slumped and his hands fell to his sides. "You cannot believe she could choose me of her own free will?"

"No—she could not. You and your mewling coven of unnaturals will not steal this crown." Valin's index finger shook, inches from Seryn's nose. "This is treason!"

"You speak nonsense." Seryn slapped his brother's hand from his face. With a fluid move, Valin grasped Seryn's tunic by the shoulders and shoved him. Seryn landed hard, as books rained on his head.

With a swing, Seryn swatted his brother's hands from his garment. Valin balled a fist and swung back. Seryn ducked as Valin punched a volume on Calderian farming, his fist but grazing the top of Seryn's head.

Seryn launched, tackling Valin over a bench, sandwiching his brother between himself and the furniture as they tumbled to the floor. Prone and grimacing, Valin glanced a fist off Seryn's cheek. Seryn responded with a rib strike—in precisely the spot where Valin landed on the bench. The wind left Valin with a futile whine. Seryn struggled to stand, but Valin, despite his gasping, grabbed hold and kept Seryn on his knees. *Just won't give up, will you?*

So Seryn reared back and hit him in the ribs again.

Valin wheezed, struggling to suck air into his empty lungs. He slumped from Seryn, buying time to catch his breath. Seryn used the bench to leverage himself to his feet. As Seryn stood over his fallen kin, Valin squirmed to the other side of the bench. *He's had enough,* Seryn thought.

Regaining his breath, Valin's gray eyes sparked. On his backside, the elder Vardan spun and kicked the bench into Seryn's shins, returning him to the floor. Valin swung wildly, and Seryn lurched out of harm's way. Valin swung again, before Seryn regained his balance.

Landing a fist squarely in Seryn's eye, Valin's punch knocked Seryn flat on his back. *Devil's luck, he's quick!* Valin pounced atop Seryn, pinning him to the ground.

"Warned you," Valin said, letting fly another blow as a knowing grin escaped his bloody lips. Elbow high, he cocked his arm again.

"Wouldn't listen," Valin chided. The next shot bloodied Seryn's nose.

Seryn writhed to unseat his brother, to no avail. *Devil take you!*

"Impertinent maggot-pie—now you'll learn!" Valin's next punch split Seryn's lip. *I'll not submit!*

Valin landed three more punches before Seryn blacked out.

Alma shrieked when she spotted Seryn and raced to his side, hopping over the strewn tomes. He stared at the ceiling, struggling to focus while tasting a mouthful of blood. Rather than spit in his beloved library, he swallowed. *Get up,* he urged himself.

His first attempt at standing landed him back on the floor.

"Oh, my," Alma said. "'Twas not yer clay-brained brother, was it?"

Seryn nodded.

"Tis an ill omen fer kin ta fight like this." She shook her head, examining Seryn's injuries. "That logger-headed brother 'o yers done ye good this time." On her knees next to Seryn, elbows wide, she rested her fists on her narrow hips. "Don't move, pignut. I'll return in a blink with proper unguents."

I've no inclination to move. His head pounded and face throbbed. Even his ears rang.

Before he realized she'd left, Alma returned, hands full.

"This'll help," she said, wiping his split lip with a cloth dipped in her vinegar-based tonic. Seryn winced, doubting the efficacy of her homemade treatments. Yet, as far back as his memory reached, he recalled Alma treating him with her remedies. And it always seemed to help. *At least a little.*

"There, now," she said, her cloth now mottled with crimson. Alma tossed the bloodied rag aside and opened a clay jar. "This'll help the swelling." Her wrinkled fingers dipped into the container, extracting a dollop of ointment. Seryn grimaced at the sickly odor. "Hemlock and henbane," she replied. "Ye'll get used ta the smell, ninny-hammer," she said, wiping the balm on his puffy skin.

I believe her not one bit. "As if I didn't feel bad enough," he said, "now I smell of rotting flesh."

"'Tis that flap-mouth that earned ye this beating, I bet." She wiped a strand of red hair behind her ear. "Let's try an' get ye on yer feet." Knees popping, she stood and with a tug, pulled Seryn up. He planted a hand on the wall to steady himself.

"The room's in shambles."

"Don't fret, puttock," Alma cooed. "I'll tidy it up good as new."

Legs wobbly, he staggered to the stairway and, with her help, up to his bedroom. She ushered him in and promised to return with a healing elixir as soon as she brewed it.

Seryn shuffled to his mirror. Eyes blackened, lips swollen, his face looked twice its normal size. He wiped crusty blood from his inside his nostrils. *Alma had not ventured quite so far.*

Contrary to his training at Eh' liel Ev' Narron, he cast a spell to ease the pain and reduce the swelling. *Don't really know how badly I'm injured,* he rationalized. The illuminae instructed their students that magic was reserved for times of dire need. *This is dire enough for me.* The incantation provided a measure of relief, but drained his stamina. He stumbled to bed and dropped in a heap.

Alma returned with a steaming carafe, interrupting Seryn's attempts at slumber. As soon as his mind wandered from Valin's cruelty, his thoughts returned to Ioma. *It shames me to think of her finding out about today.* Alma poured a mug of her hot brew, distracting Seryn from his self-pity.

"Smells worse than the henbane," he whined, only half-serious.

"Will make ye see straight, dizzy-eyes," she replied. Seryn grasped the pewter mug and sipped the frothy concoction. He contorted his face, mostly for show. *Can't let her think it's anything less than horrible.*

"Finish that and rest till dinner. I'll summon ye when it's ready."

"Don't bother," he replied. "Food's the last thing I want." *I'll not give him the satisfaction of seeing me like this.*

"Yer gonna have ta face 'im sooner or later."

"Not tonight—not like this."

"Aye." She nodded, squinting. "'Tis yer father yer avoidin' ain't it?"

"There's hardly a difference. They're of the same mind."

"No father wants ta see his son suffer. Valin'll get a stern reproach for certain."

Seryn peered at Alma and shook his head. "Father'll say I was asking for it, and I got what I deserved. He'll probably hope Valin knocked some sense into me." Seryn chuckled half-heartedly. "You know I'm right."

"Drink up and get rest," she said, closing the door behind her.

The following morning, Seryn examined his reflection. *Feel worse than yesterday, and look it as well.* The swelling receded somewhat, but the coloring deepened. *If only I knew a spell to remove the bruising.*

Stiff and sore, Seryn shuffled to his desk. *I cannot face Ioma like this.* He opened an inkwell and dipped a quill, then put the dripping feather to fresh parchment. *Not my best penmanship.*

He summoned Alma to have his message delivered. *I'd rather she think me ill than know the truth.* Upon seeing his mottled visage, Alma covered her mouth. *Lovely,* he lamented. *I look the monster.* The startled housekeeper traded the rolled note for another serving of her steaming tonic. *Still pissing out last night's batch.*

Seryn skipped breakfast, and still neither his father nor brother called to check his condition. *It's as though I were dead.* Once his family left, he slunk to the kitchen, ravenous.

Filling up on soft foods and wine, he decided to stay home. *No school, no Ioma.* Despite his pain, his mind kept drifting back to the princess. *Who's courting her today? Is Valin feeding her lies about me? Is father conspiring with Nargul and the king to seal Valin's future?* His heart ached more than his battered head. Sprawled on the bed, he buried his face in his blanket.

Upon hearing soft knocking, he couldn't stand the thought of company.

"Go away!" When the door crept open, he glared.

"Seryn?"

His swollen jaw dropped as he watched Ioma slip in. When their eyes met, concern draped her face as she rushed to his bedside.

"What happened?" Ioma caressed his battered face, sliding on the down-filled mattress next to him. He winced at her touch, yet it sent shivers of pleasure through his wracked form.

"Long story," he slurred through his puffy lips.

"I'm in no hurry," she said, staring into his glistening hazel eyes. "Who *did* this to you?"

"Valin," he bullfrog-croaked. She stiffened.

"That jealous bastard. How could he look me in the face after doing this?"

"You saw him?"

"Yes, but not by choice. Father's pressuring me." She spoke the next words with difficulty. "Your father and Lord Nargul met this morning." Ioma looked ashamed. "He says Valin intends to propose."

Seryn's heart stuck in his throat as his heart raced. The blood rushing through his swollen veins ran red-hot.

"You cannot marry him!"

"I will not marry him!"

Seryn sat upright, failing to hide the discomfort the effort caused. He slid from the mattress and took one knee at her feet. *The time is now,* he told himself. He swallowed hard. "Ioma, I love you dearly. Will you do me the honor of accepting me as your husband?"

The princess paused not even a moment to consider.

"I *will* marry you, Seryn Vardan!"

He rose to the bed, no longer a pain in his body, took Ioma in his arms and kissed her. She returned the embrace, running her fingers through his long locks. His scalp tingled at her touch. Pulses accelerating, their hearts pounded in rhythm.

She unfastened her cloak, letting it slide off her shoulders, over the mattress edge, to the floor. The falling garment wafted her scent into Seryn's room. An aroma of rose-water and oil tantalized his nostrils as his eyes grew saucer-wide.

His fingers fumbled with her bodice strings while her warm hands slid inside his robe and caressed his aching ribs. Her soothing touch melted away his jitters, and her blouse ties fell victim to his now-nimble fingers. Encouraged by her fearless hands, his loose gown slipped from his shoulders and pooled around his waist. He kissed her neck, tasting her soft skin and inhaling her scent. Ioma took the lead, freeing him from all but the most pleasurable exertion.

They wound together, the warmth of their bodies spurring them on. Emboldened by youthful passion, they explored each other with inexperienced clumsiness. Were the heavens to rain fire, the couple would not relent.

Ioma did not leave until the morrow.

85914385R00173

Made in the USA
San Bernardino, CA
23 August 2018